A Necess.... ,

Jane Emersson
5/15

A Necessary Fiction

by

Jane Emerssen

JAYSTONE PUBLICATIONS

Copyright © Jane Emerssen 2013
First published in 2013 by JayStone Publications, Bewdeill, Ashtree Avenue,
Keswick, Cumbria, CA12 5PF

Reprinted 2015

www.jane-emerssen.co.uk

Distributed by Gardners Books
1 Whittle Drive, Eastbourne, East Sussex, BN23 6QH
Tel: +44(0)1323 521555 | Fax: +44(0)1323 521666

The right of Jane Emerssen to be identified as the author of the work has been
asserted herein in accordance with the Copyright, Designs and Patents Act 1988.

All rights reserved. This book is sold subject to the condition that it shall not,
by way of trade or otherwise, be lent, resold, hired out or otherwise circulated
without the publisher's prior consent in any form of binding or cover other
than that in which it is published and without a similar condition including this
condition being imposed on the subsequent purchaser.

All the characters in this book are fictitious and any resemblance to actual people,
living or dead, is purely imaginary.

British Library Cataloguing in Publication Data
A catalogue record for this book is available from the British Library

ISBN 978-0-9574310-0-3

Typeset by Amolibros, Milverton, Somerset
www.amolibros.com
This book production has been managed by Amolibros
Printed and bound by T J International Ltd, Padstow, Cornwall, UK

Salad Days

On a particularly wet Tuesday afternoon in the summer of 1952, when life was much less complicated, Laura had abandoned her paintbox and half-finished study of harebells in a jam jar, to reluctantly turn her mind to the history project set by Miss Wolstenholme, designed to keep wayward fourteen-year old girls occupied during the long school holidays. Laura had no great interest in local history: there were far more fascinating things to attract her attention at that age; Clark Gable for one; the arrival of a new gardener for another.

But Miss Wolstenholme would expect an essay of at least a thousand words at the beginning of term, so there was nothing to do but face up to the necessity of knuckling down and getting the wretched thing done.

The little-used archives in Lingford Library revealed Meeston itself had once been known as Merestown in the Middle Ages on account of the several small lakes in the area around the village. Apart from the pond at Nether Meeston Farm however, these were no more, lost to land reclamation and drainage schemes over the years between.

Meeston Lodge itself, she discovered, was only built in the eighteenth century, principally as a hunting lodge for guests visiting Meeston Hall, the fine Georgian residence six miles to the east. The previous manor house, an elegant Tudor mansion modelled on the architecture of Hampton Court – according to the woodcuts of the period which Laura thought might be worth the trouble of sketching – replaced an even earlier structure on the same site. This grand mediaeval edifice, built by Hugh de Granville in solid sandstone rather than flimsy brick sometime in the early twelfth century, apparently included a castellated tower and battlements designed to repel more unwelcome visitors – such as advancing hostile armies. It was a pity, Laura thought, that its Tudor replacement lacked these essential qualities: it was consequently burnt to the ground not long after the start of the Civil War and reduced to a ruin.

The prosperity that ushered in the beginning of the new century however, reawakened interest in the estate. William Granville, a distant descendant of Hugh's, ordered the site cleared, and the splendid new manor house in the Palladian style of the period rose from the ashes. Surrounded by its elegant landscaped gardens, parkland and woods, it became a fashionable place to visit, and Meeston Lodge, a modest five-bedroomed property of comfortably domestic proportions and pretty walled garden, was built to accommodate the demands of the age.

Inevitably, pestilence and wars took their toll on the Granvilles and their direct line petered out, the estate passing through the hands of distant cousins to be broken up and sold off as debts mounted and times changed. The Great War had delivered the *coup de grâce*. Thus Meeston Hall and its grand estate ceased to exist as an entity, and as such, became nothing more than a dusty history at the back of the archive shelves in Lingford Library, with an occasional mention in articles on places of interest in the monthly edition of the county magazine.

By quizzing Gwen Davis, the family's cook who had encyclopaedic knowledge of the area, Laura discovered the Hall was bought in the '20s by George Ryecroft, who set up and ran a successful haulage firm in Crewe. His son, Gerald and his wife, Maisie, still lived there – the new lord and lady of the manor – or so they liked to think. At the same time, the Lodge fell into the hands of Alfred Byford, something of a mystery man. He lavished a small fortune on the property, according to Gwen, renovating and improving, turning one of the smaller bedrooms into a bathroom – very avant-garde for the time – and adding the wash-house to the outside of the kitchen. He then went on to invest in what gossip of the day described as "a highly speculative venture" and lost everything.

The rest of its history, Laura knew. Her father had bought the Lodge in 1933, acutely aware that on her marriage, a Harriman heiress would expect to take up residence in a property roughly similar in status to her family home, Hazeldene Court at Broxley. Meeston Lodge was perfect, its elegant Georgian proportions and tasteful decoration matched her requirements exactly. The hallway was spacious, half-panelled in a light oak with exquisite parquet flooring that extended throughout the ground floor, with the exception of the kitchen and back hall, where there were terracotta tiles. Like the hall, the two reception rooms on either side faced west, looking out across the broad gravel drive to the high beech hedge which separated the grounds from Meeston Woods. The mature oaks and birch in the wood shaded the tall windows of these rooms from the glare of the late afternoon sun, so they were never uncomfortably hot in summer, while the morning room, facing east at the rear of the house, was bright and airy. This lovely room looked out along the shrubbery and flower bed that backed against the red-brick wall of the kitchen garden, and from there across the curving drive to the old stables which, with the passing of the age of the horse, had been transformed into a serviceable garage for her father's Rover.

Originally, the morning room had through-doors into the sitting room making it possible when they were open to use both rooms at once for larger family gatherings. In the first years of her parents' marriage there had been several such occasions.

Up the curving staircase leading from the hall onto the landing, with its Victorian stained-glass window overlooking the walled garden, were the four remaining bedrooms, the fourth a smaller room at the front over the hall – originally intended as a nursery – with an adjoining door to the main bedroom. But when the expected family, with the sole exception of Laura herself, failed to materialise, this little room had been filled with a bulky Victorian mahogany wardrobe and tallboy to become her father's private dressing room.

As expectations of a larger family dwindled, and her mother sought to use her time and energy in pursuing good causes rather than producing children, the sitting room became her domain where she entertained those she wished to cultivate. Laura knew this intrusion by outsiders into her father's private world had become a source of friction in the marriage. Ultimately, while Laura was still quite small, she remembered the removal of the double doors and the opening being bricked up, plastered and redecorated. A desk was bought, bookcases acquired and sundry other items of furniture. Ever afterwards, the morning room became her father's study and very personal space. No one, not even her mother, entered without his permission.

None of this later history of course, would be mentioned in Laura's essay.

––––––––––––––––––––––

CHAPTER ONE

November 1962

The overnight gale had blown itself out, subsiding into peevishness with sudden showers peppered with hail that rattled against the stained-glass windows of the church, drowning out Reverend Talbot's adenoidal tones as he wrestled with the onset of a mid-November cold.

"…The Lord gave, and the Lord hath taken away…"

Laura, head bowed, eyes fixed but not focused on the open prayer book balanced precariously on the ledge in front of her, breathed in the chilly air filled with familiar scents of beeswax and damp plaster overlaid by the faint mustiness of hassocks, whose needlework, completed for the Coronation nine years before, was now in need of some repair. Behind her the congregation shuffled and coughed, breaking her concentration. She resented the intrusion, wanting to keep her thoughts elsewhere.

Her thoughts had in fact, been elsewhere for five days, a detachment she found both satisfactory and unsettling by turns, but a state of mind from which she had no desire to be freed. It had wrapped itself around her like a protective cloak from the moment Dr Crawley had telephoned Mr Gittings at the Bank, and he had called her into his office and given her the news.

"I'm so sorry, Laura ..."

He had sent her home with his condolences and the sympathy of colleagues, their words a jumble of sounds deprived of any relevant meaning, words that looped themselves endlessly inside her brain like a dull mantra during the long meandering bus journey home through a rain-swept countryside.

A slight ache was beginning to make its presence felt behind her eyes. Reverend Talbot's monotonous intonation was becoming irksome. She longed for silence. There had been so many words during those five days. But expressions of sympathy required some acknowledgement, however brief, and her mother had retired to her bedroom responding only to visits by her sisters, particularly her younger sister, Cynthia, and Cynthia's husband, Richard.

"I really don't feel I can see anyone outside the family..."

Enquiries by friends and acquaintances – although in truth Daphne's friends were all acquaintances – had become, by default, Laura's responsibility. In this unwelcome role, she had pieced together the most appropriate phrases to express the right degree of gratitude to those who called with cards or flowers.

"Terrible news, my dear..."

"How is your mother..."

"Please give her our condolences..."

As the days passed however, she discovered she could

deliver her replies by rote, while behind the wan smile she found best suited to the occasion, her emotions could remain untouched. But it troubled her there was no grief to touch, no tears, no sense of loss – just a void. And what troubled her more was the thought, the really dreadful thought, that she was indeed her mother's child.

Her mother, sitting next to her: Daphne Driscoll, a force to be reckoned with; buxom and well-corseted, wearing beneath her A-line coat trimmed with astrakhan, a tailored suit of the finest wool bought especially for such occasions from Morton's in Chester; the ivory silk blouse with a neat bow at the neck; the pencil skirt just the right length to display to their best advantage her well-rounded calves and slim ankles; her shoes, of course, of patent leather. A stiff curtain of black lace hung suspended from the brim of her brushed sable hat – an elegant creation from Adeline's in Lingford. It obscured her carefully powdered face – lightly rouged, with just a touch of lipstick – hiding the lack of visible emotion. In her black leather-gloved hands however, she held a delicate cream silk handkerchief which she occasionally, and ostentatiously, lifted to tearless eyes. It was a performance of great distinction.

Mr Davis struck up the opening bars of Psalm 23 on the organ, the notes reverberating upwards through the chill air to the vaulted ceiling of ancient oak with its curved beams arching together to meet like hands in prayer. Throats were cleared and from somewhere at the back of the church Laura heard a fine male tenor lead the singing, his voice sending shivers of quiet ecstasy running through her, an exquisite sensation that diverted her attention from the now persistent ache in her head.

"… Yea though I walk through death's dark vale …"

She lifted her gaze to the coffin, a beautiful polished oak box with finely-wrought brass handles reflecting the pale lamplight in the church. Along its length stretched a magnificent wreath of perfectly-formed cream lilies and an abundance of maiden-hair fern. Someone must grow cream lilies just for funerals. Like man that is born of woman, they had but a short time to live. Such a terrible waste.

The Psalm finished and dutifully following the example of the rest of the congregation Laura sat down, feeling the hard, unyielding wood at her back reminding her to sit up straight.

Reverend Talbot climbed unhurriedly into the pulpit, blew his nose and surveyed the assembled company through rheumy eyes. The reading, he told them, was from the First Book of Corinthians. It went on at great length. Laura kept her head bowed and listened instead to the rain spluttering against the windows.

"… Amen."

She looked up. Reverend Talbot was riffling through several sheets of paper preparing to embark on his carefully prepared homily. He cleared his throat and began. "James Driscoll is a sad loss to our community," he said solemnly, his words echoing around the rafters in the pause that followed.

The full force of this dreadful lie cut through Laura's inattention like a knife. No! No, that simply was not true! In twenty-nine years of married life, James Driscoll had *never* been part of the Meeston community. He had studiously avoided involvement in any of his wife's fundraising efforts or 'worthy causes'. Even his attendances at St Wilfrid's had been conspicuously limited to Christmas, Easter and the occasional Harvest Festival. His working day revolved around his office in Lingford; his weekends and evenings to the pleasure of listening to the radio or reading the paper in his study, with occasional forays into the garden with Mr Moray, their gardener. Reverend Talbot was heaping compliments on someone he barely knew; trying to please the black-veiled woman in the front pew whose commitment to the church, and sizeable donations, had been vital to the restoration of the bell-tower in the past, and would, no doubt, be equally important for the maintenance of the organ in the future.

For the first time, Laura recognised the full extent of her father's anonymity among her mother's circle: he was almost invisible. It was as if her marriage had been an irrelevance. In the pews behind, stretching to the back of the church, sat the evidence – Daphne's Harriman family connections: her sisters; the Gorsts and Parrs – young and old; her retinue from the Mothers' Union, the Flower Club and flower rota; the numerous St Wilfrid's appeal groups, the Parish Council, neighbours and sundry other hangers-on who, despite everything, were prepared to tolerate her inflated sense of self-importance to bask in her aura of prestige and influence. Here they all were, paying their respects to the widow, not the man. There was no Driscoll here to mark his passing.

Reverend Talbot's empty rhetoric distressed her. A burst of anger sprang from nowhere, making her heart race. She wanted to stand up and silence him; to denounce him as a hypocrite; to point the finger and expose this eulogy for what it was – a disgraceful sham – that had nothing to do with her father, dead in his coffin – there, in front of them – and everything to do with his widow – and her money.

The moment passed, her rage smothered by the dull knowledge of her own cowardice and the throbbing in her head. Who was she to cast the first stone? Had she not learnt subservience herself – and at what cost? She shuddered. What could *she* say to contradict the beneficence heaped upon her father's memory? Why should she? Who was James Driscoll if not the much-admired professional gentleman, loving husband and father? – this quiet man who lived in his wife's shadow dominated by her family's dictates, past and present – like herself; a man caught in the Harriman web of influence from which there was no escape.

The movement of those around her refocused her attention. The congregation was standing. The pall-bearers in their black tail-coats and silk top hats had moved silently out of the shadows and were lifting the coffin from its resting place before the altar with the smooth efficiency of those accustomed to the task.

To the strains of an unidentifiable fugue, Laura followed behind the bobbing lilies, her mother rigidly upright beside her, the silk handkerchief clutched tightly, and unnecessarily, to her face.

In the pews across the aisle, a scattering of well-heeled men in business suits and black Crombies – presumably her father's associates or clients – bowed their heads as the procession passed. Laura acknowledged them, grateful for their presence. They at least had come to mourn the man.

By the door at the back of the church stood more familiar faces: Gwen Davis, who cooked for them at the Lodge, her soft plump features unusually tense and drawn; young Elsie Fleming, their daily help, red-eyed from weeping; and Mr Moray, taking time off to pay his respects, his unruly chestnut hair combed down, his head bowed as the coffin passed, his thoughts held close, no doubt remembering another place and another time.

Outside, the watery sky had given way to sullen ranks of steel-grey cloud with ragged edges, and above them, patches of forget-me-not blue held out the promise of a brighter afternoon. The air was fresh and clear.

The procession followed the old path between worn headstones, its cracked slabs greasy beneath a wild mosaic of autumn leaves caught in a sudden shaft of sunlight, a palette of exquisite colours. The burnt siennas and terracottas of the giant beech that dominated the churchyard mingled with the cadmium yellows of the ash fronds blown there from the adjoining field, while the startling crimson and vermilion tints of the wild cherries in the hedge by the lane lay in tumbled clusters. The trees were almost bare now, the last remnants of their summer glory hanging like tattered rags from their branches. Sad reminders of the passing of the year.

Was it just two short weeks ago she had walked here, searching through the new-fallen leaves seeking out the best? – later that day capturing their brilliance in water-colours in the safety of her room? The memory lay much further off, surely? – in another time; another life, when she could hear the distant sound of an afternoon concert on the radio in her father's study?

The newly dug plot lay open to sky, close by the ancient yews. Mr Barnaby had taken time and trouble with his work: the sides were cut with geometrical precision; the excavated soil lay in a tidy heap to one side protected from the overnight rain by a large green tarpaulin: and the wooden slats across the void had been placed there in perfect parallel symmetry.

Groups were gathering on the fringes of the family circle taking care not to intrude. Voices were hushed.

There was a pause while the pall-bearers removed the lilies and set them to one side. The trees moaned softly, and the breeze ruffled Reverend Talbot's cassock, rippling the hem across his well-polished shoes. Laura watched the fabric move: the shifting pattern of the folds; the curve of light reflected in the glossy black of the leather...

"... In the midst of life we are in death ..."

The coffin was being lowered. Her mother had removed her gloves and was stepping forward to pick up a handful of soil from a small pile left for the purpose.

" ... earth to earth, ashes to ashes dust to dust ..."

The grains fell from her hand pattering onto the brass

plaque. She stepped back, wiping away the dirt from her fingers with brisk, decisive strokes. Duty done.

Laura hesitated.

"… in sure and certain hope of the Resurrection …"

From somewhere close behind her, the familiar voice of Oliver whispered in her ear. "You have to do it, Laura," he said. Oliver being supportive, as was expected of a fiancé, while she kept him at a distance, requiring nothing of him.

The earth felt cold and damp to the touch, the cloying sweet odour catching in her throat. It was the smell of autumn: of fungi; of decaying leaves; of Death itself. Soon her father would be buried in it; would become a part of it.

The earth trickled between her fingers, like the sands of time. She saw it falling, spreading out across the coffin. Then others were stepping forward, following her example, stooping to pick up a handful for themselves, and the beautifully polished oak lid, with its brass plaque, began to disappear from view. Soon it would be smothered. He would be gone for ever.

CHAPTER TWO

Despite the adequacy of the new heating system in the Lodge, Elsie had laid a fire in both reception rooms. "A good blaze will help to cheer the place up," was her reasoning.

Daphne, divested of her hat and coat, her light-brown hair without so much as a wisp of grey and combed into place in the style of Her Majesty, took up her position in the sitting room waiting to be consoled. There, enthroned in the armchair nearest the fire, she could be seen by those entering the room, and approached as one might approach someone whose status was so evidently superior. Admittedly, the sitting room hardly equated to the gilded opulence of a State Room – its carpet, wallpaper and furnishings owing much to William Morris – but nonetheless, Daphne's ability to generate an aura of authority inevitably gave her immediate surroundings a certain grandeur.

Cynthia, elegant in a charcoal-grey suit with the addition of a delicate rose-shaped brooch at the shoulder with earrings to match, was installed next to her sister. Cynthia had none of Daphne's acerbic character, but had however the same hauteur, a useful quality when others might need reminding of what was expected of them during their audience. She was also adept at saying all the right things to dissuade less suitable individuals from outstaying their welcome, and could bring into the circle those who would act – quite without their knowledge – as a useful buffer zone. Of these, Isabel Barnes, a widow of modest means, and Dorothy Villiers, her spinster neighbour at Meeston Green, both staunch members of several of Daphne's fund-raising groups, were soon enrolled to play their part and invited to stay. Thus, surrounded by her most devoted adherents, Daphne was preserved from the twin social horrors on such occasions of having too many people around her, or none.

"I can't think why Reverend Talbot doesn't do something about the heating," Daphne was complaining. "I'm chilled to the marrow. Where is he, Laura?"

Laura had been hovering in the doorway. Her answer, she knew, would be unwelcome. "He asked to be excused," she began. "His cold—"

"Tush! Really! A simple cold. Well perhaps he'll turn up the boiler next time I mention the heating."

Daphne had never considered the replacement of the ageing Victorian boiler at St Wilfrid's as an appropriate project for her fund-raising activities. A boiler was much too prosaic. As for making an outright donation – heavens, no! Who would see the brass plaque acknowledging her generosity in the boiler room?

A steady stream of sympathisers was gathering in the

hall, stopping to admire the abundance of cream and white chrysanthemums in outsize Chinese vases on the window ledges. Soon there was quite a crowd, including a number of people who, regarded by Daphne as belonging to *hoi polloi*, would not normally be granted access to Meeston Lodge.

To her relief, Laura was dismissed to usher visitors into the sitting room to pay their respects, and her mother's expression slipped effortlessly from irritation to one of regal composure under duress.

"… a lovely service, Mrs Driscoll …"

"… a dreadful shock for you …"

"… so sudden …"

In the dining room, with its Lloyd Loom chairs of an earlier era and reproduction Chippendale, Gwen had laid out a generous buffet on the long, extended table in accordance with instructions. She was to use one of the better damask table-cloths, but not the best, in case someone accidentally spilt something on it. The large oval white Staffordshire pieces that rarely saw the light of day, would do for the cold meats ordered from Lawson's, the butchers in Weaversham – Lawson's could always be relied upon to send only the best roast ham, ox tongue and beef – and the smaller ones could be used for the scotch eggs, sausage rolls and neat triangles of salmon sandwiches Gwen was to make herself. The lemon cheesecake could remain in its stoneware flan dish, and the large quantities of fruit salad could be served up in the cut-glass bowls only brought into service when catering for those outside the immediate family circle. There would be no tears shed if they were damaged. And at the far end of the table, were two orderly piles of white every-day plates with interleaved white paper napkins next to neatly assembled ranks of assorted cutlery.

Soon, those who had exhausted their repertoire of expressions of condolence, or been dismissed with faint smiles and condescending nods, began to drift out of the sitting room in the direction of the dining room, where the conversation level rose from hushed tones of a sympathetic nature to a more general hubbub of everyday topics and concerns over the state of the world. Groups formed and reformed as people came and went, and through all the comings and goings, Gwen and Elsie circulated unobtrusively, removing plates, passing round tea cups, or offering refills. Laura, balancing the need to appear welcoming to the many strangers in the house with her deeper desire to remain as uninvolved as possible, followed their example, weaving between discussions on the latest women's fashions and the frightening brinkmanship of the American President over his handling of the Cuban missile crisis.

In the kitchen she found Gwen stacking china ready for washing. Gwen was a refuge in times of stress. She had been at the Lodge since Laura was three, and her simple presence, especially in recent years, had been enough to defuse the many occasions when friction between mother and daughter threatened to break out into open warfare.

Gwen looked up from her task. "My – you're looking pale, Laura. Everything all right?"

"A slight headache."

"There's some aspirin in the cupboard. No point in making life harder than it is, is there?" She ran the tap and filled a glass.

Laura pressed it to her forehead and closed her eyes. She was in no hurry to return to the hubbub in the hall, or be drawn into unnecessary conversations. "Thanks for all your help today," she said.

"Nonsense," Gwen said, tossing the compliment aside and plunging her hands into the foaming sink in front of her. "The least I could do. Your father was a steady man. Not many of them about these days. I said to Harry this morning – Mr Driscoll was a real gentleman. We'll all miss him."

Laura put down the glass and picked up a tea towel. She wanted to echo Gwen's sentiments but the right words proved elusive. "Yes," she said finally. "We will."

Elsie came bustling in balancing another tray of used plates. "Oh, Miss Driscoll, your uncle's asking for you."

Richard Gorst had done well for himself by marrying Cynthia Harriman. They made a good couple from the start, everyone said so: he, polished and professional; she, pretty and wealthy. The years since their marriage had treated them well. He was still a tall, slim, distinguished-looking man, now in his mid-fifties sporting a neat military moustache. On most occasions he carried about him an air of gravitas appropriate for a solicitor who regularly attended Lingford Magistrates Court. As a prospective father-in-law, he was potentially forbidding – not in the same league as Grandpa Harriman, of course – but Laura had never felt ill-at-ease in his company. Quite the contrary. There was an unspoken understanding between them which was difficult to define, but which existed nonetheless: a recognition perhaps that they were both outsiders.

Her uncle was leaning against the Adams-style fireplace in the dining room dividing his attention between reading the condolence cards on the mantelpiece and conversing with his business partner, Horace Parr. Horace, a tubby and affable man with rosy cheeks and receding hairline, had the softly-spoken manner and concerned expression ideal for commiserating with bereaved relatives, which was his principal role in Gorst & Parr, Trusts and Wills being his forte. Horace had married Richard's younger sister, Phyllis, and consequently, had himself become enmeshed in the outer strands of the Harriman web.

Mr Parr saw her first. "Here she is, Richard."

Her uncle turned and smiled. "Your mother seems to be bearing up remarkably well, Laura," he observed dryly.

"Yes. Everyone's been very supportive."

"So I see. How about you?"

"Oh – I'm all right. Plenty to keep me busy at the moment."

"Mm." He replaced a card he had been reading and studied her. "You look a bit peaky. Perhaps you should take a holiday. Get away for a while."

"No – that's not possible. Mr Gittings expects me back on Monday."

"Well, just remember what I said. Anyway – Mr Parr wanted a word." And with that he drifted off to join another group of men, none of whom Laura recognised.

Mr Parr rubbed his forehead thoughtfully. "It's your father's Will, Laura," he said, pausing to look earnestly at her as if trying to impart something of greater importance. "I've suggested Monday evening to your mother," he went on. "I think it better to discuss matters here rather than in the office, don't you? Much too impersonal." He ventured a faint smile. "She seems happy enough with this arrangement – and I've explained it would be useful to have Mr Jackson here as well – to discuss one or two matters she might not be clear about. Of course, I didn't exactly say that – I don't want to offend." Another nervous smile.

Arthur Jackson was the sole surviving partner of Driscoll & Jackson, Chartered Accountants of 6 Market Square, Lingford. Younger than her father by several years, but looking older, his presence too was always unobtrusive, never to the fore in the company of others. He was here, somewhere in the crowd surrounding them that afternoon, his diminutive form hidden from view by more robust visitors, his face, no doubt, wearing its usual care-worn frown, his myopic, pale-blue eyes peering at the world through well-worn tortoiseshell spectacles.

"Will Monday evening do?" Mr Parr was asking.

"Yes – yes, of course."

"There's something I'll need to discuss with you separately – afterwards," he added.

Laura nodded, uncertain how to answer.

Their conversation was interrupted by two middle-aged ladies from Upper Meeston with whom Laura had only a nodding acquaintance.

"We've said our goodbyes to your mother," said one, intent on sounding important. "Terrible shock for you both." And she patted Laura's hand indulgently.

"Terrible," chimed in the other, her eyes still darting around the dining room taking in the details of the furnishings. She seemed particularly impressed by the brocade curtains.

Others were drifting away too, their curiosity and hunger satisfied, and the men in their dark business suits took their leave with due deference, their duty done.

" ... our company will miss your father's professional services, Miss Driscoll..."

" ... such a reliable man ..."

" ... a great loss to us ..."

To which Laura replied uniformly – "I'm sure Mr Jackson will continue to provide you with all the services you require" – shook their hands, and wondered afterwards who these strangers were who thought so highly of her father.

The afternoon wore on. Soon, only a smattering of Meeston residents were left. The remainder of the guests were the usual inner circle of family connections, dispersing into more convivial and exclusive groups.

The younger generation of Parrs and Gorsts had long since given up their funereal air and had found congenial places to pursue their separate interests. Antonia, the vivacious younger of the two Parr sisters, was engaging the attention of Oliver's younger brother, Stephen, in an alcove by the fireplace. Rosemary Gorst, a year younger than Oliver, and very sophisticated, was looking stunning in an all-black woollen dress with white piping round a low scooped neckline, a view which was captivating the headstrong Julius, eldest of the Parr siblings, as they stood in the shadows by the stairs. While Oliver, accepting Laura's wish that he should not 'hover' around her all day, was making polite conversation with Phyllis and her sultry, but moody elder daughter, Claudia, who, although visibly trying to maintain a show of interest, was nonetheless obviously bored stiff, stifling a yawn behind her teacup.

Members of the older generation were engrossed elsewhere. Mr Parr and her Uncle Richard had joined Arthur Jackson in the chairs by the dining room window. Mr Stockdale and some of the other influential members of the Parish Council were detaining Dr Crawley by the door into the hall, while Daphne continued to hold court in the sitting room surrounded by those she prized most.

Unwilling to settle and find herself besieged by acquaintances from whose attentions she would be unable to escape, Laura kept herself occupied, searching out discarded plates and cups and ferrying them into the kitchen.

From across the hallway, a richly mellow female voice called after her. "Laura, my dear!"

She turned to find her elderly Harriman aunts, Millicent and Sylvia, resplendent in outfits of purple and violet to match their respective 'blue' rinses, advancing towards her like stately Spanish galleons in full sail.

"Laura," Millicent was saying, taking hold of both her hands and pressing them fondly. "Sylvie and I have to be going. Your old Aunt Hetty will fret if we leave her much longer. Daphne quite understands."

Sylvia leaned forward to give Laura a quick peck on the cheek, engulfing her in a wave of expensive perfume. "When do you go back to the Bank, my dear? You look so tired."

"Next week, Auntie."

"Too soon," Millicent said, shaking her head disapprovingly. "Far too soon."

"Mr Gittings said he could survive without me until then."

"Well, if you must, you must. Should I arrange to take Daphne out for a spin on Monday? Do you think she would like that?"

"I'm sure she would."

Sylvia patted her arm, leaning forward confidentially while giving a meaningful look over her shoulder in the direction of Oliver. "Of course what would really pick her up would be some good news – a wedding perhaps."

"Oh, Sylvie – really!" her sister scolded. "Not now! Come along with you."

Laura felt the heat in her face betray her embarrassment.

"Ignore her, my dear. Sometimes she can be so tactless." And with that Millicent kissed her enthusiastically on both cheeks and ushered her sister out of the front door. Laura waved them off. The car doors slammed, the engine spluttered into life, and the Morris Minor sped down the driveway at great speed, scattering gravel in all directions.

CHAPTER THREE

The promise of a brighter afternoon was short-lived. Banks of rain-sodden cloud gathering over Meeston Woods to the west were swept in on a blustery wind.

"Not much left to do now," Gwen was saying, surveying the freshly stacked plates on the kitchen table with satisfaction. "Elsie and me can finish this lot off in no time."

Elsie was busy drying the last of the plates, gazing out of the kitchen window. "Oh – there's Robert," she said. "He said he'd fix that apple this afternoon."

Gwen craned her neck to see him. "There's tea and sandwiches left if he wants some. Go and tell him will you, Elsie."

"I'll go," Laura offered. The dull ache in her head had eased but left a fuzziness which made it difficult to concentrate. Escaping into the fresh air was suddenly attractive.

Outside, there was a raw edge to the wind that took her by surprise. The fine woollen fabric of her dress gave little protection against the sudden gusts, and she hugged herself close as she hurried down the curved steps into the comparative shelter of the garden. There was a faint drift of drizzle in the air. "Mr Moray," she called out. "There's tea and sandwiches if you'd like to come in when you're finished."

The smart Mr Moray at St Wilfrid's was transformed again into the man she recognised, his hair wind-blown and disordered, his tweed jacket with leather elbow patches showing signs of wear and tear, and his thick cord trousers mud-spattered at the bottoms from the thick clods on his boots. Although he must have heard her calling, he made no attempt to acknowledge her, concentrating instead on securing the wayward branch of the espalier against the trellis. Eventually, he turned to face her. "Thanks for the offer, Miss Driscoll," he said in his soft Scots burr. "But I wouldn't want to intrude." His expression was a perfect blank.

"Goodness, Mr Moray, you're not intruding!"

"No, if you don't mind," he insisted. "I'm not dressed for company." He smiled apologetically and turned back to check that the remaining fastenings on the trellis were secure.

There was something odd about his refusal that made her persist. "Is anything wrong, Mr Moray?" she asked, wondering if her mother had been short with him again, as she so often was, resenting the time her husband spent with him in recent years. But for all her disapproval of him, she had never denied him access to the kitchen – as long as he removed his boots.

Mr Moray's back remained stubbornly turned in her

direction and there was a long pause before he answered. "I got on well with your father, Miss Driscoll," he said at last. "He was a great help to me ..."

She should have known. Old ghosts.

Ten years earlier, Robert Moray had left his roots in the North and arrived out of the blue to work for William Benyon at Nether Meeston Farm. He was a young man of twenty-five then, fresh-faced, with unruly chestnut-hair and melancholy green eyes. He was almost mad with grief – according to William's wife, Ann – fleeing from places too close to the memory of his dead wife and child. He had taken up the tenancy of the smallest of the farm's cottages on Nether Meeston Lane, a one-up-one-down affair with a kitchenette and bathroom added to it in a simple lean-to construction at the back. He had settled there, living his solitary life among the Meeston community, keeping largely to himself until that spring. It was common knowledge now, frowned upon in certain circles – not least by her mother who regarded the liaison as utterly incomprehensible – that he had taken up with Susan Holbrook, the infant teacher at St Wilfrid's Primary, an attractive young woman in her late twenties who lodged at the Benyon's. The relationship had begun, by all accounts, when he had offered to provide conifer branches in lieu of palm fronds for the Easter play Miss Holbrook was organising at the school. With the closeness of their respective places of abode, what had begun as a casual friendship had over time become something more serious, and seemed to be blossoming. There was even talk they might marry. "What she can possibly see in a farm worker, I do not know," Daphne had opined to anyone who cared to listen. "Such an educated girl too."

Shortly after his arrival in Meeston, Mr Moray had started helping out at the Lodge, doing the heavy maintenance work in the garden on a casual basis. In return, Laura's father had offered him the use of the large vegetable patch beyond the walled garden as an allotment. The produce he grew there was shared between the Lodge and himself – a mutually beneficial arrangement.

Ten years ago, Laura remembered coming home from school for the summer holidays and being surprised to discover old Mr Timms, the gardener at the Lodge for as many years as she could remember, had retired. In truth, for several years the job had not required someone full-time, but Mr Timms was not a young man. He had steadily become increasingly frail and allowances had been made, perhaps for too long. His sudden departure nonetheless was a shock to her, and in his place she found this strangely silent man, coming and going like a phantom, not given to much conversation beyond necessary politeness. She was fascinated by him. His past had an air of mystery about it that appealed to her over-active adolescent mind, and she hung around the garden that summer whenever she could, hoping he might be there. With the natural curiosity of a fourteen-year old, she was inquisitive to know more, but her father had been adamant – "Don't ask him personal questions, Laura, it's not kind," – a rule she had dutifully followed then, and since, restricting her topics in those early days to the wild flowers she picked as studies for her first attempts at water-colours, when he would help her identify those she did not know. But with the passage of time and her long absences at school, her curiosity died away. And by the time she left Hunters Lane at sixteen, her life was being directed towards Oliver and their future together. Hobnobbing with the casual gardener was frowned upon by her mother, and their paths rarely crossed for more than a few moments, limited to brief exchanges of commonplace greetings. So it had come to this: he was a familiar sight to her, but only as someone living on the margins of her world; someone who remained as much a stranger to her now as he had been ten years before.

A gust of wind caught her. She shivered, wishing she had brought a coat. He was still occupying himself checking the trellis, making no attempt to fill the awkward silence between them.

Despite her thoughts lingering on the warmth of the kitchen, she felt obliged to continue the conversation in the hope of persuading him into the house. The effort was something of a struggle, the words in her head unwilling to untangle themselves. "My father enjoyed talking to you about the garden," she began, adding pointlessly in view of the quantity of debris and leaf litter everywhere, "The shrubbery looks very fine just now." The drizzle was becoming more persistent. If he would not come to the house now, then so be it.

Unhurriedly, he finished refastening one of the ties. "Your father wanted something to last after he'd gone," he said, turning slowly and very deliberately to face her, giving the statement an emphasis she could not fail to notice.

There was a brief moment when the full weight of his words failed to register before she felt herself shiver – not from any lack of warmth – but from the kind of dread that comes from the sudden discovery of something purposely kept hidden. Had she misunderstood him? "Did *you* know he was ill?" she asked, thinking the fuzziness in her head was making her slow-witted.

He stuffed his hands into his jacket pockets and briefly studied the mud on his boots. "Yes," he said. "Heart disease isn't uncommon if you've had rheumatic fever as a child. But I expect you knew that." He was looking straight at her now. A challenge?

She was nodding in agreement – a purely automatic reaction. She had known nothing of the sort. Neither, she was sure, had her mother. Daphne's reaction to her husband's death had been one of unmitigated shock. Foreknowledge would, at the very least, have blunted her reaction.

Why had her father confided so fully in this man? – she was asking herself behind a facade of bland acknowledgement. Why had he left his wife and daughter in such terrible ignorance? It was unforgivable!

The dull thudding behind her eyes was growing louder as the same thought wheeled through her mind over and over again: her father had *known* he was dying.

She began to feel very strange indeed. Light-headed. Aware of an intense focusing of her vision on the top button of Robert Moray's shirt, and around it, a darkening halo threatening to engulf her.

"It's starting to rain," she heard him say through the roar of blood at her temples. "You should go in."

Her own voice came to her from a great distance. "Yes – yes, of course. You're right."

That was the moment, she decided later, her life began to change. Even as she stood, cold and damp, her mind still not fully engaged, not fully comprehending the enormity of his words, she knew the sudden revelation of her state of ignorance was more, much more than first it seemed. A box had been opened – and revealed beneath – another box.

CHAPTER FOUR

With the exception of Dr Crawley, prevailed upon by Daphne to stay a while longer by the lure of a glass of sherry, everyone had finally gone home. Gwen had returned to Back Lane to cook Harry his supper before Friday evening choir practice, and Elsie was tending the needs of her housebound mother, Florence, in one of the weavers' cottages in Alehouse Lane behind the Meeston Arms. Cynthia and Richard were the last to leave, Oliver having been delegated the responsibility of taking Rosemary back to Dyers Green a little earlier. Laura had encouraged him to go.

Dr Crawley had ventured into the sitting room at Laura's suggestion while Daphne said her goodbyes. He was hesitant. Although no stranger to the house, the sitting room was not his usual haunt.

It had been his custom to visit the Lodge occasionally, when he and her father would cloister themselves away in the study, particularly on winter weekday evenings when Daphne was occupied with Cynthia or others in the sitting room. They would settle into the comfortable old brown leather armchairs rescued from the previous suite – the sofa was discarded after the War – enjoying a blazing fire, smoking their pipes and talking about goodness knows what. But he was always on call, his doctor's bag left in the hallway, just in case, and, as often as not, the telephone would ring and his wife, Audrey, would be on the other end of the line summoning him to some emergency or other in Weaversham or elsewhere.

Now he was standing with his back to the fire, looking slightly ill-at-ease in strange surroundings. "I haven't seen much of you today, Laura," he said, making obvious small-talk. "Going back to work on Monday, are you?"

"I was only given a week's leave."

"Mm. I think another week wouldn't do you any harm. Too much left for you to sort out, by all accounts – all the funeral arrangements et cetera. You need to take care of yourself. Your mother will rally quickly enough, I'm sure."

"I'd rather go back to work, Dr Crawley."

"Understandable – but perhaps not wise – not just yet. Look, I'll be seeing Mr Gittings at the Old Lingfordians Reunion tomorrow evening. I'll let him know how things are. Tell him it would be better if you had a bit more time to get over this."

There was no opportunity to argue. Daphne's return interrupted the conversation. "Do sit down, Philip," she said, taking up residence again in the armchair by the fire with an uncharacteristic air of languor about her. "Laura, pour Dr Crawley a sherry, will you? And one for me as well."

Dr Crawley settled down in his armchair, accepting the

generous glass Laura offered him with obvious pleasure. "I was just saying to Laura she should have another week off," he said.

"Tush, Philip. What nonsense! Of course, I could do with her here at the moment. So many letters needing to be written." A brief look of surprise registered on Dr Crawley's face. He glanced in Laura's direction. "And she is the typist in the family after all," her mother added with the usual disparaging tone of voice she used whenever Laura's occupation was mentioned.

The telephone rang in the hall. Unbidden, Laura got up to answer it. "It's for you, Mummy. Mrs Spencer is wondering if you would like her to chair the Christmas Fayre committee on Wednesday."

Daphne's languor evaporated. "Good heavens, no! What can she be thinking of? Let me speak to her."

Mrs Spencer had not been able to come to the funeral to pay her respects because of work commitments in Lingford and an unsympathetic employer. The conversation was likely to become protracted while suitable explanations were offered and received, and Daphne's emotional well-being established. To Laura, the interruption was a godsend. Quite suddenly, her mind had become pin sharp.

In all the confusion that had surrounded her father's death, one person alone among close family and friends had not expressed any surprise whatever over the apparent suddenness of the event. Philip Crawley.

"Dr Crawley, can I ask you something about my father?"

He was sipping his sherry delicately, lost in the pleasure

of rolling the liquid around his tongue. "Of course, Laura. What is it?"

"How long had Daddy known about his heart condition?"

Dr Crawley paused, twirling the glass very slowly between his thumb and index finger contemplating the contents. He frowned. "He came to me about five or six years ago. I was surprised he recognised the symptoms. Most people don't." He looked up sharply, glancing at the door into the hall. "He was adamant your mother shouldn't know."

"Why was that?"

"You know your mother. She's not very good at handling illness."

There were memories of being isolated in the sick bay at Hunters Lane with chicken pox, and then later with German measles. Any notions of returning home to be nursed were peremptorily dismissed.

She let him return to enjoying his sherry for a moment. "Had it anything to do with having rheumatic fever as a child?" she asked innocently, throwing this pebble into the pond just to see what ripples it would produce.

Dr Crawley looked genuinely surprised. "He told you? Goodness me. I never would have thought it."

Laura shrugged off his concern, adept at lying by omission where necessary. "I never mentioned it to Mummy, of course."

"No, of course not. I'm glad you didn't." He drained his glass and placed it carefully on the side table. "No point in raising unnecessary questions, is there?"

"It's not something you hear much about," she said casually.

He took the bait. "Certainly not in Harriman circles, that's true. I suppose that's why he didn't want to make it general knowledge. Not the sort of disease you find in well-to-do families."

"I don't know much about it."

"No, of course not. Why should you? It's usually associated with poor nutrition, bad housing – that sort of thing. Not always of course. I know James was orphaned as a young child, but he came from a good background. And Mr Watson, his guardian, took him to live with his family at Upper Ossington, so goodness knows how he came by it."

"But it damaged his heart?"

"It's a serious illness. He must have known there was the possibility of heart failure for many, many years – long before he came to see me." He paused, lost in thought for a moment. "I have to say, Laura, I really am surprised he mentioned it."

Under his scrutiny, Laura feigned ignorance with a sigh and a smile, released from the need to dissemble further by her mother's return. Pleading tiredness with Dr Crawley acting as her unwitting accomplice, she retired upstairs to her room and lay on her bed in the dark staring up into the blackness, contemplating Robert Moray's revelation, and now, the absolute certainty it was true.

This was important, she told herself. She must try to remember if there had been even the smallest hint she might have overlooked. Something her father had said, or done in the past, that might have been in any way out of the ordinary. Anything that might have told her, with the benefit of hindsight, that he had recognised the onset of the inevitable blow that would strike him down, as it had, that Monday morning in mid-November.

She cast her mind back five or six years, only to reflect her concerns had been very much bound up with herself. Hunters Lane and her formal education were already two years behind her, her mother insisting there was no point in her staying on after 'O' Levels. "You aren't going to be a career girl, Laura," she had said in that particular nuanced tone that indicated there was something vaguely distasteful about girls who espoused such ideas, despite the inconvenient fact that cousin Rosemary – and for that matter – Claudia and Antonia, were all determined to be just that. But of course, they were destined to have to make their own way in the world, whereas she was going to marry Oliver. Miss Annabel Westlake, her Form Mistress – whose flamboyance Laura had found utterly fascinating – was particularly upset she would not be taking 'A' Level Art. "Such a dreadful waste of talent, Laura." And Miss Arbuthnot, the inspirational Headmistress everyone admired, had done her best to shake Daphne's resolve, to no effect. Her parting words were suddenly far more pertinent now than they had been at the time. "You leave Hunters Lane with a store of basic facts, Laura. Learn to be curious to know more."

But at Meeston Lodge curiosity was stifled by habitual reserve and severe strictures on what was, and what was not, an acceptable topic of conversation. So just as she had been instructed not to raise the subject of Mr Moray's family, equally taboo was enquiring into the loss of her father's parents, or taking an interest in his business affairs. Her life had been entirely dominated by her mother. School friends were replaced by relatives and the narrow rituals of visiting or entertaining the Harrimans, the Gorsts and the Parrs – or other socially acceptable ladies of the village. Academic subjects were relegated to bookshelves in her bedroom, her spare time devoted to helping out at fund-raising events for St Wilfrid's, embroidering napkins or table cloths to sell on her mother's personal stall, or helping Gwen bake fairy cakes. Even her beloved art had slipped into abeyance under the need to be permanently on hand when required. For two years she had let her mother fill her head with what was expected from her as Oliver's 'intended', constantly reminding her of the size of the inheritance that would be hers from Grandpa Harriman on the occasion of their marriage. It was to be a fortune – but it left her in limbo waiting for Oliver: waiting for him to complete his National Service in a RAF Maintenance Unit somewhere in the South of England; waiting for him to decide when they should become officially engaged; waiting for him to become a junior partner in Gorst & Parr. Just waiting. And throughout those two years, she reflected, her father, shut away in the sanctuary of his study when he was at home, had not demurred. Not once – until she had finally rebelled. Was that the significant moment he had first consulted Dr Crawley?

She had been eighteen and was becoming restless. Oliver had returned from his National Service, but instead of seeing more of her as she had anticipated, his spare time was increasingly taken up by study for his law examinations. Uncle Richard was proving a hard taskmaster. He expected his son to concentrate on qualifying, not to fritter away his time at weekends in jolly jaunts around the countryside in the car. And weekdays were entirely out of the question for socialising.

Boredom set in, mingled with envy, as Laura saw those around her widening their horizons with their parents' blessing. Rosemary, equipped with three 'A' levels, and two years abroad studying French and Italian at a smart international college in Lucerne, had just returned and secured employment with a company in Manchester that imported Italian fashions. Claudia, always determined to make her mark in life, had embarked on a full-time secretarial course with the intention of joining Morgan & Buckingham, the new legal partnership in Lingford, professional associates of her father. While Antonia, bubbling with enthusiasm as usual, had announced to everyone who cared to listen that she had decided to become a journalist and had enrolled at night school for shorthand and typing and was doing very well.

Laura remembered feeling insignificant; a mouse with nothing to say, her life empty, surrounded by peers who were vibrant, witty and taking life by the ears and giving it a good shake.

"Night school!" Her mother's combined indignation and incomprehension had shattered the quiet Sunday afternoon tea on the terrace. "Quite impossible! I don't know what you're thinking of!"

"I'm bored, Mummy."

"Nonsense! – in any case, how would get home from Weaversham at nine o'clock at night?"

And what had her father said from behind his Sunday paper? – "She could always catch the bus, Daphne." Yes. She could almost hear his quiet, unruffled voice, a voice that was no longer there to stand between herself and her mother, now, or at any time in the future. It must have been the very first occasion he had expressed an opinion that ran counter to his wife's wishes. Why had this momentous incident not fixed itself more firmly in her mind? He must have known it would be ill-received. And it was. There was a chill in the atmosphere for several days.

And afterwards? – when she was newly turned twenty and armed with her certificates – when she had triumphant-ly returned home with the news she had been offered the position of shorthand-typist at the Bank in Weaversham? While her mother had expressed profound reservations, her father had planted a small, tentative kiss on her forehead, an uncommon act for a man not given to open displays of affection. "Well done, Laura," she remembered him say-ing, adding the inexplicable rider to his congratulations, "Inheriting a fortune isn't everything in life, is it?" What had he been trying to tell her? It was too late to ask him now.

And then six months later, there had been Martin. And when she most wanted his support to strike out on her own, he had chosen not to give it.

Chapter Five

Laura sat at the breakfast table, conscious it was the first Saturday her father was not there to join them.

Opposite, her mother, immaculately groomed as always, was spreading a fine layer of Seville marmalade over her toast. "I'm surprised Oliver isn't taking you out for the day, Laura."

"I asked him not to."

"How very perverse of you."

"I don't feel like socialising at the moment, that's all."

"Life goes on, Laura. You're becoming morose. It won't do."

There was little to be gained in putting forward a contradictory point of view. A silence settled and pervaded the room, filling the space between them. In the hallway, the grandfather clock struck nine.

Daphne finished her tea and replaced the cup delicately onto its saucer. "I thought I'd telephone Millie after breakfast and ask her to take me over to Broxley. Hetty will want to give me her condolences in person," she said. It was a flimsy excuse to impose herself on her sisters in the absence of a direct invitation, and typically thoughtless to expect Millicent to drop everything at a moment's notice to drive over and collect her. It was also hypocritical. Henrietta was twenty-six years Daphne's senior, and because she was 'only' her half-sister – which Daphne clearly regarded as putting some distance between them – she was rarely given the time of day beyond a perfunctory enquiry as to her health. It was an unnecessary snub to a lovely old lady for whom Laura felt a particularly fondness.

"Millie said she would take you out on Monday," Laura reminded her.

Daphne dabbed at the corners of her mouth with her napkin. "I can't expect Hetty to wait until then, can I? It would be most remiss of me."

Laura wished she had the energy to contest the deceitfulness of this little speech, but thought better of it. What was the point? There was going to be friction enough in the months to come.

"Well, if you aren't going out," Daphne was saying, "you may as well deal with the letters that need attention. You can use the study, I suppose."

The King is dead, Laura thought, but there was no male heir to step into his shoes, and already her father's beloved study had become just another room in the Lodge.

Later that morning, Millicent dutifully arrived from Hazeldene Court, cheerfully obliging as usual, and collected her sister. Laura waved them off and closed the door on an empty house, the steady ticking of the clock in the hall her only companion.

She retrieved the assortment of brown envelopes

addressed to 'J Driscoll, Esq' she had carefully removed from her mother's sight by secreting them in the little drawer of the hall table, and opened the door to her father's study. It swung easily on its hinges, opening wide, leaving her standing awkwardly on the threshold, reluctant to enter his private world without his permission. Foolishness, she knew, but during his lifetime, she would never have dreamt of intruding, and even now it felt as if she were doing something unacceptable.

A pale November light reflected the tall window in the glass-covered fronts of the bookcases. The air was still, the room filled with the heavy scent of pipe tobacco, thick, and smelling faintly of warm chocolate. In the grate between the two armchairs, the dead ashes of the last fire to burn there on the previous Sunday lay cold and grey, Elsie, in floods of tears, vowing she couldn't begin to think of entering the room to clear them away until after the funeral. Behind the grand mahogany desk facing the window, the well-loved, and well-worn, black leather swivel chair was pushed back, slightly askew, as if he had just got up from its comfortable warmth and left the room for a moment. And on the desk itself, his favourite possessions were waiting for his return: the Imperial portable typewriter to the left of the immaculate blotter; the exquisite paperweight of Venetian glass streaked with crimson, cobalt blue and yellow strands, a present from a grateful client, holding in place a sheaf of papers requiring his attention; the elegant silver letter opener with chased ivy leaves on the handle, lying next to the carved wooden pencil box, with its intricate pattern of animal heads peeping out from behind lush vegetation; and, in pride of place on the blotter itself, his favourite fountain pen, with its blue-marbled shank and fine gold nib with which he crafted to meticulous perfection his exquisite copperplate handwriting.

His absence was almost a presence.

"May I come in?" she heard herself whisper into the silence.

By mid-afternoon the daylight was already fading. Daphne had not returned, and it was clear she had managed to extend her stay at Broxley until after tea, and very probably until some time later in the evening. By such a stratagem, she could be absent from the house until she retired for the night, and would only have to cope with breakfast the following morning before Richard collected her after church to spend the rest of the day with Cynthia at Dyers Green. Laura suspected this would be the pattern of all weekends to come, a change, she knew, that Gwen for one would be happy to see, the obligation to provide Sunday lunch at the Lodge increasingly onerous now she had grandchildren to visit on Sunday afternoons. The weekday rituals, of course, would simply continue as before.

The finished letters lay in the wire basket ready for posting. Laura drew the heavy brocade curtains against the early winter evening and returned to the comfortable old swivel chair. She settled her head against its high back, her eyes closed against the darkness, leaving the lamp unlit. The room no longer felt strange, nor unwelcoming. The scent of the furniture polish mingled with old tobacco, a scent that would forever evoke her father's presence in a room. It had a comforting familiarity; it blocked out the need to think too much about the future, or where her life was taking her.

In the darkness, behind closed eyes, she could see more clearly. Life could not just 'go on': it was neither rational nor responsible to remain so passive, to drift so aimlessly. There had to be a new beginning.

From somewhere in the past, she could hear her father asking quietly – "Who is he, Laura?"

She felt the heat rising in her cheeks at the memory, and her heart stumble.

Six months after she had settled into her position at the Bank, Martin Evans, the new cashier – and only a year older than herself – had arrived on the scene. He was everything Oliver was not: unsophisticated; merry in a mad-cap sort of way; and occasionally boisterous. He was well-turned out – of course, but not particularly good-looking. But that did not matter. He had that 'something' which had chimed with her spirit of restlessness, and the attraction between them had been mutual from the start. What her mother had feared most, had happened. Her daughter had found life outside the confines of the family offered more satisfactory and interesting diversions. "Inheriting a fortune isn't everything."

Their romance had blossomed quickly. At first it was nothing more than spending lunch times together in The Spinners' Café off Weaversham High Street. But soon it flowered into more than holding hands. There were clandestine meetings in the evening after the Bank closed; trips to the cinema; even days out to Chester when Oliver was immersed in his studies or busy with his father. For Laura, the liaison engendered a new skill: learning to use subterfuge and guile. She started in a small way, commandeering the name of the young typist in the office, Betty Bailey – without her knowledge or consent – to fabricate a non-existent friendship. Once it was established Betty came from 'the right sort of family' – another fiction of Laura's imagination – Daphne had no reason to question the regular nights out at the Odeon. She even encouraged them to keep Laura occupied while Oliver concentrated on his studies. Lying to her mother, she found, came easier with practice.

But if lying became easier, the realisation a genuine romance had grown out of it was harder to handle. Their feelings for one another were becoming increasingly intense. Tentative fumblings in the back row of the Odeon were no longer enough. Martin had lit a spark and stoked a fire in Laura she had never known before – and it threatened to consume them both. She ached for him. Given the opportunity, they would have, without a doubt, taken things to a natural conclusion: the passion was there; the willingness was there. They were in love. He wanted to marry her – and she wanted to marry him. They began to make plans. She would abandon her inheritance and cut herself off from her family. They would be poor – Martin's salary was modest and her own a pittance, there would be no allowance from her parents, and the Bank did not allow husbands and wives to work together – but they would manage. In the way of such affairs of the heart, it mattered not how.

Oliver, still engrossed in his final year of articles and the demands of Gorst & Parr, remained blind to any change in her conduct towards him, their contact dwindling to little more than a series of regular visits between the families, punctuated by Sunday afternoon walks with the cousins, usually accompanied by the younger Parrs and their three Labrador dogs, and by more formal occasions such as Christmas and birthdays. Lying to Oliver therefore was completely unnecessary.

But the best laid plans go awry. It was early Spring only three short years ago. Now, from the perspective of this dark November evening, it seemed like another lifetime. At the Lodge, the daffodils were beginning to nod in the borders, and the flower boxes in Weaversham were brim full of brightly coloured primulas. Martin had taken her to their usual rendezvous at The Spinners' Café after the Bank had closed that Saturday lunch time. They had been totally absorbed in one another, intoxicated by counting the days until she became twenty-one that June, when they could openly declare their love and marry as soon as possible. They had kissed across the table, oblivious to everyone and everything around them.

"Been anywhere special with Betty this afternoon?" her mother had asked casually over the tea table that evening.

Laura remembered feigning an interest in a slice of Gwen's sponge cake, still warm from the oven. "Just the usual place for lunch."

Her mother had put down the tea pot with a deliberate slowness. Laura could still feel the dreadful tightness encircling her heart as she sensed her world was about to crumble into dust.

The glacial stare across the table told her everything was lost. The silence had probably been little more than a moment, but overwhelmed by the sensation a trap was closing in around her, it had seemed like an eternity. Her mother had stood up, a towering Fury. "How dare you! How dare you lie to me! I saw you. In that café. With *that* man!"

Her father had looked up from reading his paper, bewildered, searching her face for answers. "Who is he, Laura?"

Defiance had made her bold enough to try to justify herself. "He's Martin Evans, Daddy. He's a cashier at the Bank – and we want to get married."

He had just stared at her, speechless and troubled.

From across the table, her mother's wrath reached new heights. "Have you taken leave of your senses? You are going to marry Oliver!"

"I don't want to marry Oliver!"

"Don't be silly, girl. Of course you do."

"No, I don't. I don't love him!"

She remembered getting to her feet, and the briefest of pauses before her mother struck her, a single stinging blow across the face. No one had every struck her before, and the shock of it stunned her into silence. It was followed immediately by a catalogue of the consequences of her folly, spelt out in great detail over several minutes. And when the tirade had finished, without a second thought, she had obeyed the imperious command to go to her room and stay there. Throughout this little scene, her father had said absolutely nothing.

By the Monday morning, Mr Gittings had been telephoned and informed an inappropriate relationship had sprung up in the office. Laura was kept at home under the guise of a bad cold, a fiction which allowed Daphne to keep Oliver at arm's length for the duration, and within the week, Martin had been transferred to another branch in Yorkshire. Denied access to one another – all telephone and written communications intercepted – their beautiful romance swiftly, and painfully starved to death, although for months afterwards, Laura had cherished the hope all was not lost. But by the time of her twenty-first birthday, the door on such wishful thinking was irrevocably shut.

What her father thought of the affair, he never revealed to her. He simply took up the duties expected of him, delegated the responsibility of taking her to and from the Bank each day to ensure her compliance with the strictures laid on her. Perhaps he had known what was planned for her twenty-first birthday. If he did, he had remained resolutely silent on the subject, although clearly still troubled. "Let's not talk about it," he would say, when she had tried to explain her actions, but his pained expression left her feeling she had somehow let him down.

CHAPTER SIX

Aunt Millicent had decided Daphne's visit at short notice on the Saturday had relieved her of her obligation to take her sister out for the day on Monday. Daphne, somewhat peeved by this retraction, consequently had the whole day in which to anticipate her visitors that evening. She was, as a result, visibly on edge for most of the time. There was no pleasing her. Gwen had laid out a plate of sandwiches in the kitchen and covered them to keep them fresh. They caused no end of anxiety. Should she have chosen beef rather than ham? – beef was so much nicer with a little dash of dark French mustard – or horseradish. And English mustard was much too commonplace. But what could be done? It was too late to contact Lawson's at six o'clock and expect a delivery that evening.

From her concern over the choice of food, her attention shifted to what drinks she should offer her guests. The sherry glasses were freshly washed and polished and the decanter next to them replenished. But she had forgotten Horace preferred whisky, and was thrown into a flurry of activity organising Laura to ensure the lead crystal tumblers in the drinks cabinet were pristine while she went upstairs to change.

She took longer than usual, appearing at last in her rose-pink twin-set and pearls, with a royal-blue skirt and matching court shoes with a semblance of self-confidence restored. Everything was as it should be, but she was still restless, plumping up cushions, poking the fire, or adjusting the ornaments on the mantelpiece. A large sherry settled her at last on the sofa with enough time to gather her composure before seven o'clock.

Mr Parr was no stranger to the Lodge, but his visits were always social occasions with Phyllis and the children – or the Gorsts, and Mr Jackson rarely came to the Lodge at all, other than to spend an hour or so in communication with her father. Faced with meeting them in their professional capacity, her usually unshakable social competence appeared to have deserted her.

A light frost was glistening on the gravel when the black Rover swept up the drive just as the hall clock struck seven, and Mr Parr, with the diminutive figure of Mr Jackson in tow, emerged quickly to hurry up the steps to the front porch of the Lodge.

"A cold evening tonight, Daphne," Mr Parr observed as she ushered them both into the hall.

"Indeed it is, Horace," she said, perhaps a little over-brightly because of the sherry, and taking their coats and hats as they divested themselves, immediately handed these to Laura to take care of. "Do go into the sitting room, won't you – and take the chairs by the fire. Would you prefer a sherry – or whisky?"

Laura hung up the coats with their respective hats on

the hall-stand and followed them into the sitting room to provide the hospitality expected of her.

Daphne had positioned herself once more at one end of the sofa and was straightening her skirt. "Laura, both Mr Parr and Mr Jackson would like a whisky. I'll have another sherry while you are about it."

Laura filled the glasses as ordered and poured herself a small sherry, remembering on other occasions, her father would have carried out this function.

Mr Parr accepted his tumbler, beaming up at her. "Not back at work yet, I hear."

She shook her head. "Dr Crawley advised against it for a day or so."

"Very wise, Laura. A trying time – and you've not looked yourself for a while now," he added. "Well, do join us, and then we can begin." He glanced briefly in her mother's direction, catching her evident surprise at such an invitation. "Laura needs to stay," he explained. "There are one or two provisions in the Will which affect her."

"Oh – I see."

Laura positioned herself at the other end of the sofa, wondering what all the fuss was about, and sipped at her sherry. It was too sweet and she put the half-drunk glass back on the table next to her.

Mr Parr opened his briefcase and took out a wad of papers, balancing them carefully on his knee. He studied them for a moment and then smiled optimistically in Daphne's direction. "As I mentioned when we last spoke, Daphne, Arthur is here as the surviving partner of Driscoll & Jackson to help explain one or two matters. Arthur?"

Mr Jackson gave a small cough and sampled his whisky before clearing his throat once more. To Laura's surprise, he began to address himself directly to her, his pale-blue eyes peering myopically at her from behind his thick-lensed spectacles with unblinking earnestness. "As you know from your banking practice and position as Mr Gittings' Secretary," he began solemnly, "a partnership is dissolved on the death of a partner unless an agreement exists to ensure the continuation of the business."

Laura confirmed this was true, glancing in her mother's direction in the hope he would take the hint and include her in his observations, but he seemed resolutely determined not to.

"Your father and I drew up such an agreement in 1946," he went on. "We thought it was in both our interests."

Daphne leaned forward to interpose herself into the conversation. "I'm sure it was, Arthur," she said stiffly.

Mr Jackson acknowledged her comment with the briefest of nods, but continued to address himself to Laura. It was an uncomfortable moment, one which revealed that, regardless of Daphne's comprehension of the minutiae of the Harriman Trusts, in the understanding of wider financial matters, Mr Jackson regarded Laura as being the more knowledgeable. It was not lost on her mother.

Apparently unaware of the irritation he was causing, he continued. "The agreement covers your father's share of the business – as you would expect – including the capital tied up in the property of Driscoll & Jackson – that is, our offices in Lingford – and of course his contribution to the goodwill of the business."

Daphne was no longer prepared to take a back seat in the proceedings. "I'm sure you don't need to go into the finer details, Arthur," she said, a tight smile pulling at the corners of her mouth.

Cut off in the middle of his flow, Mr Jackson recognised he may have unwittingly caused offence. "Of course," he said, visibly retreating into the depths of his armchair to gather his composure, and glancing nervously in Mr Parr's direction for support, which came in the form of the slight inclination of his head in the general direction of their hostess. "To put it simply then," he continued, now feeling obliged to include Daphne in the conversation, "there is money due to James's estate from the business – in the region of four-thousand pounds. This amount is to be kept in a fund to generate income for the running and maintenance costs of Meeston Lodge."

"That seems perfectly sensible," Daphne observed, and there was a momentary pause during which Mr Jackson downed the remainder of his whisky and lapsed into silence. Laura remained bemused by his need to tell her the financial arrangements for the upkeep of the Lodge.

"Right then," Mr Parr continued, shuffling through his papers. "Thank you, Arthur. I think that's made matters perfectly clear. Now we come to the Will itself." He brought the document to the top of the pile and with almost studied carefulness attached a sheet of handwritten notes to the front of it with a paper clip. "What I thought might be best," he began, making sure his words were addressed to both parties sitting at either end of the sofa, "is rather than simply reading through it – it is, I have to say, a somewhat complex and lengthy document – I would run through the basic provisions – minus the legalistic terminology – and leave the copy for you to digest later at your leisure. Is that acceptable?" He smiled in an encouraging sort of way designed to defy any contradiction without the perpetrator appearing churlish.

Daphne, still evidently wrestling with the complexities of partnership agreements and her daughter's apparent understanding of them, acquiesced with a nervous smile and sip of sherry. "Yes, Horace, that would be perfectly satisfactory."

"Stop me of course, if I haven't made myself clear."

"Of course. Please go on."

Mr Parr seemed in no hurry to begin, as if he were mentally rehearsing his lines before giving them voice. "Right then," he said finally. "The Will is dated the seventh of September nineteen-sixty-two. I'll deal with the simplest matters first and move on to the more complicated aspects that require Arthur and myself to administer. First, there are three specific bequests." He paused. "Gwen Davis, Elsie Fleming and Robert Moray are each to receive six hundred pounds."

Laura heard her mother's astonished intake of breath at such generosity. "Goodness me, Horace! What can James have been thinking of? Six hundred pounds each?

They won't want to stay on at the Lodge with six hundred pounds each."

Mr Parr continued as though nothing had been said. "Daphne, you are to retain a lifetime interest in the Lodge, provided you don't remarry."

Her mother's mortification reached new heights. "Remarry! As if I would do such a thing!" she said, visibly shocked at such a suggestion. A nervous hand played with the string of pearls at her throat and she reached for her sherry for moral support.

Mr Parr attempted reassurance, happy perhaps to deflect her attention away from weightier matters. "It does happen, Daphne. And in your case, at fifty-four – if you'll forgive me for mentioning your age – it's not entirely an unreasonable supposition. James was, as usual, being pragmatic. However," he said, keeping his eyes firmly on his handwritten notes, "in view of your financial situation as one of the heiresses to the Harriman fortune – and to reduce the burden of death duties in the future – Meeston Lodge is bequeathed to Laura."

Laura studied her hands lying passively in her lap. Mr Jackson's reasons for explaining the financial arrangements for the upkeep of the Lodge to her were now patently clear. The Lodge was hers. She sat waiting for her mother's reaction, but it never came. Perhaps the copious amount of sherry had clouded her mental faculties, but she appeared not to grasp the enormity of this bequest that left her little more than a lodger in her own home.

The fire hissed in the grate. A plume of blue flame burst

briefly into life and subsided into a lazy curl of smoke. Laura followed its upward progress until it disappeared from view.

For twenty-four years, she thought, her image of her father had been one of a benign, but remote, undemonstrative man, overshadowed by his wife and her family's forebears. At no time could she honestly say she had felt close to him, or had any indication from him that she figured very largely in his life. This fixed, solid image of him was now being steadily eroded and reconstructed into an entirely different entity – someone she neither recognised, nor could honestly say she had ever known.

"Now, where were we?" Mr Parr was musing, running a finger down his list of notes. "Ah, yes – division of assets." He engaged Daphne's attention again with an encouraging smile. "Arthur will fill in the background details for you."

Mr Jackson obliged, referring to a document he had produced from a folder in his briefcase. "As you know, Mrs Driscoll," he said – although Laura now suspected it was likely she did not – "James had a portfolio which produced a considerable dividend income. I've recommended a firm of stock brokers to Horace who will arrange for these holdings to be sold and the resultant moneys added to the estate. As a rough guideline, I believe this will raise between thirty-five and forty thousand pounds – and of course, this does not include the sums held in his various bank accounts which amount to roughly five-thousand pounds."

Laura had the impression her mother was no longer fully engaged in the proceedings: she was smoothing out the fabric of her skirt with small, repetitive movements, while her brow sank into a deep frown of concentration.

Mr Parr had also noticed her distraction. "Are we going a bit fast for you, Daphne?" he enquired, without any suggestion she might be rather slow on the up-take.

"No – no," she reassured him. "It's all just a little overwhelming."

"Of course. Of course. Quite understandable."

The fire was dying down. Laura took the opportunity to add more coal and then ask if either of the gentlemen would like their glasses refilled. Both declined. Her mother, however, required another sherry.

"Now," continued Mr Parr once everyone was settled again. "The moneys Arthur has just mentioned form the basis of the rest of the Will. James made very specific arrangements for your both." There was a significant pause, as if he were signalling he was about to import something of great consequence. "Firstly," he began, turning to Laura, "all the moneys realised from the sale of his stocks and shares are bequeathed to you unconditionally. Secondly," and he turned to Daphne, continuing perhaps before the full implications of this gift had sunk in, "the combined total from his bank accounts is to be placed in a Trust operated by myself and Arthur for your benefit. You can access these funds on request at our discretion, but the intention of the fund is to provide a financial safety net in the event of your needing additional finance in your old age. I realise this is unlikely, of course, but nonetheless, life is uncertain, and a little extra is always welcome. On your death, however, the Trust will be wound up and any remaining funds transferred to Laura. Should she die during your lifetime without issue – as they say – the Trust would again be wound up and you would receive all the funds unconditionally. However," he added, without allowing room for interruption, "if Laura should have any children who survive her, the Trust would remain in force until your demise, at which time the funds would be shared equally between her surviving children and administered for their benefit until such time as they reach their majority. And that," he added, without a pause, and with what might have been construed as undue haste, "concludes the Will. I hope everything's clear. I haven't rushed it, have I? Muddled anything?"

Daphne, who appeared to have sunk into a reverie, recovered herself sufficiently to respond, "No – not at all, Horace."

Mr Parr was supremely satisfied with this. "Excellent. Excellent," he said, beaming all round.

Laura suddenly felt the need to escape. "Would either of you like some sandwiches," she suggested. "Or tea?"

Mr Parr was still all smiles. "That's very kind of you, Laura. I think we might take you up on that. Sandwiches, Arthur?"

Mr Jackson nodded his assent. "Very acceptable," he said.

She got up, only too willing to oblige.

Mr Parr followed her to the door. "Actually, Laura, if I could have a quick word with you? Arthur, would you mind going over the Trust fund arrangements with Daphne again, just to clarify any aspects that might not be entirely clear?"

"Of course," Mr Jackson agreed, eager to engage

Daphne's attention while Mr Parr ushered Laura out of the room.

As they emerged into the hall, Mr Parr's smile evaporated. "Perhaps we could use your father's study?" he suggested. There was a note of urgency in his voice.

The curtains had not been pulled across when they entered, and the room was dark and cheerless. Laura went over the window to close them. "I'd have lit the fire if I'd known..."

He cut her short. "Please sit down, Laura. I need to deal with this quickly."

She obeyed his summons without question, his manner so alien, she began to suspect something dreadful.

"You know, of course, that by the terms of his Will, your father has effectively made you his main beneficiary – and given you complete financial independence."

"Yes – but I don't know why."

He took from his inside jacket pocket a thick brown envelope and handed it to her. "This is for you – and only you. It was left in my safe-keeping together with his Will." The front of the envelope was marked 'For the personal attention of Miss Laura Driscoll'. "And this," he added, producing a folded octavo sheet of paper from the same pocket, "is his covering letter to me. You will see that he asks me to let you read it."

She unfolded the letter. It was written in her father's immaculate copperplate script bearing the date two days prior to his Will.

'Dear Horace,' it began.

'The attached sealed letter is for Laura. Please ensure it is handed to her privately as soon as possible after my Will is read. I trust this will not prove too difficult to effect.

'I must stress that under no circumstances should the existence of the letter, or its contents, be disclosed to my wife at any time, now or in the future.

'I would be grateful if you would also let Laura have sight of this letter to you.

'Kindest regards

'James Driscoll'

She folded up the letter and handed it back to him, unable to make sense of anything. "Does Uncle Richard know? – about the Will? – about this?"

"No."

"I see." She looked down at the ominous brown envelope lying crisp and unopened in her lap. "Do you know what he's written in it, Mr Parr?" She hoped he did – to give her some inkling as to its contents.

"I'm sorry, I have no idea." He smiled apologetically. "But you should know there is also a second letter – and I'm instructed to hand it to you in three months time, at which point it will be up to you whether you accept it, or empower me to destroy it in your presence."

A small, incredulous laugh surfaced, which refused to be stifled. "How ludicrously melodramatic, Mr Parr. It doesn't sound a bit like Daddy at all."

"I can assure you, Laura, he was absolutely serious about his instructions."

"How odd. What can he mean by it?"

"I'm sorry – I've no idea." He reached out and took her hand. "I know this is probably deeply insensitive of me to mention at such a time, but when probate is granted – probably in six months or seven months from now – you are going to be a very wealthy young woman in your own right. Think about this. It could change your life." He made it sound almost like a warning.

"Yes, I realise."

"At the moment, I don't think your mother has quite grasped the situation, but when she does, she probably won't be in any hurry to broadcast your inheritance – it would raise too many questions about the provisions made for herself. At least, that's what your father hoped. Can I suggest therefore that a discreet silence on the subject might serve you best as well."

She nodded.

"Right – now go and find somewhere safe to keep the letter, and then we can go back into the sitting room and I can help you serve the sandwiches."

CHAPTER SEVEN

Their visitors stayed until almost eleven, and it proved impossible for Laura to excuse herself before they left. And so the contents of the ominous brown envelope remained unread.

For the whole of the evening Laura remained in a state of perpetual anxiety, constantly expecting some reference to the Will to be mentioned, even in passing, and imagining every sort of difficulty arising from this. It was very taxing. As it happened, there was a complete silence on the subject, her mother casually depositing the copy document in her writing desk during the course of an entirely unrelated conversation. It seemed to give weight to Mr Parr's impression that she had not yet fully grasped the situation.

As soon as Daphne had waved their guests off the premises, she retired, leaving Laura with a dilemma. In the interests of secrecy, she had hidden the envelope in the safest place she could think of – behind her stock of sketch pads and artists' materials in the bottom of her chest of drawers. This piece of ancient furniture, inherited from Hazeldene Court, was of robust construction, and the bottom drawer, not used as often as the others, had a habit of groaning or squeaking, or both, when it was opened or closed. If she had been able to access it again earlier in the evening while Mr Parr and Mr Jackson were still being entertained downstairs, this would not have been a problem. In the silence of the night however, the sound would waken the dead, never mind her mother, and under the circumstances, she had no wish to encourage a visit from her demanding to know what she was doing disturbing the peace at such an hour. So the envelope remained secreted away while she lay in bed fretting about its contents, and listening to the passing hours marked by the chiming of the clock in the hall, or the occasional hooting of owls in Meeston Woods. Somewhere around six o'clock she must have fallen into a deep sleep. She was still asleep when, three hours later, her mother was at the door demanding to know why she was still in bed when Elsie had arrived to do the weekly linen.

Thick-headed and longing to be left alone without interruption, there was at least some comfort in the discovery Gwen had taken the day off to visit her daughter, Penny, who was expecting her third child at any time, and Elsie was too busy in the laundry room to engage in chit-chat.

"I'm having an early lunch," her mother announced when Laura finally came down to breakfast. "There's a Village Hall Committee at two and I want to have a word with Mr Stockdale first. Take the key if you go out."

The morning stretched ahead of her in an endless succession of minor tasks, the frequent consultations of her watch confirming the theory that time can be annoyingly elastic. By one o'clock Daphne had eaten and was fussing over her appearance in the hall mirror. Laura lazed on the sofa in sitting room, ostensibly reading the latest county magazine but otherwise in a frenzy of subdued impatience waiting for her to leave.

At last, Daphne said her goodbyes.

Retrieving the bulky envelope from the back of the drawer, Laura sat on the edge of her bed and looked at it, suddenly paralysed at the prospect of opening it. She could hear her heart thumping loudly in her ears, beating much faster than usual, and a tightness in the midriff reminiscent of examination nerves. Shivers were running down her back. Pull yourself together, she told herself, and tore open the flap. Inside, the several sheets of vellum writing-paper were inscribed with her father's beautiful and precisely executed script.

She sat quietly for a moment, collecting her thoughts, letting her heart-rate settle, and her breathing drop to a slower, steadier rhythm. She must not rush this.

'My Dearest Laura' – it began.

Perplexed, she read the words a second time, noting the elegant flourish of the pen as it formed the capital letters. If she had not recognised his writing, she would have sworn he had not written such terms of endearment. Never once in her life had he addressed her with such tenderness.

'My Dearest Laura' – she read again.

'I write this now because I must. Dr Crawley has confirmed my fears that time is short, and I need to let you know my true feelings before it is too late. I have so much on my mind that needs to be said.

'I look back on my life, Laura, with a sense of guilt. I have allowed myself the luxury of self-interest, which not only cast a cloud over my own life, but yours as well.

'More than thirty years ago, I confess, I invented a history for myself as a means of advancement. There were aspects of my background which were less than savoury and I saw them as detrimental to my prospects. But facts are facts. They do not go away because you want them to.

'The truth is, Laura, I lied to your grandfather, letting him believe I was more than I was. I married your mother knowing it would be to my advantage – that by such a marriage, I would acquire wealthy clients who would have been beyond my reach. For her part, she saw me as a successful professional man, and that was enough. She has never questioned my history, Laura, either because she chose not to, or did not wish to know.

'It has not been a happy marriage. Perhaps it never could be without at least some affection in it, and overshadowed as it was by her father's desire that we should have a son. When this was denied us, from the moment you were born, your grandfather was determined that you and Oliver should marry. The only consideration for him, and your mother, was that the Harriman fortune should remain intact to be handed on to the next generation.

'You might find it difficult to understand why no one thought to challenge this philosophy, but your grandfather was not a man to cross. You may not remember him, Laura – you were very young when you last saw him – but Edward Harriman was a patriarch from a bygone age. His word was law, just as his father's and grandfather's had been before him. Your dear Aunt Henrietta could tell you more.

'It is to my eternal shame that I never stood up to him, or your mother, letting them dictate what was best for you. If you had not opened my eyes, Laura, I would never have seen that what I was doing was patently wrong. Your determination to be yourself made me take stock. I saw the world of the Harrimans belonged to the past, and the future belonged to you.

'Over the last few years, I have watched you flourish in your own right, and not sink into the shadows of someone else's dreams. Your successes pleased me. But still I held my peace. When I look back, the one defining moment that should have forced me to break my silence was when Oliver proposed to you. It was a splendid piece of theatre, and no doubt he believed he was playing his part in maintaining the Harriman tradition. Perhaps he still does. But I saw in his manner no passion, no adoration, just duty – and your face conveyed not love, nor even affection, just bewilderment – and I have seen nothing since that convinces me that you are right for one another.

'And then there was Martin. If I had given you even part of what I am giving to you now, you could have married him – if that was what you really wanted. Forgive me that I was too weak to support you when you needed me most. At the time, I knew Oliver intended to propose to you, and I lacked the courage to pursue the possibility Martin meant more to you than just a passing fancy.

'Perhaps I have misinterpreted your feelings for Oliver,

and you do truly love him, or at the very least feel some affection for him. If this is so, then you have my blessing. But if you feel nothing for him, Laura, then do not marry him. I do not expect it of you, and I would not have you go into a loveless marriage as I did.

'You will know that Mr Parr holds a second letter in trust for you. It contains details of my less than admirable family history, should you wish to know it. However, if you are determined to marry Oliver, you must destroy both letters. No good could come of keeping them. Please do not be anxious that I might have done something in my past which was in any way unlawful. I have not. I have worked hard and prospered, and can at least console myself that I am passing on to you the fruits of my industry.

'I am sorry, Laura. It grieves me I was not the father to you that I should have been. My life has left me over-cautious and afraid to show my feelings. Perhaps some of these fears were ill-founded, but I want you to know that you had my love. Let my legacy to you be the means to make your own life. My greatest wish is that you find success and happiness whatever path you choose.

'Your loving father

'James Driscoll'

She put the letter down beside her on the coverlet. There were so many emotions swirling in her head, she was dazed. He had raised memories she had smothered, preferring peace of mind, and left them like old sores needing to be healed.

So many memories. Martin, whom she had truly loved.

Her grandfather – a terrifying figure to a four-year old; eighty-eight and still as straight as a ramrod, with dark piercing eyes beneath heavy brows, and a hooked nose. He had towered above her, like a ferocious eagle in one of her story books. She had the clear recollection of him bending down, his face very close to hers, his long bony finger prodding her shoulder. "You'll be a fine wife for Oliver, young lady. Remember that." Remember that? – it had become a mantra repeated over and over again throughout her life until she could no longer think for herself.

And another memory – Saturday, the sixth of June 1959 – her birthday. She was twenty-one, still hurting from the loss of Martin, and what might have been. He was gone, and life with Oliver remained the only option.

Her mother had organised a celebration of family and friends at The George Hotel in Weaversham, and bought her a long, black silk dress with a low-cut bodice and narrow waist that flattered her figure. There had been a pair of patent leather court shoes, and a clutch-bag to match trimmed with little gold bows. Estelle, the ladies hairdresser from Weaversham, had come to the Lodge, and sculpted her hair into a perfect French pleat for the evening with a black and gold comb at one side. The image of herself in her full-length mirror had startled her, revealing the mature young woman she had become.

At the hotel, a press of well-wishers had greeted her, and Julius Parr – or Jules, as he now preferred to be called – had bustled in an out of the mêlée taking endless photographs. There had been presents thrust into her hands, those from the younger Gorsts and Parrs unremarkable: silly trinkets, teddy-bears and dolls to sit on her pillow, as if she had been a child of eight. From others, gifts of more lasting value: from her parents, a Swiss watch with a gold bracelet she wore every day since; from her Harriman Aunts, pretty pieces of jewellery; from her Uncle Richard and Aunt Cynthia, a gold pen and propelling pencil in a red leather case; and from the Parrs, a silver necklace of hearts. Friends of her mother had opted for silk handkerchiefs, perfumes and sundry toiletries. And from those who were not invited, but had sent gifts all the same – a useful recipe book from Gwen; a beautiful porcelain swan from Elsie, that must have cost her at least a week's wages – and now had pride of place on the mantel shelf in her bedroom; and a pocket-sized book with detailed coloured illustrations of wild flowers from Mr Moray, simply inscribed in his neat handwriting – 'To Laura Driscoll on her coming of age. 6th June 1959. With best wishes from Robert Moray.'

Oliver's gift had been noticeable by its absence. She had shrugged off the omission, but it had left her anxious.

After dinner, her father had made a little speech to mark the event, and sat down looking embarrassed at the need to bring himself so openly into the public gaze. There had been applause, a toast and everyone had settled once again. Except Oliver. She could see him now in his immaculate dinner suit: tall, elegant and good-looking in a film-star kind of way – a younger version of Clark Gable perhaps, without the moustache – every young girl's dream – except hers.

He had cleared his throat, looking around the assembled company, waiting for silence. She could remember him saying, "I know it has long been the wish of many of you here that Laura and I should make our way in life together." There had been polite applause and a few here-heres. "Well, I thought tonight would be the most appropriate occasion to publicly make my formal proposal." He had moved towards her between the tables, reaching out and taking her by the hand to raise her to her feet. "Laura Driscoll," he had said, turning to include everyone in the room, "Will you do me the honour of becoming my wife?" There had been cheers of approval, and Jules had stepped forward to take another photograph.

Could she have said "No"? – in the midst of this family with such fixed expectations of their marriage? She was cornered, with no way out. He had not even waited for her reply. He had smiled at her indulgently and produced a small box from his waistcoat pocket. Inside was the engagement ring she still wore on family occasions: a trio of diamonds set on a twisted gold band; it sparkled brightly, reflecting the lights in the chandeliers. With a flourish, he placed it on her finger, kissed her hand and raised it for everyone to see. To applause and general congratulations, he had reached across and shaken her father's hand and given Daphne, glowing with unbounded satisfaction, a quick peck on the cheek. The remainder of the evening had become a blur. All she could remember now was her father, watching her intently, and old Aunt Henrietta, sitting on the table next to her, gazing at her with large, sad eyes.

If she could remember little of that evening, she could vividly recall the day that followed – the most abiding memory of all. Oliver had called to collect her in his new car – a black Riley like his father's. He was more interested in driving than their final destination.

It had been a beautiful summer's afternoon, with light, fluffy clouds in a china-blue sky. After an hour or so, they had stopped in a secluded spot beyond Broxley, and got out to walk down to the river. A warm breeze ruffled the leaves of the willows along the bank. He had spread out the travel rug in the shade of an alder, and they had sat in silence watching the sunlight dancing on the water. He had lit a cigarette. The minutes had passed. The ring on her finger still felt strange, and she had been thinking of Martin. After a while, she had screwed up her courage enough to ask him, "Oliver – do you love me?"

He had laughed at her. "Good God, Laura! What a question! Of course I do." But he had turned away, finishing his cigarette and throwing the butt into the water.

"When will we get married?"

"In four years time, I suppose. When they make me junior partner."

"It's a long time."

He had studied her for a moment, then moved closer. "We don't have to wait until then, you know. We are engaged. I've got a rubber with me."

She felt sick now at that memory. She should have stopped him. She should have said, "No." But she had not. Why not? Somehow she had deceived herself into believing she had no option. She had accepted his ring. She was engaged. They were to be married.

What followed had been a series of pathetic gropings; passionless, wooden and deeply embarrassing. His mouth had fastened on hers like a leech. There had been no tenderness, no affection, just mechanical action, his hands not so much caressing or fondling, as kneading; his awkward shoving and pushing into her, painful and humiliating. Any satisfaction he might have had from this encounter, incompetent as it was, had been entirely his. For Laura, bewildered and appalled, the episode had revealed to her, in the starkest possible terms, that their engagement was a terrible mistake.

For three years now, their relationship had stagnated. Perhaps the embarrassment had been mutual, and he had decided sex was better left until they were married. It was a topic they never discussed. Instead, he remained mildly attentive, but little more, apparently believing their engagement relieved him of the need to spend too much time with her alone. The social circle of Gorsts and Parrs had closed around them. Once he finished his studies, the weekends had become predictable: on Saturday evenings there were parties 'for the young folk' in the basement of Highfield House, hosted by the Parrs, with the relief of occasionally seeing new faces as the Parr siblings spread their wings; the fortnightly dances in Lingford Town Hall – although these was less successful because Claudia was always the odd one out unless Oliver or Stephen took pity on her. Sundays likewise began to slip into a regular routine:

in summer, picnics or drinks at the tennis club and possibly a couple of matches; in winter, if the weather permitted, long walks between Weaversham and Broxley taking along the Parrs' three Labradors – and if not, listening, or singing along to records by Buddy Holly or the Everly Brothers in the basement of Highfield House, or playing darts and table tennis.

Her father had seen it all – the suffocating dead weight of other people's lives dragging her down. In the end, he had intervened the only way he could.

A great ache began to swell inside her, filling her with an overwhelming sense of loss. She could picture him sitting behind his great mahogany desk, pouring out his love to her in a letter she would only read when he was dead. And now it was too late to go downstairs, open the study door and put her arms around him. Too late for him to look up, smile and embrace her in return. Too late for anything that mattered.

CHAPTER EIGHT

Her head was buzzing. The bedroom walls suddenly seemed much closer, the rosebuds on the wallpaper pin-sharp, their pinks more intense against the beige background. The atmosphere had become suffocatingly warm, pressing in on her. She felt sick. She must get out.

Hastily, she replaced the letter in the back of the drawer and ran downstairs. At the back porch, her everyday boots were waiting by the door, her thick woollen socks stuffed into their tops. She pushed her feet into them, unhooking the old green duffle coat from its peg and scrambling into it, throwing the long grey scarf around her neck as she fled down the steps into the walled garden.

It was already mid-afternoon, and the lowering clouds of the November sky would bring an early evening. If she took the short cut through the woods there would be light enough to see her home.

The latch on the gate to the walled garden clicked shut, and she hurried down the drive, listening to the gravel scrunching underneath her feet. At the entrance to the Lodge she turned left onto Meeston Road. A few yards further on, the iron kissing-gate opened into Meeston

Woods, and for a while, the footpath followed the tall beech hedge along the western boundary of the Lodge. The ground was soft and muddy, well-trodden by those who took their dogs for walks, or young couples seeking privacy in lesser known places.

She walked briskly, her thoughts random and erratic, like a broken string of pearls, impossible to catch. Ridiculously, snatches of song kept surfacing in her memory, refusing to go away.

'Love letters straight from your heart, keep us so near while apart...'

She could not remember the singer's name. Had she heard it on the radio? Or had Betty Bailey been crooning it in the staff room during the lunch hour?

'I'm not alone in the night, when I can have all the love you write.'

She had written to Martin. He had never replied. Or perhaps he had, but the letter had been confiscated.

'Maybe Baby, I'll have you-ou-ou.'

On the juke-box at the Expresso Bar. Dancing down the street to the bus stop, singing their heads off with the sheer joy of living.

'Maybe Baby, you'll be true-ue-ue.'

Kissing and holding each other close waiting for the last bus from Weaversham to Meeston, the blood pumping through her veins.

She had missed her way. Her mind distracted, she had followed her usual route, choosing the narrower, less-favoured path that circled the outer edges of the woods, winding between coppiced hazel, sapling oaks, and stands of beech and birches where sudden clearings led to marshy ground and boggy pools. Here were her secret places, the endless source of inspiration, filling her sketch books with intricate flower studies that marked the passing seasons, giving her the chance to be herself, just for a while.

Today, the air was chill, filled with the sweet dark scent of ancient mosses and fallen timber, succumbing to decay. She looked back. She had come too far. The fork in the footpath was well behind her now; to retrace her steps would gain her nothing.

She must hurry then. No time to reflect on where the pale primroses clustered on sunny banks in the spring, or where the shy dog violets lay hidden; or recall the dappled shade between the beeches where the fragile wood anemones merged with clumps of wild garlic, their pungent aroma swirling on the breeze when they were trampled, and where, if she looked hard enough, she would find the strange forms of the Lords-and-Ladies wearing their weird spotted hoods.

She half ran, trying to make up lost time, stumbling and sliding as the path descended rapidly through taller trees, past where a haze of bluebells carpeted the clearings between the oaks and beeches in mid-May, and marsh orchids could be found along the edge of ditches; past where the purple foxgloves and white drifts of stitchworts mingled with the pinks of Herb Robert in summer, and around the boggy fringes of small pools where the sallows grew and flag irises flourished, while lush green stinging nettles and broad-leaved docks vied with the soft creams and rich scent of meadowsweet; and further on, to where in early Autumn, multi-coloured fungi pushed through dense coverings of leaves over-night, and tan flat-topped brackets, as big as saucers, sprang from the base of beeches, to turn as hard as wood with age.

She stopped to catch her breath, giddy, listening to the thudding of her heart. She looked up. Above, the trees were sullen grey-black skeletons etched against an iron sky – and nothing stirred. Everything seemed to be waiting. For what?

"What are *you* waiting for, Laura Driscoll?" A voice from the past in her head – Miss Evelyn Hay, patient teacher of English – and fourteen-year old Laura, day-dreaming as usual, unaware she had been asked to read the poem. Was it Tennyson who wrote – *Come my friends, 'tis not too late to seek a newer world*? She couldn't remember. Miss Hay would have been cross at her forgetfulness. Did it matter? The words matched her state of mind.

She reached the old stone wall leading down to the main footpath, stumbling a little, her legs unwilling to hold her. At the iron gate that opened onto Nether Meeston Lane below the row of cottages, she stopped again, and took stock. There were venerable oaks here, the ground beneath them studded with acorn cups, their treasure already harvested by mice and squirrels. That Summer, she had idly wandered here between the trees, searching for inspiration, and unexpectedly discovered Mr Moray with Susan Holbrook in his arms. They were kissing, caught in a shaft of sunlight, and oblivious to anything around them.

She had stopped in her tracks and retraced her steps rather than embarrass them. But for a long time afterwards, the image persisted, her heart catching at memories of other walks, at other times, with Martin – and she envied them.

'*Maybe Baby, I'll have you-ou-ou* some day.'

She went through the gate onto Nether Meeston Lane below the three farm cottages and headed up towards The Cross at the centre of the village. It was strangely quiet, the school-children long-since wheedled from the sweets in The Village Shop and taken home for tea and *Children's Hour*.

The brisk walk up the lane had left her hot and breathless. She stopped at The Cross, studying the simple message at its base. *Lest We Forget*. Carved in stone. The Remembrance Service had been the week before, the day before her father died. Now the wreaths of poppies, laid with loving care, were bedraggled and sad. She lifted her eyes to read the names on the plaque. Like so much in her life, she had taken them for granted. Some were familiar; some less so. Janet Woods from the Post Office had lost a grandfather at Ypres; Frank and Mary Taylor, who ran The Village Shop with their daughter, Linda, had lost a son sailing with an Atlantic Convoy; and Caroline Fawcett's husband, Duncan, had been a pilot in Bomber Command – missing, and presumably dead. She had never remarried, living alone in her sprawling Victorian mansion in Upper Meeston, waiting perhaps for his return.

War had never touched her, Laura realised – nor Oliver – not in the way of losing someone close, or knowing the horrors of a bombing raid. Her father had been in the 40th

Cheshire Home Guard, was all she knew, and presumably her Uncle Richard too, although it was never raised in general conversation. And being so young at the time, her own recollections were few: the inconvenience of rationing – a never-ending source of complaint from her mother; and the need for blackout regulations – strictly adhered to. And at an age when she might have understood things better, she was wrapped up in another world at Hunters Lane, proud of the status of 'term-boarder', while Rosemary and the Parr sisters were just 'day girls' – not nearly so impressive. And she had new friends too – Felicity Shaw, all freckles and daring, and Vivian Harvey, very 'County', who was as bright as a button, and knew a thing or two about boys, having older brothers. The three of them had grown up together, shared secrets, and had crushes on the same film stars – Gregory Peck and Robert Mitchum; they had quarrelled, made up again, and been as thick as thieves. Now there was no one she could turn to, to confide in, as her life rushed headlong into the unknown. Contact had been lost long ago. Their lives had moved on and their interests had diverged. Letters became less frequent and finally did not come at all. Felicity had joined the Civil Service, and moved to London; Vivian had got a First in English at Manchester, but was currently to be seen in the pages of *Country Life* on the arm of the Honourable Jonathan Baxendale.

'Tis not too late to seek a newer world…

She should go home, she told herself. She felt very strange. But her legs refused to go, taking her instead up Smallcross Lane.

In the windows of the post-war semis, lights were being put on and curtains closed against the coming night. The air had turned colder, and the curling smoke from the chimneys spiralled downwards into the road, filling her lungs with its acrid tang. She struck off to the right into Weavers Walk with its ancient cottages, lovingly restored but made ugly with television aerials sprouting from their roofs. At the field-gate to St Wilfrid's Meadow she stopped and looked back across the village, filled with people she knew by sight, but did not know: the acolytes of her mother; the willing workers who ran the stalls at village fêtes and were on the church flower rota; the parents of children she should have grown up with, but had not; the children themselves – some of whom had children of their own – who barely spoke to her beyond a nod. Perhaps they considered her remote, stuck-up, or both. She had been born in this village, but was not 'of it'. She had become a stranger living in their midst.

Her head was throbbing now, her eyes aching. She went through the gate into St Wilfrid's Meadow and broke into a shambling run along the muddy path for no good reason she could think of, except the need to release the dam of pent-up emotion flooding into her. A noisy flock of rooks took off and flapped ahead of her, cawing raucously as they wheeled away to their roost beyond the Vicarage. She chased after them in a futile, headlong flight, stumbling out into Vicarage Lane, breathless and hot, feeling stupid. But no one had seen her: the school was in darkness; the playground empty.

Dusk was settling. The dark shape of St Wilfrid's

rose above her to the left on its higher ground, the trees whispering with the rising wind.

She should go to her father's grave and cry her heart out on it. But she felt weak, and barely able to stand. She struggled on.

The street-lights were flickering into life as she reached Meeston Road. Across from where she stood loomed the large stone pillars flanking the entrance to the Lodge. The house would soon be hers, but it no longer felt like home.

The light was on in the porch. Her mother had returned, and would be expecting her for tea. There would be the usual inquisition – where had she been? – what had she been doing? – how could she possibly get herself into such a filthy state?'

'Tis not too late to seek a newer world...

She felt close to tears. "Where do I go to from here?" she demanded to know.

But there was no reply.

CHAPTER NINE

Influenza – or a close cousin, as Dr Crawley put it – was rarely, if ever, a blessing. For Laura however, once the drumming behind her eyes had lessened and the feverish bouts of shivering subsided, its arrival was almost welcome. The long hours drifting in an out of sleep induced a blissful, undemanding state in which her thoughts no longer buffeted around her brain, and the questions which demanded answers mattered not one jot.

The shortening days merged into a haze of semi-consciousness interspersed with nourishing broth, milky drinks, hot water bottles and regular doses of aspirin, all served up by Gwen, who had never caught 'flu in her life, she maintained – Asian or otherwise – and wasn't going to be intimidated by the latest version. No, indeed not! – despite several other cases being diagnosed in the village. Besides – as she was at pains to point out – those who had succumbed were either on the younger side of thirty, or the very old, who always caught everything, which was why Elsie had decided to stay away too, fearing for the health of her elderly mother. Daphne, of course, was far too busy marshalling her troops for the forthcoming Christmas Fayre to turn her attention to nursing an invalid, and if Gwen was happy to offer her services – even over the weekend – then this was perfectly acceptable.

Aunt Millicent however was less amenable, suggesting Daphne should cancel her Saturday visit to Hazeldene Court – just in case. "Hetty's always been a bit susceptible – ever since that Spanish 'Flu in nineteen-nineteen."

Daphne took this rebuff as a personal insult.

Friday saw the arrival of a card from Oliver with the picture of a Golden Labrador on the front, its head on its paws, looking just like Claudia's Poppy with its large, liquid brown eyes and doleful expression. "Sorry you're not well," the message read inside. "Get well soon so I can take you to the new jazz club in Lingford. Hope you don't mind if I go this weekend with the others. Love, Oliver. xx"

Why should she mind? She was content to keep him occupied elsewhere – and he seemed happiest these days when they were part of a crowd. But he must have felt a pang of guilt because, on Saturday morning, a bouquet of expensive red roses arrived with a little note from him saying, "Something to brighten up your day," and two more kisses. But they had a very strong scent which was quite overpowering.

"I'll put them in the sitting room," Gwen offered. "A bit more space for them there. Mind you," she added, "there'll be a lot going on in there later this morning."

"Oh?"

"Your mother not told you, then? About the TV coming?"

"No."

"Well, maybe she did, but you weren't really well enough at the time. You've been sleeping like a baby these last three days. Anyway, she went straight out and bought it on Thursday – just after your Aunt Millicent said she'd rather not invite her over for Saturday lunch – because of you having the 'flu that is. They'll be all over the roof this afternoon – putting up the aerial – so I'll keep the curtains closed for you."

"Yes. Thank you."

Later, when all the fuss had died down, Daphne announced the arrival and installation of the television from the bedroom doorway. "Cynthia said it was time we had one," she said, as though her own wishes had played no part in the decision. "And the radio can be so tedious on winter evenings."

The radio had never been 'tedious' in the past, but perhaps her mother had, in this one small area at least, allowed her husband to have his way during his lifetime. He had been adamant he did not want a television in the house, regarding it as second-rate entertainment. "It's for those who have no imagination," he said on the one occasion Laura heard the topic raised.

On the following afternoon, when Daphne was at Dyers Green visiting Cynthia, Laura ventured downstairs for the first time, and found the television in the sitting room, looking very smart in its elegant walnut cabinet, triumphantly occupying the place where her father's armchair had always been for as long as she could remember, and the chair itself relegated to the wall behind the door. This brutal rearrangement of the furniture, of such a seemingly minor nature to an outsider, signified to Laura not just her father's visible removal from the scene, but the deep, and as yet unspoken, resentment her mother must be harbouring over the provisions of his Will.

She returned to her bed, wrapping the blankets closer for comfort, and in a futile, defiant gesture, switched on the radio, determined to enjoy the frivolity of 'The Billy Cotton Band Show', even though its gaiety had never been to her taste. But the image of the sitting room in its sadly altered state unsettled her – and the myriad questions raised by her father's letter resurrected themselves from the forgetfulness of the last few days and demanded answers – so that in the end, she heard little of the programme. When she awoke later that evening, to the gentler strains of the Grand Hotel Palm Court Orchestra, the feverishness of the afternoon had vanished. Her head was clear, and she felt strangely calm and resolute, with a sense of purpose, ready to do what had to be done. But first, she must talk to Mr Moray.

The following morning, she went downstairs for a late breakfast, determined to get back on her feet again as soon as possible. Her mother was already busy elsewhere, Gwen had gone shopping and Elsie was still giving Meeston Lodge a wide berth, so she had the house to herself. Outside, she noticed, the walled garden had been left tidy for winter: the perennials cut back and thinned; the straggling branches of vulnerable shrubs trimmed, and the pathways cleared of leaves. The wheelbarrow, full of collected debris, was waiting to be collected by the gate in the west wall, its presence signalling Mr Moray was spending at least part of his day up at the Lodge

Her plans to seek him out however, were thwarted by Dr Crawley, who called to check her progress. Her tentative suggestion that she was well enough to take a walk around the garden met with opposition. "I'd leave any expeditions outside for a couple more days," he said. "You'll find being out of bed tiring enough." And, as usual in matters medical, he was right. She fell asleep in the armchair by the fire after he had gone, and woke to the sounds of Gwen and Daphne's voices in the kitchen, the daylight beyond the windows fading into early evening.

Aunt Millicent telephoned later to enquire after her health, and offer encouragement. "Come and see us, when you're feeling better, Laura. We miss your company."

Oliver telephoned too, although his enquiries as to the state of her health took second place to his detailed account of the splendid evening she had missed that Saturday, particularly the appearance of the latest local talent, Johnny Hayter, one of Jules' friends who "was an amazing saxophonist". She listened patiently, and made all the appropriate responses where necessary, while her thoughts drifted elsewhere to what needed to be done, and how quickly.

The following morning, she received another card, this time from the staff at the Weaversham Bank, wishing her a speedy recovery. It was a pretty picture of a vase of roses and she put it next to Oliver's on her bedroom mantel shelf.

It was a miserable day, overcast with light drizzle, and a

raw edge to the wind, according to Gwen. The wheelbarrow had gone from the walled garden and the side gate was firmly shut. There was no sign of Mr Moray, and Laura could only assume he was employed on the farm for the whole of the day. Despondent at the continued thwarting of her plans, she retired to her room after lunch when she had the house to herself, and retrieved her father's letter from its hiding place.

Sitting on the window seat – just in case Mr Moray did make an appearance – she read and reread it several times. Each reading made her feel a little bolder. Her father had given her the means to reshape her life, the rest was up to her. But she had to be rational. The moneys due would not be hers for some time, so her freedom to act was limited. Currently, she had neither sufficient capital nor income in her own right to fund somewhere else to live – and sharing a flat with someone she did not know held no appeal. So she must, in the interim, however difficult this might be, remain a resident at Meeston Lodge.

More pressingly, there was the problem of Oliver. Poor Oliver. Well-meaning and earnest, but there was no point in pretending any longer, he could not – and probably never would be able to – light that vital spark in her – not like Martin. She had to break with him. "If it were done… then 'twere well it were done quickly," as Miss Hay would have said, paraphrasing 'The Scottish Play'. There would be consequences – unpleasant consequences – and no mistake. Laura had no doubt life at the Lodge would become intolerable once their engagement was broken.

Her mother's repressed resentment, combined with the frustration of her plans, would be a combustible mix.

But the matter of Oliver was a nettle that had to be grasped.

CHAPTER TEN

Overnight, the weather cleared and left a crisp, clear morning. By noon, the sky was a cloudless pastel blue.

Laura idly sauntered into the kitchen after lunch and noticed the side gate of the walled garden was open.

Daphne was discussing cake-making for the Christmas Fayre with Gwen over a cup of tea. Laura's arrival was acknowledged with a brief pause in the conversation.

There were three stout leeks on the kitchen table, the soil on their roots still damp from being freshly lifted. "I thought I might take a stroll outside," Laura said casually, speaking to no one in particular.

Her mother raised an eyebrow. "Well, if you must. But Dr Crawley was insistent you shouldn't rush things," she said, moving towards the door into the hall, evidently deciding to drink the rest of her tea in the sitting room.

'Rushing things', of course, was precisely what Laura intended to do, starting immediately if Mr Moray was somewhere in the garden.

Gwen was studying her closely as she beat the butter and sugar together in the mixing bowl. "You mind you don't stay out too long," she cautioned.

"I won't." But she was not entirely sure that this was true.

Swathed in duffel coat, woolly hat and mittens, she stepped out from the back porch onto the raised terrace. The cold air came as a shock, and the fierce glare of the low sun made her eyes water. Her legs felt ridiculously wobbly, and breathing was painful.

She was cautious as she made her way down the path to the side gate. The usual easy rhythm of walking had become a clumsy stumbling, her feet feeling much too heavy, catching at the gravel. She paused beyond the gate, wondering if she were wise to go on. But determination is a fine thing. Gathering her strength, she followed the winding path around the side of the old stables and between the tall rhododendrons into the vegetable patch where the southerly aspect behind the walled garden had prompted the construction of the greenhouse and a robust timber garden store that always smelt of creosote.

The store was full of things she had been instructed never to touch as a child, and inevitably, as a consequence of this, it held a greater fascination for her: the lawnmower, with the shears and pruners on a shelf above; the hoes and rakes neatly stored in the racks next to the garden forks and spades; the savage-toothed wood saws hanging from their nails; the upended barrow with its wheel just the right height for a child to spin; a shelf devoted to cans of machine oil and balls of twine; and the high wall-mounted cupboard housing pesticides and fertilisers. In front of the grubby window, where spiders wove exotic webs in late Autumn, was the well-used workbench and beneath, a wooden stool.

And tucked away, against the wall, were bags of potting compost, keeping warm. Nothing had changed since Mr Timms had left. Mr Moray kept it just the same, and its old familiarity was comforting. This was where she sought him out in years gone by, armed with her flower sketches and questions needing answers.

And it was here, that afternoon, she found him, staring at the scene beyond the window, his lunch box open, his sandwiches half-eaten, and his tea part-drunk, no longer steaming in its cup.

He turned sharply, her sudden appearance surprising him.

She was embarrassed. "I'm sorry. I'm disturbing you."

He stood up rapidly, the stool scraping back against the floor. "No. Not at all." But his face betrayed a distracted state of mind and his hair looked as if he had raked his fingers through it several times.

"I've interrupted your lunch."

He studied the contents of the box for a moment then closed the lid, as though it was of no consequence. "No, you're fine," he said, downing the remainder of the cold tea and replacing the empty cup on the thermos flask.

She waited for him to invite her in, but instead, he blocked the doorway, hands in pockets. "Should you be out in this weather?" he asked abruptly.

"I needed some fresh air."

He considered this. "You'd better come in then," he said reluctantly. "Here, take a seat," and he pushed the stool across the floor towards her.

Inside, the atmosphere was almost warm, the sun heating the timbers at her back when she sat down and leaned against them. He stood opposite, propped against the workbench, arms crossed, just looking at her from under lowered brows.

His attitude was strangely hostile, and the well-turned phrases she had practised earlier that day suddenly seemed all wrong. "Are you going to spend Christmas in Edinburgh?" was all she could think of on the spur of the moment. It was his usual practice to join his mother and brothers there, so he must have thought her question very odd indeed.

Yes, he was, he said, his attention slipping away to contemplate the view of the vegetable patch beyond the open door.

She sensed he was shutting down the conversation – that her presence was a source of irritation – and his strangeness more than usual reserve. Something was wrong, and her questions would have to wait, however frustrating this might be. "I'd better go," she said, getting to her feet. "I'm keeping you. I'm sorry."

Perhaps her tone betrayed her disappointment. "No – please sit down," he said, forcing a smile. "Was there something particular you wanted?"

His change of tack wrong-footed her. Where to begin? She sat down again, trying to put her thoughts in order. "Mr Moray," she began, venturing a tentative smile. "I wanted to ask you about my father."

"What did you want to know?"

"He seems to have confided in you," she said, not meaning to sound critical, but somehow it came out that way. "About his illness," she added hastily. "And – and I wondered – if he'd told you anything more – about himself, I mean."

He weighed up her words. A shaft of sunlight crept through the door illuminating the space next to his feet. He studied it intently. "Was there anything specific you had in mind?" he asked warily.

She searched for the right words, floundering a little. "I've been given a letter," she began. "A very private letter."

He waited.

"It contains some information I need corroborating."

"Was the letter from your father?"

"Yes."

"I see. How do you think I can help?"

She pressed him further. "Did he ever mention his family?"

"Not exactly. We talked in general terms. He was interested in mine of course – being part Scots himself –" Her confusion must have shown because he stopped abruptly.

"No, I think you must have misunderstood him, Mr Moray," she said, convinced that he was wrong. "His parents were Irish."

He was clearly embarrassed at having to correct her. "Your grandfather was Irish, Miss Driscoll, but your grandmother was a Scottish lass – Annie Douglas – from a village near Coldingham in north-east Berwickshire. It was a private joke between us – The Douglas Connection," he added helpfully.

"The Douglas Connection?" She was so far out of her depth, she felt in danger of drowning.

"My maternal grandmother was a Douglas, that's all," he was saying. "Margaret Douglas – from Coldstream – on the Borders," he added, evidently feeling it was necessary to expand further on the subject.

"I see," she said lamely, the door into her father's past suddenly flung open.

"I'm sorry. Perhaps I've said too much."

"No, not at all. My father never talked about his parents. He was only four when they died, you see – and he was brought up by a guardian – Mr Watson."

He looked down at the ragged planking. The shaft of sunlight had pushed further into the space between their feet, spilling onto his boots. "Miss Driscoll, I don't know what to say. If your father wanted you to know about his past, he would have told you."

"But he has told me, Mr Moray," she insisted, feeling there was nothing to be lost by being honest with him. "In his letter. He said – he said he'd lied about it."

He considered this for a moment. "And that's all he said?"

"In this letter – yes – but he says there's more – in another letter I'm to have in three months' time."

"Then perhaps you should leave things 'til then," he advised, his tone a little harsh. "He must have had his reasons."

She was losing patience with him. "He had – he explained

them. But I've already made up my mind about something that worried him, so keeping his past a secret – from me – doesn't matter any more – honestly."

He studied her closely, trying to make out perhaps, whether she was speaking the truth. "I don't make a habit of breaking my word, Miss Driscoll," he said solemnly. "But he told me in confidence he was never orphaned as a child." He was watching her reactions very closely. "It just suited him to say he was, he said."

"Are his parents still alive?"

"No. His mother died when he was twenty-one. His father lived a good while longer."

She was reduced to silence.

"I hope you'll believe me when I say I've never spoken to anyone about this – until now."

She nodded, trying to make sense of his information. "So who was Mr Watson?"

He shook his head. "I'm sorry, I don't recall the name."

The last sliver of sunlight moved on and slipped out of the doorway, plunging the interior into a dusky gloom. The air went chill and she felt the cold seep through the fabric of her coat, making her shiver.

"You'd better be getting back," he said, changing the subject. "You've been out too long already."

She got up from the stool. "Thank you for being so open with me."

"I'm sorry I couldn't help you further."

He followed her out of the store into the vegetable garden, walking with her through the rhododendrons and onto the drive. They scrunched along the gravel in silence until they reached the side gate into the walled garden.

She stopped by the gate, struck by a thought that might explain so much secrecy. "Mr Moray," she asked, "Are we related?" Her mother, she knew, would never be able to accept such an unwelcome possibility.

He shook his head. "No, I don't think so. Douglas is a fairly common name. Does that answer your question?"

"Yes. Thank you."

The sun had sunk behind the trees and the evening light was fading fast. He opened the gate and stood back to let her pass. "Good night then, Miss Driscoll."

"Good night, Mr Moray – and thank you again." He nodded and she heard him close the gate behind her.

There was frost forming on the steps as she came up from the garden. The light was on in the kitchen, and she knew Gwen would lecture her on the perils of staying out so long.

CHAPTER ELEVEN

Oliver's black Riley swept into the drive just before two o'clock on a crisp, sunny Saturday afternoon. Sitting on her bedroom window seat, Laura watched her Aunt Cynthia emerge from the passenger door wearing her exquisite sable coat and Russian-style fur hat.

Oliver joined his mother on the drive: her tall, elegant son with everything going for him. He was immaculately dressed, as usual, like a magazine advert for expensive menswear, a tailored tweed jacket with matching cap, beige waistcoat and twill trousers, and a checked scarf hanging loosely round his neck. So why was it, Laura wondered, he failed to light her fire? – whereas in the eyes of others, he was definitely regarded as 'a good catch'? One evening, shortly after their engagement, he had waited for her outside the Bank, and Betty Bailey had openly gawped at him, wide-eyed. "Is he your fiancé, Laura?" she had asked. "He's *gorgeous*."

Daphne was already at the front door to greet them. "On time as always, Oliver," Laura heard her say. "Oh, Cynthia, your lovely fur coat – for the Christmas Fayre! I do hope no one puts sticky fingers on it. It's quite impossible to control children at these events, you know – especially when Father Christmas arrives." Father Christmas this year being William Benyon, who had the rosy cheeks, hearty laugh and girth to match the part. "Laura," she called up the stairs. "Oliver's here."

Laura had spent the morning preparing for this visit. It was important to feel both suitably dressed, and comfortable, she decided. She did not want to have her thoughts distracted by nagging doubts about the way she looked. Eventually, she plumped for the simple lambswool twinset in royal blue and her new navy slim-line skirt, and let her hair fall loose, 'flip' style, rather than pulling it up into a French pleat.

Under the circumstances, she decided it was politic to wear his ring. She took it from its little red velvet-lined box, where it lay unworn during weekdays – on the grounds it might get damaged in the office – and slipped it over her finger. It was a beautiful piece of jewellery, but it gave her no pleasure to wear it: it was as alien now as it had been the day he had given it to her.

He was tidying his hair in front of the hall mirror as she came down the stairs, a thick lock having been dislodged from its place by his cap. He turned to greet her with a ready smile, planting a light peck on her cheek as he replaced his comb in his top pocket. "Glad you're feeling better. Can't have you fading away, can we?"

"So good to see you up and about again," Cynthia added. "Richard and I were so worried about you. There are so many horrendous tales about 'flu these days."

"I'm much better, Auntie."

"I'm so pleased. I hear you're going back to the Bank on Monday."

Daphne was standing by the front door in her coat and hat, waiting for the pleasantries to be completed. "We must be going, Cynthia," she urged. "I need to be there promptly."

"Of course, darling. We'll see you two lovebirds later."

Laura led the way into the sitting room with its welcoming fire banked against the cold, and sat down. Oliver stood in front of the blaze warming his hands before perfunctorily surveying the room. The roses he had sent the week before were in the blue Chinese vase in the front window. He did not notice them.

"So – that's the new TV," he observed, fixing his concentration on it. "Very nice. Walnut cabinet, isn't it?" He ran his fingers over the wood delicately, appreciating the fine finish.

"Yes," she said. "My mother's very pleased with it."

"You don't sound very impressed."

"I don't watch much. Some of the programmes are awful."

He laughed. "Don't be such a snob, Laura. They aren't all bad."

She resented him patronising her. "I didn't say they were. But at least with the radio you can listen and do something else at the same time. With the TV, you just end up sitting staring at the wretched thing – like a zombie."

He found this amusing too. "Well, what shall we do?"

he asked brightly, changing the subject. "Pity we can't go for a walk. It's lovely in the sun."

"We could if you like. I strolled round the garden for a while on Thursday."

He looked surprised at her taking up his suggestion. "Ah – well, perhaps not. I've not brought my sheepskin. I didn't think you'd be up to it – and anyway," he added as if to reinforce his decision, "I've not brought my walking shoes either." He indicated the fine Oxford brogues he was wearing and shrugged apologetically. "Sorry."

"It doesn't matter. I was only agreeing with you it would be nice to go for a walk."

There was an awkward silence, the conversation ending up in a cul-de-sac and shuddering to a halt. He looked uncertain about what he should do next, then sat down suddenly in the chair opposite her. Had it always been like this? – Oliver talking for talking's sake – filling the space between them without saying anything of note? Yes, it had, she realised.

"I should have suggested inviting the others round as well," he said, resorting to rubbing his hands together in an automatic, pointless sort of way. "We could have had a game of cards."

"Or Monopoly," Laura found herself suggesting, the idea springing into her head from nowhere, possibly because it was a game you could play for hours without talking about anything else.

He frowned. "Well, perhaps not Monopoly," he said finally, looking at her in a helpless sort of way. The last time they had played, Claudia had been declared bankrupt after only half-an-hour and sulked for the rest of the evening while Stephen teased her, and Rosemary and Antonia had gone on to amass property empires.

The silence reasserted itself while he sat looking around the room searching for inspiration.

"Your flowers have lasted well," Laura observed, thinking he had at last noticed them in the window.

He looked blank.

"The roses."

"Oh – yes." But he did not turn to look at them, or even seem aware of them. Instead, he sat on the edge of the chair, leaning forward on his elbows, clasping his long, elegant fingers together. His evident discomfort was almost tangible. "There's a good film on later this afternoon," he said finally.

"In Lingford?"

"No – on the TV. *Ice Cold in Alex*. Shall we watch it? We can't do anything else."

Laura swivelled the ring on her finger, the diamonds catching the firelight. The thought crossed her mind that Martin would have known what to do with three hours in a house all to themselves. She stifled the memory. "Oliver," she began, "I need to ask you something."

"Oh – right. Anything in particular."

"Well yes, actually." Go on, a voice in her head urged her. Do it now. But it was still difficult to take that final step. So she paused before she asked him, "Oliver, are you in love with me?"

He looked genuinely shocked. "What?"

"Are you in love with me?"

"Good God, Laura! What's brought this on? Of course I'm in love with you!"

"Of course? Why 'of course'?"

"We're engaged, aren't we?"

"But if we weren't engaged, would you still say you were in love with me?" He looked bewildered, so she continued without giving him the chance to concoct any sort of reply. "Look – I don't think either of us have thought very seriously about this. We've grown up with the idea we would get married, that's all – and – if you aren't in love with me, I really don't mind." She tried to keep herself sounding matter-of-fact, but she was aware she was stifling a bad attack of nerves when she came to the bit that mattered most. "Because, if I'm honest, Oliver," she managed at last, "I don't think I'm in love with you."

There was no immediate response: he just sat there mutely, staring back at her, as if he had looked on Medusa and been turned to stone. "Is there someone else?" he asked quietly, " – at the office?"

She could at least be honest in her answer. "No – no one."

"Then tell me – what's this all about?"

She floundered a little, searching for the right words. "I suppose I've just decided it would be silly to go on like this – if I don't really love you. Let's face it, we aren't exactly a pair, are we?"

"In what way?"

"In every way. We don't have the same interests. You enjoy having lots of people around you all the time –

socialising. I don't. You're into jazz clubs and parties – that sort of thing."

"And you aren't?"

"I'm not saying I don't enjoy them occasionally, but not all the time. Sometimes I want some space around me – without other people always being there. Do you understand?"

He nodded.

"So, we don't really have that much in common, do we?" She could have added – and I think we both bore each other rigid – but refrained from being quite so brutal.

He looked down at his hands, frowning in concentration. There was silence again. After a while he looked up. "So where does this leave us then?"

"Oh – I think you know the answer to that, Oliver. I think we should be grown up about this and agree to end our engagement. We're just not right for each other."

It was a tremendous relief that he made no effort to contradict her. Instead, he sat back in his chair and considered the matter. "I don't know what to say," he said eventually.

"How about just admitting it's the best thing to do? – that it won't work for us?"

He blew out his cheeks and looked away. "God, Laura, you're going to hate me for this. I knew that the day after we got engaged."

"Maybe that's when we both knew."

"I thought about it – afterwards. I realised I'd rushed things. I thought it was what you wanted. You didn't, did you?"

"No."

"I wish you'd said."

"I didn't know how to. I thought it was expected."

"Yes – well, I should have known better."

"We didn't – click – did we? We never have."

"No," he admitted. "We never have. I just kept hoping things might change. I would have gone ahead, you know – married you. Some people grow to love each other. I thought maybe – maybe we might … but …"

"But we haven't – and we won't."

"No."

"Then we should stop pretending."

"Yes, perhaps we should."

The coals in the grate collapsed in on themselves and she got up and added some fresh pieces. The flames lapped lovingly around them.

"What will you do," he asked, " – if we don't get married?"

"I don't know yet. I'll think of something. You're not to worry on that account."

"There's going to be one hell of a fuss, Laura. I go cold just thinking about it. Our mothers will go ballistic."

"They'll get used to it. They'll have to."

He raked his hands through his hair. "Oh God! All that business about the Harriman Fortune! You realise, if we don't get married, I still get my share – you'll get nothing – absolutely nothing?

"Yes, of course I do."

"It's so unfair."

"I'm not going to marry you for money, Oliver. I'm sure I'll manage without it," she added, her conviction sounding convincing, not least because it was true, although he was not to know that.

He sighed and studied the flames for a while. "How are we going to break the news? It's not a good time to do it. You know you're both invited to Dyers Green for Christmas Day – and there's the New Year's party at the Parrs?

"Yes, my mother said. I think she was relieved we wouldn't have to spend Christmas and New Year here without my father."

"We'd better leave the announcement until after New Year then. Do you mind? It means dragging things out a bit."

"I don't suppose another three or four weeks are going to make much difference. We just need to carry on as usual – as though nothing's happened."

"Antonia's organised carol singing for a crowd of us next Saturday. Raising money for one of the *Herald's* good causes. Homeless Families at Christmas, I think she said. Would you want to come? I'd understand if you didn't."

"I think I'd better. My mother will start suspecting something if I don't."

"Yes, you're probably right. We'll have to play things by ear. In the meantime, I'll try to work out the best way of telling everyone – maybe after one of the Sunday lunches when we're all together, then it's all done and dusted in one go."

"Yes, maybe that would be best."

They sat in silence, both of them staring at the fire for several minutes. The clock in the hall struck three.

Laura stirred herself. "Come on," she said, pulling him to his feet. "Let's just forget about everything for now. We can't do anything today. Gwen's left us some of the lovely buns she made this morning for the Christmas Fayre. I'll put the kettle on."

"I suppose we could watch *Ice Cold in Alex*," he suggested.

"Yes, we could."

How civilised they both were, she thought afterwards. How very British. They were dismantling the hopes and dreams of generations of Harrimans over cups of tea and butterfly cakes.

Later, they sat on the sofa together waiting for the television to warm up. The diamonds in the ring sparkled in the firelight, catching her attention. "I'll give it back, you know – when it's all over," she said.

He put his arm around her. "I don't want it back, Laura. Keep it – to remind you of my folly."

"No, I can't keep it. I should never have accepted it in the first place. I just couldn't turn you down in front of everyone."

"God, that was thoughtless of me."

"My father thought it was a very dramatic gesture."

He was amused. "Did he indeed. I wonder what he really thought."

The screen lit up and the music and opening credits began. Her concentration drifted, her father's words running through her mind. She would never let Oliver know what her father really thought. It would be a hurtful, unnecessary thing to do. They had made an amicable break – something she had never dared to hope for – and that was more than enough.

On Sunday, after morning service, Laura left her mother in the church porch basking in Reverend Talbot's eagerness to assure her that the great success of the Christmas Fayre had been entirely due to her excellent organisation, "a sterling effort in view of such a recent sad loss", and walked quietly down the path between the headstones to her father's grave. The lilies had long gone and the spot was naked, as yet unmarked. The turves had been replaced, and the earth beneath was starting to settle. It looked forlorn, she thought. Unloved.

She wrapped her coat closer against the wind, not wanting to rush away. His presence was close. "It's over," she whispered to a freshening breeze. "I can start again." But her heart ached, and she wished she could have told him this while he was still alive.

CHAPTER TWELVE

"Nothing succeeds like success, Laura," as Miss Arbuthnot would have said. And she was right.

Laura's state of quiet introspection was believed by her colleagues to stem from the combination of bereavement and her slow recovery from illness. Cocooned in this protective shell, she spent her days gratefully submerged in a backlog of work Betty had not been able to complete, and the occasional conversation on office matters, while inwardly contemplating what to do with her future.

And so the first week back at the office passed off reasonably well, and Laura was content.

On Saturday, the weather turned quite blustery, the wind becoming wilder as the evening drew on. But despite this, there were crowds of festive drinkers packed into the smoke-filled pubs in Weaversham, happy enough to be carolled by a group of lively young people – and equally happy to be parted from their money.

For Laura, it turned out to be an unexpectedly jolly occasion, with many new faces – mainly friends of Antonia's from the *Lingford Herald*, who had come out in force to support their paper's good cause, although there were others who were apparently colleagues of Jules and Stephen. With so many people she did not know, Laura was, for once, only too glad of Oliver's company. Strangely, the break between them had produced an oddly satisfactory situation: both of them were now much more at ease with one another than before.

By closing time, in an alcoholic haze, but still in good voice, the group of merry songsters trooped back through the howling wind to Highfield House, clinging on to woolly hats and scarves, laughing and joking, and leaning into the teeth of the gale with arms outstretched. vying with one another to see who could keep their balance longer than the rest.

At Highfield House, Mr Parr opened the door to this rowdy throng, and the three Labradors, Ben, Poppy and Daisy, came bounding down the hall to greet the visitors with enthusiastic barking and much wagging of tails.

"Everyone in for a coffee," Julius ordered over the din. "Coats and things over the bannisters," he instructed, "and into the cellar with the lot of you. Can't have you disturbing the parents."

Mr Parr, well-used to these events, although perhaps not quite prepared for such a large invasion, hovered on the fringe of the melée with a hopeful smile. "Everything all right, Laura?" he asked as she was ushered past him.

To anyone else, this would have been a polite enquiry as to her health. To Laura, it had a greater significance. "Yes, thank you, Mr Parr."

"Good. Good," he said, patting her on the shoulder affectionately. "That's what I like to hear."

Julius was in no mood to have his father interrupt the decanting of his friends into the cellar. "Come on. Come on," he chivvied, directing the tardy members of the group through the door under the stairs. "No time for chats."

The cellar was where the Parr brood let their collective hair down with friends and acquaintances. It was their private club. There was an old piano in one corner for vamping, for which Julius was renowned; battered sofas and chairs to collapse on; pin-ups and pop idols pinned to the walls, which everyone used as alternatives to the darts board; a fold-down ping-pong table, and a record player that had seen better days but still had enough go in it to provide plenty of noise when required. At the far end of the cellar was a short hallway leading to the toilet and small kitchen area with a sink, and on an adjacent wooden shelf, a selection of chipped mugs, a jar of instant coffee, some dried milk next to a bag of sugar, and an electric kettle.

By the time everyone had been shepherded downstairs, Oliver and Stephen had elected to make the promised coffee, and were in the kitchenette sorting mugs onto trays, and Julius, acting as mine host, was trying to tot up the number of merrymakers who would need to be refreshed.

Laura leaned against the piano by the wall, glad to merge into anonymity among the sea of new faces as the general crush of bodies gradually coalesced into groups. The racket of raucous laughter continued undiminished and the atmosphere grew hotter and smokier.

"How much did we collect tonight, Toni?" bawled out a gawky young man in drainpipe trousers, who was lolling on one of the sofas.

Antonia, flushed from several Babychams and the sudden warmth of the cellar, was flirting outrageously with one of her colleagues from the *Herald*, a good-looking fly-boy who appeared to be serious competition for Stephen, in Laura's opinion.

"Fifty-three pounds five shillings and sixpence," came back a chorus of several voices from around the room, clearly proud of their ability to remember such a sum after so much alcohol.

Disengaging herself, Antonia scrambled, somewhat shakily, onto a chair and raised her hands to silence everyone.

There was lots of 'shushing', and the crowd settled down.

"That's exactly right," she confirmed. "Fifty-three pounds five shillings and sixpence. And Barry here –" she indicated her new friend, "tells me he's got some first-rate pics for the paper. So I'm hoping we'll get a good spread in next week's edition. Thanks everyone for coming out on this rotten evening and helping to raise such a fantastic sum." She clapped her audience, and there were whoops and whistles of acknowledgement while she scrambled back down from her perch and the former level of noisy chatter and laughter resumed.

"A tidy sum," said a velvety male voice behind Laura. She turned to look at its owner. She had no idea who he was – nor could she remember him from earlier in the evening. Her instant reaction was one of shock. How could she not have noticed him? He was about Oliver's age, she judged, not quite as tall, but with a more athletic build. His thick, dark brown – almost black – hair fell forward in studied carelessness onto a broad forehead above well-shaped brows; his eyes, she noticed, were a deep liquid brown, like dark chocolate she could drown in; his nose was straight, with slightly flared nostrils, and these strong, attractive features were enhanced by the generous shape of his mouth. "Hello," he said, introducing himself with a lazy smile that combined dangerous self-assurance with blatant sensuality. "I'm John Rufford. I've not seen you here before."

Laura smiled back, guardedly. "I suppose that's one better than 'do you come here often?'" she said.

He smiled again, unabashed by her obvious rebuff. "Do you?" he asked, his eyes never wavering from her in their concentrated gaze. "Come here often, that is?"

"Quite a lot, actually."

"Right," he said softly, still giving her the benefit of his undivided attention. "That puts me in my place. But you've not been here the last few weeks, have you? I think I might have remembered if you had."

"A family bereavement," she explained, forcing herself to feign an interest in the Dean Martin poster on the wall opposite.

"I'm sorry to hear that." His voice had taken on a decidedly husky quality that made her turn to took at him again. He was standing much too close, invading her space.

"So what's your name?" he was asking her. "I presume you have one."

This is animal magnetism, she thought, suddenly assailed by a waft of aftershave designed to ensnare unwary females – or perhaps, even wary ones. "Laura Driscoll," she said brightly, "and the Parrs are my cousins' cousins. You get a prize if you can work that one out."

"Sounds interesting," he said, clearly enjoying the verbal jousting. "If you tell me what the prize is, I might be tempted."

Into this strangely delightful tête-à-tête barged Julius, with a tray of mugs precariously balanced on one hand. "Sugar's in the kitchen," he announced through the barrage of noise, thrusting the tray in Laura's direction. "Hello, Johnny. Eyeing up Oliver's fiancée are you? Put her down." And he turned to Laura, grinning at her. "I work with this –" and he adopted an expression of mock distaste, "this – Lothario. Don't let him anywhere near you. Here – have a coffee." And having dispensed refreshment and advice, he moved off into the crowd, weaving between the groups with all the expertise of a professional waiter.

John Rufford continued his unabated interest in her. "I hope you'll ignore your cousins' cousin," he said, raising an eyebrow as he spoke. "I am actually a perfect gentleman."

This verbal sparring, Laura decided, was worth the trouble for a while longer, but probably better not to encourage, however tempting that might be. "And are you the gentleman who plays the saxophone at the jazz club?" she asked nonchalantly.

He shook his head. "Afraid not. That's Johnny Hayter. He's not here tonight. Are you a jazz fan?"

"How fanatical do you have to be to be a fan?"

He was studying her very closely now. "Do you want some sugar?" he asked suddenly.

She followed him into the kitchen where Oliver was busily lining up another set of mugs on a tray. "Oliver," she said artlessly, "this is John Rufford."

Oliver glanced up. "Oh – yes," he said, not taking very much notice. "Didn't I see you here a couple of weeks ago?"

John Rufford nodded.

"You're the new Assistant Solicitor in the Town Clerk's Office, aren't you?"

"For my sins."

Laura took the opportunity to remove herself from their conversation and slip back into the crowd. She was rather pleased she had managed to extricate herself so easily, and looked around for someone she could join who would prevent any further intrusions.

Claudia, dressed in a figure-hugging holly-green dress with a cowl neck, was perched cross-legged on the arm of a sofa smoking a cigarette with exaggerated ennui, and showing a charming amount of shapely leg to one of the press men sitting on a nearby chair who was appreciating the view.

Laura sat down on the sofa next to her. "Am I in the way?" she asked, indicating she had noticed the young man's interest, and preferring not to become a gooseberry.

Claudia tossed back her glossy auburn hair and passed

a languid hand through it, adopting what could only be described as a provocative pose. "No, not at all," she said, sounding bored, and dragged heavily, almost savagely, on her cigarette, blowing a cloud of smoke towards the ceiling.

"Are you sure?"

Claudia made no attempt to answer. Instead, she turned her attention elsewhere, scanning the room in a restless sort of way, perpetually seeking out something, or someone she could not see. The young man clearly held no interest for her. So who did? John Rufford, thought Laura. Still in the kitchen talking to Oliver. John Rufford – the ideal man for Claudia. Was she jealous he had shown an interest elsewhere?

Someone had switched on the record player. The Beatles. 'Please Please Me'. Everyone began singing along, loudly, and not very expertly.

"Oh God!" Claudia said, stubbing out the cigarette in a saucer next to the sofa. "I think I'm getting a headache." And she pulled herself off the sofa, smoothing her dress out with a glance towards the kitchen, and wove her way across the room between gyrating couples, while the young man's eyes followed her progress up the stairs and out of the door.

The record was played again.

"You're as slippery as an eel, Miss Driscoll," said the now familiar husky voice as John Rufford, appearing as if from nowhere, made himself comfortable on the sofa beside her.

Laura sipped at her coffee, trying to ignore him. She had enjoyed their earlier encounter, but his insistence was becoming tedious. Oliver was negotiating his way through the perilously fluctuating spaces between dancers to the other side of the room with his tray of mugs, and Laura began to wish he would come to her rescue. But he was too busy with the job in hand. Denied a knight in shining armour, she felt obliged to acknowledge her unwanted companion. "You've missed her," she said, without looking at him.

"Who?"

"Claudia."

"Ah – Claudia." He did not seem too concerned. Instead, he leaned back against the sofa, one arm nonchalantly placed along the top behind her. "Have you known Oliver long?" he enquired casually.

"Since the beginning of time."

"My – that is a long time," he said, pausing apparently to reflect on the information. "When's the Great Day?"

Someone had put on Frank Sinatra's 'Night and Day'. Couples were beginning to smooch.

She resented his curiosity. "Why do you want to know?"

He smiled – that slow, lazy smile. "Just wondering," he said. Frank Sinatra crooned on. "If you finish your coffee, we could have a dance."

Fast worker, she thought, briefly imagining smooching her way round the room with him. Definitely someone she might be glad to dance with in the future. And why not? But not now. The fiction of her engagement had to be maintained a few weeks longer. "Thanks for the offer," she said, surveying him over the rim of her mug, "But as Jules pointed out – I'm already spoken for."

He looked serious for a moment, apparently considering her reply. Then, with a very deliberate movement, allowed the hand on the back of the sofa to slip down onto her shoulder. "You're not wearing a ring," he said, his other hand delicately tracing the length of the bare finger of her left hand as she held the mug.

With great care, she moved away from him slightly, downed the rest of the coffee and leaned forward to put the mug on the floor. Her heart was thumping. This was Martin Evans territory – only moreso. She hoped no one had seen what had happened. Rosemary was draped around Jules not far away, but was too busy whispering into his ear. Stephen was by the record player in full view, but mercifully, he too was preoccupied, keeping an eye on Antonia. John Rufford's hand was now down on the cushion immediately behind her – not quite touching – but very close. If she leaned back again, he would almost certainly be in intimate contact. She was amazed at his boldness. "Would you mind moving your hand," she instructed, swivelling round to admonish him.

"If you insist," he said.

"I do."

He complied, still smiling at her.

Frank Sinatra had been taken off the turntable and a stack of 45s was being piled onto the auto-load. He was still contemplating her. "You deserve better," he said quietly.

"What do you mean?"

"What I said. You deserve better," he repeated. He was being deadly serious, and suddenly, without warning, he put an audacious hand on her thigh. "Believe me," he added, before suddenly getting to his feet and making his way over to where Julius and Rosemary were locked together, their arms around one another's necks. There was a brief conversation; Julius nodded, and John Rufford left, climbing the stairs two at a time with an easy grace. Laura watched him go. He turned at the top by the door and looked back at her, smiling.

She ventured to smile back. No doubt Claudia would be waiting.

Later, when Oliver drove her home, he seemed preoccupied. The wind was even stronger, and he was concentrating on avoiding debris torn from the trees and strewn across the road. When at last he stopped the Riley on the Lodge driveway, he took out his silver cigarette case and offered her one.

"I don't smoke, Oliver," she reminded him.

"Sorry – silly of me," he said, lighting up one of his own, evidently lost in thought. "Wasn't a bad night, was it?" he said at last, addressing the windscreen.

"No," she said, cautious about how she should reply. "Antonia must be pleased with the fund-raising."

He opened the window slightly, and blew the smoke out of the car. "Mm. She said she wanted to do it again next week. Try some of the Lingford pubs for a change."

Thoughts of John Rufford flitted briefly through her mind. "Do you want to go? I don't mind keeping up appearances."

"I'm afraid I can't. One of our clients has invited Horace, my father and I out to a dinner next Saturday evening.

Sorry about that. How about I pick you up one night next week after work and bring you home? That should keep our mothers happy. It won't look like I'm neglecting you."

She agreed, aware of feeling distinctly disappointed. "I should probably go over to Broxley next weekend and visit Aunt Hetty," she said, hiding her true feelings. "I haven't seen her in ages."

"I'll pick you up on Wednesday evening then. Five-thirty?"

"That would be fine." She gave him a light peck on the cheek and got out of the car.

He did a neat three-point turn, and drove off without looking back.

It had been a strange evening, she thought later, studying herself in the dressing table mirror. Claudia's predatory friend, John Rufford, had made a blatant pass at her, which in view of Claudia's stunning good looks was nothing short of ridiculous. Of course, it could well have been down to an excess of alcohol on his part. Except she could not quite rid herself of the feeling that alcohol had nothing to do with it. All of which left her contemplating the memory of his sensuous smile, his obvious interest in her, and the audacity of his hand resting on her thigh.

CHAPTER THIRTEEN

The single-decker bus picked her up from Meeston Cross and deposited her half-an-hour later in Broxley. She turned down Chartris Lane for half-a-mile between straggling hedges bright with scarlet hips and crimson haws until she reached a high wall which continued for a hundred yards or so before curving inwards in a semi-circle to the two imposing stone pillars topped by globes. From this imposing entrance, Hazeldene Court could be seen, set in its four acres of gardens at the end of a wide gravel drive flanked by lawns with shrubberies on either side. This mid-Victorian edifice with its steep gabled roofs and tall chimneys, spoke of solid Victorian values and money. Its architect had thoughtfully placed the small attic windows of the servants' quarters to the rear, so as not to offend the aesthetic sensibilities of it worthy visitors.

To the side of the house, a wall enclosed the kitchen garden, and an elegant archway, large enough for a coach and pair, led through into the spacious cobbled yard of the service buildings. The stables and tack room were empty now, and Aunt Millicent's Morris Minor was parked in the coach-house. The glory days were long gone.

Millicent, all smiles, opened the door wide to greet her. "Come in, Laura – come in. Oh, how lovely to see you," and Aunt Sylvia, not wishing to be found wanting in her own welcome, rushed forward to embrace her and kiss her on both cheeks.

It was always difficult not to respond to their enthusiastic welcome, but for Laura, visits to Hazeldene Court always conjured up the dread she could trace back to her frightening encounters with Grandpa Harriman when she was a small child. She still half-expected to see him glaring down at her from the landing. There was something about the dark oak panelling lining the reception rooms and staircase that intimidated her, while from old oil paintings in heavy gilt frames, men and women in a range of nineteenth century fashions, looked on enigmatically with faintly derisive smiles, or downright disapproval. And there was that distinctive smell: accumulated dust, old floor polish, heavy drapery and the thick closeness of Persian and Chinese carpets of a certain age. The suffocating atmosphere was intensified by the efficiency of the heating system with its ugly, bulbous radiators. These monstrous objects drained the place of air, leaving her breathless and anxious.

Millicent ushered her into the sitting room with its chintzy furnishings and tall windows with their lovely views across the south-facing lawns, and sat her down in front of a small, but unnecessary fire. "You must have a cup of tea," she insisted, and hurried away to make the necessary preparations before Laura could decline the offer.

"Hetty's still having her afternoon doze," Sylvia

explained, "but she was terribly excited about your visit."

Millicent returned with a tray already set with their delicate bone china tea service with its pretty rose pattern, and a large cake, cut into generous portions. "Do help yourself to some Victoria sponge, Laura. I bought it at Ellersons this morning."

The usual, gossipy chit-chat went on for several minutes until both sisters were satisfied with their hospitality. Then Millicent dabbed at her lips with her napkin, and looked inquisitorially at her niece. "So do tell us, my dear, why this sudden interest in the family history?"

"Oh, I don't know really," Laura said, reduced to telling a white lie by such a direct question. How could she admit the thought had never crossed her mind until her father had suggested it? "I suppose I've just realised I don't know much about it."

"Oh – I suppose you mean the Harriman Fortune," Millicent said with her unerring ability to home in on a topic without it being specifically mentioned. "Not a happy story," she added, glancing at her sister. "It dominated our lives, you know."

"Yes indeed," Sylvia agreed with a sad shake of the head.

"The First World War didn't help, of course," Millicent went on. "With David and Hugh being killed." A noticeable silence descended on the room after this observation. Sylvia sought her handkerchief and blew her nose delicately, and Millicent appeared to be preoccupied by something in the fireplace.

Laura was uncertain how to proceed, not having heard

of either of these names before. "I'm sorry, Auntie – who were David and Hugh?" she asked.

Millicent looked up and put her smile firmly back in place. "Our cousins, my dear – David and Hugh Harriman. David was lost when HMS Vindictive went down at Zeebrugge – St George's Day 1918."

Sylvia was nodding. "And Hugh died at Arras the same year," she added, her eyes suddenly brimming with tears. "Twenty-first of March. He was with General Gough's 5th Army, you know."

"I'm sorry – I didn't."

Millicent reached over and patted her hand. "Don't fret, my dear. We weren't the only ones to lose sweethearts, were we, Sylvie?"

Sylvia shook her head and dabbed her nose again with her handkerchief.

"Of course it was worse for Uncle William and Aunt Ann," Millicent continued, seemingly determined to be as stoic as possible. "They'd lost both their sons."

David. Hugh. William. Ann. Names conjured out of the air as far as Laura was concerned, but they had been flesh and blood to her aunts. Her ignorance of their existence seemed to somehow diminish the importance of their lives, and she felt ashamed.

Millicent soldiered on, regardless of her silence. "Of course, after the War, eligible young men of our age were in short supply, so Sylvie and I had to make new lives for ourselves. I won't say it was easy, but it did make things more difficult for Daphne and Cynthia a few years later.

Our father was forever trying to ensnare suitable young men. Do you remember Peregrine Tavistock, Sylvie, the heir to that enormous estate in Somerset? Father was absolutely set on him marrying Daphne. In the end, the poor man took fright.

Laura had never heard of Mr Tavistock either.

"Our father absolutely terrified him," Sylvia confirmed.

"Dear me – if he had only just let things take their course – but he would keep pressing the poor man. Such a shame. Your mother was distraught."

"And she was twenty-five when Peregrine left," Sylvia added. "Everyone said she'd end up on the shelf, just like us."

"So you can imagine, my dear, when your father came along ..." Millicent stopped herself abruptly in mid-flow and looked terribly flustered. Sylvia coughed, and hastily put down her cup of tea.

Laura looked between them, realising the source of their discomfort: her father had been seen as any port in a storm. No wonder no one wanted to enquire too deeply into his past! Here was a successful professional man prepared to offer marriage to a woman already regarded by most as an old maid. Even Edward Harriman had learnt his lesson. No one was going to frighten off James Driscoll.

"Oh, Laura," Millicent said, genuinely upset she may have said something unforgivable. "That was terribly silly of me."

Under the circumstances, it was difficult to find the right words of reassurance. "It's not important, Auntie," she said, hoping she sounded convincing.

"I'm not sure your mother would see it that way, my dear. Please don't breathe a word of this to her, will you?"

"No – of course not."

The carriage clock on the mantelpiece chimed three and saved everyone from further embarrassment.

"Good heavens! Is that the time? Hetty will be wondering where I am." And Millicent was out of her seat, hurrying from the room, still visibly flustered.

Sylvia began plumping up the cushions on the sofa, trying to look busy.

Laura was left wondering what she could possibly say to defuse the situation. "Auntie," she said at last, convinced she had found a useful topic to pursue. "Why didn't Aunt Hetty get married?"

Sylvia hesitated and sat down again, frowning. "Oh dear," she said. "How can I put this without sounding terrible. Hetty has always been – well – to be honest – quite plain. And of course it didn't help that she looked so much like her mother – Maud. Father said no one would be interested in her."

"So why did he marry Maud if he thought she was so plain?"

Sylvia sighed. "My dear Laura, you really are an innocent at times. Maud had a fortune settled on her when she married. Father had no intention of settling anything on Hetty except a small allowance."

Millicent came bustling back into the sitting room. "I've given Hetty her tea and cake, so you can pop up and see her now if you like. Remind her to show you the family Bible."

Like so much of Hazeldene Court, Hetty's room was a little faded, the flock wallpaper no longer rich crimson and cream, but dulled to a reddish-brown and beige by years of coal fires and down-draughts; dusky red velvet curtains caught their hems on a worn Persian carpet dominated by monumental pieces of Victorian mahogany furniture; and the over-heated atmosphere was filled with the sickly sweet scents of old age.

Henrietta was sitting in her easy chair by the fire. She was dressed to receive her visitor. She wore her rose-coloured twin-set with a string of pearls, and a heather-mix skirt which covered her bulky knees, but could not disguise the thickened ankles and large feet encased in a pair of wide satin slippers of a strikingly deep violet hue. Her steel-grey hair, which had not turned white like Millicent's and Sylvia's, had been beautifully set in soft waves swept back from her forehead, but no amount of elegant styling could divert the eye from her bulbous nose, or the fleshy folds beneath her chin.

With Sylvia's observations fresh in her mind it was hard for Laura not to see what Edward Harriman had seen: a daughter not blessed with the pretty oval face or dimpled cheeks of her younger half-sisters. And time too had not been kind to her: whereas advancing years had added a voluptuousness of sorts to them, to Henrietta it had simply added shapelessness. She was undeniably something of a dumpling, which was a dreadful thought, Laura decided, and made her regret ever letting this cross her mind when her aunt's face lit up with pleasure at seeing her. "Hello,

Auntie," she said, leaning forward to kiss the soft downy cheeks smelling of face powder and rouge mingled with the overwhelming scent of too much lavender eau-de-cologne.

Her aunt held on to her hand, the podgy fingers unwilling to let her go. "It's so lovely to see you," she said, her voice still remarkably strong for her age. "Millie's brought the chair over so you can sit next to me – but before you do, go over there and fetch the family Bible." She flapped her hand in the direction of the bookcase by the window. "The bottom shelf, my dear – the large, leather-bound thing at the end."

Laura sat down with the heavy volume on her knees while her aunt turned her attention to the remainder of her afternoon snack on the side table between them. "I hope Millie gave you some of this cake, Laura. It's really very good," she said, tucking into the last piece with evident relish.

Laura assured her she had been well provided for, and Hetty, satisfied her niece had been properly fed and watered, drained her tea cup and pushed everything to one side out of the way. "Now, Laura, put that great clumsy thing on the table and we can start." But once the Bible was on the table, her aunt seemed reluctant to open it. Instead, she clasped Laura's hand again, her mood shifting suddenly into seriousness. "I was so sorry I couldn't come to your father's funeral, you know. He was always so kind to me."

"He wouldn't have wanted you to catch pneumonia, Auntie."

"I know – I know. But I get to so few places nowadays.

It's my hips, you see. Soon I'll be confined to this room like a naughty child." She patted Laura's hand and tried to look a little more cheerful. "But let's not talk of such things. Millicent says you want to learn about the family history." And her watery blue eyes lit up a little at the prospect of being useful.

"Daddy said you were the best person to ask."

"Did he? Bless him – how nice." And she pondered this compliment for a moment before turning her attention to the thick tome before her, examining the frayed corners with a critical finger. "Not a very pretty thing, is it?" she said. "It really needs rebinding. My step-mother, Alice, gave me this after Father died," she added. "Said I should have it. So I suppose you could say it was my inheritance." She smiled, rather sadly Laura thought, and opened it.

On the flyleaf was the Harriman family tree, recorded in a variety of writing styles beginning with a beautifully executed Gothic script. With the passage of time, less precise hands had followed, until, nearer the bottom of the page, the writing had become little more than a scrawl. The whole page was filled with names and dates threaded together by horizontal and vertical lines. It was difficult to fathom, except one thread could, with a little attention, be followed as it progressed, with some deviations, across the page, from the top – on the marriage of Charles Harriman and Charlotte Grosvenor in 1794 – to the bottom, where, at the far right, on the very edge, and in danger of not being recorded at all, was the name 'Henrietta, born 1882'.

Laura let her eyes drift across the page. So many people!

So many people she knew nothing of! Significant lives, she realised, as she looked back up the main thread of the history, without whom neither she nor her Aunt Henrietta would have existed. These lives mattered – to both of them.

"Where would you like me to start?" Hetty was asking.

"From the beginning, Auntie. With Charles. I want to understand why the Harriman Fortune meant so much to Grandpa."

"I only know what my Aunt Mary told me, you understand. She and Uncle Christopher brought me up, you know, after my mother died."

Laura nodded, knowing for the second time that afternoon that she was ignorant of so much.

Hetty's podgy finger was at the top of the page. "Charles Harriman, gentleman farmer with land around Melton Mowbray. Married well – Charlotte came from a wealthy family, you see. Two sons – Henry dying quite young – so George, my great-grandfather, was the sole heir. He's the rather splendid young fellow in the oil painting over the fireplace in the dining room."

"I must pay him more attention, Auntie."

"Aunt Mary said he was very attractive – even as an old man. Anyway, he was a clever businessman, made a fortune by investing in canal building in the 1820s, married Isobel Travers – I'm sorry, I don't know anything about her – and moved to Loughborough. When his father, Charles, died in 1847, he became one of the wealthiest men in Leicestershire."

"And they had six children," Laura noticed.

"My grandfather, Henry, was the eldest, which made him a very eligible bachelor. George wanted to make sure Henry married well – and he did – Adelaide Webb – only daughter of a wealthy industrialist. Her father had invested in railway stock during the 1830s, and done very nicely. Henry followed his example – bought railway shares on the rise and sold them at the top – just before the bubble burst. Then he put all his money into the engineering workshops in Crewe and moved to Lingford."

"So now the Harriman's are even richer."

"Their finest hour, as Mr Churchill might have said."

Her aunt's finger had moved down the page. Laura followed its progress. "So Henry and Adelaide had seven children?"

"It was the fashion in those days, Laura. But this is when things started to go wrong for the family. You can see here," she said, and pointed to three names. "My father – your Grandpa Edward – had two older brothers, Charles and Henry."

"They both died in 1855. They were very young."

"Five and four years – and little Louisa their sister, the baby of the family at the time, was just one."

"What happened?"

"Diphtheria, Laura. Not unusual at the time. That left my father – a three-year old – the only child. Which is why, so my Aunt Mary said, Henry and Adelaide had more children."

"To make sure their was an heir to the family fortune?"

"Exactly. So my Uncle James was born the next year, Aunt Mary two years later and Uncle William in 1860."

"Is that the Uncle William whose sons were killed in the Great War?"

"Yes, dear, but you're running ahead of the story."

"Sorry, Auntie. So what happened to James? There's no date of death for him?"

There was a twinkle in Henrietta's eyes as she whispered, "Black sheep of the family, Laura. He was posted to the Punjab when he was eighteen – as an administrator." She paused, dragging out the tale to give it more spice.

"Oh, Auntie, stop teasing."

Henrietta's blue eyes were full of mischief, giving her face a delightful merriment that briefly overcame the dumpling effect. "He went native," she confided. "Set up home with a local woman, left his post and just disappeared!"

Laura burst out laughing. "Oh, Auntie – I think that's wonderful. Good for him!"

Her aunt suddenly became very serious, cocking her head on one side and studying her closely. "Are you going to go native, Laura?" she asked abruptly.

"Heavens, Auntie, what do you mean?"

"Are you going to kick over the traces?" She gripped Laura's arm with an intensity that belied her age. "You can't marry him, you know just because your mother and Cynthia expect you to."

The image of Aunt Hetty's expression when Oliver had proposed flashed briefly through her memory.

Henrietta was still holding on to her. "There's no love between you. I can feel it. And none of this," she said, her free hand sweeping across the family tree, "is worth a loveless marriage."

Laura had no idea how Hetty had come by her precise understanding, but she needed to deflect it for the time being. She patted the hand still holding her in a vice-like grip and attempted to shrug off the matter as best she could. "Heavens, Auntie! You don't think I'd marry someone I didn't love just to please my mother and Auntie Cynthia, do you?" It was the glorious truth without the need to stoop to deception.

Henrietta's hand continued to hold fast for a few moments longer before relaxing its grip. "Well, think about what I've said. This family doesn't need any more heartache." She turned to look back at the spidery handwriting that filled the bottom of the page.

Laura followed her gaze. Edward had married Maud Somerville in 1874. There had been five sons – and then Henrietta. With so many potential heirs, why had Edward Harriman felt compelled to marry a second time? It did not take long to see why. It was all there: a list of dates; a catalogue of family disasters recorded in scratchy, ill-formed writing; the destruction of the House of Harriman.

CHAPTER FOURTEEN

Oliver, in a rare moment of humour, once commented that Aunt Millie's driving technique was 'Byronic' – mad, bad and dangerous to know. This colourful description readily resurfaced whenever Laura was forced to accept a lift in her aunt's car, the journey home from Hazeldene Court that Saturday evening being no exception. Millicent revved the engine fiercely, and they sped down the driveway at high speed, the car's headlights on full beam.

"I hope I didn't tire her too much," Laura said, trying to ignore their erratic progress.

"No, my dear, I'm sure you didn't."

The gears crashed, and the car lurched out onto Chartris Lane.

"I didn't realise there'd been so much tragedy. All those children dying so young."

Millicent was pragmatic about such matters. "Lots of children died young in those days," she said. "And lots of mothers too, of course. Poor Maud. She was only twenty-nine, you know." Adding by way of explanation, "That's what having six children could do to you. She wasn't as strong as she looked."

There was an unflattering portrait of 'Poor Maud' on the staircase at Hazeldene Court, painted in thick oils to mark her engagement. She was only twenty at the time, with an unattractive, severe hairstyle parted in the middle, and heavy-set features that gave the impression she was twice her age. It was indeed Henrietta's misfortune that she had inherited her mother's looks.

The car shuddered to a halt at the junction, and after a cursory glance in both directions, Millicent wrestled it out into Broxley's High Street. The headlights stretched ahead of them, lighting up the hedgerows towards Redbridge in the distance.

"I often say to Sylvie, we don't know how lucky we were, you know. Marriage isn't always a bed of roses."

They lurched over the packhorse bridge to the next junction, turned left and joined the main road heading north to Weaversham.

Laura tried to concentrate on the topic she wanted to pursue. "I didn't get the chance to find out what happened to Hetty after Maud died. She kept avoiding the subject."

The engine whined piteously and Millicent decided to go into top gear. There was a surge of power, and they sped along the straight stretch before the bend at Dyers Green. "It's left its mark – no doubt about that. Did she tell you Maud was eight months pregnant with her when little Henry died."

"No, she didn't."

"A dreadful accident. There was a big old chestnut in the front lawn in those days. He'd been told not to climb it. Of course he did. Fell and broke his neck. He was only six. They say shock brought on Maud's labour. Father had the tree chopped down."

Millicent braked hard to round the bend by The Old Mill. Laura noticed Oliver's car was in the driveway.

Millicent noticed too. "Any reason you're not out with Oliver tonight, Laura?"

"He's with Uncle Richard and Mr Parr," she said, casually. "They've had a dinner invitation from a client."

"I see. Don't want him neglecting you, do we?"

Laura saw no need to reply.

The fork in the road lay just ahead. With barely twenty yards to go, Millicent flicked out the right indicator, and veered off into Meeston Road without changing gear.

Laura gripped the front of her seat out of habit. "What happened to the children after Maud died?"

"Hetty got farmed out to Aunt Mary and Uncle Christopher – I suppose you could say they adopted her. They certainly brought her up as one of their own. But our father blamed her for Maud's death – and never let her forget it – for nineteen years! I've often thought about this. I fancy he must have gone a bit crazy at the time. Little William and Edward were packed off to boarding school – and John, of course, had died the year before – he'd only lived a few weeks after he was born, poor mite."

"So he just sent his children away?"

"I don't think he could cope, Laura."

Laura tried to remember the dates under the names written in scrawly handwriting. "Edward died in his twenties, didn't he?"

"January 1899 – in India. He was twenty-four. He went looking for Uncle James – the Black Sheep of the family. I'm sure Hetty told you about him."

"Yes, she did."

"He didn't find his uncle, I'm afraid – no one has. He'd only been out there two months when he caught dysentery."

"So there was only one son left – and Hetty."

"Exactly. Grandpa Henry of course nearly had a seizure at the news. He wasn't going to leave his money to a man with only one surviving son. Goodness, no! He made it very plain that our father should remarry and get breeding, or he'd leave everything to William. After all, William and Ann had David and Hugh by then. Two sons are better than one."

"So your father married Alice Foxgate."

"Yes, my dear, and it was very fortunate indeed that Grandpa Henry died two months before I was born. I'm sure he'd have changed his Will if he'd known his prospective 'grandson' was going to be a girl!"

They were nearing Highfield House. Millicent braked again as she negotiated two bends, revving up to gain speed as she passed the front entrance. All the lights were blazing in the house, and there were several cars in the drive. Laura wondered if John Rufford's might be one of them. They had passed the house in a trice, and sped on with only a few miles to go before they reached Meeston.

"How did Grandpa meet Alice?" Laura asked.

"The Foxgates owned Chartris Farm, my dear – at the end of our lane – and a good deal more besides. Alice was their youngest. They were very happy to see her married off. She was twenty-one. Edward was forty-seven. No doubt they were hoping she'd be a young widow."

"They wouldn't expect him to reach ninety."

"I don't think she did either. There was a rumour she took a fancy to young William early on. They were the same age, and he'd come back to live at Hazeldene Court after he'd left school. Uncle Christopher got wind of it apparently, and advised him to leave home."

"So he joined the Army."

Millicent gave out a long sigh. "And got killed in the Boer War," she said. "At Spion Kop – in Natal – January 1900."

Names and dates in scrawly handwriting. Her grandfather's? A record of his unimaginable loss. All his sons. And the only child left – Henrietta – the unloved, unwanted daughter.

Meeston Cross came into the headlights, and her aunt braked, ready to swing the car into the Lodge driveway, scattering gravel in her wake. She pulled up the car with a jerk outside the front door and turned off the engine. "After William's death, of course, having a son became an obsession with Father," she went on, her attention focused on the rhododendrons illuminated by the headlights. "And you can imagine, when Sylvie arrived in 1901, it made things worse. Mother had a string of miscarriages for seven years after that before Daphne was born. She was worn out. Henrietta was brought home to be our nanny. Father treated her like a servant," she added. "Something I never forgave him for."

"I never liked Grandpa very much," Laura confessed.

"He wasn't a very nice man, my dear. Our mother was nothing more than a brood mare to him." She paused to reflect on this. "Mercifully, after Cynthia was born, the doctors said it was unlikely she would ever conceive again. And I can tell you this in confidence – she told me she'd made sure she never would." In the faint light from the porch lamp, Millicent's face looked strained. Beneath all the froth and light-hearted banter, lay a great swathe of bitterness.

The front door opened and Daphne came out onto the top step. "Are you two going to sit out there all night?" she demanded.

Millicent grasped Laura's arm urgently. "You won't say a word about Mr Tavistock, will, my dear?"

"Of course not! My lips are sealed, Auntie."

CHAPTER FIFTEEN

Other people's lives. The revelations. The expectations. All the heartache. Boxes within boxes.

Laura was keeping a record: a shorthand notebook filled with carefully written notes in neat Pitman script kept at the back of the drawer with her father's letter. It was her secret world, one which occupied her thoughts more and more as the days wore on.

Christmas and the New Year – and what was to follow – loomed closer. Surrounded by preparations for the Festive Season, Laura was quietly triumphant that she and Oliver were managing to maintain the fiction of their engagement with relatively little effort. But while everything was calm on the family front, a storm was brewing elsewhere.

It broke the Friday before Christmas on the last day of term. Mrs Ashworth, Head Mistress of St Wilfrid's Primary School, chose the final school assembly to announce that Miss Holbrook was leaving the following term, and would be taking up a temporary post at Lingford Primary. This information, coming out of the blue as it did, initially produced ripples of consternation confined to parents who had children at the school – and in Gwen's case, grandparents, as her favourite grandchild Lucy, aged five-and-a-half, was particularly fond of Miss Holbrook. But by the following morning, rumours and gossip were flying around like wildfire, and the whole of Meeston was agog with the news.

Laura, travelling home after a successful Christmas shopping trip to Lingford, remained in blissful ignorance. She had planned to spend the rest of afternoon and evening wrapping her purchases, as Oliver was usefully occupied at a Law Society function. She was, as a result, in a contented frame of mind. She was also rather pleased with herself. Finding token presents for Gwen and Elsie, was always something of a challenge, but she had found a selection of luxury English Garden soaps – Lily of the Valley, Honeysuckle and Jasmine – in a pretty presentation box, that she knew Elsie would love; and a de-luxe assortment of biscuits in a large square tin emblazoned with the words 'Home is where the Heart is' in a mock sampler design – which Gwen would certainly appreciate as she was having her extended family staying over Christmas now she was a grandmother once again.

In the past, Laura had never for a moment thought of buying a gift for Mr Moray. He was not, after all, an employee at the Lodge. But on this occasion, she felt compelled to make some gesture to mark his friendship with her father.

Initially, she was hampered in her quest by not having the faintest notion what he might like, but eventually found a robust penknife, and chose this on the grounds that the dilapidated version kept in the garden store for cutting garden twine should have been retired long ago, along with Mr Timms.

As she closed the front door, she became aware of her mother's animated tones in the kitchen.

Daphne was dressed in her best coat and matching pill-box hat, apparently either on the point of going out, or having just come in. She was in full flow, while Gwen, brow furrowed in concentration, was bent over the kitchen table attempting to ice the Christmas cake. "It reflects very badly on us," Daphne was saying. "And the Benyon's too, of course. It's quite dreadful."

"I've obviously missed something," Laura said casually, hoping Gwen might be forthcoming.

"There's been a bit of a fuss," was all Gwen would say, casting a quick sideways glance in Daphne's direction while manoeuvring the icing bag.

"Bit of a fuss!" Daphne was incandescent with outraged decency. "You call Miss Holbrook having to resign 'a bit of a fuss'?"

"Resign? Whatever for?"

"There's been a complaint," Gwen said, completing the shell pattern around the edge of the cake with some difficulty. "About her and Robert."

"What did she expect behaving like that?" Daphne added, with that particularly nuanced tone of voice that Laura recognised too well.

"She was seen," Gwen said, looking awkward. "Leaving Robert's place one morning – very early."

Laura made light of it. "It's probably just malicious gossip," she said, not paying much attention to her mother's indignation: it was too regular an occurrence.

"There's been a *complaint*," Daphne emphasised. "Mrs Ashworth can't ignore a complaint. And she knows Miss Holbrook's parents, which makes it so much worse. She had to tell them why she was asking her to leave."

Laura was astonished. "What on earth for?"

"I should have thought that was obvious, Laura. Imagine what they must be feeling – their daughter having an affair with a farm labourer – an educated girl like that."

"It's not an affair, Mother," Laura corrected her. "You have to be married to someone else to have an affair."

"Whatever you call it, Laura, it's grotesque."

"Being in love with someone is *not* grotesque!"

"It is if it's inappropriate," Daphne retaliated. "And I certainly won't have him coming here again," she added. "This is a respectable house."

Gwen caught Laura's eye briefly, giving her a clear warning that silence might be the better option.

But Laura had heard enough. "Oh, I see," she said, adding sufficient sarcasm to penetrate her mother's indignation. "So, do I take it you are volunteering to look after the garden when he's gone? The sprouts are just about ready to harvest, I notice."

Daphne blinked, taken aback. "I'll find someone else," she said, visibly uncomfortable that Gwen was a witness to this very obvious challenge to her authority.

"No, I don't think so," Laura said quietly, realising she

must curb the impulse to remind Daphne that Meeston Lodge was no longer hers to organise without reference to herself. "I think we should leave things just as they are. Anyway," she added, thinking of her father's letter and her aunts' revelations, "I don't think we should be so quick to pass judgement on other people."

"That's as may be," Daphne said, not to be outflanked so easily. "The Benyons will probably ask him to leave in any case."

Gwen straightened up from her task, standing solidly between them, like a referee in a sparring contest. "There!" she said, triumphantly surveying her handiwork in white icing, and smiling at both of them as if she had not heard any of the previous conversation. "All finished!" On the smooth upper surface, little silver balls spelt out the words 'Happy Christmas', and cut-out pieces of green marzipan snuggled close to red jelly beans, pretending to be holly. "What do you think, Laura?"

What Laura thought was that Gwen had neatly defused a difficult situation. "It's lovely," she said, mentally thanking her for being so tactful. "Much too nice to eat."

Gwen beamed. "Are you staying for tea, Mrs Driscoll?" she asked, turning her attention to putting on the kettle.

Daphne had recomposed herself and was readjusting the silk scarf at her neck. "No, thank you, Gwen. Eileen is expecting me at the Vicarage. Reverend Talbot wants to discuss the flower displays for St Wilfrid's at Christmas." And with that, she left, leaving in her wake a sense of righteous indignation.

Gwen waited until the front door had closed. "She's been up on the ceiling for the last hour," she said, setting out two cups and saucers.

"Is it true, Gwen? Or just gossip?"

"I don't think Miss Holbrook would have resigned if it'd been just gossip, do you?"

"No, probably not. Who complained?"

"Nobody really knows. It's all third hand as far as I can tell. But it won't make it any easier for him."

"So it was just gossip?"

"No smoke without fire."

"But who saw her?"

Gwen shrugged. "I don't know, but she's moving out of the Benyons today, by all accounts. Taken a vacant cottage up at Smallcross."

"It's all so sudden."

"Who's to say? I heard Janet Woods telling Mrs Spencer in the Post Office this morning. She said she'd heard it blew up a couple of weeks ago. It's just been kept secret until the end of term, that's all."

Laura remembered Mr Moray in the garden store; his strange demeanour, and hair all awry. He must have known there was going to be trouble. How her interruption must have galled him, asking so many questions while his world came crashing down. But he must not be forced to move away: he was the only one who knew about her father.

Gwen warmed the pot before putting in a large scoop of tea. "I shouldn't think the Benyons will want him to go," she said, as if she were reading Laura's mind. "He's a good worker, and William's not one for listening to gossip."

"Why didn't they just get married?"

Gwen shrugged. "Who knows?" she said, pouring out the tea. "But I suppose your mother's right about one thing – it was a bit queer a school mistress going out with a farm hand."

Laura was unwilling to concede her mother might be right about anything, and Gwen's attention moved on to other matters, saying how it was a real shame this had happened – the nativity play had been so lovely – and Robert had helped out building the set on his days off – and Lucy had been the perfect angel – for once.

Laura drank her tea, her thoughts elsewhere. She would not condemn Mr Moray for being in love. She would have spent the night with Martin if she could have done. No, she would not condemn him. She would wrap his present, and take it to him. She would stand by her father's friend – and she would not play the hypocrite.

With this clear idea in mind, as soon as Gwen had gone, she hurried to her room, found some wrapping paper with small silver stars on a midnight-blue background, and parcelled up his little gift as quickly as she could. The tag presented problems. How could she wish him a 'Happy Christmas' when his life had been turned upside down? The best she could devise with so little time to be more inventive was to write the simple message, 'To Mr Moray from Laura Driscoll, Christmas 1962', and leave it at that.

A grey wash covered the winter sky when she set out, draining everything of colour. She hurried, listening to her footsteps on the tarmac as she struck off down Nether Meeston Lane from The Cross. They beat time to her heart, and she realised she was angry. Angry at the tittle-tattle. Angry with people who enjoyed spreading it. Angry he might feel the need to leave.

By the time she reached Nether Meeston Cottages her mind was full of possibilities. Had one of Molly Smith's three unruly youngsters seen Miss Holbrook? Or Peggy Higson's? They caught the early bus to Lingford on their way to school. More than likely.

Peggy was letting out their black-and-white cat as Laura passed, and she looked up to see who was walking down the lane.

"Afternoon, Mrs Higson," Laura called over to her, wanting to show she was not averse to being seen in the vicinity of Mr Moray's cottage. "Do you know if Mr Moray is at home?" A question she could well have answered if she had walked ten yards further on, but there was a perversity inside her that made her want to challenge everyone.

Peggy, her hair in curlers, came out onto the path, hugging her cardigan close against the chill, while the cat slipped silently past her across the lane and into the hedge. She craned her neck to look next-door. "I don't think so, Miss Driscoll," she said, somewhat puzzled by the question. "His front light's not on. Of course, he could be at the back."

"I'll call anyway. Thank you."

In the few steps it took to reach the little wooden gate of No.3, all the well-rehearsed phrases of support she had practised earlier, all the self-confidence in her decision to see him, drained away. She paused before lifting the latch, and with some effort walked down the narrow gravel path to his front porch. For a few moments, she stood under its pitched roof studying the bench seats on either side, and the stack of wood stored neatly underneath them.

The half-glazed door with its old brass knocker stood solidly in front of her, deep in shadow. She knocked twice, the sound seeming unnecessarily loud to her ears. No one answered. No lights came on. She was relieved to find him not at home. What had possessed her? How did she know he would want to see anyone? He might have been embarrassed. Ashamed, even.

Eager to be gone, she fumbled in her pocket and took out the gift, lifting the flap of the letter box to ease the package through the narrow opening. She heard it land with a soft thud on the doormat on the other side.

It was almost dark now, the pale lights in the lane flickering into life. In her haste to be gone, she hurried down towards the gap in the wall that would take her home through the woods. She ran the last few yards, and, as fate would have it, collided with him coming out the gate.

He was hunched inside his work coat, hands deep in his pockets. Even in the half-light, she could see the tautness in his face: it had a closed-down look. He stepped away from her and said absolutely nothing – just stared at her.

Her mind went a blank.

He continued to stare at her. "Where do you think you are going?" he asked, his voice harsh and uncompromising.

"I – I was on my way home ..."

"You can't go through the woods," he said sharply. "The path's blocked. We're taking out fallen timber."

The gales, of course. She had forgotten. She stood searching for the right words, eager to explain she was not one of those who thought badly of him. "Mr Moray," she began. "I wanted to say – I'm sorry."

"For what?"

"For – for what's happened – about Miss Holbrook – leaving."

A terrible stony silence wedged itself between them.

"I thought you would be getting married," she blurted out, noticing a small tic at the corner of his mouth. She blundered on. "You shouldn't let gossip keep you apart," she urged him. "Not if you really love each other."

She could hear him breathing – a hard, ragged breath. "Miss Driscoll," he said, barely able to control his anger. "This is none of your damned business! Go home!" And with some force, he unexpectedly gripped her by the arm and spun her round, propelling her back up the lane at some speed until they reached his gate, where he pushed her roughly away. "Go home!" he repeated. "Now!" And without another word, he stalked down his path and round the corner of the cottage. She heard the back door slam shut.

She stood shaking for a moment, shocked by the ferocity of his response. Her arm was hurting. She had made a fool of herself and there was no way she could undo the damage.

With great self-control she walked briskly up the lane back to The Cross, hoping neither the Smiths nor the Higsons had witnessed her humiliation. But their curtains were closed, and the flickering blue glow of televisions told her they were occupied elsewhere.

The primrose path to Hell is paved with good intentions – Miss Arbuthnot would have said.

CHAPTER SIXTEEN

"Hail, the heaven-born Prince of peace

"Hail, the Sun of righteousness!

"Light and life ..."

The descant soared and echoed round the rafters, the choir's enthusiasm and Mr Davis' rendition on the organ, compensating for any deficiency in the singing. The atmosphere was hot and stuffy, the press of bodies in the pews and around the walls readily providing what the ailing boiler could not, the regulars outnumbered by those whom Reverend Talbot described, with a heart-felt sigh, as "The Three-Times-a-Year Congregation". Her father had been among their number. But on this Christmas morning, he was absent, no longer among the half-hearted who were happy on this occasion to fill the church to overflowing. "He's been called to Greater Glory," Reverend Talbot had said, attempting comforting words after Communion the previous Sunday.

Was he? Laura was no longer sure. His faith had never been deep. He had been ashamed. Had he been found wanting?

Behind her, two women from the cottages in Weavers

Lane were singing with great gusto in high soprano voices, as they might on any Saturday night in the Meeston Arms. In the pews across the aisle, the Higsons and the Smiths had turned out in force, even the boys, fidgeting and eager to get back to their newly opened presents.

"... Hark! the herald-angels sing

"Glory to the new-born King."

There was the shuffling of feet, the sound of the congregation settling into the pews, hymn books dropped accidentally, a child wailing and being scolded, and the inevitable coughing.

Reverend Talbot, with evident pleasure, was surveying the increase in his flock from his vantage point in the pulpit. "The reading this Christmas morning is from St John's Gospel, Chapter One. 'In the beginning was the Word, and the Word was with God, and the Word was God...'" His voice, fully restored to its mellifluous tones, rang out, encompassing everyone with his sense of wonder and joy.

Below the pulpit, and surrounded by yew boughs, intertwined with holly and ivy tastefully arranged by her mother, was the Nativity scene modelled by the children at St Wilfrid's Primary. Miss Holbrook's class. Pipe cleaners made flesh to live among us, twisted into shape, clothed in coloured crêpe paper; the angels with silver foil wings and gold tinsel haloes; the Virgin Mary with a startlingly crimson mouth and two blue blobs for eyes; Joseph, standing lopsidedly beside her; and baby Jesus, a small, pink plastic doll wrapped lovingly in a piece of white cotton handkerchief, lying cradled in straw from the Benyon's farm, provided by Robert Moray.

How many cheerful, Christian souls crammed into the church that morning celebrating the birth of God made Flesh had traded gossip about Miss Holbrook and Mr Moray? – she wondered. Probably most of them.

Prayers. More shuffling and coughing. "... And forgive us our trespasses, as we forgive them that trespass against us..."

Would Mr Moray forgive those who had trespassed against him? Possibly not. He was gone now, taken by William Benyon to catch the train north to spend Christmas among friendlier faces. Would the New Year bring him back to Meeston? And if it did, would he stay – or simply collect his possessions and move out of their lives? Oh, why did this wretched business have to happen? And why had she made such a fool of herself trying to be so self-righteous?

"...and the blessing of God Almighty, the Father, the Son, and the Holy Ghost, be amongst you and remain with you always."

The chorused "Amen", and the service was over, everyone hurrying home to stuffed birds cooking slowly in the oven and vegetables waiting to be boiled. In previous years, Laura and Daphne would have done the same. Christmas at the Lodge was a relatively quiet affair, unchanging in its little rituals: the choice of goose, rather than turkey; sherry trifle instead of Christmas pudding; the family presents under the tree, opened after listening to the Queen's Speech on the radio; ham sandwiches and Christmas cake for tea; sherry by the fire in the evening.

Boxing Day, and the drive over to The Old Mill at Dyers Green for lunch, to spend the afternoon and evening with the Gorsts and the Broxley aunts.

But this year, the old order had been swept away. This year, Richard and Cynthia – or rather, Cynthia – had thought it more appropriate to hold the family celebrations on Christmas Day itself. "We can't have you on your own at Christmas, Daphne," she had said, and meant it kindly.

So Laura and her mother were propelled out of the house at noon by Richard who had called to collect them, and they, and their presents, were deposited at The Old Mill in time for a grand Christmas lunch.

Cynthia, wearing an exquisite powder-blue silk dress and the hint of expensive French perfume, ushered them into the sitting room, bright with festive garlands and Christmas cards pinned to ribbons on the doors. A Christmas tree, festooned with tinsel and baubles, and surrounded by gaily-wrapped packages, reached up to the ceiling, and a yuletide log blazed in the grate, crackling and hissing, filling the air with the heady scent of resin. In the background, carols were playing softly from the radiogram. "Oh, it's so lovely to see you," Cynthia was saying, kissing them effusively in turn, while Rosemary offered to take their coats, and Oliver suggested a small sherry before lunch.

Daphne, already a little emotional after a large glass of sherry before morning service, was visibly overwhelmed by so much attention. Laura, preferring to have stayed at home, wished she could rise to the occasion and stop feeling so wretched. She saw herself a fraud, a hypocrite like all the others in the congregation at St Wilfrid's, who were outwardly one thing, and inwardly quite another. It really ought not to be too much for her to show her appreciation for all the affection and kindness being lavished on her, but she could not push from her mind the prospect of the not too distant future, when all this gaiety – and her own part in it – would be seen in a very different light. How would she be regarded by her hosts, accepting their hospitality – and their gifts – knowing full well she was not going to marry their son? Nor did it help when Rosemary, thinking perhaps that Laura's melancholy was rooted in feeling the loss of her father during the Festive Season, decided to engage her in spirited conversation about the games they had devised for the afternoon. And Stephen, terribly earnest, and becoming more like Oliver every day, felt it necessary to provide further details on the charades and a quiz of his own devising, with prizes for correct answers and forfeits for the wrong ones.

All Laura really wanted was for them to leave her alone. Unable to reciprocate wholeheartedly, she was reduced to a semi-mute passivity, making brief, appropriate comments where necessary while her mind wandered elsewhere seeking consolation, her guilt being replaced by embarrassment at the memory of that dreadful scene outside Mr Moray's cottage, an image which refused to budge, even after a second glass of sherry.

"Luncheon is served," Cynthia announced with a flourish, and for once, Laura was grateful when Oliver came to collect her and take her into the dining room.

The table was resplendent in gleaming silverware and crystal wine glasses on a snowy-white damask tablecloth. There were crimson napkins and golden crackers with holly motifs, and at each end of the table were finely wrought triple candlesticks with scarlet candles, already lit, courtesy of Oliver, to welcome the diners.

Richard brought in the oval platter with the turkey, surrounded by roast potatoes, stuffing and sausages, and began carving with well-practised ease. Oliver poured the wine. Plates were filled; tureens of steaming carrots and sprouts were opened; and the gravy boat and cranberry sauce passed round from hand to hand. There was much merriment and laughter; the crackers were pulled and paper hats put on at rakish angles; jokes were read and groaned over, and the silly trinkets mocked or treasured, according to taste. Amid the gaiety, Laura sat quietly next to Oliver conscious his laughter sounded uncharacteristically loud. Her mother, sitting opposite, her face glowing, perhaps the result of so many generous servings of sherry and wine, occasionally glanced across at him, a small frown registering her perplexity at such behaviour. Richard, sitting next to her, was showing much the same reaction, and even Rosemary was beginning to notice. Laura could do nothing to stop him, reduced to trying to pretend it was perfectly normal for Oliver to be so boisterous.

Cynthia's voice, clear and commanding, addressed her from the far end of the table. "Do have some more turkey, Laura," she said, deflecting attention to her niece. "A sparrow would eat more than you do." So Laura obliged, only to ensure her presence faded all the quicker from the limelight.

The meal progressed through the enormous Christmas pudding which arrived all aflame; the brandy sauce; the mince pies, and the selection of cheese and biscuits. At three o'clock, everyone trooped back into the sitting room to watch the Queen's Speech on the television, and afterwards, Oliver took the Riley down to Broxley and collected his aunts while everyone else piled into the kitchen to clear the mountain of dishes. The frenzy of activity mercifully obscured Laura's self-absorption.

The arrival of Millicent, Sylvia and Henrietta heralded the opening of the presents. There were expressions of delight, flurries of excitement and many kisses all round, Laura's discomfort increasing with every gift from her hosts: the fur mittens; the silk scarf; the pretty silver rose on a chain; and Oliver's cashmere sweater in royal blue. Her only consolation was her own gifts to them were cooed over and received with genuine pleasure. Perhaps, when the time came, they would forgive her duplicity.

The wrapping paper disposed of, cups of tea were brought in and a hubbub of conversation sprang up. There were the usual reminiscences: other Christmases at Hazeldene Court; the well-rehearsed tales of burnt turkeys and other culinary disasters; embarrassing incidents and moments of reflection. Laura listened with more attention than usual, the familiar stories set now against the background of her wider knowledge. Behind the laughter – or lack of it, in some cases – there was still no mention of Hugh and David, the untimely deaths of Aunt Hetty's brothers, or Alice's years of misery with her husband – and definitely no mention of Mr Tavistock – all 'Things that Must Not Be Mentioned' at family gatherings. Even when Laura spent time with Hetty, once her half-sisters were deep in conversation among themselves, her aunt made no reference to their afternoon together those few short weeks before, and when Laura strayed a little into talking family history with her on a deeper level, Hetty smiled, patted her hand and said simply, "Not now, dear."

The distribution of Christmas cake and more sherry was the signal for the games to start, accompanied by a great deal of hilarity, excitement and general clamour. Oliver was working too hard at being humorous while Laura tried to sink ever further into the background. Alas, there was no hiding place once the quiz started, everyone having to take part, and she found herself the object of unwelcome attention when her distracted state resulted in having to sing a verse of 'Ding dong merrily on high' as a forfeit for failing to name three countries beginning with 'G', and on another occasion, being required to recite a poem for forgetting who wrote *Robinson Crusoe*. Thoroughly discomfited, her brain a complete void, she stood up and delivered the only lines she could think of on the spur of the moment. "'Ulysses', by Alfred, Lord Tennyson," she said, fighting to remember what little she knew. "Come, my friends, 'tis not too late to seek a newer world …" and she stumbled on, floundering under the interested gaze of Aunt Hetty. "…It may be that the gulfs will wash us down: It may be we shall touch the

Happy Isles, And see the great Achilles, whom we knew."
She sat down again to enthusiastic applause, flustered and
hot, relieved no one had noticed her recitation was nothing
more than a brief extract of the whole, and wishing she had
not eaten so many mince pies.

Mercifully, the games were brought to an end at nine
o'clock when Hetty became tired and asked if she could
go home. Millicent and Sylvia were happy to accompany
her, and Oliver volunteered to act as chauffeur once again.

The party broke up. Stephen excused himself on the
grounds there had been no chance to telephone Antonia
earlier, and he disappeared into the hall to begin what
became a protracted, very private conversation. Rosemary
and her mother elected to clear the dining room, refusing
help from anyone else, and Daphne asked if she could lie
down for a while, as she was feeling in need of a little rest.
Laura unexpectedly found herself alone in the sitting room
with her uncle.

Richard was in his favourite fireside chair contemplating a
well-rounded port. The fire crackled, and Laura sat watching
the pattern made by the flames against the firebricks, feeling
no urgency to begin a conversation. The general rowdiness
of the last few hours had left her head spinning, and she
welcomed the silence.

Her uncle shifted slightly in his chair and cleared his
throat. "I'm glad we're alone for a few moments, Laura,"
he said quietly. "I wanted to talk with you – about your
engagement."

Laura focused hard on the grate, her heart missing a beat.

"I couldn't help noticing," he went on without looking at her, "you're not wearing your engagement ring." There was no trace of criticism in his voice.

She studied the offending hand in her lap, its bare fingers a testimony to her distracted state of mind that morning. She could think of nothing to say to him by way of explanation that would sound remotely convincing.

He put down his port and lit a cigarette with an elegant slowness. "Is anything wrong between you?" he asked, almost casually.

She repeated his words silently to herself, mulling over her options while her heart continued bumping away against her ribs like a demented tennis ball. There really was only one answer she could give him. Better to discuss the subject rationally with him than suffer the histrionics of her mother – and possibly her aunt – at a time not of her choosing.

"We don't want to get married," she said at last, hearing her voice catch in her throat as she said it. "We don't know how to break the news."

A simple statement. An even simpler explanation.

A pause. No drama. No indignation. Her uncle inhaled deeply and exhaled in slow motion, letting the smoke drift in lazy curling strands towards the grate. "Understandable," he said, turning at last to look in her direction. "Well, at least that explains Oliver's strange behaviour today. But I'm not surprised. I've known there was something wrong for a while. I've even mentioned it to him on a couple of occasions. He's always denied there was a problem."

"It's a very recent decision, Uncle."

"Since your father died?"

"Yes."

He nodded. "Sometimes a trauma makes us take stock of our lives."

"Yes."

"Does your mother have any inkling of what's afoot?"

"No. It's not going to be easy telling her." An understatement that needed no elaboration.

"The Harriman inheritance," he said wearily, finishing his cigarette and stubbing it out in the lead crystal ashtray at his elbow.

"Yes."

"It means nothing to you?"

"No. I couldn't marry for money, Uncle."

"I should think not – not under those terms, anyway."

There was the sound of Oliver's car returning, its headlights raking across the curtains as he swung into the parking area by the front door. Her uncle got up and went into the hall to meet him. She heard the front door open and close, and Stephen's voice still in earnest conversation with Antonia, then the lower tones of Oliver and her uncle.

A few moments later, they entered the sitting room. Oliver was deathly pale. "I suggest we go into my study," her uncle said. "We can have this conversation there."

They followed behind him as he led the way.

"Sit down," he said, and they did as they were told. He chose to remain standing, leaning back against his desk, his long legs crossed at the ankles, nonchalantly. He let several moments lapse before speaking. "Well, Oliver," he said at last, "I'm glad this has finally come to a head. Not everyone's as blind as you apparently think they are. I just wish you'd had the courtesy to give me an honest answer the last time I asked you if this marriage was going ahead. I've been obliged to ask Laura instead." There was a decided chill in his tone.

Oliver had all the appearance of a small boy caught out stealing apples. He seemed to physically shrink into his chair. "We only discussed it a couple of weeks ago," he said, looking wretched. "With all the family celebrations coming off, we thought it best not to mention anything before the New Year."

"Under other circumstances, Oliver, I would have agreed with you. But there's a small problem. I happen to know Julius and Rosemary intend to announce their engagement at New Year. If you defer matters until after their announcement, you'll take all the gilt off the celebrations."

Oliver swore and put his head in his hands.

"Not the most useful observation," his father commented caustically.

Laura did not know what to say. It had been so simple to make the decision; easy to say that everyone should be told; easier still to recognise the importance of picking the right moment, but much, much harder to face the moment itself. Consideration of the consequences and the aftermath had been pushed to one side, disregarded perhaps because they were fraught with inevitable anger and disappointment.

Bringing matters to a head sooner than anticipated was a fearsome prospect.

"Any ideas, Laura?" her uncle was asking. "Your mother will be difficult to handle, I've no doubt. Are you up to it?"

"I don't know. She has such fixed views on the matter."

"Would it help if I told her?"

"That's very kind of you, Uncle, but this is our problem. I suppose we should face it."

"Not entirely your problem," he said. "I think your father might have agreed with me on that point. In his absence, can I at least act as your advocate?"

Had her father shared his reservations with Richard? He had mentioned nothing of this in his letter. Perhaps her uncle had simply seen what her father had seen – a mismatched pair thrust together at the behest of others. "It's a generous offer. Thank you – I'd be most grateful."

"Then can I suggest we get this over and done with on Sunday? Daphne will be coming to lunch. Oliver, it might be helpful if you are here. You can deal with any flak from your mother. I'll try to defuse the situation as best I can with your mother, Laura, before I bring her home. It won't be easy, I know, but I need to say a few things myself on the subject that might just help a little. No doubt, she will not be interested in attending the Parr's New Year's Party once this news breaks – it would be too embarrassing for her – and no doubt, Laura, you will feel the same."

She nodded. "I need time to myself, Uncle."

He smiled wanly. "Yes, you do," he said.

CHAPTER SEVENTEEN

Snow. Deep and crisp and even, the flakes still falling from a leaden sky, unhurried but persistent. From her window seat, Laura watched them floating in wayward, hypnotic, downward curves through the still air, like feathers.

She had woken to an eerie silence and flung back her curtains, surprised by the overnight transformation of everything familiar into shapeless mounds of whiteness. Breakfast suddenly seemed unimportant compared with witnessing this exquisite spectacle. Huddled inside her dressing gown, she curled up on the window seat, letting her thoughts drift with the flakes, aimless and unhurried, losing track of time.

The telephone was ringing in the hallway.

"Laura!" her mother called up to her. "It's Oliver."

The spell was broken. Reluctantly, she went downstairs to take the call. "Hello," she said. "I was watching the snow."

"Can you talk?"

Her mother had retired to the dining room, but was still well within earshot, and no doubt would be listening. "It depends," she hedged.

"I got a rollicking off my father after you'd left. Sorry I didn't handle things better."

"That's all right. Don't worry about it."

"Do you want to go out on Saturday? One last time?" His voice betrayed his lack of enthusiasm.

She forced herself to laugh for the benefit of her mother. "No, I don't think so, but thank you for asking."

A pause. "I'm sorry, Laura."

"Don't be."

"Good luck on Sunday then."

"Yes. We'll both need it. 'Bye."

"'Bye."

She put down the phone, knowing the next time they spoke, their lives – and those of others – would be changed for ever.

" 'Come, my friends, 'tis not too late to seek a newer world. Push off, and sitting well in order smite the sounding furrows'." She could hear Miss Hay's ringing tones extolling the class to reach out into the unknown with Ulysses, " 'To strive, to seek, to find, and not to yield'." It was an exhilarating, if terrifying, prospect.

Her mother drifted into the hallway holding her cup of tea. "I do hope Oliver wasn't suggesting coming over in this weather." She paused in her critical assessment of such a notion, noticing Laura's state of undress and feeling compelled to comment on it. "You do know it's after ten, don't you?"

By mid-day, the snow was thicker. From the kitchen, the walled garden had become a hazy blur, lost in flurries of thick, whirling flakes. There was no longer any distinction between paths, flower beds or lawns, just a thick quilt of whiteness spread over everything. Only the espaliers stood out, stark against the red of the cottage bricks, their naked branches grotesque, like pinioned skeletons, arms outstretched. It was a scene of contradictions: great beauty, but menacing and eerie, all at the same time.

Wanting to indulge herself in doing absolutely nothing, and being answerable to no one, Laura returned to her lookout on the window seat, folded herself up into a comfortable huddle, and let the afternoon slip by to the haunting refrains of Tchaikovsky's *Swan Lake* while she watched the snow. It was peaceful, undemanding and she had no need to think of anything.

Early the following morning, Mr Gittings telephoned to say the Bank would be closed until New Year's Eve, the following Monday. Weaversham was cut off, he explained, as was much of the rest of the country, and there was no certainty the snow ploughs would be able to open all the roads before Saturday at the earliest.

Enforced idleness, while pleasant enough in the short term, paled somewhat with the prospect of inactivity spread over several days. Laura had not planned on being marooned with her mother for the interval between Boxing Day and the fateful Sunday ahead. It made her fretful and fidgety, all the moreso when she considered the possibility that circumstances might prevent her mother's visit to the Gorsts when all would be revealed – *must* be revealed – before Rosemary and Julius made their announcement at New Year.

Sometime during the night it stopped snowing, and by mid-morning a bright, cold sun was creeping over Meeston Woods casting a sharp white light into the garden.

In the kitchen, Gwen was busy making bread, kneading a large lump of dough with vigour. "There'll be no deliveries for days," she was saying to Daphne. "Even the milk tankers can't get through, Ann Benyon says. It's a good thing we've got some vegetables in the garden to fall back on if needs be."

Except that Mr Moray was not around to lift them, thought Laura. "I think I'll go out for a while," she said. "Unless you'd like me to help with anything, Gwen."

"No, I'm fine. It's a lovely day. You make the most of it."

Daphne said nothing, and by the time Laura was muffled up against the cold in her old green duffel coat, and had pulled on her wellingtons, her mother had retired to the sitting room, where Elsie was busy lighting a fire and chattering away like a sparrow.

The snow was deep, and made walking difficult, throwing her off-balance as it scrunched under her feet. Progress was slow and often erratic, but great fun. In the shelter of the rhododendrons, she turned to see her footprints zig-zagging up the drive in a crazy pattern, and laughed at them. The rolling English drunkard, she thought, finding her spirits lifted by such a notion.

Beyond the rhododendrons, the vegetable patch was strange and beautiful – all light and shade, and steeped in silence. The sun shone low through the lattice-work of trees at the edge of the wood, throwing long, distorted shadows onto the snow-covered rows of brassicas, hillocks of white, the ice-crystals on the surface reflecting a rainbow brilliance into her eyes. And when she looked across the broad sweep of the scene, she saw that nothing was black and white, like a photograph: it was a world where shadows took on subtle undertones of greys, greens and yellows, bruised purples or deep indigos. The trees, scratching a silver-blue sky, were dark chocolate etched in charcoal; the shrivelled oak leaves still clinging to the branches, a dull bronze; the fallen beech leaves, gathered in sheltered nooks and crannies by the wall, a brilliant shade of copper in the sunlight. Her mind's eye saw it all, as if for the first time, already mixing colours on her palette.

By the warmth of the wall, the garden store looked comical, the snowy covering on its sloping roof lopsided, like a badly iced cake, and the plant pot, under which the key was kept, wore a fluffy white hat, which fell off when she disturbed it. The lock yielded reluctantly, stiff with cold, and she stepped into the welcome dark interior, warmed by the sun through the grubby cobwebbed window. There was the comforting smell of leafy compost and creosote, and she stood for a while lost in thought, surveying the well-ordered contents of the store in their silent vigil, waiting for Robert Moray to return. She wished him back, if only to apologise – to explain herself. But the thought lingered that for all her wishing, he might never return, and the doorway into her father's life might be closed for ever. She locked the store and put the key back under the plant pot, retracing her steps into the house.

That afternoon, with her mother preoccupied with watching television, she entered her father's study. When she opened the door, the movement sent a flurry of sunbeams tumbling through the shafts of sunlight spilling onto the carpet. She closed the door behind her. The room was like the garden store, silent and waiting. The clock on the mantelpiece had stopped long ago.

For a while, she sat behind the desk breathing in the warm aroma of old books mingling with polished wood and aging leather, watching the sunbeams' unchoreographed dance as they rose and fell to soundless music. Already, the dark chocolate smell of pipe tobacco was fading. The room was peaceful but unloved, and her mother showed no inclination to reclaim it, abandoning it to the past and the husband that was no more. Here, at least, thought Laura, she could hold on to her father's memory. She would make it her room too.

Idly, she wandered over to the bookcases, their contents a mystery. She turned the key in the glass-fronted doors and opened them. Most of the books were on accountancy or banking practice, as she had expected, but there were others that tugged at her curiosity: a fine set of leather-bound encyclopaedias; the complete works of Shakespeare in very small print; several of the more popular novels of Charles Dickens; a shorthand tutorial with pencilled annotations in the margins; Home Guard instruction manuals; a selection of *Readers' Digest* condensed stories; and tucked away on the bottom shelf, a small red cloth-bound book of sea shanties, most probably second-hand from the state of it, with a faded inscription in blue ink on the flysheet – 'From Andrew, April 1920'. She put everything back and locked the doors.

In the cupboards under the shelves, were yellowed copies of the *London Illustrated News*, and professional accountancy journals dating back several years. She pulled these out to discard them. Unexpectedly, behind these and tucked away at the back of the cupboard, she found a pile of sketch pads. Opening one at random, she discovered exquisite water-colour studies of wild flowers and butterflies, painted with painstaking precision. Another contained beautifully detailed pencil sketches of the Lodge, and a third revealed hastily executed, but perfect likenesses of her mother when she was much younger, Aunt Cynthia and Phyllis Parr, the Gorst and Parr children, and some of herself about the same age. She laid out the open pads on the desk feeling a profound sense of loss. Why, when she had shown an interest in art, had he remained so obstinately silent on the subject? – encouraging her, but that was all? Did he think his efforts of so little consequence there was no need to share his talent with her? They could have been so much closer. Now these exquisite testimonies to his ability were the sad echoes of what might have been.

What else had he hidden?

In the centre drawer of his desk, she found an unexceptional assortment of stationery items: paper clips and treasury tags, pens and pencils, rulers and rubbers, and three bottles of ink – one permanent black, another emerald green, and the third a vivid scarlet – all tools of his profession.

The drawers in the left-hand pedestal were filled with unused ledgers, boxes of good quality foolscap and octavo paper, and variously sized envelopes. The companion drawers in the right-hand pedestal contained stiff buff folders, black and blue carbon paper of differing sizes, flimsy copy paper, and typewriter ribbons wrapped in cellophane.

The larger bottom drawer had a lock, and when she tugged at it, it refused to open. There was no sign of a key, and a cursory re-examination of the mish-mash of assorted objects in the centre drawer failed to find one. Nor was it in the exquisitely carved pencil box. Determined not to be beaten, she searched every possible hiding place in the room: in the vases on the mantelpiece; under the chairs; on the wide upper ledge of the door frame; even under the hearth rug, all without success.

Reduced to impotence, she indulged in swinging from side to side in the swivel chair wondering what to do next. Taking a screw driver and wrenching open the drawer seemed overly dramatic, and possibly very damaging. There had to be a key – somewhere.

In the drawer of the hat-stand in the hall, her father used to keep his house keys on an old brass ring. When he left in the morning, he would take his coat and hat from the stand, and the keys from the drawer. It was such a familiar ritual, it barely registered – until that moment.

Making sure her mother was still in the sitting room, she tiptoed across the hall, listened for any likely interruption, and opened the hat-stand drawer. The keys were where he had left them, forgotten, ready to be collected the morning he collapsed in the hall. She slipped her hand into the drawer and retrieved them, wrapping her fingers tightly around them to stop them jingling, and returned to the study.

On the ring, beside the house keys, were several others, probably belonging to his office. They were all shapes and sizes, some much smaller than the rest. She inspected these closely. They looked promising, and she selected three as the most likely. The first would not fit: it was too thick in the shank. The second surprised her by sliding easily into the lock. She turned it carefully. At first, the lock resisted, and she hesitated to apply too much pressure in case the key became stuck fast. Her hand was shaking when she tried again. There was a slight movement, and then an audible click. She sat back in the chair, triumphant but equally cautious. The drawer had been locked for a reason. Was she sure she wanted to open it? Her father's life was shrouded in mystery. What dark secrets might be revealed here? She felt no sense of urgency to find out.

Her concentration drifted to the snowy scene beyond the window. The shrubbery along the wall was striped with golden light. The delicate layers of snow had begun to slip from the latticework of branches onto the ground, leaving water droplets sparkling in the sun.

Open the drawer. Better for her to discover its contents than her mother. She slipped her fingers through the curved handle and pulled. The drawer gave only slightly, then jammed. She peered through the narrow crack but could make nothing out, so she tugged harder. It opened with a sudden jerk, taking her by surprise. She heard herself gasp.

The drawer was empty.

CHAPTER EIGHTEEN

There had been no more snow, just a brief thaw, then intense cold with four days of frost. The snow-plough had pushed its way through from Weaversham to Meeston the day before, and Daphne embarked on her visit to the Gorsts in blissful ignorance of what would lie ahead.

Laura had occupied her idle days in painting to the constant companionship of the Light Programme, experimenting with different techniques to mirror the colours in her snowscapes. In moments of reflection, she had rehearsed her response to her mother's anger, seeking the right words or phrases to placate or quell her; a different tone of voice; wondering if it would be better to sit or to stand, until she had exhausted every combination, and no longer felt any emotion except exhaustion, and a profound desire to see the whole matter out in the open at last.

It was mid-afternoon when Richard's car returned from Dyers Green. Laura went downstairs feeling oddly calm and collected.

In the hallway, Daphne swept past without a look, or a word, and went upstairs.

Richard closed the front door behind them and hung up

his hat and coat on the hall-stand. He called up after her. "Don't be too long, Daphne. I'd like a word with both of you before I go."

There was no reply.

"Shall I make some tea?" Laura suggested.

"Something stronger may be needed," he said.

They went into the sitting room and waited, her uncle standing with his back to the fire.

"Was it dreadful?"

"I think she's more shocked than angry at the moment. She hasn't said a word all the way back."

"What about Aunt Cynthia?"

"She'd rather suspected things weren't going well, but she's concerned Daphne might think she's responsible. There's always been rivalry between them – and it doesn't help that Oliver inherits his share regardless."

They waited in silence for several minutes. Her uncle checked his watch.

"Perhaps I'd better go up," Laura said.

In the bedroom, her mother was sitting in front of her dressing table still wearing her hat and coat. Her face, reflected in the mirror, was as white as a sheet.

"Uncle Richard's waiting," Laura said.

Her mother remained silent. She stood up, removed her hat and coat, and laid them on the bed with exaggerated carefulness. Then, still without a word, led the way downstairs.

Laura poured her a sherry, and Daphne sat down with great dignity wearing an expression of tight-lipped composure.

Richard waited until she was seated, and nodded to Laura to do the same. He remained standing, hands behind his back, with an air of court-room gravity. "What I wanted to say," he began, "I wanted to say to both of you, and I would beg you to hear me out before you say anything." His words were general, his attention was focused on Daphne. "For as long as I can remember," he began, "both James and I had reservations about this marriage. No, Daphne – let me finish. We were both, in our own ways, responsible for letting things go on as they did – maybe through a sense of duty, however misplaced, to do the right thing by our respective wives. But that is no excuse. The real – the only – reason for our lack of action was cowardice."

Her mother frowned, tutting to herself, as if she regarded this as nonsensical.

"Yes, Daphne – cowardice. We were too weak to challenge the notion that the bulk of the Harriman Fortune should be kept intact by the simple expedient of marrying off our children to one another – regardless of their feelings. That somehow – in the Twentieth Century – it was perfectly natural for this prearranged marriage to take place without any questions raised." He paused, so that Daphne could fully appreciate what he was saying, but there was little sign of it. Her expression of granite disapproval remained firmly in place. "But you know," he went on, his voice softening, "It was perfectly obvious to both of us that Laura and Oliver weren't in love, had never been in love, and most likely would never be in love. And the terrible truth dawned on us – we should never have allowed the idea to be fostered in the first place. So, what I'm saying, Daphne, is that if your husband – and I – couldn't bring ourselves to express our doubts, you mustn't blame Laura or Oliver for doing the same. What's important now, however, is that you feel able to give Laura the support she'll need to make a fresh start in difficult circumstances."

This proposition seemed highly unlikely. Daphne was still sitting bolt upright, the image of dignity under duress. Eventually, she stirred herself to answer. "It was what our father always wanted," she said, with a certain peevishness of tone.

Richard leaned forward. "Exactly," he said with a slight smile. "It was what Edward Harriman wanted." The Counsel had made his point. "With the greatest respect to your father, Daphne, his wishes seem somewhat irrelevant in an age when the United States is exploding nuclear bombs in the Nevada Desert and Russia is sending men into space." He gave her a light kiss on the cheek and an encouraging pat on the shoulder for good measure. "Now, if you'll excuse me, I need to to get back and have a word with Cynthia. I'm sorry this has blown up over the Festive Season, but there was probably never a good time to raise the subject – not after so many years."

Daphne did not answer and he did not wait to see if she would.

Laura followed him out into the hall, closing the door behind her. "I can't thank you enough, Uncle."

"I didn't say anything I didn't mean, Laura. Your father and I were concerned we'd let things slip, and neither of us knew how to unravel the mess. It's a pity the burden ended up on your shoulders instead of ours. Give her time," he added with a nod in the direction of the sitting room.

"Will you take Oliver's ring back for me? I don't want to make a big thing of returning it."

He nodded and began to put on his hat and coat. There was no sign of Daphne intending to see him off.

Laura brought down the little box from her room and handed it over.

Her uncle slipped it into his coat pocket, as he might a handful of loose change, and embraced her gently. "I don't suppose we'll see much of you at The Old Mill for a while?"

"No – I don't think so."

"I shall miss you at our gatherings." He leaned forward and kissed her on the cheek. "A Happier New Year to you, Laura."

"Thank you, Uncle."

He let himself out and she followed him onto the porch into the cold air, drinking in its stinging freshness as he got into the car, and with a wave of his hand, drove away down the icy drive into the rosy twilight of the early evening.

In the sitting room, Daphne was still sitting stiffly in the fireside chair.

Laura poured herself a small sherry and sat on the sofa listening to the clock ticking in the hall.

"I don't know what to say to you," her mother said at last. "I can't believe you let me go to Cynthia's today with no warning of what to expect. It was unforgivable."

Laura had no defence against this line of attack: Daphne was too practised in the art. Silence seemed the best option.

"Have you nothing to say?"

"Nothing you'd be interested to hear."

"Don't be so obtuse!"

A cul-de-sac. Laura sipped at her sherry, feeling strangely light of spirit, and not in the slightest concerned by her mother's irritation.

"All those years wasted on you! You're a fool, Laura. A spoilt, ungrateful child. Always were. Always will be. You seem to take delight in destroying everything I do for you. Well – there's no going back this time. You've lost your grandfather's inheritance. I hope you're pleased with yourself."

"I don't care about the money."

"Oh – I see. Now your father's left you well-off you don't care about the fortune your grandfather left you? Remarkable!"

Laura had wondered how long it would be before her mother raised the topic of her husband's Will. Six weeks. Quite a feat. "It's all rather beside the point, isn't it?" she said. "I don't love Oliver – and he doesn't love me."

"Well let me tell you, Laura, at your age you're not likely to find yourself a better man than Oliver – or one who isn't just after your money."

There were echoes of Mr Tavistock and her father, but Laura bit her tongue. She had promised Millicent. "Then I shall have to take great care not to mention it, won't I?" she said, passing off the comment lightly.

"Eligible bachelors don't grow on trees. You'll end up an old maid – like your aunts at Broxley. Do you want that?"

"I might decide not to get married."

"Oh what nonsense! What are you going to do with your life?"

"I have no idea at the moment, Mother, but I'm sure I'll think of something."

"I despair of you – I really do! You're quite feckless. Your grandfather will be turning in his grave."

Another cul-de-sac. Laura got up and put on the lights, closing the curtains against an early frost.

Daphne seemed reluctant to let the subject drop. "He made sure you would want for nothing," she continued. "I can't believe you're prepared to sacrifice everything he worked for to make you happy."

"Happy?" Laura was incredulous. "Mother, Grandpa Harriman didn't care whether I was happy or not!"

"That's a dreadful thing to say!"

"Is it? He never worked for anything. All he ever did was inherit money – and hoard it. Look what he did after poor Maud died – he married Grandma Alice to protect his inheritance."

Daphne was indignant. "That's not true!"

"Oh, but it is."

"You're wrong. He put the family before everything!"

"I can't believe you're saying this – you're so blind, Mother! He put money before everything. The Great Harriman Fortune. He couldn't think of anything else. And what happened? He ended up with no son to inherit it. So he did the next best thing – he decided Oliver and I should marry to keep it all in tact. Then he dangled this over you and Auntie Cynthia until neither of you could think straight. Don't you see how pathetic it is? – he never realised – with all his planning and scheming – that his 'Great Fortune' would never be inherited by a Harriman."

"Goodness, Laura! What nonsense."

"My God, Mother, listen to yourself! Has it really never occurred to you? Oliver's a Gorst and I'm a Driscoll – neither of us are Harrimans! The whole thing's been a colossal fraud. A monumental deception by a crazy old man! And you believed it!"

There was an ominous silence. Daphne sniffed, as if she had detected a bad smell under her nose, finished her sherry and recovered her equilibrium. "Well, Laura," she said at last, as though the previous conversation had never taken place. "I really don't know what to say to you. You seem to have given no thought at all to what I'm supposed to tell people. Indeed not," she added with a little shake of the head. "It's all very embarrassing."

"Embarrassing? It's only embarrassing if you say it is. Some people will think it's for the best."

"Well, I can't imagine who," she said indignantly.

But it was not long before she found out, to her considerable discomfort. A telephone call to Millicent confirmed that no one at Hazeldene Court was remotely troubled by the end of the engagement, and she was obliged, at Millicent's insistence, to pass on the message, "Hetty sends her love to Laura," without fully understanding its significance. While at Meeston Lodge, there was a discreet silence on the subject by Gwen and Elsie, who would not be drawn when they heard the news; and Reverend Talbot merely nodded wisely over his cup of tea, and observed that "young people were very independent these days".

With no moral high ground left to stand on, Daphne retreated into resentful silence. She now had two causes of complaint: her husband's misplaced generosity to their daughter – which was hard to bear, and Laura's wilful disregard of her grandfather's much larger provision for her future well-being. Resentment bred resentment, and their daily lives moved ever further apart.

CHAPTER NINETEEN

New Year. Rosemary and Julius were engaged. The announcement appeared in the *Herald* the following Friday. The cold remained unrelenting with no sign of any thaw to come. The same could be said of the atmosphere inside the Lodge.

Daphne's grievances multiplied. She felt betrayed by everyone. Her weekends were in ruins. Millicent did not want to drive while Chartris Lane was a nightmare of rutted ice, and invitations to Sunday lunches at The Old Mill were neither forthcoming, nor likely to be accepted. The Parrs, whose New Year's invitation had been declined, remained noticeably silent. Cut off from her inner circle, literally and metaphorically, she chose to extend her bounty elsewhere, in the direction of the Vicarage, where she was always assured of a warm welcome – at least by Reverend Talbot – and to Meeston Green, with its attraction of the enthusiastic attentions of Dorothy Villiers and Isabel Barnes, who had no knowledge of more intimate family matters.

For Laura, there were comforting rituals of daily routines at the office, but the weekends were empty, and the contrast with the hustle and bustle before Christmas was all the more stark. She retired to her father's study, kept a fire burning in the grate, and sat in his old armchair rereading *Great Expectations,* a reminder of happier times at Hunters Lane, and the cheerful companionship of friends and teachers who had brightened up her life.

Of Robert Moray, there was no sign – and no word either. "Most likely cut off in Scotland," Gwen said, finding no mystery in his absence when Laura asked if she had seen him. "There's telephone lines down all over the country, Ann Benyon says. So likely as not, that's why they've not heard from him. Could do with him lifting those parsnips mind," she added. "I don't like to think of good food going to waste out there." But still he did not come.

A few evenings later, the telephone rang. Daphne answered it. "Laura," she called upstairs testily, "it's Horace Parr – for you. He didn't seem at all himself – terribly garbled. Can't think what's the matter with him."

By the time Laura came down, her mother had already returned to the quiz show she had been watching, and the sound of muffled audience laughter drifted out through the closed door.

Laura's mind was still upstairs with the melodies of the evening concert fresh in her thoughts. She could not imagine what Mr Parr needed to speak to her about.

"Laura – I'm sorry," he said, his voice tremulous as he spoke. "I really don't know where to begin – except to apologise. I thought I should telephone – before you heard it from anyone else. And of course it could make your visits to the office very difficult." He cleared his throat. "You see – it's Oliver and Claudia."

Oliver and Claudia. Laura considered their juxtaposition. Not the most obvious combination. Chalk and cheese. Seriousness and sultriness. No immediate connection. "Mr Parr, I'm afraid I don't follow you."

She could hear him struggling to find the right words. "I can't make this sound any better, I'm afraid," he apologised. "They've been caught out," he added somewhat opaquely. "In fact, it seems they've been seeing each other for a while – although 'seeing' is perhaps the wrong terminology – even while you were engaged. It was unforgivable of them. Phyllis and I are extremely embarrassed, Laura – and as you can imagine, your Uncle Richard is very angry – which is why I realise it would be deeply humiliating for you – or your mother for that matter – to visit me in my professional capacity at the office." He paused for breath.

"Well, yes, I suppose it would," she agreed, finding it difficult to digest so much confusing information all at once.

"In which case," he continued at great speed, "I will have to arrange to meet you either at Meeston Lodge – or in the case of your father's 'other business'," he emphasised the words, "perhaps at the Bank – with Mr Gittings' consent, of course."

"Yes, if you think that's best."

"They will, of course, be getting married," he added, as if this explained everything. "Richard has agreed to telephone your mother to explain the situation – about Oliver. We thought this would be best – although, forgive me – 'best' is hardly the right word either – and I quite see this isn't going to make life any easier for you – under the circumstances. I really am so very, very sorry, Laura. I do hope you believe me when I say neither Phyllis nor I had the remotest idea this was going on."

"Yes, of course."

"Thank you for being so understanding. It's a great weight off my mind. And, of course, I want to assure you that this will in no way prevent me from discharging my duties to you as your father's Executor with all possible diligence and speed."

"Of course – yes. Thank you." She replaced the receiver and sat on the stairs, confused, while the sounds of the television programme continued to drift into the hall. Oliver and Claudia? Caught out? Getting married! There had never been even the smallest hint of any romantic attachment between them. And surely Claudia was far more interested in John Rufford? – he was much more her type? This was ridiculous!

Usually there was nothing that would prompt her to disturb her mother's evening addiction to the television, but this was the exception that proved the rule.

In the sitting room, Daphne was riveted by the image of a bright young woman, hair and make-up immaculate, extolling the virtues of a soap powder.

"I think you need to know Uncle Richard will be ringing shortly. He'll want to speak to you."

"Oh. Whatever for?"

"I think he'll explain."

"Well, I hope so. Horace Parr was incoherent."

At which point the telephone rang again.

Laura turned off the television and waited. It was not a long conversation, and when Daphne returned, her expression said everything. She poured herself a very large sherry from the decanter and returned to her chair clutching the glass. Her hand was shaking, but for once, she was speechless.

Laura remained silent. It was only a matter of time.

The storm broke. "How dare he! How dare he come round here playing the gallant fiancé when all the time he was two-timing you with that wretched Parr girl! I can't believe it! I shall never speak to him again." Daphne was visibly seething, her indignation reaching a crescendo in a very short space of time. "I never liked that girl," she added, addressing the hearth rug. "Always pouting and putting on airs. Throwing herself at anything in trousers. Well, we can all see what she was after now, can't we? A rich husband. More fool him!" She downed a very large mouthful of sherry without noticing. "Cynthia *must* have known this was going on," she added bitterly. "How could she do this to me?"

Laura noticed the shift in emphasis. Oliver's infidelity was no longer a humiliation to her daughter, it had become another triumph of Cynthia over her older sister.

Daphne's anger remained undiminished. "Well? I suppose you're going to tell me you had no idea this was going on?"

Laura was astonished. "Of course I didn't! How can you think such a thing?"

"I don't know what to think any more, Laura. First there was you with that penniless Evans boy – and now there's Oliver with that trollop. You're both as bad as each other! Heaven knows what Father would have thought!"

Laura had no appetite for a pointless argument: her head was still reeling trying to understand how she had managed to misread whatever signals there might have been to warn her; and wishing Oliver had had the courage to tell her honestly and openly his interests lay elsewhere. Too late now.

"Well, I suppose as far as Oliver's concerned," her mother observed cuttingly, finishing the first glass of sherry and helping herself to a second, "one cousin's as good as another." And with that damning observation, she downed her second sherry and switched on the television. "You do realise," she added as she waited for the screen to warm up, "that's the end of any future invitations to Dyers Green or the Parrs? We can be sure of that."

The programme on the television had changed. Laura stared at the fire, ignoring the gunfight raging in the corner of the room, and the hectic music that went with it. How typical of her mother, she thought. No word of genuine regret that her daughter had been treated so shabbily, even if Laura herself felt almost indifferent to the turn of events, and was merely confused by them. Daphne saw only a wider gulf between herself and her younger sister, and a further diminution in her social life with the removal of evenings at Highfield House.

When the telephone rang the following evening, Daphne

flatly refused to answer it, and it was left to Laura to respond to its insistent ringing. "Hello. Meeston 457." The beeping sound of coins being fed into a public phone box followed, and a velvety male voice – unmistakable – answered. "That is Laura Driscoll, isn't it?"

"Yes. Who's calling?" But she already knew the answer.

"John Rufford. We were ships that passed in the night just before Christmas.

Her spine tingled. "I vaguely remember you," she said, lying brilliantly and slipping automatically into her other, hidden, self. "Aren't you the 'gentleman' who doesn't play the saxophone?"

"The very one," he replied, and she could picture his level gaze and the quirky smile that would accompany the words. "I thought I might give you a call."

"How did you get my number? From Jules?"

His easy laugh came down the telephone. "No – the directory." He was caressing her with his voice. "There's only one Driscoll in Meeston."

"That's true," she agreed, feeling decidedly light-headed. "We're quite unique."

"Well, *you* are," he corrected her. "I wondered if you'd like to come out with me on Saturday evening – now you're off the leash – so to speak."

"Am I indeed? Who says so?"

"Little birds," he said.

This time she knew it was Jules.

"I could pick you up about seven."

"And where would we be going?"

"Oh – out for a meal – cinema – club. Whatever you like."

Laura closed her eyes and remembered the aftershave; the languid pose; the smile, and the audacious hand on her thigh. Did she really want to go out with this man? – this Lothario, as Jules had described him? Did she really think a meal, the cinema or a club was all he had in mind? She was not so naive, but neither could she fool herself. This gift was hers, if she wanted him. And she decided she did.

"That's very thoughtful of you," she said, amusing herself at his expense. "You can take me out for a meal, if you like. Somewhere special, as I seem to remember you saying I deserved something better."

His voice was quite husky when he replied. "Whatever you want."

She had no doubt about what *he* wanted. If she accepted his offer, she accepted the whole package. So be it.

CHAPTER TWENTY

Choosing what to wear for the evening required attention to detail. Sparston Hall was, by all accounts, a rather stylish establishment. Trendy, it was not. Elegance and sophistication was the look to aim for, and she spent the Friday evening mulling over various possibilities in her wardrobe. After much indecision, her midnight-blue cashmere dress seemed the best choice. She checked her reflection from all angles. Perfect. The apparently modestly scooped neckline belied the altogether more provocative effect of the soft fabric accentuating her figure. At her neck, she would wear the little rose pendant on its silver chain given to her by Uncle Richard and Aunt Cynthia at Christmas, and add the merest hint of perfume.

How to wear her hair was equally troublesome. A French pleat – both tasteful and refined – would have been her natural choice. But on this occasion there were other priorities. She went through the ritual of sweeping her hair up into place and surveyed the result critically. Much too formal, she decided. And more importantly, much too difficult to keep immaculate. She let her hair fall naturally to her shoulders again and swept it back from her face to one side, holding it in place with a simple silver clasp. The addition of her little silver and diamond stud earrings completed the effect. She would need only the minimum of make-up. Simplicity had its charms.

The following evening, her image in the mirror met with her approval. She glowed, anticipation adding a vivacity missing for far too long. It was pointless pretending: she relished the prospect of seduction. She felt wilful and volatile; she did not want to be rational, or prudent; she wanted excitement and intoxication. John Rufford, she had no doubt, would provide it.

Daphne had not welcomed the news of her evening out. "Where did you meet this man?" she had wanted to know. And discovering he was a friend of Julius Parr had done nothing to reassure her. If anything, it had damned him by association. She was already on watch, waiting for him, when he arrived punctually at seven in a two-seat MG Roadster in British Racing Green. He got out, drawing his Crombie closer against the cold, and came lightly up the steps to ring the bell. She opened the door to him, ensuring he remained outside under the porch.

"Mrs Driscoll?" he said, offering her his hand. "I'm John Rufford. Glad to meet you."

Anyone else would have been dazzled by his smile, but Daphne did little more than acknowledge him with a cursory nod, shaking his proffered hand with a noticeable lack of enthusiasm. He appeared not to notice the slight. "I do hope you'll take care, Mr Rufford," she said, casting a jaundiced glance in the direction of his choice of car

– evidently far too flashy. "The minor roads are still icy between Lingford and Chursley."

"I'm a very careful driver, Mrs Driscoll," he assured her. "You need have no fears on that account."

Daphne appeared not to notice the implications of what he had said, although his meaning was not lost on Laura. She could barely look in his direction without experiencing a jolt under her ribs, and the sensation of sudden wild exultation that comes from doing something dangerous. She had never felt like this before, not even with Martin.

John took her arm, smiling at her, and led her down the steps with a level of solicitousness Oliver had never shown.

"Don't wait up for me," Laura called back as he helped her into the passenger seat. "I'll let myself in."

He closed the door, looking at her very intently.

He was, Laura discovered, despite his choice of car and Daphne's doubts, an unshowy driver. There was none of Jules' recklessness, and his concentration was focused on his driving, not idle conversation. She soon relaxed in his company, enjoying their steady progress through the web of country lanes beyond Lingford to the north-west, where the snow, still banked high on either side, loomed up like frozen waves in the headlights as they rounded bends, and icy ruts scrunched beneath the tyres.

"Been to Sparston Hall before?" he enquired casually after a while.

"No."

"I think you'll like it."

"I'm sure I will."

A mile or so later, they passed through Lower Chursley, and he turned the car into a private tree-lined drive, pulling up beside several Bentleys already parked outside a grand Victorian mansion, now a secluded, and very obviously, high-class hotel. Lights blazed from its windows welcoming visitors inside.

"Do you bring all your dates here?" she asked, mocking him.

"No – just those who deserve something better. Here, let me help you out. There's ice on the gravel." His grasp was firm.

Inside, the spacious reception hall was furnished with Georgian antiques and thick-piled carpets. The atmosphere was warm, hushed and intimate; the staff unobtrusive, but attentive when needed. In the ladies' cloakroom, the young woman on duty took the trouble to carefully arrange Laura's coat on a hanger before it was placed, with equal diligence, next to several fur coats already on the rail.

Her hair and general appearance meeting with her approval, Laura sauntered back to the bar where several couples were sitting at low tables smoking and enjoying pre-dinner drinks. The men were mainly middle-aged with an air of well-heeled affluence, cigars and spreading waistlines from too many business lunches. Their women had sculpted hairstyles, lacquered into place, with heavily made-up faces, all mascara and bright lipstick. They sported expensive jewellery and fashionable evening wear, sipped at cocktails and smoked king-size cigarettes. Their laughter was brittle, and their sharp eyes watched her progress, as did their companions' over the rims of their whisky glasses.

John was leaning nonchalantly against the bar, a menu in one hand, a tumbler of what appeared to be whisky and ice in the other. She paused, simply to enjoy the sight of him. He was magnificent, she thought, compared with the others. He was sleek and totally at ease with himself; perfectly assured; impeccably dressed in a dark grey suit, a white shirt with woven stripes in the fabric, and a plain wine-coloured tie. On his feet were unmistakable Italian leather shoes. He looked up, seeing her approach. "Would you like a drink?" he asked, unashamedly evaluating her.

Under his close scrutiny, she chose a Martini rather than a sherry.

They sat down at one of the corner tables and he handed her a menu. "You look stunning," he said casually, his attention apparently on the list of *hors d'oeuvres*.

"So do you," she said, slipping effortlessly into the rôle of verbal sparring partner, and relishing the challenge.

He glanced up, raising an eyebrow. "Well, now we've both agreed on that, what would you like to eat?"

The Martini was already making her feel light-headed. Concentrating on the menu was becoming difficult. There were several courses on offer. Too many. She wanted to keep it simple. "Oh – just the soup and steak, please."

"Are you sure?"

"Mm. The desserts look very tempting."

He turned and summoned the waiter hovering discreetly by the bar, and after a brief consultation over the choice of wine, chose a rosé because it was her preferred option. The waiter bowed slightly, and slipped away.

"Would you like a cigarette?" he offered, taking out a gold cigarette case and flicking it open. The cigarettes were lined up in orderly rows. Peter Stuyvesants.

She shook her head and thanked him. "I don't smoke."

He flicked the case shut and put it away without comment, choosing not to smoke either. A little touch of thoughtfulness she noted.

He engaged her in casual chit-chat, enquiring about her interests, and unlike most men, who usually preferred to talk about themselves, he wanted to know more, especially about her painting and the subjects she chose, while the occasional smile and raised eyebrow beguiled her without any apparent effort on his part. His mannerisms, his way of expressing himself, and the little hand gestures that accompanied his conversation, were all utterly charming. She was fascinated by him, while the Martini appeared to be encouraging her to become increasingly talkative, and she was relieved when the waiter finally arrived to show them to their places.

The dining room was spacious, the intimate candle-lit tables set in secluded alcoves ranged around the walls, some already occupied. In the centre of the room, a parquet dance floor with a mirrored globe suspended above it, had already attracted two couples, and on a raised platform nearby, a spot-lit trio of musicians in evening suits were playing a medley of slow-tempo Thirties dance tunes in muted tones on a piano, saxophone and bass. The ambience was delightful, and slightly decadent. Oliver, she realised, had never taken her anywhere remotely like this.

"I'm hoping I can persuade you to dance with me this evening," John said once the waiter had slipped away. "You rather gave me the brush-off the last time."

"That's because I was otherwise engaged."

He smiled. "Indeed you were."

When the first course was cleared, he led her onto the dance floor. The melody was a slow waltz. He held her lightly round the waist, his hand barely touching the small of her back, guiding her with an effortless grace. There was not the slightest hint of impropriety but the effect made her feel ridiculously weak, and it was clear from his unambiguous gaze, he knew precisely what he was doing.

They had two more dances, both decorous – and unsettling, in equal measure. The music stopped, and the musicians took a break to polite applause.

Everyone returned to their seats. The main course was served, and the wine poured, the waiters moving between their customers with choreographed precision and exaggerated courtesy.

John thanked them politely, waiting until all the fussing about them had finished, then raised his glass. "To Laura Driscoll," he said softly. "To the start of her new life."

"Mm," she agreed. "To the start of my new life."

The conversation drifted for a while, discussing the quality of the food, and his solicitous enquiries as to whether her steak had been cooked to her liking. It was enough simply to bask in his company.

"You've gone very quiet," he said. "Are you enjoying this evening?"

"Of course. But tell me honestly, why did you ask me out?"

He frowned. A mock frown. "Honestly? Honesty can be dangerous. Are you sure you want to know?"

"Was it because you thought I was on the rebound – that I'd be an easy catch?"

He laughed softly. "No," he said. "I told you – you deserved better."

"Better than Oliver?"

"Uh-huh."

"Why are you better?" she challenged him.

"You ask very direct questions, Laura Driscoll. I hope you're prepared for the answers."

"Try me," she said, watching his reactions to her boldness.

He gave her the benefit of his lazy smile. "What you see is what you get," he said, leaning back casually in his chair, the same pose he had adopted that evening in the Parrs' cellar those few short weeks before: provocative; inviting. "I'm a short-term arrangement with no strings. I don't date more than one girl at a time. I don't make promises I can't keep. And I don't pretend to be the marrying kind – because I'm not. I'm a pastime. Nothing more – nothing less." He was looking directly at her again, potent and utterly amoral. "You can take it – or leave it. It's entirely up to you."

"Did Claudia want more?" she asked, trying to break the power of his magnetism.

He laughed and returned to eating his steak. "Claudia? I've never been out with Claudia."

"Never?"

"No," he said, very firmly. "Not my type. Too obvious."

"Oh."

He looked sympathetic, a small frown creasing his brow. "You never suspected, did you? – about her and Oliver."

She shook her head, embarrassed by her lack of insight.

He reached across and took her hand, stroking her fingers. "Well, if it's any consolation, it came as a surprise to me too – when Jules said you were Oliver's fiancée."

"Why?"

"Because I'd seen Oliver and Claudia together several times before Jules invited me round to Highfield. They'd not noticed me. Too bound up in themselves."

"Where did you see them?"

"In restaurants – at lunch times. In Lingford. Obviously a pair. I couldn't work out why they were so indifferent to each other with the Highfield crowd – until the night you turned up. Then it all became very clear. I did try to tell you."

"Yes, you did – and I didn't understand. I thought you left early to find Claudia."

"I left early because the only girl I was interested in was someone else's fiancée." He poured her more wine. "I admit, I was intrigued. You weren't in love with him, were you?"

"Was it so obvious?"

"It was to me. So – to go back to your original question

– if you weren't in love with him, you're not exactly on the rebound, are you?" He cocked his head on one side and smiled, quietly triumphant.

"Touché, Mr Rufford," she said and raised her glass to him.

He acknowledged her appreciation with a slight nod. The musicians had returned and there was an introductory tinkling on the piano before the saxophonist stepped up to the microphone and began crooning 'You do something to me'.

John pushed back his chair and stood up. "Can I have this dance, Miss Driscoll?" he asked, all mock seriousness.

With equal seriousness, she obliged.

They danced between the main course and the dessert; and between the dessert and the coffee and mints; and then afterwards, as the evening drifted on. The trio switched seamlessly between styles, slipping into slower rhythms, when the only lights in the room were those reflected from the mirrored ball above the dance floor, and couples hung around each other's necks. He held her closer now, but not too close, oddly decorous under such circumstances, she thought, the scent of his aftershave more intoxicating than the wine.

At midnight, the trio drew their repertoire to a close with thanks and more polite applause, and the diners drifted away, the residents to the bar, and the others to their waiting cars.

Laura collected her coat and inspected her make-up. "What now?" she asked her reflection with its smoothed-out complexion and heightened colour. She felt very much alive, and responsive to the slightest touch.

He was waiting for her in the reception hallway, standing with his back to her in a comfortable, languorous sort of way. His hands were deep in his coat pockets, and he was studying one of the many old oil paintings in elaborate gilt frames displayed round the oak-panelled walls. It was a hunting scene, the lead riders surmounting a field hedge and the others straggling behind them, hounds at their heels. A small plaque embedded in the frame bore the title – 'The Chase'.

"How apt," she said, moving up to him and taking his arm.

He said nothing, just smiled, and led her out into the frosty night, shepherding her across the icy gravel and into the car. Above them was starlight and a waning full moon high in the sky.

Without any sense of urgency, he put on his driving gloves and turned on the ignition. "I can drive you straight home, if you want," he said quietly, addressing the windscreen. "And you'll be back before one. Or," he paused, turning to look at her, "you can come over to my place – and you may be home for breakfast."

"Do I really have a choice?"

"Of course." His face was half-lit by the moonlight, his eyes hidden in shadow. "But," he added meaningfully, "you do understand, don't you – if you come back to my place, it won't just be for coffee and a friendly chat?" The softness of his voice was quite explicit.

Chapter Twenty-One

It was gone four o'clock when he brought her back to
Meeston. The driveway was washed clean in moonlight,
brilliant blue-white in the intense cold. The Lodge itself was
in darkness, a brooding silhouette against the strangely-lit
sky.

Laura spent the journey home lying half-asleep against
the headrest, existing somewhere between exhilaration and
exhaustion. If he chose never to see her again, she could live
a lifetime on those three hours spent sprawled on his bed.
There had been no shame; no artificial coyness; just honest
intimacy; his love-making adept and finely tuned; his touch,
exquisite, feather-like in its delicacy – a revelation to her
after Oliver's clumsiness. He lifted her into an unforgettable
realm of ecstasy with such perfect ease, it was breath-taking,
and at times, alarming. He taught her things she had never
dreamed of, and she learnt well – too well, perhaps. He
had made her hungry for more. "You're a beautiful, sensual
woman," he told her afterwards, lying next to her, stroking
her hair. "Don't ever forget that." And to prove it, he had
made love to her again.

When he brought the car to a stop, he kept the engine

running. His hands – which had explored her so thoroughly only an hour before – remained firmly on the steering wheel. He turned to smile at her, the outlines of his face etched in the moonlight. "Are you all right?" he asked.

She was still suspended in the dream-filled space between sleep and wakefulness. "Yes – perfectly," she said, listening to her body's quiet exultation. "Thank you for tonight. For everything." She had no expectations. He would simply say 'good night' – and nothing more. No strings attached. She would be sorry, because she would have liked more of him now, but, if it was not to be, it was not to be.

The engine continued to purr softly. He was still looking at her; still smiling. "I wish you could have stayed over," he said quietly, lulling her, making her want him again. "If I asked you to – would you – next time?"

Images danced in her head. "Do I qualify for a 'next time'?"

"Of course."

"That would be nice." She was remembering how he looked in the lamplight, astonished at how much she found pleasure in his nakedness; how he felt, the hard muscles under the smooth skin of his back, and the long slope down his spine to the gentle curve of his buttocks; the scent of his aftershave, and his sweet, insistent movement deep within her.

"Next Saturday?" he was asking.

"Yes."

"I'll telephone Thursday evening then."

She remained quiescent, her head against the headrest,

unwilling to break the spell. She was satiated; her limbs heavy, her body tingling, her mind floating. He was dangerously addictive, she decided.

"What are you thinking?"

"Oh – about this and that – about how you made me feel."

He was studying her closely. "You'd better go in," he said, and swung himself out of the car to help her up the steps, steadying her on the frosty ground. At the door, he did not kiss her. He had not kissed her all evening – not on the lips – he had been occupied elsewhere. "Until next Saturday then," he said softly.

"Yes," she said.

She watched him drive away before opening the front door. His going was a loss, and she wanted nothing more than to sink into the comfortable chaos of her bed and relive the glorious confusion of sensations he had revealed to her, over and over again.

A light came on upstairs almost as soon as the door was closed, and Daphne appeared on the landing, her dressing-gown hastily thrown over her nightdress. "Do you have any idea what time it is, Laura?" she asked, her irritation palpable, even at such a distance.

Laura closed her mind to the sudden and unwelcome harangue, wanting the magic to last, not to have it shattered into a thousand fractured pieces under a barrage of questioning. She would not, she decided, absolutely would *not* be interrogated.

In no great hurry, she took off her coat and checked

her image in the hall mirror, surprised to find herself so outwardly unchanged. How could that be? "We went on to a party," she lied effortlessly. "I told you not to stay up."

Her mother swept down the stairs. "I didn't stay up, Laura. I lay awake worrying about where you were."

Laura shrugged off her concern. "I'm sorry. What more can I say?"

Daphne was not to be placated so easily. "You don't know anything about this man – all smooth talking and nice manners, grant you. It's not sensible to take such risks."

"What risks?" There had been no risks: he had taken every precaution. Did her mother want the details? She doubted it.

"You know exactly what risks!"

"He didn't rape me, if that's what you mean."

"This is no matter for flippancy, Laura! It does happen." Her mother's voice was becoming ever more strident.

A thousand needling grievances Laura had subdued over the years bubbled to the surface and boiled over; unstoppable. "Oh for heaven's sake! Stop treating me like a child!

Daphne bridled. "While you're living in my house, you'll have the decency to listen to what I say!"

Regrets can never undo the harm of the unguarded moment. If only she had been more alert, Laura thought later, she might have held her tongue. But her mind was elsewhere, lying with John Rufford, luxuriating in his delicate touch, her body still exulting in his delicious sensuality, so the words escaped, uncensored, and there was no going back. "Well, Mother," she said, bursting with irritation and the petulance of the child she claimed not to be, "Come to think of it, this is *my* house now, in case you hadn't realised."

"Laura!" Daphne reached out, grasping the bannister rail to steady herself. She had turned deathly pale.

They faced one another, like combatants across a field of battle, years of animosity rising up between them. A vast, impenetrable silence descended and engulfed them both, leaving the steady ticking of the clock to fill the space, measuring the passing seconds with its ponderous beat.

The moment passed. Laura felt the heat rushing into her cheeks. Angrily, she pushed past her mother and ran quickly up the stairs. "I'm sorry," she said, aware she did not sound it. "I shouldn't have said that. But you don't know when to stop, do you?"

The Rubicon was well and truly crossed.

Lying in bed, hugging her hot water bottle, she pushed her mother's indignation aside, and let herself slide into the warm contemplation of the following weekend – and all that it would bring.

She woke to the hall clock striking eleven, and opened her eyes to a pale sunlight on the wall beside the curtains. She stretched, as a cat might, smug and well-satisfied after a long, uninterrupted sleep, too comfortable to stir itself. Her mind drifted, content to let the day slip by. It was Sunday. Her mother would be at church. Reverend Talbot would be concerned she was not there beside her in the pew, and Daphne would feel obliged to concoct a satisfactory explanation for her daughter's absence – and that too would be held against her. There would be no reconciliation that day – or perhaps even the next – or the next – if ever. No matter. This would be the necessary parting of the ways. In future, she would be answerable to no one but herself. Her mother's power over her was no more. Nor, she decided, would Reverend Talbot find her in St Wilfrid's every Sunday praying for forgiveness of her sins. Such sins! Such joy and delight! There was no repentance. No guilt. Quite the opposite. She felt liberated, and incredibly alive.

She watched the progress of the sunlight on the wall as it slipped along the margins of the curtains and through the crack between them. Remorseless progress – like John Rufford's delicate touch sliding down her body from her eager breasts to the deep, dark heat between her thighs. Was this ecstasy hers alone? Did Claudia feel this way with Oliver? Was it possible? Was Oliver like herself? – she wondered. Was he as passionate in the arms of someone who could light his fire? Perhaps he was. It was a curious notion. But there were others. What of Mr Moray? Had Susan Holbrook lain tumbled in his bed and felt the same, glorious satisfaction? Perhaps she had, but not enough, it seemed, to marry him.

The hall clock struck twelve. Daphne would not be long returning from St Wilfrid's, brimming with self-righteous indignation, no doubt. Her lips would be pursed, a taut line of disapproval to match her frown, and she would busy herself in the kitchen, fussing over this and that with a brisk efficiency designed to demonstrate her sense of outrage.

Laura threw back the covers, suddenly invigorated by her

clarity of purpose. She would clear the air between them, and that would be the end of it.

Daphne, still dressed for 'going out', was already in the kitchen. Nothing was said, but there was an icy glance in Laura's direction indicating it had been noted she had not yet eaten breakfast, whereas she, Daphne, had not only eaten but also found time to attend the House of the Lord for morning service.

Laura did not rise to the bait. "Is Millie driving over?" she asked casually, slicing up the bread to make some toast. "I presume you're spending the afternoon at Broxley?"

There was a curt nod.

"We need to talk – about last night."

Daphne had laid out a tray with tea and biscuits ready for Millicent's arrival. "I don't wish to discuss the matter," she said, picking up the tray.

"I think we must. We can't go on like this. Please sit down."

Daphne pondered the request for a moment, implying it was greatly inconvenient, then complied, her dignity still ruffled. "I don't know what's come over you, Laura," she said stiffly. "You've changed."

"I've learnt to assert myself."

"Whatever you call it, you've become unpleasantly aggressive."

"I'm trying to survive, Mother, that's all."

"You don't have to be so offensive."

"I've already apologised for last night. It was – uncalled for.

"Indeed it was."

"Very well – the subject of Meeston Lodge is closed. We both understand the implications of Daddy's Will. But now I'm not marrying Oliver things have to change."

"Oh – in what way precisely, may I ask?"

"We need to manage our lives differently."

"And what do you mean by that?"

"I mean I want us to live separately – divide the Lodge between us."

"What nonsense!"

"No, it's not nonsense. I want some privacy while I'm living here, that's all." She tried to sound eminently sensible. "I thought I'd turn Daddy's study into a studio. Somewhere for my art-work. My special place – no interruptions – somewhere to entertain, if I want to – without disturbing you. Naturally, the sitting room would be entirely yours –"

Daphne's expression visibly hardened. "That's very kind of you, Laura."

"Please – I'm trying to be civilised."

"Well that's very nice of you. Are there any other rooms you would like to exclude me from? You will let me know, won't you?" Her voice was laced with sarcasm. "Of course, I realise you've inherited the house, my dear, which obviously gives you *carte-blanche*, but it's still my home. I hardly expected to be dictated to in my own home."

There was the smell of burning toast. "I'm not dictating to you, Mother," Laura said, rescuing the sad remains. "I'm trying to suggest sensible living arrangements until I decide what to do with the rest of my life. I'm not a child any more," she added, wondering if the toast was worth saving, "How I spend my time and who I spend it with is for me to decide, not you."

Their eyes met, determination in Laura's, affront in her mother's. "I see. So – I'm not to trouble myself when you return home at all hours? I must put aside a mother's concern for your welfare and disregard your recklessness? Is that it?"

"Yes. Precisely."

"How very novel. And what do you suggest I say to Reverend Talbot when you are absent from Sunday morning services as a consequence of your 'interesting' lifestyle? This morning, I had to tell him you were a little under the weather. He was most concerned."

"Then tell him the truth," Laura suggested, enjoying the slight frisson she felt at recommending such an outrageous proposal.

There was a momentary pause while Daphne digested the impracticality of telling Reverend Talbot anything that might remotely hint at impropriety. "You are quite beyond the pale, Laura," she said at last. "I'm at a loss what to say to you."

"Then don't say anything."

The front door bell rang. Daphne rose from her chair with dignity to answer it, and Aunt Millicent's cheery tones drifted into the hallway.

Laura spread the marmalade generously over her toast and felt well-pleased with herself. It had been easier than she had expected to slay the dragon.

The mid-afternoon sun, circled with a silver haze in its powder-blue sky, was still too weak to penetrate the deep chill in the garden. The lock on the store was stiff, and by the time Laura opened it, her fingers were numb with cold. She stepped inside, hoping for a scrap of warmth, and found the windows crazed with frost.

The racks of garden tools remained untouched. A light fork, easy to handle, seemed the best choice, and clutching it in gloved hands, she picked her way carefully across the frozen ground between the brassicas. Here and there, the slight thaw of previous days had inched back the mantle of snow, revealing the feathery tops of the parsnips. Around them, patches of earth had been revealed, like dark haloes.

The ground was unyielding, and the fork bounced off the surface with a high, protesting metallic ring, jarring her wrist. She swore under her breath and tried again, still to no effect. She would have to be more subtle. Wriggling the fork back and forth eventually opened up the solid crust to broken ground beneath. The first roots came up with care. She laid them out by her garden trug to thaw, pleased with her efforts. It was slow work but a pleasant, wholly absorbing occupation, and it suited her triumphant state of mind.

"Miss Driscoll." The familiar burr in the voice seemed to come from nowhere.

She turned around. "Goodness, Mr Moray – you startled me!"

He was standing on the rutted gravel path watching her. He cut a sad figure, she thought, his collar turned up against the chill, his hands deep in his pockets, his expression, as usual, a perfect blank, revealing nothing. His anger had gone. "I owe you an apology," he said.

"No, not at all. I just didn't hear you."

He shook his head. "No – I didn't mean that. I meant about what I said – before Christmas."

His unexpected arrival deprived her of making sensible conversation, her mind very firmly fixed elsewhere. "Oh – that," she said, uncertain what else to say.

"I hope you'll forgive me."

"Yes – of course. Perfectly understandable – under the circumstances," she added. And as so often happened with Mr Moray, the conversation shuddered to a halt. "Gwen didn't want the parsnips to go to waste," she went on, noticing him frowning slightly at her endeavours.

He seemed prepared to accept the change of topic. "You'd better give that to me," he said, reaching out and taking the fork from her, critically inspecting the alignment of the tines.

"Have I damaged it?" She was afraid she had, and he would be cross at her meddling in his domain.

He glanced up at her briefly. "No – but it's too light for the job."

"I wanted to do something useful."

He seemed not to hear, or feel the need to answer. Instead, he crunched his way back to the store, returning with the larger fork, and set about lifting the rest of the row with quiet, resolute determination.

Feeling she was unwanted, Laura retreated with her

trug, threading her way back between the cabbages to where the rows of sprouts stood in disordered, drunken ranks beneath the weight of frozen snow. The tight green buds were icy to the touch, but soon the trug was full and there was nothing left to do but wait for him to finish so they could share the spoils between them. He worked on silently, uncommunicative and withdrawn, and she wished she could find something useful to say that might help to lift his spirits. But perhaps, she thought, recalling their earlier, overheated conversation before Christmas, it was wiser to say nothing. So she simply waited, burying her hands in her pockets.

He straightened up and began cleaning the soil from the fork, running his fingers down each of the tines in turn.

"Was there much snow in Scotland?" she asked, feeling compelled now to start some sort of conversation.

He nodded, but added nothing more to explain his prolonged absence.

"We were cut off here for a while too."

He seemed preoccupied.

She tried another tack. "I hope you got my present," she said, wishing immediately she had not drawn attention to his lack of gratitude.

He looked up, evidently embarrassed. "Forgive me, I should have thanked you sooner," he said. "It was a nice thought." He reached into his pocket and brought out the penknife. "I'll treasure it."

"It was just a token. I wanted you to know I valued your ..." She was stumped for the precise word she was seeking.

"… openness – about my father," she added, feeling this was not quite what she meant.

He nodded. "It must have been a difficult Christmas, Miss Driscoll – without him."

"Yes, it was. Difficult for you too, perhaps?"

Silence.

Why, oh why had she said that? She had not meant to – it just popped out – like the sudden unstoppable rush of irritation at her mother's unwarranted and unwelcome questioning. Had she no self-control?

He was looking at her: green eyes filled with hurt.

"Oh, Mr Moray, I really didn't mean to be so thoughtless. It's been so easy for me – I didn't want to marry Oliver in the first place – and now I'm free to start again …" She trailed off, wishing she had never started.

Chapter Twenty-Two

"Good night, Mr Gittings." She stepped out into another early evening frost, wrapping her scarf tighter against the chill.

"Hello, Laura." Oliver was standing a few feet away, hunched inside his Crombie, its collar turned up and his trilby pulled forward. In the pallid blue of the street lights, he looked gaunt, less sure of himself, and not how she remembered him. "Can I give you a lift?" he asked.

She wondered what he wanted. "I'm not going straight home, Oliver," she said, having no inclination to encourage him.

"Oh – can I give you a lift somewhere else?"

"No. I'm having tea at The Spinners' Café."

"With anyone?"

"No, I just enjoy changing my routine."

"Can I join you?"

"If you like. You can buy me an omelette."

"Yes – of course."

They walked in silence, and he seemed uncomfortable in her company, keeping his distance. At the café, he chose a corner table, well away from the brightly lit window and the casual gaze of passers-by.

They placed their orders with the tired-looking girl who oozed resentment at having customers so late in the day, and from beyond the door into the kitchen, tones of equal irritation could be heard.

Oliver appeared in no hurry to begin a conversation. His gaze was firmly fixed on the salt and pepper pots sitting in the middle of the red gingham tablecloth.

"Well, Oliver – what do you want to talk about?"

"I wanted to explain."

"About you and Claudia?"

There was a trace of a wince at her directness. "I wanted to apologise for not being honest with you."

"Very refreshing of you. It did come as something of a surprise."

"You're very calm about everything."

She reached out and patted his hand reassuringly. "That's what everyone says. But why do you want to talk now, Oliver? I might have been more impressed if I'd heard about your – liaison – from you, and not Mr Parr. He was terribly embarrassed."

He looked away. "I can't excuse myself. I just couldn't face you."

Her omelette arrived, and two cups of tea. "Is that all?" asked the waitress.

"Yes – for now, thank you," he said, and she retreated behind the counter to stare at them balefully.

Laura waited for him to continue.

He watched her eat, stirring his cup long after the sugar had dissolved.

The omelette was already half-eaten. "Well?" she asked, wondering if he was ever going to make a start.

"Where should I begin?"

"How about the beginning?" she said. "When did you fall madly in love with her?"

He cast a furtive glance at the waitress, who pretended to be inspecting her nails. "Don't make fun of me, Laura. This isn't easy."

"I'm not making fun of you, Oliver – honestly. I want to know, that's all. You must have fallen madly in love with her – or was it the other way around?"

"No. No. It sort of happened," he said, helplessly. "We drifted into it, I suppose."

"Go on. I'm listening."

"Maybe it goes a long way back – I don't know. I never saw much of you when you were at Hunters Lane."

"And Claudia was a day girl." She finished the omelette. "Could I have a piece of chocolate cake?"

"Oh – yes, of course." He summoned the waitress and placed the order without noticing her undisguised irritation at his request.

The cake arrived, and Laura cut it into little pieces to make it last for as long as possible. She was enjoying making him feel uncomfortable. "So, there we are, you and I, plodding along, destined for the altar. Then we get engaged – and we know that was a bad move. So what happened?"

"I knew then we weren't right for each other. I didn't really feel any…"

"Passion?" she offered helpfully. "No, don't be embarrassed, Oliver. I never felt any either. It can't have helped."

"I just thought it was because you hadn't –"

"Any experience?"

"God, Laura, you're making this difficult."

"Sorry. I thought I was being helpful. Go on. When did you discover you were interested in Claudia? Three months ago? Six? A year?"

He fiddled with the teaspoon. "I can't put a date on it. We began seeing more of each other after she started at Morgan & Buckingham's. Sometimes she'd bring round urgent letters from their clients to ours – to save time. Most evenings she'd come to the office to get a lift home with her father. We started talking while she waited." He shrugged. "Then we met by accident one lunch time. I suppose it became a habit."

"Someone saw you together," she said casually.

He looked up sharply. "Christ! Laura. Who?"

"It's not important. Anyway – I only heard about it after we'd broken up."

"I suppose that's something to be thankful for."

"Is it?"

He looked away.

"When did it start getting really serious?"

There was a long pause. "A few weeks before your father's death," he confessed.

"Not exactly the best time to discuss calling off an engagement."

"No, it wasn't. It made things a lot harder."

"It must have been a godsend when I didn't want to go on with it," she said, his bumbling attempts to explain his reservations before Christmas taking on a new dimension. He had got off rather lightly, she thought. He had never needed to confess his interest lay elsewhere. But she should have seen the signs: the get-well card of a Labrador; his forgetfulness in offering her a cigarette the night she met John Rufford. She finished the cake. "You can take me home now, if you like."

"Yes, of course." He paid the bill and they left, to the relief of the waitress who was regularly checking the time on her watch.

They picked their way between the remnants of compacted snow clinging to the pavements down the side streets, to where his car was parked discreetly in the shadows that lay between two pools of light. He helped her in, embarrassed at having to hold her arm, and when he closed the door, she noticed Claudia's perfume lingered on the upholstery of the seat.

He fussed around making himself comfortable on the driver's side.

"Why the rush for you two to get married, Oliver?" she asked innocently. "She's not pregnant, is she?"

"Good God, Laura! No she isn't!" He started the engine savagely and crashed the gears.

"It's the usual reason, isn't it?"

"Things happened, that's all."

"Mr Parr said you'd been caught out. Sounded like a cricket match."

He concentrated hard on the road ahead. "Phyllis came home unexpectedly," he said.

The laughter just slipped out. "Oh, Oliver! You mean she caught you at it?"

"It's not funny."

"Of course it is! It's hysterical."

"It was horribly embarrassing."

"Well, yes – I suppose it was." She let the subject drop, and he seemed in no mood to discuss it further. "Does Claudia know – about you meeting me tonight?" she asked as they drove into Meeston. There had to be a reason for him being so peculiarly on edge.

"No."

"Why ever not? Shouldn't she know you're meeting your ex?"

"I want to keep things simple."

"Do you mean she's jealous of me?" Memories of the pre-Christmas party at the Parrs' came to mind; Claudia's petulance, and sudden departure. There was satisfaction in discovering one's worth in another woman's eyes – especially when that woman was Claudia.

"I mean, I want to keep things simple," he repeated. "Things are bad enough between our parents without adding to the mix." He pulled into the Lodge driveway and left the engine running.

Laura reached across and turned off the ignition. "Listen,

Oliver, frankly I won't lose sleep over the possibility of never seeing either you or Claudia again, but I'd like to think Aunt Cynthia, Phyllis, and my mother too, of course, were on speaking terms. If anyone has the right to be angry, it's me. And I'm not, so I can't see the point of this – this silly nonsense."

"You try telling my mother that – or Phyllis Parr for that matter."

"Why not? Why don't I telephone your mother – and Phyllis – tonight?"

"Good God, Laura! You must be mad!"

"Not at all. What's to be lost in mending fences?" It was such a delicious plan, she was quite elated by it, recognising its duplicitous nature without a moment's qualm. On the surface, she would appear amazingly forgiving and unselfish. Quite a coup, she thought, but that was not her motive. Once Daphne was back in the comfortable routine of family visits, there would be less time for her to fret over what her daughter might be doing. And she intended doing quite a lot.

CHAPTER TWENTY-THREE

John telephoned as promised. "I thought we could go for a drive on Saturday afternoon," he suggested. "Take a stroll perhaps – have a meal at The Narrowboat. It's an old inn by the canal at Farley Heath. Do you know it?"

His voice revived more intimate conversations. "No," she said.

"Just wear casual," he added. "And stout shoes. You do have stout shoes?"

"I'm known for my stout shoes."

He laughed softly. "They're not one of your more obvious attributes." There was a pause. "Would you like to stay over?" It was a casual enquiry without the slightest hint of anything improper. "I thought we could go to Rothwell Mere on Sunday – if the weather holds."

"I've never been there either."

"Then I must try to expand your horizons," he said.

"Yes, I think you should."

On Saturday, Aunt Millicent's Morris Minor was in the driveway when Laura arrived from work at lunch time.

Millicent came out from the sitting room into the hall to greet her. "How wonderful!" she enthused, smothering her in a warm embrace and French perfume. "Daphne tells us you have a new young man!" adding *sotto voce*, "But I can tell she doesn't approve of him. My, my – you are the dark horse, Laura, aren't you?"

"He's just a friend, Auntie, nothing more."

"Well, of course he is, my dear. But you never can tell, can you? Things could turn out differently."

"I can assure you, Auntie, they won't."

"If you say so, my dear. But Sylvie and I are all agog to see him."

Laura had no intention of putting John Rufford under the microscope of her aunts' inspection. She was packed and waiting for him in the hall when he arrived punctually at two.

He smiled as he stowed her weekend case into the boot. "I see we have a farewell committee," he said, not looking directly at the sitting room window, but evidently able to make out the three figures trying not to be seen.

"My aunts are visiting."

"Do you think they'll approve?" he asked. He was wearing a three-quarter length camel duffel coat with a college scarf, dark slacks, an Arran jumper – and his most attentive smile. It was difficult to imagine what they could possibly disapprove of.

He drove west, into the web of lanes weaving between snow-filled fields until they reached the canal, following its lazy progress through the countryside. There was ice along its margins, as pale as frosted glass. On the towpath, in hollows sheltered from the bright sunlight, small pockets of snow lingered among low grasses, and the low hawthorn hedges were jagged silhouettes, uncompromisingly stark against the silver-blue sky.

"You're very quiet," he said. "What are you thinking?"

"I'm remembering the landscape – the colours – the shapes – the winter light."

"You must show me your paintings sometime."

"If you're really interested."

"Oh, I am," he assured her.

She was never certain if he was being serious, but it hardly mattered: harmless banter added to the pleasure of his company. It was a novelty: Oliver was incapable of such frivolity. "It's only fair, I suppose," she said, enjoying the thought of teasing him a little. "After all – I have seen your etchings."

He laughed softly. "Yes – indeed you have, Miss Driscoll, at very close quarters if I remember rightly."

"Very close," she said, with considerable satisfaction.

"Ah – but I haven't shown you my photographs."

She frowned, wondering if they were still playing word-games or not.

He was not. "Mainly landscapes," he said. "A few portraits. Nothing improper – or 'artistic'," he insisted, with heavy emphasis. "If we go to Rothwell Mere tomorrow, I shall take my camera."

They had reached a small car park, just large enough for half-a-dozen cars or so, beside a long, low double-fronted red-brick building, with bull's-eye glass in its sash windows. Smoke curled in lazy spirals from its chimney where two jackdaws sat, huddled against it – and each other – for warmth. Above the porch, a painted sign depicted a black shire horse with white fetlocks hauling a bottle-green narrowboat. There was an crudely executed image of the inn in the background.

They got out of the car into the chill of the late afternoon.

"A quick walk?" he suggested. "As far as the bridge and back?" He threaded his arm around her waist, holding her comfortably against him, and they set off at a brisk pace down the towpath, their breath swirling around them.

When they reached the bridge, the sun was already sinking fast, and they turned back to cover the half-mile or so to the inn before it grew dark. They talked little, the sharp air catching at their breath, and they kept up a good pace to stave off the cold. There was no need to talk: they walked in step, and the easy rhythm was a pleasant reminder of another, closer, union.

The small lounge bar was empty, too early for other customers. On its plastered walls between the windows, well-burnished horse brasses on old leather straps hung from hooks, and pewter mugs of every size and shape filled the high shelves above the bar. Years of smoke had stained the low beamed ceiling, and high-backed dark-oak pew seats with deep crimson cushions and tables between, made intimate spaces. In the arched brick fireplace, a log fire crackled in its black iron basket, ashes spilling onto the red-tiled hearth. The room was hot, filled with the thick, rich scent of wood smoke mixed with beer.

The barman, middle-aged, balding and cheerful, made them welcome, suggesting they take the cosy inglenook. "No sign of a thaw any time soon," he said, making small-talk and rearranging the beer mats on the table. "What can I get you? A whisky, is it, sir? And something warming for the lady?"

Laura noted the easy familiarity between them. John must come here often.

"A double, please – with ice. A schooner of sweet sherry for the lady."

They discarded their coats and scarves and settled into their private corner, sitting across the dark oak table bearing its scars of time.

"So," he said. "What have you been doing with yourself this week?"

"Mending fences."

He raised an eyebrow. "I didn't know I was dating a Land Army Girl."

"Metaphorical fences, John. Trying to get my mother, Aunt Cynthia and Phyllis Parr on speaking terms again."

"I'm impressed. That must have taken some courage."

"Not really. Self-interest, that's all. I don't want my mother's social circle getting smaller. I need to keep her occupied. That way, she won't notice my comings and goings so much – or, if I'm honest, miss me being around once I decide to leave home."

He leaned back, a quizzical expression on his face.

"Don't panic," she reassured him. "I'm not planning to move out and move in with you."

The drinks arrived, interrupting their conversation, and the topic was not pursued.

He raised his glass to her. "Good health," he said, savouring a large draught as he studied her. His gaze was very direct. He put down his glass and reached across to take her hand, suddenly serious. "I wanted to spend more time with you this weekend for two reasons. I think the first one is probably obvious – the second is ..." he looked slightly embarrassed, rather obviously giving careful consideration to what he was about to say. "The second is – I won't be able to see you next weekend."

She tried not to show her disappointment, angry with herself for feeling vexed at the prospect, but it proved difficult: it was like being dropped from a great height onto solid ground. She sipped at the sherry, trying hard to think of something to say, and eventually managing a very lame, "Oh."

"I'm visiting my parents," he explained.

"Do they live far?" she managed, half her mind listening to her heart thudding.

"Shrewsbury," he said, stroking her fingers delicately. But his eyes were watching her reaction. "I go down once a month."

"They must look forward to your visits." It was getting harder for her to find the most appropriate words.

"They do," he said with a smile: still watching; still evaluating.

She took another sip of sherry, hiding behind the glass to mask her confusion. "You're making me feel uncomfortable,

John," she said, deciding he needed to be told. "What do you want me to say?"

"I want to know what you're really thinking."

How could he ask that? – she thought. What was she supposed to say? Was he somehow trying to trap her? "Why?" she asked, throwing the ball neatly back into his court.

"Just wondering," he said, raising an eyebrow just to provoke her.

She extracted her hand from his attention and decided on boldness: there was nothing to be lost. "Well, I suppose I could say, I'll be glad of the chance to recover from your attentions," she said, feeling light-heartedness was possibly the best option. "Or – on the other hand – I could offer you the prospect of my being utterly distraught at the thought of not being riveted to your bed. Which would you prefer?"

He was gloating. "Whichever's the truth. As I recall, you wanted me to tell you honestly why I'd asked you out for a date."

"Oh – in that case," she said, throwing caution to the wind, perhaps under the influence of too much sherry, "if I have to give you an honest answer, I'm utterly distraught."

He leaned back, smiling broadly.

"Have I passed some kind of test?" she asked irritably. He was spoiling the pleasant euphoria the afternoon had given her. She finished her sherry and decided on silence.

A log slumped in the grate sending a shower of sparks up the chimney and bringing the barman over to tend to it. Satisfied with his handiwork he seemed in no hurry to return to the bar. He and John exchanged glances. "Would you like any more drinks, sir?" he offered, casting a sideways look in Laura's direction. "Another sherry, perhaps – for the lady?" On reflection, she thought, the barman had a sly look about him, and she disliked the implication in his choice of words.

"No, thank you," she said, wanting him out of ear-shot as soon as possible.

John declined the offer with a small wave of the hand. His own drink was only half finished. The barman took the hint.

The door opened, and a group of three couples came tumbling out of the cold into the warm interior, chattering and laughing. They hurried over to the fire, warming numbed hands and stamping their feet, their closeness much too close for an intimate conversation to continue.

Laura contemplated her empty glass. She had drunk the sherry much too quickly. Her head felt very light. John was still leaning back against his seat, contemplating her, reminiscent of the evening at the Parrs.

The jovial group were directed away to another table and were soon absorbed in ordering their drinks.

Her mood shifted. She felt increasingly defiant and not a little angry at his evident smugness. The complicity between him and the barman only added to a sudden urge to challenge him. "Do you bring all your conquests here?" she asked, fixing him with an equally direct gaze.

"A few," he acknowledged, still watching her closely.

She wanted to goad him. She leaned forward. "Are we in the tens – or the hundreds?"

He pulled a face. "I think 'hundreds' would be pushing it."

"Oh, I thought you might be flattered."

"Flattered? I'd be exhausted."

"Come on," she taunted. "Don't duck the question."

"A few," he said, refusing to be drawn. "I don't keep count."

"I'm disappointed. There weren't any notches on your bedpost either."

He was thoughtful for a moment. "You're cross with me, aren't you?"

"Yes, I am."

"I didn't mean to spoil the afternoon."

"Well you have."

"Then I'm sorry. It wasn't my intention. Am I forgiven?" He looked contrite enough – but maybe that meant nothing.

"I don't know," she said, still irritated. "I'll think about it."

CHAPTER TWENTY-FOUR

She woke to early sunshine and John sitting on the bed swathed in a blue towelling dressing gown. He was tousled, unshaven and relaxed; his features softened; his dark-brown eyes partly masked by the after-glow of sensual pleasure.

"Sleepy head," he said softly, leaning over and kissing her forehead. "Wake up. It's a lovely day, and I want to take you out to Rothwell Mere."

She stretched slowly, heavy-limbed from his loving, and reluctant to leave the warmth they had made together. She was too comfortable; too content; her irritation with him lost in the tumbled sheets. She reached out for him.

"Later," he said. "I'll go and make breakfast. I want you downstairs in quarter of an hour."

"Or else?"

"Or else I'll come up and pull all the bedding off you."

Reluctantly, she let him go, wondering if others had woken in his bed and felt the same sensuous pleasure that suffused her now. Strangely, there was no jealousy, or genuine curiosity about these other women in his life. They were no more substantial than shadows. Perhaps because they were invisible. There were no signs of them around her in the room: no photographs; no obvious gifts; no apparent mementos; no trace of female presence in the bathroom either, where all the toiletries were singularly masculine, and a solitary toothbrush stood sentinel in a tumbler next to a tube of toothpaste. He was a careful man.

There were sounds of him moving around in the kitchen, and the rich aroma of fried bacon drifting up the stairs. With little enthusiasm, she emerged from the warm bed into the cold morning. By the time she joined him, he was already washed, dressed and shaved; immaculate; busy packing sandwiches and a thermos flask into a hamper.

"Sit down please," he instructed.

"Do you always serve your guests?"

"Always," he said. "I insist."

He ate quickly and finished first, waiting for her to do the same.

She was in no mood to hurry, enjoying the sense of having done something truly outrageous: she had spent the night with him. Would he be discreet? Or had her reputation gone the way of Susan Holbrook's? And if it had, did she care? "John, does Jules know about us?" she asked, merely curious.

"No – and he won't."

"He seems to know about the others."

"He likes to think he does. I flirt around the office. Keeps the typists happy. Nothing serious."

"No liaisons behind the filing cabinets?"

"Not to be recommended."

"So what does he know."

"There were a couple of telephone calls – at the office – a while back now." He did not elaborate, but she deduced someone had made a nuisance of herself after he had drawn the line.

"Is that why you don't have a telephone here?" she asked. "To keep ex-lovers at arm's length?"

He regarded her quizzically. "You don't miss much, do you?"

"You rang me from a phone box, John – twice. I'm not stupid."

He just smiled. "I can see I won't be able to hide much from you, Miss Driscoll."

"You don't need to. I promise – I shan't be a leech." It felt like the truth.

"Are you going to eat that toast, or not?" he said, changing the subject. "We're wasting the morning." He began collecting the empty plates and stacking them in the sink ready for washing. "There's a tea towel on the radiator," he said, running the hot water. "Make yourself useful when you've finished."

"You're a hard task-master."

"I like everything tidy. No mess to sort out later."

"I noticed," she said.

If he sensed her meaning, he ignored it, piling the clean plates in orderly rows in the rack to drain.

"Were you always house-trained?" she teased.

"Not always. It's what two years as a squaddie in Her Majesty's Forces does for you. It puts some order into your life. Talking of which," he added, wiping his hands dry, "I'll make the bed."

She returned the tea towel to the radiator. "Do you want me to help?"

He smiled. "No I do not. Go and occupy yourself in the living room. I left some magazines for you – nothing salacious, of course. I'll be down shortly."

The room was as she expected: tidy and uncluttered; the furniture comfortable but functional. There were no ornaments, and the painting over the gas fire was a print: an unexceptional country scene of little artistic merit. Had it been a gift he felt unable to disown?

She ignored the magazines, more curious about the contents of his bookcase and what they would reveal. She had learned to be inquisitive about such things. They were intriguing mix: a section on local government law, which she had expected; crime and spy novels; a sprinkling of classics; road maps and car magazines; practical guides to DIY jobs around the home; several books on photography and astronomy; old theatre programmes; reference books covering an astonishing range of subjects, and a very large dictionary. On the bottom shelf lay half-a-dozen photographic albums with different coloured bindings, and labels on the spines with dates. She decided not to touch them: Pandora's Box was better left unopened. Instead, she selected an elegantly brown leather-bound volume of *Famous Quotations* propped up next to them. Inside the front cover, she found a dedication. It read '*De Montfort School, Shropshire, 6th Form Prize 1951*'. Underneath, inscribed in black ink, in beautiful italic handwriting, were the words, 'To John Leighton Rufford – Head Boy 1950-51 – For exemplary academic achievement'.

She heard him coming down the stairs and closed it quickly, but had no time to replace it before the door opened and he entered. He was dressed in his duffel coat and scarf, and carrying his camera case, ready to leave.

"You weren't tempted to look at the albums?" he enquired casually, taking the book from her and replacing it where it belonged.

"Yes – but I didn't."

"You're not interested in landscapes? I thought you were." He was mocking her.

"I don't want to pry."

"My photographs of girlfriends are elsewhere."

"Ah – so you do have some."

"Some," he admitted with a wry smile. "But for my eyes only. Now – get a move on, or we'll miss the best of the day."

Lower Chursley was still stirring when they drove out of the village into a blaze of morning sunshine and hoarfrost. They passed through small hamlets and larger villages, with their black-and-white architecture and rustic brick. She could envisage her father capturing the confusion of building styles jostling side-by-side in the high streets and alleyways. Soon hamlets became isolated farmsteads, then semi-wilderness with occasional copses and wetlands. A few miles further on, by a weathered wooden signpost, he pulled off the road into a small lay-by where a stile led through a gap in the hedge.

It was intensely cold out of the warmth of the car. She pulled on her woollen hat and mittens, and wrapped her scarf several times around her neck, while he settled his camera strap under the hood of his coat.

He helped her over the stile, offering his hand to steady her. Ahead of them, a field curved over a slight rise and out of sight, flanked by hedges of hawthorn and elder cut back for the winter. In the full glare of the sun, the snow had all but vanished here, but the footpath was rock-hard between the rough, cropped grasses.

At the crest of the rise, he stopped, wanting her to admire the view. Below them, the path curved down for a quarter of a mile or so. There, in a shallow basin, lay the mere, the silver-blue of the sky reflecting dully on the surface of its frozen face. A thin mist clung to the ragged margins where reed beds stood, locked in an icy grip, some broken by the high winds of autumn, their tops cast down, trapped beneath the ice, waiting for the thaw. Beyond, stretching out along the southern flank, a dense wood of majestic oaks and beeches formed a backdrop, the dark interior, mysterious and forbidding, plunged in shade.

There was absolute silence. Nothing stirred.

"It's magical," she whispered.

He squeezed her hand lightly. "I thought you'd like it."

Memories stirred: Miss Hay reciting poetry to the Fifth Form English class, her rich contralto delivering the lines to great effect; dramatic; despairing. " 'And no birds sing'," she said, feeling the shiver of hopelessness the words evoked.

" 'La Belle Dame Sans Merci'," he said. "John Keats."

"Something about sedge being withered by the lake – and a pale knight loitering."

"The pale knight in thrall to a beautiful lady," he said, bringing her mittened hand to his lips to kiss in mock gallantry.

If it had been a lazy summer's afternoon under a hot sun, would he have led her down to some secluded spot between the trees and made love to her? She would have liked that. He made her want him.

There was a sudden commotion from the midst of the reeds, and a heron took flight, flapping lazily away into the tall trees. It was gone before he could take the camera from its case. He stood gazing after it, lost in thought.

"Maybe it'll come back," she said, sensing his disappointment.

"No," he said softly, turning to look at her with quiet intensity. "No. It's flown away."

His mood was disconcerting. She left him to his thoughts, and followed the path down to the edge of the mere. Here, at the margins, there were strange patterns in the ice trapped in small pools between the pebbles: curving shapes where water had refrozen over several days; some transparent, fragile as the thinnest glass; others opaque, dense and solid, unyielding when she touched them.

He followed her down, in no hurry, stopping every now and then to photograph whatever caught his eye.

She kept ahead of him, wanting to capture her own memories of this day; to hold them in her mind for ever.

"Laura," he called from a little way behind. She turned in time to hear the soft click of the shutter.

"Does that make me one of your secret collection?" she asked.

"Most definitely," he said, moving to catch up with her.

"I hope I wasn't pulling a face."

"No, you weren't pulling a face. I took one earlier, but you didn't notice."

"That's sneaky of you."

"Par for the course," he said with a smile.

They continued to follow the path round into the trees, but it was colder there, out of the sun, and the view across the mere to the rising ground had less to recommend it, so they did not linger.

They returned to the car hungry and eager for warmth. He brought out the hamper from the boot and opened it. "Nothing special," he said, evidently pleased with his preparations nonetheless. "Tea, sandwiches and some chocolate. Will it do?"

That's the look of him she would remember, she decided: the slight smile; the raised, questioning eyebrow; the inner warmth that made his touch so special.

He handed her a mug of tea. "Penny for your thoughts."

She wrapped her hands around the mug, watching the steam curl upwards in unhurried spirals, each minute droplet rainbow-coloured. "It's a strange place, isn't it?" she said.

"The mere?"

"Yes. Something mystical about it. Am I being silly?"

He shook his head. "It draws you back. Every season's

different. In Spring – there's a strange quality about the light in the evenings ..." He frowned. "I can't describe it. You'd have to see it for yourself." He handed her a sandwich and she ate it automatically, her mind drifting.

Spring. She would never see the mere in Spring with John. He would be gone from her life by then, a warm, but distant memory.

"Do you think I should learn to drive?" she asked him, the need to think beyond their time together suddenly important. "Aunt Millicent drives – and Daddy's car's just sitting in the garage, doing nothing. It seems a shame."

"The world would be your oyster."

"Yes. New horizons." She finished the sandwich and drank the rest of the tea. It was going cold. "I meant what I said yesterday – at The Narrowboat. I need to leave the Lodge – find a place of my own. I know my mother – she'll never forgive me for not marrying Oliver."

"It's a big step."

"I'll get by, I'm sure.

He laughed. "I'm sure you will. I can see you now – up there in your artist's garret –"

"Penniless?"

"No – not at all – paint-spattered, madly dashing off another masterpiece commissioned by someone terribly famous, surrounded by a mountain of clutter – a real Bohemian." He made a mock toast with the cup from the thermos flask, and downed its contents.

"And I shall come and go as I please, with whoever I please, whenever I please – like you."

"Like me?"

"Yes – like you. And I shall invite all my lovers to stay – one at a time, of course – and become the scandal of the neighbourhood."

"Men can get away with more than women," he said sagely, replacing the top on the thermos flask.

"That's not true. Mr Moray couldn't."

"Who's Mr Moray?"

She told him, and he listened with a quiet gravity to the story. "La Belle Dame Sans Merci," he said when she had finished. "Are you sorry for him?"

"Yes," she said, remembering them embracing, caught in the sunlight in Meeston Woods. "I saw them kissing once. They didn't see me. I remember thinking how tenderly he kissed her. I can't understand why she wouldn't marry him." When she turned to look at him, he was gazing out beyond the windscreen, his face in profile: the straight forehead and line of his nose; the generous mouth. Did he know how handsome he was? She reached out and ran a finger lightly over his lips, following their contours as if she were sketching them.

Startled, he pulled back, frowning. "What are you up to?"

"I want you to kiss me. Why do you never kiss me – properly?" she asked. "Is it just me?" Martin would have kissed her.

"No. It's nothing to do with you."

"Then what is it? You have a lips made to kiss. They're beautiful."

He looked away again, apparently embarrassed. "I'm not sure you'd understand."

"Why not?"

"You'll think me very strange."

She waited for his explanation. It was a long time coming.

"I find that sort of kissing – unsatisfactory."

"Oh."

"You sound disappointed."

"I am. Tell me why," she insisted.

"It's a distraction. Being glued to someone's face and gasping for breath is not my idea of a passionate encounter". He pulled a face. "It's as bad as groping on the back row of the cinema – or fumbling in the car."

"Really?"

"Yes, really." He shrugged hopelessly. "I knew you'd never understand."

She remembered kissing Martin in the dark, the film an irrelevance; his hand reaching up inside her blouse; the desire to be touched; the need for that touch to become more daring – and yet more daring. And he had, once, been bold enough to touch her there, between her thighs, and she had wanted him so badly she thought she would burst with the need for him – but they had nowhere to go, and it had never happened.

He was looking at her, head cocked to one side, trying to fathom out her thoughts. "Making love," he said softly, "shouldn't be an obstacle course, surely?"

"Does it have to be?"

"It does if there's buttons – and God knows what else

to undo – never mind the balancing act avoiding the gear stick or the hand-brake ..."

"You make it sound like a farce."

"It is. It's grotesque! By the time you've wound yourself up with the kissing, fought your way through layers of clothing, contorted yourself into the only position possible – frankly, you want to get the whole thing over as soon as possible." He threw up his hands in mock horror. "Hardly an ecstatic experience for either party." His light-heartedness faded. He ran the back of his fingers down her cheek, caressing her gently. His warmth engulfed her. "When I make love to you, I want to be naked with you. To touch every part of you. To kiss you where it gives you greatest pleasure. To channel every sensation to one, all-consuming point. There's nothing to distract – nothing to hinder. Do you understand?"

"Yes."

His eyes were on hers. "So, when I come into you," he said softly, still caressing her cheek, "I know you're ready for me. Open. Completely open. There's no resistance – no force – just a sweet, smooth thrust up to the hilt. And from there the rest is timing and rhythm – to ecstasy – and completion." He paused to smile.

His words had conjured up images; her pulse had quickened. Her throat was dry.

He took her hand and placed it where she could feel him, hard and warm beneath the weave of the cloth. "Just because I won't make love in a certain way doesn't mean I don't want to make love," he said, his expression softening.

"But making love where people might see you is not a good idea either."

"Take me back, then," she whispered. "You've made me want you."

He nodded.

Chapter Twenty-Five

The warning signs were there. Laura could see them all too plainly. After only three days in his company, the prospect of not seeing him for a fortnight left its mark. She missed him, and nothing seemed to fill the great gulf that was the lack of him: not her crowded days at the Bank; nor her evenings by the fire in her father's study devoted to reading; nor the first tentative moves to set up a studio there.

January was drawing to a close, but the seemingly endless grip of winter continued, day after day, monotonous and unrelenting, leaving her dull and dispirited. The weekend without him was a void, her motivation as frozen as the ground. He had taken her vitality with him, and she felt empty and aimless.

Daphne, newly reconciled with her nearest and dearest, had accepted Cynthia's invitation to Sunday lunch, and Laura had the Lodge to herself. She mooned around the study for a while, listlessly, until a brief spell of sunshine breaking through the iron sky, drew her out into the garden. She found an unexpected patch of snowdrops braving the cold, and picked a few, putting them into a little white porcelain vase, setting them against the background of the thick red velvet curtains in the study, intent on painting them. But she got no further than the first rough outlines before the Muse deserted her and she idled away the remaining time until mid-day staring out of the window.

The telephone rang in the hall, and she did not hurry to answer it, knowing it would not be John.

Aunt Millicent was her usual bright and breezy self. "Not out today with your young man?" she asked, direct and to the point as usual.

"He's visiting his parents," she explained.

"Oh, you poor thing. Why not come over to Broxley for tea and cake with us this afternoon? I'll come and collect you."

But when they arrived at Hazeldene Court, Henrietta was asleep in her room, and Sylvia was keen to visit a friend she had not seen since Boxing Day.

Millicent was undeterred. "Oh, well," she said, cheerfully, bringing in the tea tray with her latest purchase from Ellersons, a rather large chocolate cake. "Just the two of us."

Laura was content. Exorcising the family history had made visits to Hazeldene Court less forbidding. She could sit by the fire in the grand sitting room without the fear Grandpa Harriman would burst in on them, as he had done on one memorable occasion when she was a child. Refusing to bow to the destiny he had decided for her had finally laid his ghost.

"You know, Laura," her aunt was saying as she poured the tea. "I never really thought you and Oliver were very well-suited. 'Not really a couple', I used to say to Sylvie. And he's a bit of a cold fish. Heaven knows what Claudia sees in him! Money, I suppose. Well I'm glad you've been able to move on, my dear. Now don't stint yourself with the cake. I wouldn't have bought such a large one if I'd known Sylvie was going out for the afternoon."

The conversation rambled on for a while about Daphne's and Cynthia's reconciliation, and what a blessing that had been, and then how truly dreadful the weather was, and the rumour there would be no improvement for at least a month, and how sad the gardens looked with no crocuses in sight. It was all very superficial, and Laura began to suspect her aunt was working round to the topic she most wanted to discuss – the absent 'young man' – visiting his parents.

At last, the torrent of cheerful chatter subsided, and her aunt leaned forward to pat her hand. "It's no good, my dear, I can't bear the suspense. Do tell me about him."

"There's not much to tell," Laura hedged, censoring everything as the best option.

"Oh, there must be!" Millicent insisted, positively bursting with curiosity. "I gather he works in the same department as Julius Parr?"

"Yes, he's a solicitor."

"Such an attractive man!"

Laura felt heat rising in her cheeks that had nothing to do with the blaze in the hearth.

The change was not lost on her aunt. "Oh look at you, Laura – all blushes! It must be love!"

"Not at all," she protested, keen to stifle Millicent's over-enthusiasm. "We're only friends."

"Nonsense! I can see you're bowled over by him. And the way he looked at you when he helped you into his car last Saturday, my dear – he's positively smitten!"

Laura began to panic. "Auntie, please! This isn't going to be a grand romance. We're just going out together, that's all. It's not meant to last."

Her aunt's expression developed a decidedly knowing look. "He isn't married, is he?" she asked cautiously.

"Heavens, no! – just a confirmed bachelor."

Her aunt cocked her head to one side. "Really?" she said, and a mischievous smile crept across her face. But there was something about the twinkle in her eyes that implied more than she said.

"Yes – really," Laura emphasised, wishing she could change the subject.

But Millicent was not to be diverted. She was becoming more and more conspiratorial. "Do you know what I think?" she said triumphantly. "I think he's your lover!" She was evidently as pleased as punch at the possibility. "Oh, do say he is!"

Laura's head was full of protestations, none of which came to her rescue.

Millicent clapped her hands in delight. "I'm right, aren't I? I can see," she said. "How wonderful! I promise I won't breathe a word to anyone – not even Sylvie."

If there had been any opportunity to deflect her aunt's acuity, Laura knew that time had passed. "Please,

please, don't ever tell my mother," she begged. Millicent's occasional lapses in discretion were notorious.

"Not a word, my dear. Not a word, I assure you." Her face positively glowed. "Oh, I am *so* happy for you. It's just what you need after Oliver. My – how lucky you are to find him."

Laura was beginning to suspect she had never really known her Aunt Millicent at all. This rapturous enthusiasm for what was essentially an immoral liaison left her bemused. "We agreed it should only be for a few weeks – you understand? Nothing permanent. It's not meant to be permanent."

"Oh, quite right, my dear. Quite right. Very sensible. Do have some more cake."

There was a very odd silence while Millicent, looking very much like a naughty child thinking up some devilment, stared into the fire, bright-eyed. "Oh – it's no good," she said, turning suddenly and reaching out for Laura's hand. "I'll have to tell you. It's only fair." A dreamy look came over her. "My, how you've brought it all back." She paused, her face wreathed in smiles. "I had the most wonderful lover, Laura. His name was Giles – Giles Courtney. Oh, he was lovely. Such smooth skin – and *so* considerate. No one ever knew, of course. Not even Sylvie. I don't think she would have understood – not so soon after David. But the dead don't come back, and I needed to mend my heart – and he was the perfect answer. I even went on holiday with him – for a week. To Brighton."

"To Brighton?" It was all Laura could think of saying.

"Yes, I know, it was dreadful of me, I suppose, but please

don't be critical, will you? I've kept him a secret all these years."

"How can I be critical, Auntie?"

"Well – no doubt you're surprised at any rate."

"Yes – I suppose I am. When did you meet?"

"Just after the War – the Great War, of course. When I realised David wouldn't be coming home. I was only twenty. I thought my life was over." She poured them both another cup of tea and settled in her chair, smiling secretly to herself as old memories came flooding back. "I was staying with a girl friend in Harrogate – Holly Courtney," she began. "And she had this lovely brother, Giles. He'd come through the war without a scratch. And of course, with so many men lost, a good-looking man was a honey-pot. He could take his pick of anyone he chose."

"And he chose you?"

Her aunt frowned a little. "Not exactly. I rather think I threw myself at him," she said, reflecting on the true nature of their relationship. "I was a little wild in those days – and of course, being away from home, I couldn't get enough of doing what I wanted."

"Were you in love with him?"

"Heavens, no! I was far too flighty. And I knew he had no intention of settling down. He was playing the field. And who could blame him? But Laura, what a lover! He was quite amazing." She paused to sip her tea, thrilled at the recollection. "I'd never known anything like it – even with David," she admitted. "Is John like that? I think he must be. He has that look about him."

"Yes – he is."

"How lovely. And does he make you laugh? Giles could make me laugh. Ah – I can see he does. My, my – how he's put life back into you. Enjoy him while you can."

"How long did you know Giles?"

Millicent cast her mind back. "About two months, I think. It was difficult, of course. We could only meet when I was visiting Holly at weekends. We knew it wasn't going to last – but that was half the fun – and of course, it was impossible once he took up his teaching post in Kent."

"But you had your week in Brighton."

"Yes," she said fondly. "Right at the end. It was lovely. But I'm sure the lady running the guesthouse knew we weren't married. She was very suspicious. The ring didn't fit very well. It was only a cheap thing we'd bought for the occasion." She laughed at the recollection. "He changed my life, you know. I never wanted marriage after that. It wasn't anything to do with losing David – although that's what I told Sylvie. No – it wasn't that at all. I was afraid that after what I'd known with Giles marriage would be a dull grind. I'd known passion, and I didn't want to tie myself to a man who only wanted me to have his children, and had no interest in me as a woman." A shadow crossed her face. "I'd seen enough of that kind of marriage here."

"Is that why you became a teacher?"

"Yes – he was my inspiration. He said I should remember I was a free spirit. If I had a profession, it would give me the freedom I wanted. So, I took his advice and haven't regretted a single moment."

"Did you ever see him again?"

"No – we never kept in touch."

"Do you wish you had?" It was a question she knew she would ask herself at some time in the future.

Her aunt sighed. "At first I did," she admitted. "I missed him. I missed the fun we had together. But later, I was glad we'd made a clean break of it. Relationships never stay the same. They need constant tending – like a fire – and we both knew we couldn't burn that brightly for very long. It was much too fierce. It was best to walk away while we were still ablaze – and have wonderful memories. Ah – I see you understand."

"I think I do."

"That's good. You must take what comes your way in life, I've discovered."

"Were there others, Auntie?"

"Of course there were – two or three – not a patch on Giles, of course." Millicent patted her hand confidentially. "I might be an old spinster, my dear, but I'm not a dried up old stick. Giles taught me something I've never forgotten, and I'll always be grateful for that."

The coach clock on the mantelpiece chimed three.

"Oh – my, look at the time. I promised I'd wake Hetty and let her know you were here. I won't be long."

She was gone, leaving Laura contemplating the fire and the white-hot glow at its heart. Such intense heat. Like the blazing torch that illuminated her relationship with John: brilliant; demanding. But her aunt was right – fire needed constant tending, or it burnt itself out and sank into ashes.

Their passion was something to enjoy while it lasted, and to remember with a deep well of affection when it was gone.

The flames danced up the chimney.

If she could remember John with the same joy and delight as her aunt remembered Giles Courtney, what more could she want?

Chapter Twenty-Six

Afternoon teas with Aunt Millicent, Laura reflected afterwards, would never be the same again. The relationship between aunt and niece had changed: there would always be this special bond between them; an understanding, which excluded everyone outside their shared experience – even Aunt Sylvia – or Henrietta, although Laura did wonder whether Sylvie and Hetty might not have secrets too – they simply chose not to divulge them.

Laura's spirits rose: Millicent had shown her it was possible to look beyond the intensity of passion; to use it as a stepping stone and have no regrets once it was over. It was a useful lesson. It chimed with what she needed to hear; it was 'not too late to seek a newer world'. And there was further cause for quiet satisfaction: in the space of a single afternoon, she had acquired another confidante – and two were better than one. Millicent was her willing listener in matters of the heart, and Robert Moray, however reticent, remained a much-needed link with her father. She would need that link, she fancied, in the weeks to come.

February had arrived, and with it the prospect of her father's second letter in Mr Parr's safe keeping, something she had pushed from her mind for many weeks, preoccupied by more pressing matters.

Meanwhile, there were reasons to be cheerful. A brief respite from the unremitting cold had encouraged the first yellow crocus, and the winter jasmine had burst into flower against the garden wall next to the sitting room. And for the first time in several weeks, blue tits and their larger cousins, with their black caps and gaudy yellow waistcoats, flitted from branch to branch through the orchard. It seemed, for those few days, winter's fierce grip was loosening at last.

That Saturday afternoon, when she returned from Weaversham, her mind was more on the potential pleasures of seeing John after two weeks' absence, rather than the imminent disclosure of her father's past.

Mr Moray was in the driveway stacking prunings from the shrubbery into a wheelbarrow. "Miss Driscoll," he said. "Can I have a word with you?" He had evidently been waiting for her. "It's about the vegetable patch."

Laura's immediate reaction was to politely decline. "I'm rather short of time, Mr Moray," she hedged, unwilling to be diverted from her plans for the evening.

"It won't take long," he insisted.

Reluctantly, she followed him through the rhododendrons.

He surveyed the roughly dug area, hands on hips, in no immediate hurry to say what was on his mind. "There's no problem with the crop rotation," he said at last, taking for granted it was a subject she was familiar with, "but I don't know what your mother has in mind this year ..." He trailed off, apparently seeking the right words to express the changed circumstances at the Lodge, and failing. He frowned, and turned his attention to his boots.

With the winter crops all harvested, the vegetable plot was empty. It looked twice its usual size; immense, in fact, Laura thought; and far too large for the diminishing needs of the residents of Meeston Lodge. Robert Moray had evidently reached the same conclusion. "I see what you mean," she said. "We won't need as much this year, will we?"

He scuffed the ground, giving her a nervous smile as he shook his head.

"What do you think we should do?"

He considered the question. "It's a productive patch," he said. "It would be a pity to waste it."

"I agree – but who's going to want so many vegetables?"

"Well – Alan Benyon's showing an interest in horticulture. We could work the patch between us and he could take his share –" He smiled nervously. "If you think your mother wouldn't mind," he added.

Whether Daphne minded or not was immaterial now, but he was not to know, and Laura was able to side-step the issue by stating the obvious. "The garden isn't really her forté, Mr Moray. And I'm sure my father would have preferred it being put to proper use."

"Well – as long as you think it's appropriate." He gave her a genuine smile; a rare thing. "I'll draw up a planting scheme, if you like? See what you think."

From behind the rhododendrons came the unexpected

sound of tyres on gravel, and the familiar burble of the Roadster's engine. Laura's interest in planning the vegetable patch evaporated. "I'm sorry – can we talk about this some other time? I have a visitor."

"Of course," he said, but she sensed he was disappointed.

By the time she had reached the drive, John was already getting out of the car. She was ridiculously pleased to see him. "John! I didn't expect you 'til this evening!"

"Slight change of plan," he said, all apologetic and visibly irritated. "I can't ask you to stay for the weekend after all."

Her disappointment was tinged with annoyance. "Oh, I see," she said, preparing herself for whatever excuse he might give.

He took hold of her hands. "No, you don't. My parents are coming over. They're bringing my baby brother with them."

"Baby brother?" There had never been any talk of a baby brother, an unknown quantity intruding, unbidden and unwelcome, into her life.

"Well – not exactly a 'baby'," John was saying. "He's eighteen – taking 'A' Levels. Apparently, I'm providing him with a base camp while he tours a couple of colleges and universities next week."

As an excuse, this was one she could not fault: it had the ring of truth about it. "Has he a name?" she asked, more out of conversational necessity than interest.

"Michael."

Michael. Michael, she realised, was the beginning of the end, eating into the time John would spend with her. A reality, like the existence of her father's second letter, that would burst the pretty rainbow-coloured bubble of their private world.

John appeared not to notice her self-absorption. "I came in for a good grilling last weekend," he said, forcing a smile.

"Why?" she asked unthinkingly, her concentration firmly fixed on Michael and his wretched visit.

"Oh – phrases such as 'at your age' and 'settling down' came into it," he said, shrugging off his embarrassment.

A small warning bell rang in her mind. The phrase 'settling down' was not part of John Rufford's vocabulary.

He was still holding her hands, his fingers caressing her palms. He looked hopeful. "So, as I can't invite you to stay, I thought we could spend more time together today – if you're free. We could go for a drive – maybe see a film – go back to my place later?" he added, all smiles, tilting his head to one side in that way of his designed to charm birds out of the trees. He was standing very close, his aftershave a potent reminder of him. For a moment, his gaze consumed her before his attention shifted to something, or someone, at the far end of the drive. He leaned forward. "Someone is spying on us," he whispered, his breath brushing softly against her neck.

Mr Moray had followed her through the rhododendrons and was standing by the wheelbarrow, intent, it seemed, on appearing not to be watching them.

"Who is he?" John asked.

"It's just Mr Moray," she said, keeping her voice lowered.

"Ah," he said with a wry smile, weighing up the figure in the battered tweed jacket and old brown corduroy trousers. "Your pale, loitering knight."

"No, he's not," she corrected him. "He was Susan Holbrook's pale, loitering knight."

"Well, he's definitely loitering."

She was annoyed by his assumption. "Don't be silly," she said. "He's busy pruning shrubs, that's all."

John made a wry face, evidently unconvinced.

"If we're going out, I'll need to change. Come on in."

"Won't your mother object?"

"She's out visiting. Anyway, if you like, I can show you my paintings. You always said you wanted to see them."

"Yes – I would."

John's expressions of interest in her artistic abilities had always struck her as mere politeness on his part; something to say at the appropriate time; a pleasantry, and nothing more. She was surprised when he seemed genuinely interested.

"You can wait in my studio while I change. All very proper."

"If you say so." His mood had shifted: he was his usual, light-hearted self once more.

She led him indoors, disconcerted to discover, as they walked together towards the house, that Mr Moray was indeed taking a keen interest in them.

In the studio, her portfolio lay open on the desk where she had left it the previous evening.

John selected the series of winter scenes she had worked

on a few weeks earlier. He spread them out, like a panorama, admiring them. "I like these," he said.

"They're just rough pieces," she explained, wanting them to be seen as work-in-progress and not the finished product. "I was experimenting – different techniques – you know – that sort of thing."

He nodded, still evaluating them.

His silence made her defensive. "I've never painted snow scenes before. I found them a bit of a challenge."

"I'm impressed."

Praise was not something she was used to receiving. It was an uncomfortable gift. "You don't have to gild the lily," she said, removing any obligation he might feel to say something positive. "I won't be offended."

He frowned. "No – seriously. I like them. They're tremendously atmospheric. You really should take your art more seriously."

She found his enthusiasm slightly embarrassing. "If you like them, there are more in the other folder," she said, not wanting to sound too pushy. "I'll leave you to browse through them while I get changed, if you like."

"I'll put them away afterwards," he promised. "Don't be too long, will you?"

But as usual, the choice of what to wear proved difficult. She had planned for a weekend away, not just a few hours, and she was beset by indecision.

Outside, there were voices, and from her window she could see John and Mr Moray engaged in conversation. They were still talking when she came out onto the porch, and John drifted back to the car, opening the door for her.

Mr Moray began raking together the stray prunings. "I'll clear the drive so you can turn the car around," he called across to them.

John turned to acknowledge him. "Thanks," he said.

For a fleeting moment, as the two men faced one another, Laura sensed a mutual wariness between them. Why would that be?

John was silent for some time afterwards, apparently concentrating on the road ahead. "How long have you known the Pale Knight?" he asked after several miles.

Laura had been enjoying the scenery and feeling more relaxed about their revised plans, contemplating the evening ahead in his tumbled sheets with quiet satisfaction. "About ten years," she said, not really interested in discussing Mr Moray.

"How much do you *really* know him?"

"Really? Only what I've told you. He doesn't talk much. Keeps himself to himself. Why?"

"He's not exactly your average farmworker-cum-gardener, is he?"

She had no idea what he meant.

He laughed. "You don't know what I'm talking about, do you?"

"No, I don't."

He turned briefly to look at her. "Did you never wonder why a schoolmistress would be interested in him?"

"I suppose I did – I don't know. It wasn't any of my business."

"I wouldn't underestimate him, if I were you. I think there might be more to your Pale Knight than meets the eye."

Laura felt herself shrivel inside: there must have been countless times she had been condescending in her manner towards him – just like her mother. "What do you mean?"

"Oh – nothing. It doesn't matter," he said, letting the subject drop. "So – tell me, what did you do with yourself last weekend? Were you mending fences again?"

"No, I was visiting Aunt Millicent. She greatly approves of you."

"Can I ask why?"

"She thinks it's a good idea to take a lover."

He found this amusing. "You clearly have a lot in common with your aunt."

"More than I knew," she said, pondering the truth of this.

Chapter Twenty-Seven

There was, John explained, an early evening show at Pickerton's Bijou Cinema on Saturdays, reserved for Film Club Members. "There's a French Film Season this month," he said, with casual indifference to the obvious inference to be drawn from such an observation. "Would you like to go?"

To Laura, whose entire film experience was limited to the Lingford Odeon with Oliver, Hollywood epics, Pathé News and British 'B' movies, French films were associated with – from what she had heard – a great deal of sex and nudity. They were not just risqué by all accounts, but potentially pornographic. To be actually seen *going* to one, could be regarded, in certain quarters, as disgraceful. But what did she expect? This was, after all, John Rufford, whose trademark was novelty; the fresh experience with the element of surprise, delight, or downright audaciousness; this was part of his attractiveness.

He was waiting for her reply, finishing his meal, and sitting back with evident satisfaction that her silence was proof once more that he had caught her off-guard. "Tonight's film's *Les Liaisons Dangereuses*," he added with casual nonchalance.

With one eye on the Indian waiters, in impeccably white shirts with equally immaculate white aprons over their black trousers, who were hovering discreetly in the background, Laura abandoned her efforts to chase the last grains of rice around her plate. She put down her fork, and leaned across the table to admonish him, *sotto voce*. "John Leighton Rufford, you're a depraved man. Do you know that?"

"I'm working on it." he said, perfectly content to seduce her from a distance with his lazy smile.

What you see is what you get.

"No – seriously," he added, suddenly prepared to abandon the rôle of Valmont for a moment, "it's a classic." He emphasised the point. "And – I thought it was rather appropriate – the title, that is – not the story."

They had been circling around the topic of their relationship all afternoon, wrapping it up in harmless banter and elegant word-play. But occasionally, Laura sensed his teasing went deeper, too deep to fathom. Was theirs somehow a 'dangerous liaison' perhaps? She side-stepped the possibility. It was safer to throw down the obvious challenge. "And I suppose you're going to tell me there's no sex or nudity in it?"

He pulled a face, acknowledging there might be. "It's a moral tale – of sorts. Does that convince you?"

"In that case, you may take me to see it."

Afterwards, she was of the opinion she had indeed been seduced: not by John, who, in accordance with his declared aversion to groping in the back row of the cinema, was the perfect gentleman; but by the combined effect of intense acting and the elegant, measured pace of the plot that sucked her into the world of casual cruelty and its dire consequences in a way she had never known before. It left her raw. She came out into the frosty night air feeling part of her had been left behind in Pickerton's Bijou Cinema, along with the thick, smoky atmosphere, and the aroma of old seats and faded curtains.

John put his arm around her as they walked to the car, keeping her close for warmth. "Well," he asked. "Was it what you expected?"

She had no inclination to talk, still mulling over the story and its dreadful outcome. "No," she said, keeping things simple. "It was –" She floundered, unable to find the right words to express precisely what she felt. "– unsettling," was all she could manage in the end.

This seemed to satisfy him, and he asked nothing more for the remainder of the journey back to Lower Chursley.

They arrived just before nine o'clock, John insisting on making a light supper of tea and toast "to dampen down the curry," as he put it.

Laura sat gazing into the bright flame of the gas fire, lulled by its gentle hiss. *Dangerous Liaisons*. Why had he thought the title so apt in relation to themselves?. Where did he see the danger? Not in her attachment to him, surely? She had been so careful not to be beguiled into believing there was anything permanent between them: he was a charming man who charmed women. What else was there to say?

He broke into her reverie. "I've got the photographs of our trip to Rothwell Mere," he said, squatting in front of the fire with a slice of bread skewered onto a toasting fork. "I'd like your opinion. They're in the envelope on the coffee table."

She spread them out, a series of moody black-and-white prints of the landscape around the mere, evoking the memory of their Sunday together: a poignant reminder.

"Which should I keep for the album?" he was asking.

She studied them closely. "It's difficult to say," she said, unable to come up with a satisfactory choice: he was a good photographer. "They all deserve a place."

He piled the toast in an untidy heap onto a plate and took it into the kitchen. "If you had to choose just one, which would it be?" he called back.

Before she could decide, he had returned with a tray of mugs and buttered toast. "This one," she said at last, showing him the print she had finally selected: an evocative study of the harsh winter sunlight slanting through broken reeds, casting a lattice of tangled shadows across the muted brilliance of the frozen lake. "It captures the magic," she explained.

He put down the tray, taking the print from her, a frown of concentration etched into his brow as he considered her choice. "You're right, of course," he said, pausing to study her with equal intensity. "I knew I could rely on your judgement."

His gaze reminded her of how he looked at her the first time that they met, his dark-chocolate eyes soft, uncompromisingly sensual, suggesting a desire for her that even Martin had not shown. For no reason she could think of, his overt appreciation of her was as unsettling as it had been on that stormy night before Christmas, when he had put his hand on her thigh and she had experienced something akin to an electric shock. "Thank you, kind sir," she said, retreating into mock modesty, telling herself she was being ridiculous. Why this coyness?

"No, I'm being serious," he was saying, still gazing at her intently. "You have an eye for landscape – what works, what doesn't. It's a gift."

"Nonsense!" she said, laughing off his praise. "So – where are the photos you took of me?" she asked. He had made no mention of them.

He was defensive. "Oh – I put those away."

"I think you should let me see them. I might not approve."

"You would," he said, ignoring her request and handing her a mug of tea and plate of toast instead.

"John – I'd like to see them," she insisted.

"No. They're for my eyes only. Eat up. It's getting late. I want to take you to bed."

The subject was closed.

In the subdued lighting of the bedside lamp, he lay in a light doze, half-covered by the crumpled sheets, the outlines of his body etched in pale golden light. She had propped herself up on one arm to admire him. His skin was smooth, flawless, like cream marble: beautiful to touch. She lay back again and closed her eyes, replete and happy, feeling the warmth of him against her. For the moment, it was enough: to drift back into their private world of closely-guarded secrets and exquisite sensuality. What more could she want?

In the distance, far back in her consciousness, she heard

the church clock chime. Three … four. Seven … eight. Time passing. Eleven … twelve. Glass slippers left on stairs, and golden coaches turning into pumpkins. John …

She had been dreaming.

She opened her eyes with a start, aware her heart was thumping and the words of a hymn were thundering in her head, very clearly – Mrs Whittaker in the assembly hall at Hunters Lane, assaulting the piano with her usual brio – schoolgirl voices raised in song –

> *Time, like an ever rolling stream,*
> *Bears all its sons away;*
> *They fly forgotten, like a dream*
> *Dies at the opening day.*

There was a sense of panic. Something had been said, or done, and she was frightened. Of what? Of whom? Of the past? – the present? – the future? Life itself? What? The sense of it lingered briefly at the margins of her mind, and was just as quickly gone. There was no recall, just a lingering sense of hurt and loss that would not go away. She took several breaths to calm herself, and turned her head to look at him.

He was still lost to dreamless sleep, peaceful, unaware of her anxiety, his face smoothed out from loving. She watched him, his generous lips, relaxed and slightly parted, curved upwards, hinting at a smile. What had she dreamt? She did not know, except that in her heart, she felt it had to do with him.

She sat up, careful not to wake him, fretful, knowing things had changed. Lost in this world of astonishing delight, it had been easy to forget – their allotted time had reached its high-point and was drawing to a close. Six to eight weeks – those were his conditions. She had agreed to them, content to fill the empty days of waiting with the heady brew he offered. But already four sweet weeks were past. January had slipped away. February, still dark and cold, was drifting by, and old forebodings, long buried since the chill days of November, rose up now like demons. Her father's lies, kept at bay while so much else had occupied her time, crept back into her thoughts, like unwelcome guests refusing to be gone. His other secrets too would soon be hers to know. She must deal with them as best she could, unhindered.

This then was the truth that had to be acknowledged. This was the sticking point. There was no place in this world of darkness and shabby revelations, for John Rufford: he belonged elsewhere, in a sunlit world of exotic shamelessness. She should be honest with him, as he had always been with her. She must not wait. She must do what Millicent had done – be brave enough to walk away.

His hair lay disordered on his forehead, still ruffled from her fingers running through it when she had held him close. "John, I need to talk," she said softly, brushing a stray lock back from his brow.

"Mm?" he said, shifting closer.

"Listen to me, please."

Her words penetrated his comfortable drowsiness. He propped himself up, his head on one hand, looking at her with dreamy half-closed eyes. "Sounds serious," he said, understanding nothing of what she had to say.

"It is."

"I'm all ears," he answered. But he was not: he was still wrapped in languor; softened; vulnerable.

"There are things I have to tell you," she began, knowing her little speech had never been rehearsed, and she was woefully ill-prepared to make it. "When my father died," she went on, fumbling for the words of explanation that would make things clear, "he left me a letter – a very private letter."

He leaned closer to kiss her shoulder. "Intriguing," he said light-heartedly.

She moved away. "You're not listening, John."

"I am – honestly," he insisted.

She tried again, ignoring his mock seriousness. "I don't know why but he told me he'd lied about his past. Nothing criminal," she hastened to add, "but he was ashamed of what he did."

"And that's it?" He was singularly unimpressed.

"No, it isn't. He left me to decide whether I wanted to know more. The details, he said, were in the second letter. It's in Mr Parr's safe-keeping. In two weeks time, I'm allowed to read it – if I want to."

"And will you?" he asked.

"Yes."

He ran a finger lightly down her cheek, trying to lighten her mood. "A bit melodramatic, wouldn't you say?"

"I can't help that."

"Do you think 'all will be revealed'?"

"Yes."

His brow furrowed. "I don't see how this affects us."

She turned away from him, trying in vain to find the words she needed to explain herself more clearly. "I'm not making a very good job of this, am I?" she said at last.

He shook his head.

"It's just that what he's told me has come out of the blue. I don't know what to make of it."

He took hold of her hand, attempting reassurance.

"I think the second letter will be worse. I think that's why he wanted to hold back – to give me time to come to terms with what he might reveal. Do you understand what I'm trying to say?"

"No," he said, smiling at her.

Her throat tightened. He was so beautiful, and a dull thudding filled her head. "The truth is, John, I think once I've got the letter, I'm going to need time to myself – to cope with whatever's in it."

He was quiet for a moment, letting his hand stray over her, infinitely slowly. "How long will you want?"

"A few weeks – a month – I don't know."

"And?"

"And I know you won't want this relationship to go on that long."

His silence was unfathomable, his eyes searching her face with such intensity, she could hardly bear it.

"Please say something," she begged.

"What do you want me to say?"

"I want you to tell me – honestly – knowing what I've

just told you – if you'd rather end things now – tonight – not next weekend – or –" she shrugged helplessly, "or – whenever you've decided to."

He had cocked his head on one side. "What if I don't want to end things at all?" he asked.

She was lost for words.

"Didn't you think it possible?"

"No! – of course I didn't! It's not what you said – right at the start. Remember? I'm a pastime, you said. A short-term arrangement."

"I know."

She pulled her hand away and hugged her knees. "Then don't tease me," she said, retreating into irritation for protection. "Not about this."

He reached out, stroking her back, his touch impossibly tender. "I'm not teasing, Laura."

She turned her head to look at him.

"Something's happened. I can't explain it," he said, with a sad smile.

"I can," she retaliated, trying to rescue her decision from being scuttled by his unexpected revelation. "You're being pushed into 'settling down' by your parents. They want to see you with a regular girlfriend – and you've decided to oblige – that's all."

"No, it's not like that.

She was in no mood to argue: things were getting far too complicated.

"Is it so difficult to imagine I could fall in love with you?" he was asking. He sat up and put his arm around her shoulders. "I know what I said. I know it wasn't meant to happen, but it has. I thought you'd guessed."

"A dangerous liaison?" she challenged him.

"If you like – yes."

"Oh, this is nonsense, John! We hardly know each other."

"I feel I've known you for years."

A red fog swirled in her brain. This was not what she had planned for – or even remotely anticipated – John Rufford declaring his love for her! It was impossible. "Please, don't. You're making this very hard for me."

"I can't help that," he insisted. "I knew how I felt about you, right from the beginning – from that first night at Sparston Hall. I just didn't have the courage to admit it."

"Why should I believe you?"

He looked her straight in the eyes. "Because I told you – I don't tell lies. I mean what I say."

She had no words to answer him.

"Can we at least go on seeing each other? – give you time to decide how you feel about me? – if that's what you want?"

What she wanted at that point was to weep with frustration. "You're not listening, John. I'm telling you I need time to deal with this on my own. How can I make you understand?"

"I assure you, I do understand. I'm prepared to wait."

Oh – why had he said that? She pulled away from him, her heart fluttering wildly as she scrambled from the bed, hunting for her clothes. He lay back, watching her, with deep, unfathomable eyes. His gaze unnerved her. She was all fingers-and-thumbs, her hands shaking; her head was

267

bursting. "You need to take me home," she said, making a supreme effort to calm her nerves. "It's almost one o'clock. Michael's coming, remember?"

"Damn Michael," he muttered and swung himself off the bed, moving in that easy way she loved so much. She looked away, too aware of how much pleasure she had from the sight of him.

Neither of them spoke until he stopped the car outside the Lodge. She stared through the windscreen at the pruned shrubbery, blue and silver in the frosty moonlight, feeling light-headed and giddy. It seemed a lifetime ago since she and John had stood there, hand-in-hand on the gravel in the afternoon sunshine, waiting for Robert Moray to clear the drive for them to leave.

John cut the engine. "Look, I'm sorry about tonight," he said quietly, studying his gloved hands on the steering wheel. "I never meant to drop my feelings on you like that – without warning. I just didn't want you thinking I was planning to end things."

She could think of nothing very useful to say to him.

He smiled anxiously. "Will you at least consider seeing me again? – before you get your father's letter?" He sounded hopeful.

She wished he had not asked. "I don't know."

There was a very long silence, punctuated by the shriek of an owl somewhere in Meeston Woods.

"It serves me right, doesn't it?" he said after a while. "Thinking I could always call the tune?"

"You weren't to know about my father."

"No," he said quietly, glancing briefly in her direction. "But it doesn't matter, you know – to me – whatever's in his letter."

She knew he meant it, but he could not see the obvious – that it might matter very much to her.

He took her hand. "Take me at my word, Laura. Spend next weekend with me and I'll accept whatever you want afterwards, I promise."

She wanted to say 'no'. So why, when she knew this was the honest thing to do – both for herself and John – was it so difficult to say the words? Why? The answer hovered briefly in her mind – the terrible possibility – that despite everything, absolutely everything, she might feel more for him than she wanted to admit.

"Will you?" he was asking.

She should not have looked into his eyes, or seen the hopeful smile that played around his lips. Her resolve melted under the heat of his insistence. She was not brave enough to walk away. She consented with a nod, knowing she must stand by her decision – and take the consequences.

"Thank you," he said, and kissed her hand.

CHAPTER TWENTY-EIGHT

The Lodge was bathed in silence, Daphne at the Gorsts for Sunday lunch, as usual.

Laura's mood swung from irritation to frustration, with nothing much between. On the desk in the study, her morning's work lay scattered; abandoned, ill-worked doodles, in her opinion, not worthy of completion. Her thoughts were restless, endlessly debating the folly of her actions the evening before.

In the cold light of day, the echoes of her dream had long since faded, and her urgent need to raise the subject of her father's past, now seemed pointless and overly dramatic. How could she have been so stupid? In that moment of weakness, she had spoiled everything: the lovely day she and John had spent together; their glorious love-making afterwards; the prospect of the weekend that lay ahead; and all the empty, hum-drum office days between, overshadowed now by anxiety and dread. It had been so unnecessary. But what was worse, she decided, was that as a consequence, she had forced him to confess an attachment to her, however unlikely, while she had no true understanding of herself.

She stared out of the study window, seeking diversion. None came.

Decisiveness was needed. She would tour the garden.

It was cold, but sunny, the February sun promising better days to come. From beyond the rhododendrons, the acrid smell of wood smoke drifted on the breeze. She was curious. In the middle of the vegetable patch, she found Mr Moray tending a vigorous blaze, the wood spluttering and crackling as the flames licked upwards; the smoke dispersing with a roar as the fire took hold. The heat was intense, shimmering the outlines of the greenhouse and garden shed beyond.

He looked up, seeing her approach, his features outlined in the glow. "Miss Driscoll," he said, acknowledging her presence with a nod.

"You're not usually here on a Sunday, Mr Moray," she said, wondering why he was.

"As good a time as any," he said. "A fine day's not to be missed."

"Of course," she said automatically, fascinated by the shapes and colours of the flames, feeling the heat from them on her face and the strong, resinous scent, reminiscent of incense.

He continued feeding in the prunings and dead wood that he had gathered. "Have you seen Mr Parr?" he asked casually, careful, it seemed not to mention her father expressly.

She shook her head: it was a topic she preferred not to discuss in her present state of mind.

"Ah," he said, still concentrating on the fire. "I thought that's why you'd come."

It seemed odd that he should think so. It was Sunday. She had not expected to find him at the Lodge. Did he expect her to seek him out?

"Do you want to help?" he was asking, thinking perhaps this was the reason for her being there. "You can have my gloves," he added and pulled them off, offering them to her.

They were too big, but she put them on anyway: rough, thick unyielding leather, bent to the shape of his hands.

"Stand here," he said, indicating the space next to him. "Or you'll get smoke in your eyes – or worse."

He untangled a bundle of smaller branches for her from the pile beside him. She took them, throwing them onto the fire as she had seen him do, then stepping back to watch the smoke thicken and curl before exploding into life.

"I'm sorry I cut our conversation short yesterday," she said, remembering that she had.

He was easily placated. "Plans can wait," he said, with a brief smile. "The ground's too hard to do much with at the moment."

"Perhaps it would be better if you did what you thought best," she suggested, feeling under the present circumstances there was little she could contribute.

"If you like." He bundled a pile of laurel onto the fire, and stood back, waiting for the flames to take hold. They burst into life with a roar. "Did you enjoy the film yesterday?" he asked unexpectedly.

"Film?"

"*Les Liaisons Dangereuses*," he said, his pronunciation precise and elegant, revealing an appreciation of the French language – and possibly more besides. "Your boyfriend said he thought you'd find it interesting."

"John's just a friend," she corrected him, trying to imagine how this topic had arisen during the brief conversation between the two men the previous afternoon.

He was evidently surprised. "Ah – forgive me. My mistake." The fire fell in on itself in a blaze of sparks, and he reached for the rake, pulling the half-burnt wood from the edges into the white-hot core. "It's Roger Vadim's version of the de Laclos novel, I believe," he added, after a suitable pause, feeding smaller pieces of laurel onto the top of the pyre. The leaves writhed in the heat, twisting in on themselves before collapsing into a raging sheet of flame. He handed her some smaller branches.

She threw all her pieces onto the rejuvenated fire at once. "Yes, I believe so," she said, distracted from her task by his sudden willingness to talk.

There was the briefest pause before he grabbed her by the arm, pulling her back with a jerk. She felt herself overbalance and his grip tighten, holding her steady as the wave of heat swept over them and a wall of flame exploded skywards. She came to her senses, shaken.

He let go of her arm, looking her straight in the eyes. "Take care," he said, "or you'll get burnt."

Chapter Twenty-Nine

She viewed their planned weekend with mixed emotions, too diverse to unravel from one chaotic moment to the next. As the days passed, the more anxious she became, until she convinced herself the only outcome would be all recriminations and regret. She longed for him to telephone and make some passable excuse, however flimsy, to cancel their arrangement, but when he called, only to suggest they go to Sparston Hall again, she lacked the strength of will to tell him 'no'.

And so, the week progressed, and Saturday arrived. The time for wavering had past.

She wore her blue cashmere dress again, with her hair loose about her shoulders, a conscious choice to please him, which it did, whilst he, immaculately dressed and groomed, dazzled her as usual.

He was as he always was in public: urbane and charming; witty but restrained, a ready stock of careful anecdotes on hand to bridge the gap when conversation flagged. He wined her and dined her; danced with her; wooed her with his eyes, and overwhelmed her anxiousness with simple *joie de vivre*.

Of what had passed the week before, he made no mention. While she had spent her waking hours in pointless fretting, John it seemed, had dealt with any qualms he had, and moved on, prepared to regard what came next as a necessary pause in their relationship, but not the end. He was neither maudlin, nor resentful, just himself; a stratagem, she told herself, like all the rest – designed to please.

But later, spread out on his bed, intoxicated by wine and the heady tang of him, her urgency was more than matched by his. He was different. Every look, every touch, every sweet thrust of him was more intense; and at the end, in that final moment of release, he cried out, something he had never done before. It had the sound of triumph tinged with pain. She had teased him – and he had laughed with her – but she sensed he was discomfited, and thought it best to let the matter drop. Afterwards, when he made love to her a second time, he was himself again, more obviously controlled, intent only on ensuring he was pleasing her.

On Sunday morning, she woke to sunlight shining through the bedroom curtains. Somewhere from across the fields, church bells were ringing, their cheerful exuberance intruding into the sudden sense of melancholy that came with wakefulness, knowing this might be her last morning in his bed.

John, ruffled and unshaven was propped up on one elbow, his eyes half-closed, evaluating her.

"Have you been awake long?" she asked.

"Long enough."

She stretched luxuriously, her body wanting more of

him, an urgency tinged with the knowledge of potential loss. "Don't let's get up yet," she said. "Make love to me again."

He shook his head. "No, Miss Driscoll, I will not. Even I have my limitations. I wouldn't want to disappoint you." But he leaned over anyway and kissed her breasts.

She stretched again, languorously, hoping she might tempt him, but he was not to be persuaded.

"Come out with me," he said coaxingly. "It's a beautiful day. I'd like to spirit you away to Farley Heath for lunch at The Narrowboat."

"And afterwards?"

He frowned, feigning lack of understanding. "Afterwards?"

"Promise you'll make love to me again."

He kissed her neck and shoulder, his breath light against her skin. "I promise," he whispered.

He kept his word.

Later that evening, when they were spent, and her head was lying cradled on his shoulder with his arm around her waist, she listened to the solid beating of his heart marching in step to the ticking of the bedside clock. Time was slipping by. Soon he would have to take her home, and they would part, maybe for a few short weeks, or maybe months, or perhaps for ever – who could tell? But he must give her time – and space – to work things out as best she could, and be content – and so must she.

He stirred, his arm drawing her a little closer. She did not speak, but he guessed she was awake. "Do I let you go now?" he asked softly, planting kisses in her hair.

"It's late. I think you must."

He sighed, easing her away from him onto the pillow. "Don't move," he said. "I want to give you something." He reached into the drawer of the bedside cabinet and brought out a small package, wrapped in pale-blue patterned paper dotted with forget-me-nots. "A token of my appreciation," he said, handing it to her with a loving smile. "I hope you'll like it."

"A present?"

"For someone special," he said. "Open it."

Inside, she found a slim, pocket-sized volume, bound in beautifully tooled black leather. The title, worked in gold in an exotic style of script, was emblazoned on the front. "*The Rubaiyat of Omar Khayyam*," she said, uncertain if she was pronouncing it correctly.

He guessed she had no knowledge of it. "Eleventh century Persian poetry," he explained. "The Edward FitzGerald translation."

When she lifted the cover, the pages fell open naturally somewhere near the middle. Tucked between them, was a simple, but professional-looking portrait photograph, with a white deckle-edged border.

"I had it taken by Highsmith's in Lingford," he said, looking slightly embarrassed. "I hope you don't mind. I've so many of you."

The camera had caught his likeness to perfection: he was gazing into the lens, soft-eyed, seductive, head tilted slightly to one side, his languid smile playing on his lips. On the back, he had written the simple annotation, 'To Laura from John, with love – February 1963'.

"Read the poem to me," he urged. "I want to hear you read it."

At first, she could not find her voice, and when she did, it was difficult to hold it steady. " 'Ah, fill the cup:' " she began hesitantly. " ' – what boots it to repeat How Time is slipping underneath our Feet:' " She cleared her throat, her emotions suddenly rubbed raw. She continued, stumbling over almost every word. " 'Unborn Tomorrow and dead Yesterday, Why fret about them if Today be sweet!'" She was misty-eyed and trying not to be, the page blurring in front of her. "It's lovely," she said at last, overcoming the desire to burst into tears. "I shall treasure them both."

He planted a kiss on her forehead. "My pleasure," he said softly, smiling at her. "Think of me, when you read it, that's all I ask."

She could barely speak. She had bought him nothing.

"What's wrong?" he asked gently, running a finger lightly down her cheek.

"I haven't bought you anything."

"Ha!" he said, looking remarkably sanguine over her omission. "That's the best piece of news I've had for days." His good humour sounded slightly false.

"It was thoughtless of me."

"Nonsense! It tells me you don't honestly believe this will be our last weekend together. Am I right?"

It was not what she intended. Carefully, she replaced the photograph in its appointed place and rewrapped the gift, not knowing what to say. Perhaps he was right: if she had decided this was to be the end, she would have bought him something, a farewell gift, however small.

He took her silence as consent.

Later, in the shelter of the porch outside the Lodge, he brought her close once more, and they lingered there a while, neither willing to part too soon.

"When you're ready," he said softly, "write to me."

He was breaking her heart.

"I'll wait. I won't get in touch 'til you want me to. I don't want to make things harder for you. Do you understand?" The pale glow of starlight etched out the contours of his face. He was trying to smile.

She nodded.

He held her tighter for a moment before he let her go. "I'll be thinking of you," he said, as he turned away, hurrying down the steps to the car.

"Thank you, John," she called after him. "For everything."

He waved. The car door slammed. The engine burst into life and he drove quickly away over the frosted gravel and was gone.

She stood alone under the porch with only the stars for company, listening to the silence. There was an emptiness inside she had never felt before, even when Martin had gone. John had left a greater void. But, she consoled herself, at least in spirit he was with her, in the words of a Persian poet, and the gift of a photograph. Perhaps that would be enough.

CHAPTER THIRTY

Mr Parr arrived punctually at the Bank on Thursday afternoon for his appointment, and was shown into Mr Gittings' office without any great fuss. Laura was summoned a few minutes later, ostensibly to take notes, so that none of her colleagues noticed anything unusual was taking place.

"Mr Parr is waiting for you in the interview room," Mr Gittings explained as he closed the door to his office.

Mr Parr was standing behind the desk looking nervous: it was the first time they had met since their conversation after Christmas. He was still evidently embarrassed. He shook her hand awkwardly, inviting her to take a seat.

On the desk between them, he had placed a large, thick, buff-coloured envelope and a brown paper parcel tied with string. The parcel was the size of a small shoe-box, and a blob of scarlet sealing wax sat perched on the knot where the string had been tied.

"Well – here they are, Laura" he said, forcing a smile. "These are the remaining items your father left with me." He cleared his throat. "In accordance with his instructions, I have to ask you whether you now wish to take possession of these, or not." There was a small frown in the centre of his forehead, as if dreading the possibility she might say 'no'. "I understand there is a box inside the parcel," he explained, "and you will find the key to this inside the envelope."

She was hesitant now, after being so determined for so long – perhaps because of John. What lay before her, she was certain, was the prospect of sacrificing any possibility they might have a future together. Something told her that whatever lay hidden in these pathetic remnants of her father's life, knowing them would cast a long shadow, and there would be no going back to the person she had been before – nor to John.

"Don't feel you have to accept, Laura," Mr Parr was saying. "Your father made no stipulation that you should. If you have any doubts at all, then please say so."

His pressing her for a decision cleared her mind. The fog lifted. "I'll take them," she said, with absolutely clarity of purpose. "I think I should."

He nodded, and reaching into his brief case took out a small receipt book, carefully positioning the carbon paper in the appropriate place. He wrote slowly and carefully, listing the items and adding the date. "If you'll sign here, Laura," he instructed, passing the book across to her, "I have discharged my duty as your father would have wished."

She signed and returned the book to him. He tore out the top copy and handed it to her.

"These are now yours," he said, pushing the parcel and the envelope across the desk. "Of course, probate is yet to be granted, but Mr Jackson and I are confident this will not take too long now most of the financial aspects have been completed." There was a moment's silence. His gaze was fixed on his interlaced fingers clasped tightly together on the desk top. He cleared his throat again. "I can't tell you, Laura, how much Phyllis and I regret what happened –" he began.

"There's nothing to regret, Mr Parr. Please believe me. I'm perfectly content."

He still seemed unconvinced, and Laura felt no matter how hard she tried, she would never relieve him of his sense of shame.

Shame.

Shame, she thought, was different things to different people. Her father's shame lay on the desk between them.

That evening, she locked the study door and considered her latest acquisitions. The parcel was unexpected.

She opened the envelope. The little key to the box fell out onto the desk when she turned the envelope upside down. She picked it up feeling the smoothness of it, worn down by use and age. She placed it next to the parcel and paused, contemplating the act of reading the letter. It crossed her mind she could still destroy everything and no harm would come to anyone by doing so, but it was a fleeting thought, and soon dispelled. She could see the elegant flow of the copperplate script on the page before her and her eyes were drawn to it.

His greeting began, 'My dearest daughter', and from that moment, she could not stop herself from reading on.

'What follows is the truth. When you've read everything,

you will understand why it was so important that none of this should be revealed to your mother, or anyone else in the family. I am presuming therefore, that if you are reading this, you have broken off your engagement to Oliver.

'Laura, my life was framed not by wealth, but abject poverty.'

Poverty had a chilling ring to it.

'My father,' the letter went on, 'was John Driscoll, known as Jack. He was Irish, born in Cork in 1875, one of several sons of an agricultural labourer. He came to England in his early twenties looking for work in the shipyards on the Tyne. It was while he was lodging there he met my mother, Annie Douglas – eight years his junior. She was a farmer's daughter from Coldingham in Berwickshire working as a laundress. They started courting and she was pregnant when he left for several months to work at Rosyth.'

Here, the writing faltered for a moment, and with it, Laura's concentration as she felt her heart fluttering beneath her ribs. It must have taken courage for him to write those few, socially damning, unacceptable words.

'Whatever I felt about my father afterwards, I have to acknowledge that in this at least he did the honourable thing. When he returned from Rosyth, they were married. And here, Laura, I must prepare you for the existence of someone you have never met. You have an uncle – Andrew, whom I have kept at arms' length for many years – though once he and I were very close. He was born when I was three, and the box you now have, which was our father's, has come to you through him.'

Andrew. Andrew – and the little red-bound book of sea shanties she had found in the bookcase – 'From Andrew, April 1920' – a gift put out of sight, and out of mind.

'In 1905, my father went back to work at Rosyth for a while, and my mother was left with two small children and another on the way. Jean was born later that year.'

Jean? He had made no mention of her sooner, and a slight shiver ran through her, knowing instinctively that Jean's story would play a larger part in his.

'It was during this time I contracted rheumatic fever. It left me a sickly child weakened by illness. My father would never accept this. He thought me "soft", a "mother's boy" not worthy to be his son. By then, he was a heavy drinker, prone to casual violence and fits of temper, something I became accustomed to.

'In 1913, I left school at 14 and found employment as an office boy with Mr Edwin Watson, an accountant in Newcastle. I took night classes in book-keeping with his encouragement. My successes counted for nothing in my father's eyes, particularly when Andrew joined the Mercantile Marine, and I was declared "unfit" to do my bit "For King and Country".

'Mr Watson retired when I was eighteen. He gave me excellent references and a recommendation to his friend, Mr Alfred Battersby, who ran an accountancy business in Manchester. I left home, glad to escape, but knowing my mother and sister were facing increasing violence on an almost daily basis.

'Not long after the Armistice, my mother was diagnosed

with TB. I sent her what money I could, but how much was spent on her treatment, and how much my father consumed in drink, I will never know. She died early the following year, aged thirty-seven.'

Here, there were clear signs he had been unable to continue for a while: the new paragraph began in a darker shade of ink, and the flow of the pen took several lines to return to its earlier fluidity of execution.

'What followed affected me deeply,' the letter continued. 'And I could not escape the fear that – no matter how much I tried to convince myself otherwise – I might have inherited my father's inclinations. When you were born, I was afraid to express any honest and loving affection towards you. There were so many times I wanted to – but my dread prevented me. My fears may have been unfounded, but I could never be certain.

'Laura, there's no easy way to tell you of my father's depravity, but you must know of it to understand these fears.

'Within a month of our mother's death, he turned to Jean in her place. She was just fifteen years of age. At the time, I was in Manchester and Andrew at sea. He discovered the truth several months later when he came home on shore leave, and wrote to me directly. Between us, we found Jean employment as a live-in domestic away from the area, but sometime during the following year, our father found her and took her home. Neither Andrew nor I knew this had happened: he was sailing for Australia; the letters I wrote to her were forwarded by her previous employer, unwittingly helping to hide the truth, and her replies – which were never frequent – and no doubt censored, gave me no hint of her plight. By the time Andrew returned, it was too late. She had been abandoned, seriously ill, and our father had fled to Ireland. She died not long afterwards, just twenty years of age.'

Laura felt tears pricking at the corners of her eyes. Could she read on?

Eventually, she could.

'Laura, I've never forgiven myself for my neglect of Jean. For those five years, I was too self-absorbed. I was happy to believe what I read in her short notes to me. I was discouraged from visiting, and I never took the trouble to ensure that all was well.

'Afterwards, I stifled my guilt. Once I qualified, I moved on. I was given the opportunity of joining the firm of Herbert Thompson & Co in Manchester. Their clients were wealthy and well-connected, and I did not hesitate. I knew in accepting this position I was moving out of my social class, and I would, of necessity, have to disown my humble origins. It was then that I transformed myself into the orphaned son of wealthy Irish parents taken into the care of my guardian, Mr Watson. It meant disowning the existence of my brother. My decision hurt him deeply, and destroyed what once had been a close relationship.

'One of Mr Thompson's clients was your grandfather, Edward Harriman. It was he who suggested I set up an accountancy business in Lingford – and gave me the financial means to do so. The rest you know. One lie led to another, until I found myself buried by a mountain of deceit.

'Not long ago, Andrew contacted me through a third

party with the news our father had died in Ireland several years ago, and a cousin had forwarded a box to him containing some personal possessions. This is the box which is now in your possession. Its contents are reminders of a happier time. I'm surprised my father kept them. Perhaps he felt a guilt he never showed. Among the papers, you will find the record of my parents' marriage and my birth certificate.

'Laura, I'm sure you have already realised, I was born out of wedlock. From my birth certificate you will see my mother gave me the Christian names James Driscoll, so the surname Douglas could be quietly dropped after she married my father. She sincerely believed that once they were married I would be a legitimate child of that union.'

As she turned the page, Laura needed no prompting to guess what was to follow.

'If I had been born in Scotland,' the letter continued, 'as she had been, that would indeed have been the case. But Scots Law and English Law are not the same. She did not know this. Indeed, neither did I. It was only earlier this year, through an unrelated conversation with a client, that I learnt of the provisions of the Legitimacy Act of 1926. I was curious, and made discreet enquiries. I discovered that had my father been living in England on January 1st, 1927, I would have become his legitimate son. But he was not. On that date, he was resident in the Irish Free State, outside the scope and jurisdiction of the Act. So, you see, Laura, I never was, and never would be, the legitimate son of John Driscoll.

'How can I describe how this knowledge touched me? I had such loathing for the man that to loosen my ties to him gave me nothing but joy. But later, I began to fear I had become a mere shadow. Perhaps it was Divine Justice for my hubris in creating a life built on such a tissue of lies. But what can I say to you? I took my father's name thinking it was mine; I married your mother with it, and passed it on to you. But it is not your rightful name – nor mine – and I go to my grave as the counterfeit, James Driscoll, not who I really am – James Douglas. Perhaps it is only fitting that I should. But it is not the legacy I wished for you.

'Have I indulged myself revealing this? I trust not. It was not my intention. My only wish was to make a clean breast of things and leave the knowledge in your hands to understand me better.

'May you find the goodness in your heart to forgive me all my failings in the past and think kindly of me in the future,

'Your devoted father

'James Douglas xx'

At the bottom of the page was a post-script.

'I have at last made my peace with Andrew, and done the right thing by him. You will find his reply to me in the box. I ask this one favour of you – that you let him know of my demise.'

She settled her head against the soft black leather of the chair. Thoughts came and went, unwilling to be marshalled. Too much had been revealed. The neatly written pages sat at odds with all the degradation in his life. That he had striven to overcome such obstacles should have been a cause of pride for him. But he did not see it: deceit had tarnished everything, and all his endeavours had shrunk to acts of cowardice and self-interest.

Where was she in this kaleidoscope of scarred lives and layers of deceit? She too had been transformed – from Laura Driscoll into Laura Douglas – at the stroke of his pen. Like him, she had been cast adrift on an uncertain sea. Where would this knowledge take her?

The parcel lay before her, tantalising. Instinct said, do not open this. Destroy the letter. Go back to being who you were. Forget everything. Write to John. Tell him there was nothing of any consequence at all – just the ramblings of a sick man – and let the fiction of his past live on.

Except the box, neatly wrapped in its brown paper packaging, demanded to be opened.

Chapter Thirty-One

The sealing wax broke easily, and she eased away the string. The parcel had been wrapped with care, the brown paper folded with meticulous neatness. She peeled back the edges to reveal an old tin cash-box in black-and-gold with dents in its side and scratches on the lid. Was this battered, inconsequential-looking object, what her father had kept hidden in the locked drawer of his desk? It was nothing of note, hardly something to excite casual curiosity, except perhaps by its very shabbiness, it drew attention to itself.

She toyed with the little key for a moment. Then, when she was fully resolved, she placed it firmly in the lock and felt the catch draw back.

Inside, the contents were jumble of items, disordered from jostling. She picked them out one by one, inspecting each in turn and laying them out on the desk. On top, she found the birth and marriage certificates her father had mentioned, suffering from age where they had been folded and refolded many times over. Immediately below these was a plain white envelope addressed to 'J Driscoll, Esq' marked 'PERSONAL', bearing the office address of

Driscoll & Jackson in Lingford. The writing, in blue ink, was small, evenly formed, but otherwise unremarkable. Under the envelope were assorted scraps of lined paper, brown with age, on which were written what Laura took to be the words of poems – or more probably songs. They read like lullabys. There were half-a-dozen or more of these. The writing was faint, mostly done in pencil, but care had been taken to form the letters in a proper fashion, and the capitals were not ashamed of themselves. She read the first, trying to divine what tune would turn these words into a song, to croon to, and comfort a sick child.

> Come bonnie bairn with curling hair,
> Come, close your eyes and dream
> Of all those things both good and fair,
> That come with morning's gleam.

The remaining verses promised better times to come, and the other poems were in a similar vein. Laura recognised none of them. They were probably handed down from one generation to the next, but never absorbed into the traditional canon. Who sang lullabys to children in this enlightened age? – she thought. Not many. Soon these ancient lays would be lost for ever through lack of use. There was something unutterably sad about this.

Below these in the box, all jumbled and curling at the edges, was an assortment of old photographs. They were a hotchpotch of formal and informal settings; different eras; different places. There was no obvious connection between them, just random events in the lives of people about whom she knew nothing.

The first were two mounted oval portrait photographs of a young man and woman, both postcard-sized. They might once have been displayed on a mantelpiece, or sideboard, but had long since lost their frame. On the back of the image of the man was written, 'Jack Driscoll, aged twenty-five'. Looking into his face, she expected to see traces of what he would become, but they were not there. Here was a fine looking man with the lean, sharp features of the Irish and fire in his eyes; a handsome, clean-shaven man dressed in his Sunday suit with its stiff high collar, sitting for his portrait in a studio somewhere in Newcastle-upon-Tyne. The second picture, taken in the same studio, was of Annie, her grandmother as a young girl of seventeen, with a pretty, delicate oval face and light hair pinned up in the fashion of the time. She was wearing a high-necked white blouse trimmed with lace at the throat, and a small locket in the shape of a heart on a chain around her neck. There was, even then, an ethereal air about her, Laura thought, an other-worldliness about the eyes, searching for something, or someone, in a future she would never have.

She placed them on the desk, side-by-side: images of two young people with hopes and dreams that all too soon would fade. It saddened her. She searched their features for some resemblance to her father – but found none. Was she surprised? Her earliest remembrance of him recalled a slightly tubby man already in his forties: a prosperous, well-fed man, untouched by the demands of hard, manual labour and a meagre diet. The face of an impoverished childhood had vanished long ago and left no trace. Nor had any semblance of these forebears passed through him to her. The proof was there for her to see in every mirror. In this regard at least, the Harrimans had triumphed, and she was sorry for it: she would have liked a little resemblance, however small, to Annie Douglas.

She put these aside. Below them in the box were two faded full-length photographs of a youth in naval attire, bearing the date '1916', and she guessed this to be Andrew from the marked likeness to his father. He was a good-looking youth. Beneath these was a larger photograph of maybe sixty men or more, all with flat caps, standing in tiers in front of a warship. On the back was written 'Rosyth 1917'. Somewhere in these ranks, Laura guessed, would be Jack Driscoll, but the caps obscured the faces and the image was too small to pick him out.

Next were several snapshots of a later time. They showed wiry men in shirt sleeves with Driscoll features – her father's uncles, she presumed – their breeches held in place by wide, big-buckled leather belts. They were standing cross-armed outside front doors with peeling paint, next to grim-faced women in shapeless dresses and hair scraped back in buns. Beside them, sitting on door steps, or standing with hands in their pockets, were scruffy-kneed boys in short trousers and scuffed boots, pulling faces. There were no girls. On the backs of these snaps were the words 'Freedom at last!' and similar sentiments in a bold round hand. 'King and Country' it seemed, were distant memories here.

Below these lay an old school photograph. It showed a mixed group of young children, probably between five and ten years of age. At the front, they were sitting cross-legged on the ground. Behind them, older children stood in two ranks, the back row visibly standing on low benches. They were all, without exception, ill-kempt. Many appeared to be wearing hand-me-downs from older siblings, being much too big for them; others were bursting at the seams in clothes outgrown, but still needing to be worn long after they had ceased to fit. The boys, with their pudding-basin haircuts, wore expressions of gritty determination; some were grinning. Most of the girls had an air of bewilderment, their large eyes staring blankly to the front without comprehension. Above one was a pencilled cross. All that was visible of her between two belligerent-looking boys was a small, frightened face beneath short bobbed hair held firmly in place by a grip. On the back of the photograph, written in pencil in Annie's careful hand, was the simple statement, 'Jean at Fenton Road – 1911'.

So this was Jean, her father's much-abused and much-neglected sister. Had no one seen the fear already in her eyes? She was marked out even then. Laura could look at her no longer. She pushed the photograph away.

There was only one more remaining in the box, much older than the rest, but remarkably preserved: a family group, taken, Laura judged, sometime during the 1860s maybe by the style of the clothes – everyone stiff and solemn against a background of velvet drapery; the husband and wife, possibly in their late fifties, sitting upright in high-backed chairs at the front. The man wore a well-cut tweed suit and sported luxuriant side-whiskers and moustache, which masked his face. He was holding a pair of leather gloves in one hand on his knees. The woman, a lady with a refined expression, wore her hair parted at the centre under a small bonnet. A thick cape trimmed in braid at the edges fell to her waist, and her hands were hidden in a fur muff on her lap. Her full skirt, of what appeared to be a fine, light-coloured woollen fabric – no doubt supported by many petticoats – dominated the photograph. Standing behind, and to each side of these two imposing figures, were three younger men, possibly all in their twenties, clean shaven, serious, in high-buttoned tweed jackets and knotted ties. On the back of the print in Annie's careful script again was written – 'Grandpa and Grandma Douglas, my Father – Alexander, and his brothers William and Malcolm'. There was no date.

Laura was bemused. She could understand why Annie might treasure this. But why her husband should keep it long after her death, just as he had kept the remnants of her writing and the photograph of Jean, seemed strangely out of character.

She turned back to the certificates, unfolding them with care and seeing in these tattered remnants confirmation of her father's story: the belated marriage at a Registry Office; the registration of his birth as James Driscoll Douglas; father, John Driscoll, shipwright. A sharp realisation dawned. Apart from this one, solitary item in this strange collection, her father was nowhere to be found: not a single photograph of him as a boy, or a young man was here; nothing, except his name on a certificate in fading ink. It was as if, once born, he had been eradicated from his father's memory. Perhaps then, it was fitting that the son had chosen to eradicate the father too.

What would John Rufford make of these jumbled fragments and the dreadful truth behind them? Would he still think it was all 'a bit melodramatic'? Overblown? Perhaps it was, but she was certain there were no skeletons of such dreadful magnitude hiding in the Rufford cupboard; no flotsam and jetsam of deprivation or squalor washed up on his shore. This wreckage of her father's life would lie outside his knowledge, and beyond his comprehension.

No doubt he would have brushed it all aside and found a pithy quote to ease her mind, his favourite verse from the Rubaiyat perhaps, whispered into her ear as she lay beside him, beguiled by his attentions. She could close her eyes and see him smiling; hear his voice caressing her, enunciating every word with heart-stopping clarity –

> *Ah, fill the Cup: – what boots*
> *it to repeat*
> *How Time is slipping underneath*
> *our Feet:*
> *Unborn To-morrow and dead*
> *Yesterday,*
> *Why fret about them if To-day be*
> *sweet!*

And afterwards, he would have made elegant love to her, and everything would have been right with the world – except that now it never could be. A cold light had broken in and lit up the reality of ugly truth that could not be dimmed or blotted out. John Rufford did not belong here in this tangled mess of broken lives – she must accept that and understand why.

The hall clock struck ten. Soon, Daphne would return, and they would exchange a few, pointless pleasantries that were the norm of late, a form of words devised to note the other's presence, nothing more. That evening, more than any other, Laura had no wish to prolong this social nicety. She felt too burdened by her sudden knowledge to be certain of herself, while Daphne, ignorant of so much, might sense a change in her and look for reasons.

There was no time now to read her uncle's letter. So be it. This solitary item among so many belonged to someone living. For this reason, if no other, it demanded her attention, uncluttered by the sad remains of long-dead others. She left it for another day. Today belonged to the past.

Her father's letter was easily tidied into the bottom drawer, but the contents of the tin box refused to be managed. The photographs jostled one another, their curled edges refusing to be neatly stacked. Several escaped her grasp and fell to the floor. She retrieved them irritated by her clumsiness, and in being altogether too rushed, allowed the picture of the family group to fall once more, this time into her lap. She ignored it until all the rest were safely stored away.

The photograph had landed face down, and for no reason she could fathom, her attention fixed itself on Annie's words, their gravity demanding she should note them. Here, she realised with a start, was not just a record of Annie's long-lost family – her father, her uncles and her grandparents – but of her own distant Douglas relatives, about whom she knew nothing. Curiosity stirred. She picked up the photograph once more, eager now to study it more closely. The parents, evidently well-heeled, stared back at her, as did their three strapping sons, one of whom was Annie's father. But which? The youngest-looking on the right? A splendid young man with a hint of defiance in the tilt of his head. Possibly. But how, Laura wondered, had Annie come to such a low estate from this? A laundress. A life of drudgery and long hours. It was incomprehensible. One mystery had revealed another. How many more might lie hidden here?

William, Malcolm and Alexander. She smiled at the faces of their parents, well-pleased enough, she thought. She looked back at their sons. Yes, they were young men to be proud of.

And then she saw him – really saw him – as if he had spoken to her and obliged her to take notice of him – the young man on the left, with his penetrating gaze. Her concentration fixed on him until her eyes began to ache. She heard herself gasp, and held her breath.

Before her, in this image of the past, were the familiar, solemn features of the man she knew as Robert Moray.

Chapter Thirty-Two

Sleep was impossible: her head was full of endlessly unanswered questions and countless presumptions, some wildly improbable.

Her mother of course, with her ability to detect the smallest change in anyone's demeanour that might give her some advantage, had challenged her.

"You look quite flushed, Laura," she had said, fixing her with a steely gaze. "Are you ill?"

"No, not at all," she had replied, perhaps too brightly. And she had hurried to her room, aware she had sounded brittle and wholly unconvincing, and that Daphne had watched her go.

The hours dragged, their snail-like passage marked by the clock striking in the hall.

Her father's revelations had been the stuff of nightmares, but her own discovery – if 'discovery' was what it really was – caused her more concern. What was in the past could not be undone, the future was something else. She must be careful not to jump to wild conclusions without thinking through the consequences. It was too easy, she kept telling herself repeatedly, to become carried away by the romantic notion of The Douglas Connection. And as the hours passed, doubts crept in. Perhaps she had been too susceptible, seeing a resemblance that was not there, wanting to believe it simply for her father's sake – or perhaps her own. It was possible. Mr Moray had been quite adamant there was no relationship between them. Would be lie? Improbable. But if he had, why would he? Out of delicacy perhaps? Or was it possible he had never known the truth – if truth was what it was? How could she question him without implying he had been dishonest in his dealings with her father – and with her? She had no idea. And if she found a way, would he welcome any link between them? He might resent it, or be embarrassed by it. How was she to know? Of course, she could be completely wrong in her assumptions, and he might tell her so, give her proof, and make her feel a fool.

The clock struck five. Feverishly, she threw aside the coverlet and got up, dragging it around her shoulders, seeking refuge on the window seat. She curled up in its voluminous folds and sat staring at the stars, yearning for answers that were not there to be had.

She must be calm, she told herself. Let time pass and wisdom prevail. Friday was dawning – a working day, filled with demands more urgent than her own – and Saturday would keep her in Weaversham until early afternoon. Nothing would be lost by waiting – except her patience.

And when Saturday came, and she returned from her morning at the Bank, Laura found Millicent's car in the drive, and her aunt, newly arrived, waving to her from the steps to the porch.

"Hello, Laura, my dear," Millicent said, embracing her enthusiastically and kissing her on both cheeks. "I've come to collect your mother. How are you?" By which it was clear she was referring to niece's love-life.

Laura hedged. "I'm very well thank you, Auntie. Are you?"

Millicent was not to be distracted by social niceties. "Going out with John this afternoon?" she enquired as Laura let them both into the hall. "It's a lovely day."

Laura shook her head. "We've agreed not to see each other for a while," she said, making light of it. "I may go for a walk later."

"Gracious, Laura! So soon? What a shame. Weren't you tempted to let it run a little longer? He was such a lovely man."

"I'd like to concentrate on other things, Auntie."

"Oh. Anything in particular?"

Daphne appeared at the top of the stairs, resplendent in her latest tailored two piece, ready for afternoon tea at Hazeldene Court. "Millie – I didn't expect you until half-past at the earliest!" she said, abruptly interrupting the interrogation, and Millicent felt obliged to let the matter drop.

"Sorry I'm early, Daphne," she said. "Estelle had a cancelled appointment. How do you like the new colour?" She delicately touched her immaculately styled hair, now a slightly lighter shade of blue than previously.

Daphne surveyed her sister critically. "A definite improvement, Millie. The other was a little on the loud side."

"I thought so too. Well – we'd better be off. Sorry to hear you've given up your beau, Laura," she added, patting her niece on the shoulder affectionately.

Laura was aware of her mother's attention focused on her, and an intense interest in the unexpected intelligence that Mr Rufford was no longer to be expected.

Millicent was unstoppable. "No doubt we'll find out in good time, Daphne, what – or who she wants to concentrate on instead."

"I thought I'd start driving lessons," Laura said, saying the first thing that came into her head which sounded feasible to both her listeners. "Now the weather's better," she added for good measure.

Millicent was delighted. "Oh, that's wonderful! Just think, Daphne, once she's passed her test, she'll be able to use James's car. It's such a waste having it sitting in the garage doing nothing."

Daphne made no comment. Instead, she began putting on her gloves with an air of detached indifference. "Are you ready, Millie?" she asked with a tight smile. "We mustn't keep Sylvie waiting."

Millicent shrugged, gave Laura a quick peck on the cheek and a cheery wave good bye.

Laura breathed a sigh of relief.

There were days, she knew, where nothing would go right, no matter how much you might will it to be otherwise. Saturday proved such a day. Having resolved to find Mr Moray in the hope that casual conversation might lead to more pressing topics, there was no sign of him around the

Lodge. The vegetable patch showed signs of activity and the window in the garden store had been cleared of cobwebs, but the door was locked. Instinctively, she knew that if she wandered down through Meeston Woods to Nether Meeston Lane, he would not be at home. She went down anyway, and, pretending she was walking to The Cross as she so often did, noticed the lack of smoke from his chimney, and the general air of stillness that empty houses have.

Disheartened, she continued on her way, resolving to extend her walk up Smallcross Lane to Wilfrid's Meadow, hoping something of interest would lift her spirits. But the early promise of the day had gone, and the sun had slipped into a milky haze leaving a chill breeze. Wilfrid's Meadow was deserted, the small birds seeking shelter in surrounding hedges, and the rooks already in their lofty perches up behind the Vicarage. And so, without anything of note to mark her expedition, she reached Vicarage Lane and the short walk back to the Lodge.

At the side-gate to the church yard, she paused, and on impulse went through, climbing the steps and making her way to her father's grave. It was still unmarked, waiting for the earth to settle, and its very anonymity seemed suddenly more poignant, emphasising, so it seemed to her, his lack of true identity. His headstone, when finally erected, would record the passing of someone who had never been, and she alone would know, and could never speak of it.

As she turned to leave, Reverend Talbot appeared at the end of the path from the church, taking a short-cut to The Vicarage.

"Laura!" he said with a ready smile as he reached her. "How are you? We don't see much of you at church these days."

"No," she said, searching for the right words to tell him why without offending, and ultimately failing.

He studied her closely. "A crisis of faith, perhaps?" he suggested tentatively.

She nodded.

"Quite understandable," he said. "It happens sometimes when we lose someone we love. But, as they say, 'The Lord moves in mysterious ways'. His Love never dies." He paused, apparently waiting for her to respond, and finding her silent, recognised the need for a tactical retreat. "Your father was a fine man," he said, addressing his words to the disturbed ground at their feet. "A fine man." He smiled nervously. "Well – I'll leave you to your thoughts. Remember – you are always welcome at St Wilfrid's." He bustled away without looking back.

She went home to an empty house, and wondered where John Rufford was that afternoon – and who he was with.

Chapter Thirty-Three

She had woken up that Sunday morning feeling more positive. Without any doubt, she assured herself, she would find Mr Moray at home that afternoon. And so he was, much to her satisfaction: wood smoke billowed from his chimney, drifting on the breeze as she stood outside his gate.

Her resolve to face him had over-ridden caution. She had hurried through the woods, heedless of the softened ground, almost giddy with a heightened sense of purpose that had left her breathless, and a little flushed. When she knocked at his door, she had no idea how she would proceed, and the photograph, carefully stowed inside a coat pocket, suddenly became an object of potential embarrassment.

It seemed a small age before he answered. He was dressed casually in a pair of nut-brown cords with a thick plaid shirt open at the neck, the sleeves turned back at the cuffs, and his usually tousled hair almost tidy. He was holding, clutched to his chest, an open book he had evidently been reading, and the sound of classical piano music wafted out from behind him into the cool afternoon air. He was evidently surprised to find her on his doorstep. "Miss Driscoll?" he said, frowning slightly.

"I wondered if you could spare me a few minutes," she began.

"Has something happened? – at the Lodge?" he asked, evidently expecting to deal with a problem that demanded his attention.

"No – no, there's nothing wrong."

Having cleared this from his mind, he remained standing in the doorway, waiting for an explanation for her visit. Behind him, the music continued playing, the delicate, tinkling notes reminiscent of water trickling over mossy stones into little pools.

"Can I come in?" she asked in the absence of an invitation. "I'll leave my shoes in the porch, if you like. I came through the woods. They're a bit muddy."

He was clearly not at ease with the notion of offering her hospitality, and then, seeing she had no intention of leaving, gave way with as much grace as he could muster. "They'll be fine there," he said, and stepped back to let her through as she slipped out of her shoes, leaving them next to the wood under the porch seat, padding into his living room in her thick woollen socks.

He closed the door behind her. The piano music swirled around them in the warmth of the small white-washed room with its low ceiling and bright log fire. The air was heavy with the scent of wood smoke and resin.

In the ten years she had known him, she had never once stepped across his threshold, and now she had, she was surprised by what she found. John Rufford had been right: Robert Moray was more than he claimed to be – a humble farmhand-gardener. All around her was the proof: the thick rugs on the flagged floor; cottage-style furniture; the beautiful original watercolour of a rural scene above the mantelpiece; the modern radiogram; the astonishing number of impressive-looking books on the shelves in the inglenooks. And everywhere – on the window sill and side-tables, elegantly framed photographs of individuals and groups were reminders of other people in his life.

She was conscious he was watching her evaluate his home. "What a lovely room," she said, hearing herself sound horribly condescending.

"I'm glad you like it," he commented, as if whether she liked it or not was a matter of supreme indifference to him, and he went over to the radiogram to switch off the music.

"Oh – please don't turn it off on my account," she begged.

But he switched it off anyway and put his book face down over the arm of the chair he had occupied before she came. "It doesn't matter," he said, stuffing his hands into his trouser pockets and turning to face her with his usual implacable gaze. There was a strained silence.

"I'm sorry to turn up just like this," she began, wishing he would stop making her feel like a naughty child. The room was hot, and she was already over-heated from her walk. She scrambled out of her coat, feeling light-headed. "Can I sit down?" she asked, clutching the coat awkwardly, and without waiting to be invited, sat in the nearest chair.

"You could have telephoned," he said, indicating the existence of the handset on the table by the door with a slight nod in its direction.

"Oh – I didn't know you had one."

"Meeston 588," he said bluntly. "It would have saved you a journey."

"Well – no – not really. I needed to see you."

He shifted his position, removing his hands from his pockets and folding his arms instead. "You do realise," he said, emphasising the point, "that if anyone has seen you come here, your reputation is now in shreds?"

"Oh," she said lamely, dimly aware this had never entered her head. "I'm sorry, I never meant to cause embarrassment –"

"I don't think it's me that's likely to be embarrassed," he observed dryly. "I'm fairly immune to embarrassment now. But I wouldn't want you becoming the subject of idle gossip in the Meeston Arms."

"Surely not – you work at the Lodge!"

He shrugged, dismissing the topic, and bent down to tend the fire. "Anyway," he said, placing a fresh log in the grate, "You should be out with your gentleman friend this afternoon, not wasting your time here with me."

His observation seemed remarkably impertinent, and reduced her to an irritable silence.

He straightened and refolded his arms, surveying her critically. "John, was it?" he asked.

"Mr Moray, John and I aren't courting, I thought I'd made that clear. I'm not even sure I'll ever see him again."

He frowned. "You've broken up?"

"Not exactly," she hedged, trying to remain civilised under his persistent interrogation. "We never intended to get serious."

He was still frowning. "Well I have to say you both looked pretty serious to me."

This conversation had to stop. She bridled. "Mr Moray," she said curtly, "As you once said to me – this is none of your damned business!"

He cocked his head slightly at her outburst and considered his reply. "It may or may not be my business, Miss Driscoll, but I know what I saw."

"John Rufford is not the marrying kind, Mr Moray. He made that very plain right from the start – and I was perfectly happy with that arrangement. Now please – I really don't want to talk about him." She was angry now, not just with him, but with herself. She had blundered into his afternoon, and everything had gone horribly wrong. She had certainly never expected to be interrogated about John Rufford, and had the uncomfortable feeling she may have unwittingly given the casual onlooker the impression of being more emotionally involved than she intended – or believed herself to be. Millicent had implied as much only the day before. It was all very irritating. How could she proceed from this point on the matter of The Douglas Connection? The atmosphere between them was now much too fraught to make any conversation amicable. "I think I'd better go," she said, gathering up her coat in something of a rush, determined to remove herself as soon as possible from this predicament. "This is obviously not a good time."

"I'm sorry," he said, genuinely contrite. "I didn't mean to offend. I spoke as I saw – and if I was wrong, please forgive me. What was it you wanted to see me about?" And he reached out and took hold of the coat, detaining her. "Was it about your father? – his second letter?"

She turned, and looked into his solemn face. The resemblance to the image in the photograph was quite astonishing. She hesitated.

"Please – won't you sit down," he said, forcing a smile. "Let's start again." And releasing the coat from his grasp, promptly returned to his chair by the fire, waiting for her to do the same. "Was there something in his letter?" he prompted.

Reluctantly, she returned to her seat, still clutching her coat. "Yes – and no," she said, trying to find the right words. "There was something else – a box with photographs and other bits and pieces."

He waited for her to continue.

In the end, she simply blurted out her presumption, raw and uncensored. 'Mr Moray – I think we might be related after all.'

He sat back in his chair and considered her revelation. There was a long pause before he answered. "I know," he said finally, his expression not altering one single jot.

"You know! You said we weren't!"

"I didn't think we were," he said simply. "I was wrong. Our grandmothers were cousins."

"When did you find out?"

"Over Christmas."

"Why didn't you tell me?"

"I wasn't sure I should. How did you guess?"

She retrieved the photograph from her coat pocket and passed it to him. "I thought I saw a likeness," she said, pointing at the young man on the left. "Here – he's just like you. Was I right?"

He studied the photograph for a moment, then passed it back. "No one's mentioned it before."

"It's unmistakable."

He got up, taking down from one of the bookshelves a large brown leather volume: an old-fashioned photograph album with a gold silk cord around the spine and a tassel hanging from it. "I'd better show you this," he said, placing it on her lap. "My mother gave it to me at Christmas. It belonged to my grandmother."

She opened the thick, richly-tooled cover. Inside, on the flyleaf, written with great care, was a family tree, the work of a single hand. Opposite, someone had affixed an exact copy of the photograph Laura had found in the little tin box.

She felt strangely light-headed.

He leaned forward, pointing to the husband and wife in the photograph. "This is Gilbert Douglas and his wife, Janet Fairburn," he said. "The young men behind them are their three sons – William – my great-grandfather, Malcolm and Alexander." He picked out each of them in turn. "It was taken in 1865."

She looked up at him. "Alexander was my great-grandfather," she said.

"He was the youngest. He married Elizabeth Greive

five years after this picture was taken. Their youngest child was your grandmother, Anne Douglas. She was born in Coldingham." He pointed to her name on the page at the end of a row of seven children. Two of the other children's marriages had been recorded, but not Anne's.

Anne. Anne implied someone who was valued. When did Anne become Annie – diminutive Annie? – when she left home and became a laundress? – or when Jack Driscoll began courting her?

"This is my side of the family," he was saying, running his finger down the other side of the page following the line from William and his wife, Isabella, and ignoring several of their offspring. "Their eldest daughter was Margaret, my grandmother. She married Donald Gillmuir, a local doctor in Coldstream in 1887. They had two surviving children – Grace, my mother, born in 1889 and Moira, my aunt."

There were so many other names and dates on the page, the image blurred. Here was a family tree to rival the Harrimans, if ever there was, and her father had never known of its existence. She wished he had. "What does that make us?" she asked, trying to fathom their relationship. "Third cousins?"

"I've no idea," he said with a faint smile, and made no attempt to guess at it.

"Can I look through the rest?" she asked, turning a page, curious to see more – if more there was to see that might open other doors into the past.

"If you like."

Margaret had taken great care over her album. There

were brief notes to every print in her meticulous hand: names and dates matching images of newly-weds, parents with babes in arms – then later on, as larger family groups; children in twos and threes growing up over the years, becoming newly-weds and parents in their turn. And with every image, on every page, it became clear William's family had prospered. Of Alexander's kin, beyond their names and dates of birth, set out so neatly on the flysheet, there was nothing – not a single photograph. At some point in the past, the family ties – The Douglas Connection – had snapped.

He had been watching her silently, knowing perhaps what she would eventually ask.

"What happened?"

He feigned ignorance, frowning slightly.

"Why did our grandmothers have such different lives?"

She saw him wince slightly.

"I know Annie was a humble laundress when she married, Mr Moray, and I can see there aren't any laundresses in your family, are there?" She swept a hand across the pages of the album with images of well-dressed women in elegant taffeta dresses and braid trimmings; men in morning suits and tweeds.

He leaned against the mantelpiece, one foot on the fender, and looked awkward. "No, there aren't."

She turned back to the single photograph they had in common. "So what happened after this was taken?

"What usually happens," he said. "Families break up, move apart."

"A family quarrel?"

"Not that I know of. It was just circumstances. Gilbert was a tenant farmer in The Merse. I don't suppose that means much to you."

"No, I'm afraid it doesn't."

"The Merse is just north of The Border," he explained. "The best farming country in Berwickshire – maybe the whole of Scotland."

"He looks very prosperous for a tenant."

"Merse tenants weren't subsistence farmers," he was keen to point out. "They were pretty well off by the standards of the time."

"How did that happen?"

"A combination of forward thinking lairds who wanted tenants who'd use the latest agricultural methods, and men who knew how to get the best from their acreage. Merse farms were hundreds of acres – they weren't small. They needed a good number of agricultural labourers to work them."

"So Gilbert was an employer?"

He nodded.

"Did the tenancy pass from father to son?"

"Not always. When Gilbert died, William was lucky. He was given the tenancy and carried on the farm."

"What about Malcolm and Alexander?"

"Malcolm had already emigrated and Alexander seems to have left shortly after."

"Why would he do that?"

He shrugged slightly. "I don't know. Maybe he just wanted to be his own man."

"He was a ploughman – according to Annie's marriage record. It doesn't sound like skilled work."

There was trace of a smile. "You'd be surprised," he said. "A well-ploughed field could make the difference between food on the table and hunger – or worse – on smaller farms. Alexander would be a skilled ploughman if he'd been working on The Merse. He'd hire himself out to the highest bidder every year."

She turned back to the family tree: Elizabeth and her seven children. "But what about his family?"

Another smile, this time more forced. "They would go with him," he explained. "They were part of the hiring. The wife, sons, daughters. Everyone worked on the farm. In return they got a home and a percentage of the crops they raised."

Laura thought of the cold winds from the North Sea in winter; the hard frosts; and heavy snows; of bent backs and frozen hands and feet. "It must have been a hard life," she said. "Perhaps being a laundress was a better option?"

"She'd be working indoors – and settled. No more travelling." He bent down and fed another log onto the fire.

"Is there anything else you know – about my grand-mother?" she asked, "– that you haven't told me?"

He prodded the fire, repositioning the log, seemingly in no hurry to say whether he did or not, his thoughts wrapped up in themselves. His silence spoke volumes. If he knew only part of what her father had revealed, he might not feel free to say so.

"I have my father's birth certificate," she offered, coaxing him. "Does that help?"

"Then you know what I've been told," he said simply, his concentration still fixed on the hearth. "Which is why I never spoke of it before. I didn't want to cause embarrassment."

"Thank you for being so considerate."

He acknowledged her thanks with a brief nod and took the album from her, returning it to the space in the bookshelf.

Neither of them spoke for a while: he, seemingly unwilling to talk further; Laura, because she needed time to think. So they sat in silence listening to the crackle of the flames, and let the time drift by. Outside, the afternoon faded into dusk.

She stirred herself. "It's getting dark. I'd better go. I want to walk back through the woods."

"I'll go with you," he offered, getting to his feet.

"No – I've taken enough of your time already – but thank for the offer."

"I'll walk you back," he insisted, retrieving her shoes from the porch to warm them by the fire. "Unless you'd prefer I didn't – for obvious reasons," he added, handing them to her once they had warmed.

She slipped them on, considering her options. "Which is worse, do you suppose? – someone seeing me come out of here alone? – or coming out with you?"

"They're both equally damning," he said solemnly.

She shrugged. "Then you may as well walk me home."

It was a strange progress: he, a few paces behind her all the way, following Indian-style, like a shadow, until the end of the path came into view by Meeston Lodge. It was almost dark now, and the blue-white glow of the street lamp outside The Village Shop silhouetted the lower branches of the beeches fronting Meeston Road.

He called to her, softly. "I think I can safely leave you here, Miss Driscoll," he said.

She turned, surprised at his formality. "Won't you call me Laura from now on?"

"No," he said. "You know I can't do that – just as you can never call me Robert. No one must ever know that we're related. It would raise too many questions."

He was right, of course. She should have recognised the need for silence. But the secret jarred: another falsehood to be hidden; another lie to be sustained. There were too many in her care already, and she wished them gone.

"You do understand, don't you?" he was saying.

"Yes – of course. You're quite right. Good night then, Mr Moray."

"Good night," he said, and she stood and watched him turn and walk into the darkness.

CHAPTER THIRTY-FOUR

It was, of course, an anticlimax: the satisfaction of being right, followed by – what? A dull recognition that nothing was resolved – not really. Exhilaration had blinded her to what might come afterwards: the emptiness; the confusion. What had she done? Were there not enough shadows in her life? – an uncle she could not admit existed? – an aunt whose short life had been clouded by abuse? – a father, so weighed down by guilt, he had ensured his shame outlived him? – and a lover, who may, or may not feel some genuine attachment to her, despite his past? Now, into this heady mix, of her own free will, she had added Robert Moray, a man with troubles of his own and evidently no wish to complicate his life still further. What had she been thinking of? If she had not pressed him, he would have held his peace because he was discreet, and saw no necessity in muddying pools best left undisturbed. But she, filled with too much certainty of purpose, wanted to know more. Well, now she did, and little good it did to know it. She had learnt to her cost that knowledge of the truth was just that – knowledge; it led nowhere; it hemmed her in and cut her off at the same time, so she must make the best of it – move forward and not dwell upon the past. Inaction would solve nothing. There must be no more putting off; no more prevarication. She must 'push off…and smite the sounding furrows', as she had known she must back in the darkening days of November.

The telephone call to Wadham's Driving School in Lingford was, at least, a start, and gave her the satisfaction of having something tangible to demonstrate her serious intent. Millicent, no doubt, would be pleased at such a show of grit.

Mr Gittings however, was very sorry to learn she wanted to resign, but understood why it was she felt she must.

Laura knew she would miss the comfortable rhythms of the office and the faces she had come to know. But it was necessary. Her inheritance would let her choose a new path, and she needed to be free of any hindrance that might prevent her striking out afresh, although she was only too aware of seeming feckless in abandoning employment without a clear idea in view. But in the meantime, she was able to say that she was considering enrolling at an art college, with the possibility of training as a teacher – which was true, except, as yet, she had no idea if this were possible. It was a plan of sorts therefore, in what was otherwise a quagmire of muddle-headedness.

Feeling positive was one thing, but it could not hide her lack of willingness to face a more unwelcome task – the unfinished business of her uncle, and the letter she must write to him. She had delayed long enough. But beneath her reticence lay a quiet dread, and she had no idea why.

Steeling herself to the task, she slit open the envelope. Inside, she found a solitary sheet of white paper folded in two. At the top, it was dated 'September 1st, 1962', from an address unknown to her – '17 Heddon Road, Collingsby Bay, Northumberland.' There was no telephone number, and below were three short paragraphs.

'Dear James', it began.

'Got your letter yesterday and I'm sorry to hear you're not so well just now. I'm not doing too badly – just a touch of bronchitis at present.

'I've been to the Bank and they say they'll tell me when the money's in. Yes – it'll make things a bit easier for me, so thanks for that.

'Sorry you're not able to come and see me like you hoped.

'Best wishes anyway –

'from

'Andrew'

A strange letter: opaque. She could make nothing of it beyond the acceptance of the gift of money. It was a riddle, strangely formal with its use of proper names – James and Andrew – not Jamie and Andy – or even nicknames that might have stemmed from childhood. Once, when she read it, she thought she heard resentment in his tone. The next time, self-pity. After that, a terrible sadness that bordered on despair. Sometimes, it was all three.

How to respond? Should she keep things simple? – just brief details of her father's death, perhaps? It seemed too brutal. Here was a man who had been denied, but once loved as a brother. Could she somehow make amends? But how, when she too must deny him? Would this make matters worse? Most likely, yes. But she felt compelled to show some interest in him – and in Jean, about whom she knew so little. Perhaps if she suggested they should meet – in Collingsby … She reached for her notebook.

She began, knowing she would spend the remainder of the evening pondering the right words, the best turn of phrase, the right tone to be adopted, and the finished piece would demand more than a single draft.

Some considerable time later, and after several false starts, she was able to satisfy herself at last.

'Dear Uncle Andrew' – she read.

'I've only recently come into the possession of some of my father's papers, as well as your letter to him of September last and the little box you sent him. I'm sorry to tell you Daddy died quite suddenly not long afterwards, on November 12th, from heart failure. It was a great shock to us all.

'He left me details of his past in a personal letter, and until then, I'd no knowledge of either yourself or Auntie Jean. I'm sorry he felt it necessary to be so secretive, particularly as he has asked me never to divulge any of his family history to my mother, and I know this will continue to distress you. Consequently, I feel a little embarrassed about asking you a favour. Would it be possible for us to meet sometime? I'll be free to travel to Northumberland after March 22nd if you would like to suggest a time and place. Can I suggest you write to me c/o my father's previous business address in Lingford, and I'll arrange to collect your letter there?

'I realise you may not be able to reply immediately if this is delivered while you're at sea.'

It took her some time to decide how to phrase her leave-taking. In the end, she opted for 'With kind regards' as the most appropriate under the circumstances, and signed herself simply 'Laura Driscoll'.

She sealed the envelope with a sense of melodrama she could not explain; nor could she account for her hesitancy when posting it.

CHAPTER THIRTY-FIVE

Winter was not yet done: in the last week of February, clear skies at night left the mornings with a dusting of frost outlining the laurels, and the gravel frozen on the drive.

Wadham's Driving School instructor, a Mr Fielding, was a robust, middle-aged gentleman, with a thin, greying moustache, and a manner reminiscent of how she imagined a regimental sergeant major would respond to rookies. And it was only a few minutes into her second lesson that she discovered his toleration of lame excuses was minimal. "If you want to succeed, Miss Driscoll," he had said crisply. "You will have to concentrate."

Now the evenings were lighter, she had set herself a punishing timetable of three lessons a week – on Mondays, Wednesdays and Fridays – with the intention of taking her driving test as soon as possible. Mr Fielding, while acknowledging her commitment, emphasised learning to drive required more than just the ability to handle a car and know the Highway Code – although these were both vital elements – she had to be both competent as well as confident. He implied, although he did not actually say as much, that enthusiasm alone did not always equate to ability, and, as a result, after the first week, Laura seriously began to question whether her decision to subject herself to his authoritarian regime so frequently was quite such a good idea. But it kept her busy – and busy was what she most wanted to be while she waited for the rest of her life to begin: waiting for probate to be granted – now set for March 12th, according to Mr Parr; her time at Weaversham Bank to come to an end a week later; and the possibility her uncle might agree to meet sometime after that.

But when she was not busy, time hung heavy on her hands, and her thoughts wandered. At the weekend, when the house was quiet, she became restless, and no matter how hard she tied to concentrate, pouring over the driving manual which guaranteed success – which Millicent had kindly bought her together with a set of 'L' plates – was not enough.

She roamed from room to room in solitude, without hindrance or question, seeing the place as if for the first time. It was a queer feeling that cast a shadow, and made her see the Lodge in a new light as a sad and lonely house. Who lived here? – she asked herself. There were no photographs of family members on desk tops or window sills; no bookshelves crammed to overflowing with favourite volumes, except the small collection in her father's study; no family record collection to fill the house with music; no paintings of any merit hung on any walls. There was nothing of significance. Meeston Lodge was a museum of outdated magazines and daily papers; indifferent china ornaments; and faded prints of landscapes by unknown artists in dark-brown frames. There was no visible evidence of who might live there beyond those few sketches her father had drawn of his family many years ago, then put away, out of sight.

She was chilled by her discovery, remembering the photographic images of others: John Rufford's portrait, kept safely in the bottom drawer with his copy of the Rubaiyat; Millicent and Sylvia's albums they had shown her one Sunday afternoon of the Harriman sisters as bright young things; the curling prints from Andrew in the tin box with historical significance; and Robert Moray's living room, filled with reminders of those he cherished most. She had nothing to hold on to. She had no image of her father. Already, his face, so long taken for granted, was fading from her memory. In a year, she wondered, would she still remember how he looked beyond a vague impression?

There was hope – a single wedding photograph, kept on the chest of drawers in her parents' room, an image of its time: her father in his double-breasted, not very well-fitting suit; her mother, slim-waisted and neat ankled, her Marcel-wave hair just visible beneath the voluminous folds of her veil; two people looking into the camera with slightly strained expressions, as if they had been left standing too long in the cold on the church steps before the picture had been taken. But when Laura ventured into the room, it was missing, and searching through the drawers, like a thief, careful not to raise suspicions of intrusion, she could find no trace of it. It had been discarded. Her mother had put her father – and her marriage to him – in their place – wherever that might be: out of sight and out of mind.

She went downstairs into the hall and telephoned Julius Parr. He was her last resort.

He was his usual cheery self, careful, however, not to engage in casual chit-chat that might lead to the subject of his sister – or Oliver.

"Jules," she said. "Do you remember taking photos at my twenty-first? You don't still have them, do you?"

He was obviously puzzled. "Haven't you got them?" he asked.

"I never saw them."

"I think I gave them to your mother."

"Oh – I didn't know."

"Look, don't worry, I've got the negatives somewhere. Lord knows where – but I'll find them. It's not urgent, is it?"

"No – I just wondered if I could see them."

"I'll dig them out for you. Bring them round one evening, if you like."

"Yes, please – if you don't mind."

"Not at all. Sorry – must go. Got a party lined up later. Oh – hang on." She heard the doorbell ring and muffled voices in the hall. "With you in a tick, John," he said, talking over his shoulder, and the unmistakable tones of John Rufford in the background acknowledged him.

"Jules," she said, trying to detain him.

"Sorry, Laura – guests arriving. I'll be in touch." And the line went dead.

She replaced the receiver aware she was light-headed simply from hearing his voice, and disconcerted, wandered out onto the front porch into the night. It was cold. March had crept in like a lamb seeking warmth. She hugged her cardigan closer, listening to the silence, and stepped down onto the gravel to look up into the star-studded sky. It was perfect, stunningly perfect, as it had been that night at Sparston Hall with John's arm around her waist.

She shivered. Her life was on the brink of change and she had no real sense of what this meant, or what it might bring. She turned and went inside, knowing only one thing was certain – she was missing John, his potent physicality and everything that went with it – and it hurt. Would it ever stop hurting?

Chapter Thirty-Six

That night she dreamt of John. He had been making love to her, passionately and unrestrained as always. When she woke, the memory was so vivid, so intense, her expectations were she would find him there, lying beside her, replete and warm, until, on opening her eyes, the faint glimmer of dawn revealed she was alone in the familiar surroundings of her room, not his, and very much without him.

The dream remained, illuminated by imagination and desire. She was breathless, hot, burning for him, and only too aware that no amount of self-induced sensation would fill the lasting void his absence left inside.

She rolled over, staring at the wall. This febrile state undid all her hard-fought resolutions, reducing them to little more than smouldering ruins. She had made a promise to herself the night they parted – she would recognise their time was over; that she would set him free to look elsewhere because she must, despite his willingness to wait; that she would learn to bear the loss of passion in his arms, as Millicent had learned to bear the loss of Giles. And that would be that. Except that now, after three short weeks, she could not hide the truth: his voice alone had been enough to undermine her good intentions. She still yearned for his touch.

It will take time, she told herself, getting out of bed and dressing quickly to prevent any further longing for what was patently not there.

Downstairs, she could hear Gwen talking to her mother, and found them both busy in the kitchen, the inviting smell of rich broth escaping through the open door. By the range, Gwen was ladling brimming scoops into large white enamel canisters under Daphne's supervision, while Harry, in his Sunday best to play the organ later, hovered by the door, ready to be useful.

Gwen beamed. "'Morning, Laura," she said, fastening a lid on one of the canisters. "Coming to the Lenten Lunch then?"

Laura caught her mother's gaze: hard, like flint. She shook her head.

"Oh, that's a shame," Gwen went on, determined to sound cheerful. "We don't see much of you these days at church."

"No," Laura said, keeping things as simple as she could.

"Laura has far more important things to do, haven't you?" Daphne said with a taut smile, her attention shifting immediately to Gwen. "Shall I take one of these?" She fingered the handle of one of the canisters gingerly with an elegantly gloved hand, but made no attempt to lift it.

"Oh no, Mrs Driscoll – Harry can manage them, can't you, Harry?"

Harry, aware the atmosphere around him was turning chilly, stepped forward quickly and took the canisters, one in each hand. "I'll be off then," he said, looking around nervously, and took his leave a little hurriedly.

Daphne adjusted her leather gloves. "I'll see you later, Gwen," she said briskly, turning to go. "I need to have a word with Dorothy about the tablecloths."

"Right you are then, Mrs Driscoll. Do you want me to bring the table decorations?"

Daphne paused at the door. "Oh – yes, if you wouldn't mind."

Gwen waited until the door was closed, then rolled her eyes. "Robert brought up some pussy willow and hazel catkins, yesterday – like he does every year for the church. They look ever so pretty on the tables with the daffodils. Brighten things up a treat. Of course he would pick the one time your mother was in the kitchen. You could have cut the atmosphere with a knife." She began stacking the pots and pans ready for washing later. "Who would have thought it this time last year that he and Susan Holbrook would have split up?" she went on, pondering the twists of fate. "Elsie says he doesn't go anywhere near the school now, of course. Can't blame him. He'll be glad when she's gone by Easter, I reckon. Still, as I was saying to Harry only the other day, life goes on." She paused, inspecting one of the pans. "There's some broth over, if you'd like it for your lunch. It'd be a pity to waste it."

"Thank you – that would be nice."

"I'll put it in the smaller pan then. You can heat it later." She finished tidying things into an orderly pile while Laura made a pot of tea, and then found it necessary to sit down with her for a little chat. "We do miss you, you know, at the Church," she said, patting Laura's hand consolingly. "There's plenty of folk to keep you company, if that's what you need. You do seem a bit –," she struggled to find the right words, " – on your own these days."

Laura smiled, but felt disinclined to talk.

Gwen tried another tack. "Well, I know it's not for me to say whether you should come or not. You have to do what's right for you. But you know, you're always welcome." She waited, expecting an answer, and seeing none forthcoming, added brightly, "Elsie says you're learning to drive."

Laura nodded.

"Robert says the next thing we'll know, you'll be packing up and leaving Meeston – heading for the bright lights. And why not? – I said. Lots of girls getting their own places these days." To which, Laura nodded again. "Well, must be off or I'll be late for service. Oh – mustn't forget Robert's decorations. I left them at the back door." And finally, to Laura's relief, she bustled off and the back door closed behind her.

She ate her solitary lunch, relishing the peace and quiet that demanded no explanations as to her singular state of mind. She wanted space to understand why this dream, unlike others which vanished like snowflakes in summer when she woke, had seared itself into her brain and left its mark. It did not take much to realise erasing it was difficult because, if she were honest with herself, there was pleasure in the memories it had stirred. It was not good enough. She must pull herself together.

But determination was not enough. Action was required. She left the kitchen spotless, the pots and pans all washed and put away, the utensils hung up on hooks where they belonged, the towels left neatly drying by the range, so that Gwen should not spend her Sunday afternoon toiling at the sink while Daphne was whisked away to Dyers Green and an unlikely Lenten tea with Cynthia of ham sandwiches, fruit cake and buttered scones.

The afternoon lay ahead, empty. Listless, and with no great aim in mind, she put on her old duffel coat and wandered into the garden. The cold, clear morning had been blown away by a breeze from the west, bringing with it milder air and the promise of much warmer days to come. The sky was china blue, with scattered smoke-grey clumps of cumuli that gathered and dispersed with equal speed in unexpected showers.

Beyond the rhododendrons, the vegetable patch was glistening with rain in a sudden burst of sun. The ridge tops of the neatly marked-out rows where potatoes had been planted, were etched in light. A rainbow arced across the sky above the woods and the wind began to rise, bringing on its back the first fine hint of rain.

She retreated to the garden store for shelter, sitting on the stool listening to the raindrops pitter-patter on the roof. Around her, the familiar smells of creosote and peat mingled with the metallic tang of well-oiled tools. She felt safe. The lisping sound of rain was comforting. She leaned against the workbench and rested her head on her arms. Outside, somewhere from its perch close by, despite the sudden shower, a robin was determined to be cheerful. She closed her eyes and listened to its song.

She had dozed and woke with a start to the sound of her name.

She stirred, confused, blinking against the light. Robert Moray was standing silhouetted in the doorway.

He came in, his hair wet and stranded falling on his brow, the chestnut turned to almost black, and the shoulders of his work coat drenched.

Only half-awake, she straightened. Her back ached, and there were pins and needles running down her arms. "I'm sorry," she said, not entirely sure why she felt it necessary to say she was. "Am I in your way?"

"No, you're fine. I was just checking Alan had locked up after he'd finished this morning – and I saw the door was open. Didn't want to find we'd got a tramp making himself at home here." He smiled briefly, then paused. "Is there something wrong?" he asked, studying her closely.

"No – nothing," she said, ill-prepared to explain what it was she truly felt.

He stood, leaning against the far edge of the workbench, and folded his arms. His scrutiny remained undiminished. "You know," he began, " – and I can say this now only because you're kin – you're a terrible liar. No one sits in a garden shed with their head in their hands if there's nothing wrong. I should know – I've done it myself – as you well remember."

Yes, she could remember – the day she had first asked him what he knew about her father. He had been distraught, trying to have a civilised conversation with her while his world fell apart around him.

"I know you told me that it's none of my business," he was saying, "- and I'm sure you're right – but is this anything to do with ..." He floundered, searching for the right form of words that would not cause offence.

"John Rufford?" she prompted him, not caring now whether her love-life was his business or not. As he said, he was her kin after all; he could afford to be concerned.

"Well – is it?" he persisted.

She shrugged off the problem. "I miss him, that's all."

Her answer puzzled him. "Then for heaven's sake, girl, what's stopping you doing something about it?"

She shifted on the stool and stared out of the window at the rain running helter-skelter down the pane. What *was* stopping her? Obstinacy? Pride? Shame? No – none of those things. Just herself. "My doubts," she said finally, looking up into his intensely serious face. "His life is permanently sunny. No shadows lurking in the corners. Nothing to cloud his view of the world. But life isn't like that, is it? It's not permanently sunny."

"No," he said quietly, studying the planks on the floor for a moment. "No, that's true."

"There are things I can't share with him now – you know what they are. He'd want to brush them aside – make light of them. I can't do that."

"Sometimes, you have to let go of the past for the sake of the future."

"Is that what you tried to do?" she asked. "Forget the past?"

He cocked his head to one side slightly. "With Susan?" he asked.

She hesitated. Susan was really no more her business than John was his.

"You don't have to worry," he said with a wan smile. "I can say her name now without going weak at the knees." He was thoughtful for a while, studying his mud-spattered boots. "Yes, I wanted to put the past behind me. I thought I had – I know I tried. Maybe I didn't try hard enough – or I tried too hard. Maybe she couldn't believe me when I said I had." He looked up suddenly. "But I've learnt something – you can't make someone love you just because you want them to."

It was an uncomfortable moment. She sensed his meaning: he was referring not to himself and Susan, but to herself and John. "No, you can't," she said warily.

He smiled awkwardly. "He does love you, doesn't he?" he asked straight out.

"He says he does."

"You don't believe him?"

"No – not really."

"Why's that?"

"Because of what he told me – at the start."

"Love can change a man."

"Can it? Why are you so sure?"

"I saw the way he looked at you."

"That's just John," she said, dismissing him as best she could. "It's what he does – makes a girl feel special for a while – then moves on. It's what he's always done. I understood that. I asked for nothing more."

"Do you love him?" he asked bluntly.

She flinched, struggling to be honest in her answer. "I don't know," she said finally. "I miss his company – his laughter – the things we did – his passion..." She stopped herself, feeling heat rising into her cheeks.

He looked away to spare her blushes.

She sat, listening to her heart thudding; to the deep urgency the very thought of him had conjured up; the desire for his touch; his tenderness; his body against hers. He fed the fire in her that he had lit. He always would. It was unquenchable. But was it love? No, she decided, it was not. She wanted him with every fibre of her body – but that was something different. That was lust.

Robert was silent, expressionless, waiting, anxious perhaps he may have strayed beyond the bounds of kinship. "I shouldn't have asked," he said at last, casting a quick glance in her direction.

"It doesn't matter," she said, rising from the stool and deciding she should leave. "I'm not offended – really. I'm glad you did. You made me think – more clearly."

He nodded, but said nothing, stepping aside to let her pass.

The rain had stopped. She walked out into the brilliance of a late afternoon sun, accepting there were some things in life that could never be resolved. Her feelings for John Rufford would be one of them.

CHAPTER THIRTY-SEVEN

Mr Fielding's bright red Mini, parked outside the Bank with 'Wadham's School of Motoring' emblazoned on its roof, was becoming a regular feature on the Weaversham High Street at five-thirty on Mondays, Wednesdays and Fridays.

Betty Bailey had taken to standing tip-toe, craning her neck above the obscure glass in the front window, just to see if he had arrived. It was her opinion Laura was very daring in deciding to take lessons. "I'm sure I'd never get the hang of it," she kept insisting, although from her questions, she clearly had more than a passing interest in being very daring herself – although perhaps not with Mr Fielding.

Laura had begun to find him less intimidating – just very definite about his expectations – and they were beginning to rub along quite well most of the time.

Settling into the driving seat that Wednesday evening, she was feeling particularly positive about her progress. He had been almost complimentary two days before. In a perfectly calm state of mind, she set about completing the necessary rituals expected of her. It was then, when she least expected it, as she adjusted the interior mirror, she caught a glimpse of what she thought was the unmistakable racing green of a Roadster parked further down the road. In the time it took for this to register, the No.51 bus to Redbridge drew up behind her, blocking her view, and when it pulled away several minutes later, there was no sign of any green car – of any description. It seemed it was a figment of her imagination. But the damage had been done. Her concentration was quite gone.

"When you're ready, Miss Driscoll," Mr Fielding was saying.

It was almost inevitable she would stall the engine, which she promptly did, much to her vexation.

Mr Fielding was not impressed. "Perhaps we should start again," he said dryly. And though he made no further comment, Laura felt his censure radiating from him for the remainder of the lesson. Consequently, her performance was decidedly below par, and she was relieved to be let off lightly by his brief comment that it had perhaps been a difficult day at the office.

The incident upset her. She was cross she was apparently still so besotted as to imagine John had driven over from Lingford to see her: he could never have travelled to Weaversham in so short a time. At least, not as a matter of course. Nonetheless, she was relieved when Mr Fielding deferred their Friday lesson by half-an-hour, and there was no sign of either John or his MG Roadster at six o'clock.

Mr Fielding earned her unspoken thanks for not mentioning her previous poor performance, but expected perfection in return. He took her on unknown roads outside the town before suggesting she drive home, then invited her to execute a three-point turn in the driveway at the Lodge, which she did to his satisfaction, and to her relief. She turned off the engine feeling a distinct sense of achievement.

"Well, Miss Driscoll," he said, taking out his pocket diary and flicking through the pages, "if you're happy to continue with three lessons every week, I could book you in for a test sometime round Easter. Would that suit?"

She was delighted.

"By the way, what car will you be driving once you've passed your test?"

"A Rover – it was my father's."

"Mm," he said. "Bit of a step up from a Mini. You could do with getting in a bit of practice. Could anyone sit in with you?"

Laura's first thought was to ask her Aunt Millicent, a thought she quickly discarded.

"Well, don't worry if there isn't. It might just be helpful."

Behind drawn curtain, the lights were on in the sitting room. Her mother was at home, and when Laura opened the front door, Daphne emerged into the hallway from the kitchen dressed to receive company: her well-tailored charcoal-grey suit and cream blouse – very elegant – very business-like. "You've had visitors," she said, her tight smile firmly in its place.

Laura hung up her coat and checked her image in the mirror, buying time. Her mother was clearly in combative mood, a sure sign of at least one sherry. "Oh," Laura said disinterestedly, pretending to remove a speck of dust from her eye.

Daphne was not to be out-manoeuvred so easily. "I told them you were usually home by seven," she said. "But of course you weren't, so they said they couldn't wait."

The plurality of the anonymous visitors evidently had some significance, but Laura had no intention of rising to the bait unless she had to. "Mr Fielding had a dental appointment," she said, still pursuing the non-existent speck and mentally arming herself to meet whatever line of attack her mother was devising.

Daphne was in no hurry. "Julius said you'd mentioned photographs. I was surprised."

"Oh – yes."

"You were expecting them?"

"He said he'd drop them off for me."

"Really? How sweet of him. I put the envelope in the kitchen."

Laura went to retrieve it and found Gwen vigorously kneading a large lump of dough on the pastry board, pretending not to have overheard the conversation in the hall. "Thought I'd make some rolls for Sunday," she explained with a nervous smile. "Your mother said they'd go nicely with the soup."

Daphne had followed Laura into the kitchen, and was hovering in the doorway. "I didn't know he'd taken any recently," she observed, and turning to Gwen, added with unmistakable condescension, "He was always such a hopeless photographer, you know. Quite hopeless. I don't remember a single photograph that was worth the keeping."

Gwen looked up anxiously for a moment, evidently

fearing she was about to be drawn into the tournament.

"They're not recent," Laura intervened, determined Gwen should not be inveigled into what was a private battle between mother and daughter.

Julius' large brown envelope was propped against one of the blue-and-white china dogs on the dresser. Inside, there were about twenty prints. He had gone to the trouble of having them enlarged. In all honesty, most of them had little merit: some were a little fuzzy, out of focus; others were simply unremarkable, lacking composition. But the one that really mattered most, the snapshot of her father and herself, although a little grainy, caught the moment. And what she saw was something of a shock: his expression was filled with such tenderness and fond regard, it took her breath away. If only she had seen this love, written so clearly, she would never have needed to be told he cared: she would have known.

"I said – when were they taken, Laura?" her mother was asking, evidently for a second time.

Laura pulled herself together. "At my twenty-first."

Daphne advanced, hand outstretched. "Goodness. Ancient history. May I see?" She took the photos from her, handing them back after a cursory glance. "Just as I remember them," she said dismissively.

"So you have seen these before?" Julius had been right.

"Julius gave us a set, if I remember rightly – but I threw them away."

"You threw them away!" Laura was incredulous. "Why? I never even saw them!"

341

"Well, as you can see – they weren't particularly good, were they? Just typical Julius Parr snaps."

"I would still have liked to see them."

Daphne put on her long-suffering look and said, "Well now you have – for what they're worth." She paused for effect. "It's a pity you weren't here when they called. You could at least have thanked him for his trouble."

It was now quite evident her mother was pushing to be asked who the mysterious 'they' were. Thoroughly vexed, Laura determined on a stratagem of delay, studying the prints once more, only this time more slowly. There were two photos of her Broxley aunts she would certainly keep; and a candid foursome of Uncle Richard and Aunt Cynthia chatting with the Parrs which had turned out rather well, but the rest, she had to admit, were hardly worth the keeping. There were obvious omissions too: she noticed there were none of Oliver – or Claudia.

From her station in the doorway, Daphne cleared her throat rather pointedly. "Don't you want to know who came with Julius?" she asked.

Whatever trap her mother had devised, Laura recognised it had been set, and she was being invited to walk into it. "I've not seen Rosemary for ages," she said lightly, wondering what this reply would trigger. "How is she?"

"Oh, it wasn't Rosemary," Daphne said, making no attempt to disguise her triumph. "It was that man you used to go out with – John what's-his-name."

If her mother had actually struck her, the effect would have been the same: it had all the force of a blow.

"Rufford," Laura said, quickly redirecting her attention to the photographs, knowing, without a shadow of a doubt, that her face was on fire and her ability to remain unruffled was rapidly diminishing.

"Yes – of course. You know, I couldn't remember his name. It was quite embarrassing. And he's such a charming man, don't you think, Gwen?" she said, pulling Gwen into the front line for the second time. "And so handsome," she added for effect.

Gwen looked visibly appalled at being drawn into giving an opinion.

Daphne rattled on. "I was surprised he called – particularly as you'd said you weren't going out with him any more. Of course, I was very tactful and didn't mention it. But I did wonder whether you were seeing him again."

Laura kept her eyes fixed on the photographs while her head boiled. "Mm?" she said, feigning indifference. "No, not at the moment." What she really wanted to do was thump the table in sheer annoyance. What in heaven's name did John Rufford think he was doing coming to the Lodge? – with Jules? Of all people! Had he lost his senses? If she had been at home, the situation would have been impossible. Was he trying to force her hand? – to make her openly acknowledge a relationship? – in front of Jules? How dare he!

Daphne was watching like a hawk, a small, but very definite gleam in her eye. "Oh well, in that case, it doesn't matter," she said, with a little shrug. "I rather thought they were hoping you might join them," she added, twisting in the knife a little further. "They were going on to some office 'do', I think. I really can't remember."

Mercifully, as far as Laura was concerned, the door bell rang.

Daphne's attention was diverted. "Ah," she said, her manner dissolving into brittle sociability in the blink of an eye. "That will be one of the Bowling Green Committee. If you would like to join us later, Gwen, we'll be in the sitting room." And with a departing ghost of a smile, she left, closing the kitchen door behind her.

Gwen stopped kneading the dough.

Laura knew it was better to explain rather than have Gwen's curiosity put its own interpretation on events. "My mother wasn't quite so keen on John Rufford when I was going out with him," she said, straightening the photographs and returning them to the envelope.

"He's a fine looking man, I must say. Can't see what she would have had against him."

"I think she resented someone other than Oliver wanting to take me out."

"Well, I know it's not for me to say, but good riddance, on that account," she said, setting the dough to one side on the range to rise. "Not what you'd expect from a Gorst. Elsie said the same."

It was the first time Gwen had raised the subject of Oliver since the engagement had been broken, and it threw a light on how much gossip could be generated in the kitchen at the Lodge.

"Now – that John Rufford is something else, I must say,"

Gwen went on, wiping her hands. "A sight for sore eyes, he is," she added for good measure with a mischievous smile. "Can't see why you would want to stop seeing him."

"Too much of a good thing, Gwen, that's all. Now, if you'll excuse me, I've things to do."

Safe in the sanctuary of the study, Laura slumped into the swivel chair and waited for her heart to stop bouncing around like a rubber ball. It took some time. When at last it did, she retrieved the treasured photo from the envelope and propped it up against the paperweight. She would buy a special frame for it, and keep it there, on the desk, as a permanent reminder that when you love someone, you should not only show it, you should always let them know.

Chapter Thirty-Eight

After the Bank closed on Saturday, Laura took the first bus to Lingford to collect her car insurance papers from Longsworth & Longsworth, Insurance Brokers, in return for the princely sum of six-pounds-ten-shillings-and-sixpence. Later, in Frogmore's Department Store, she found a simple, but elegant silver frame with a sturdy stand to house her father's photograph. It would not look out of place, she thought, next to his paperweight and silver letter opener.

She travelled home feeling distinctly well-pleased with herself. Mr Fielding's confidence in her had already raised her spirits, and the expectation of probate being granted the following week added to her sense of satisfaction. At last, she could begin to move forward into a new, and exciting future. The waiting was finally over.

The one loose end in all this progress, however, was the lack of any contact from her uncle. She had alerted Mr Jackson to the possibility of a letter arriving for her attention, but now, after two weeks, she began to fear it might never come. Of course, she told herself, mulling over several possibilities, her uncle could be away at sea, and she might not hear from him for months; or he might be unwell again. But her real uneasiness lay in the possibility he might have no wish to see her at all, not now, nor in the future, and she might never have the chance to heal old wounds and close the door on resentments from the past.

Meanwhile, there were other things to occupy her mind.

The padlock was stiff, and the double doors into the old stable block creaked wearily on their hinges when she tugged them open. Inside, the atmosphere smelled faintly of oil, musty fabric and accumulated dust. Her father's car sat looking forlorn and abandoned. A grey film had settled over its once shiny paint-work, and an old spider's web hung from the wing-mirror, swaying in the light breeze from the open doors.

She unlocked the car and eased herself into the driver's seat. The steering wheel felt chill to the touch and she could not quite rid herself of the thought her father had been the last person to hold it, four long months before. For a second time, she was an intruder into his world: first his study; now his car. His presence was all around her: the road map left on the back seat with the travel rug; the spare pair of driving gloves in the glove compartment; a partly-used note pad with pages torn out; a propelling pencil with a new lead, barely used; and some treacle toffees in a paper bag with several empty wrappers sticking to each other.

The leather seat felt cold, and was pushed too far forward to be comfortable. She altered its position and changed the angle of the driving mirror. Tentatively, she worked her way through the gears, keeping her eyes on the view through the windscreen, practising shifting her foot from the accelerator to the brake until she was confident of moving between them smoothly without hesitating.

The battery of course was flat, as she expected, but no doubt William Benyon would have the answer if she asked him.

"I've got a charger in the back barn," he said when she telephoned him later. "I'll hunt it out for you. Bring it up after milking."

But it was not William Benyon who came up to the Lodge.

"Laura!" her mother called sharply from the hall. "Mr Moray's here. Something to do with the car."

Leaving Robert Moray and her mother together for even a few moments was not a situation to be encouraged. Laura hurried from the study.

She found her mother resolutely guarding the doorway. She had never forgiven him 'his unsavoury affair' which, in her eyes, had tainted everyone at Meeston Lodge simply by association. She was even less likely to be forgiving given his appearance.

He was, to say the least, grubby, dressed for farm-work, his thick tweed jacket laced with strands of straw caught in the weave. Beneath his jacket, the dark-blue overalls were creased and stained black at the knees, tucked into mud-caked wellingtons. "William's waiting for the vet," he said, addressing his explanation to Laura. "He said you needed this."

In the face of evident hostility from her mother, a lesser man would undoubtedly have shrivelled, but Robert Moray was unmoved, dignified, and unyielding, standing foursquare on the porch, head up, holding the charger in both hands, like a gift from one of the Magi to the babe in the manger.

Daphne was evidently unimpressed.

"The car battery's gone flat over winter," Laura was quick to explain.

Her mother raised a disdainful eyebrow. "Your father would have asked Nuttall's to come over from Weaversham to deal with it," she said casting a damning glance in Mr Moray's direction. "There was no need to trouble Mr Benyon." She sniffed, frowning at the unwelcome visitor on her doorstep who was leaving clods of earth on the steps. "You smell of the cowshed, Mr Moray. I'd be obliged if you didn't get into the car in your condition." And with that very definite instruction, she took her leave with a curt nod, and returned to the sitting room and the television programme she had been watching before she had been so rudely interrupted.

It was demeaning to have to apologise for her mother's behaviour, but Laura felt it was entirely necessary. "I'm sorry," she said. "If I'd known William wasn't coming, I'd have suggested meeting you at the garage."

He shrugged, apparently indifferent to the possibility of being humiliated.

She led the way to the old stable and switched on the lights so he could see better what had to be done. He took off his jacket and hung it up on the old harness rack, then turned back the cuffs of his shirt at the wrist.

"It'll take a few hours," he said, lifting the bonnet and

plugging in the connections, "especially if the engine's not been turned over since November."

"I should have thought about it sooner."

He glanced up at her. "Yes – well, you've had other things on your mind."

She ignored this comment.

He was still bending over the engine, checking this and that. "It might be worth asking Nuttall's to give it the once-over before you drive it," he conceded. "It could probably do with a service. I could take it over sometime next week, if you like."

His suggestion surprised her. "Have you driven it before?" It seemed unlikely.

He continued his inspection for a few moments longer before straightening up. "A few times," he said, wiping his hands on a rag from his overall pocket.

"When?"

He continued wiping his hands, concentrating on them. "When your father asked me to," he said and promptly changed the subject, stuffing the rag back into his pocket. "Have you got a date for your test yet?"

"It might be Easter week."

"Your instructor must be pleased with your progress."

"He seems to be."

He refastened his cuffs and retrieved his jacket, standing well away from her as he put it on. Daphne had been right – he smelled of the cowshed. "So, once you've passed your test, what else have you got planned?" he asked, apparently making conversation for the sake of it.

"I'm thinking of taking a course at one of the art colleges," she said, "starting in September. Maybe go on to teacher training afterwards. My art mistress always said I should."

"You're leaving the Bank?" He was surprised.

"Yes. I need to start again."

He nodded and appeared to be weighing up what this might mean. "So you'll be leaving Meeston?" he asked after a brief reflection.

"Probably."

He gave this some thought as well, drawing into himself for a while before realising she was waiting. "I should be getting back," he said, casting a quick glance in the direction of the car. "Leave it on charge over night – that should do it."

"Shall I take the charger back to William?"

"No, leave it," he said, switching off the stable lights. "I can pick it up when I take the car to Nuttall's." He was suddenly very eager to go.

Chapter Thirty-Nine

"Whatever was your father thinking of, Laura?" Gwen asked in hushed tones. She and Elsie had ushered her away from a knot of local women clustered outside the Village Shop. "Six-hundred pounds! I said to Harry, 'Mrs Driscoll will be thinking I won't want to be staying on, you mark my words.' I don't know what to say to her, I really don't. Elsie says the same, don't you, Elsie?"

Elsie nodded.

It was difficult to be honest with them. If she were in their shoes, she would not have given the matter a second thought. But neither Gwen nor Elsie seemed to be contemplating leaving the Lodge, and who was she to suggest they should? Instead, she confined herself to the simple observation her father must have wanted to express his thanks for all their help over the years.

The previous day, Mr Parr had left her in no doubt about her own situation. "Mr Jackson and I have already started the process of transferring property and shares into your name, Laura," he had said while Mr Jackson's brow had creased in concentration. "In the meantime, you already have a considerable sum at your disposal. I'm sure you understand why it would be wise if you didn't allow this to become common knowledge." He had paused, appearing to suffer a mild attack of embarrassment. "It could attract the wrong sort of person," he had added awkwardly. Perhaps he was thinking of his daughter's sudden interest in Oliver. "Until you feel confident in handling your own affairs, do feel free to consult Mr Jackson about any financial undertakings you might wish to consider. He will always be here to advise you."

Mr Jackson had nodded again.

"There is, of course, the matter we discussed briefly last November – namely making a Will yourself. Don't leave this too long, Laura. I'm sure you'd wish to see your inheritance – how shall I put it – directed to the appropriate persons – if anything unforeseen were to happen."

She had promised she would, and he had been satisfied.

But to Laura's way of thinking, the more immediate matter demanding her attention was the already stormy relationship between herself and her mother. From now on, she knew she must expect Daphne's resentment of her altered status – effectively a tenant in her own home – to heighten the friction already existing between them. The need to leave Meeston Lodge was likely to become more pressing.

Meanwhile, she allowed herself a moment of euphoria, exulting in the knowledge that she was now truly free to do exactly as she wished.

When she pulled open the stable doors, she was delighted to find the Rover back to its old self, clean and polished. She made herself comfortable in the driver's seat, imagining the days to come. The freedom of the open road. The thrill of going where her fancy took her. Oh, the joy of it all!

The engine spluttered into life and purred contentedly; the indicators flicked in and out; the windscreen wipers arced back and forth in graceful curves, and the lights came on and lit up the old stable doors with sudden brilliance.

She wanted to thank Mr Moray for his trouble, but he was not around, and phoning him that evening required Daphne's preoccupation with the television in the sitting room. Annoyingly, her mother felt it necessary – perhaps to salve her wounded pride – to spend a large part of the evening on the telephone, giving her opinion to Mr Stockdale on which items should appear on the agenda at the next meeting of the Bowling Green Committee.

It was almost nine o'clock when Laura was able to dial his number. By then, she suspected, if he were helping with the milking the following day, it was possible he was already asleep.

He was a long time answering, and when he did finally pick up the receiver, he sounded tired.

"I'm sorry. Did I disturb you?"

"Not really," he said.

"I couldn't phone earlier," she explained. "But I wanted to thank you – for everything you've done – with the car."

He accepted her thanks.

"It was very kind of you," she added, feeling it was important to extend the call a little longer to make it worth his while.

"My pleasure," he said. There was a noticeable pause before he unexpectedly asked, "Will you be taking it out this weekend?"

She hesitated. "I'd love to, but … it's difficult."

"How so?"

"I don't really want to ask Aunt Millicent, you see," she said. "I know she would if I asked her – but – she's such a dreadful driver." She felt this confession was a terrible act of betrayal: her aunt would be mortified if she knew.

There was a very audible sigh before he said, "Then I think you should overcome your reluctance and ask Mr Rufford."

This was probably the least welcome suggestion he could have made. "I've no intention of asking him," she heard herself saying in what could best be described as a less than gracious manner, and possibly more accurately as irritable tetchiness. "And you know perfectly well why I won't."

She could almost sense his exasperation. "How long is going to take you to realise he won't give up so easily?"

"I know nothing of the sort."

"Then why do I keep seeing his car touring Meeston in the evenings?" he asked pointedly.

It was unwelcome intelligence.

"I thought you should know," he was saying.

A ridiculous silence sat solidly between them and seemed to go on for ever.

Was it this that prompted her? – the need to fill a void? Or the simple expedient of making use of him? She had no idea afterwards. "I know I shouldn't ask," she said, wondering why she was, " – and it's awfully presumptuous of me – because I realise you don't have much time to yourself – but could *you* possibly spare me half-an-hour or so – tomorrow?"

The silence was almost tangible.

Having put him in this situation, she felt obliged to give him a way out. "Mr Moray? Please say if you can't."

A long pause. "Two o'clock?" he suggested, without any audible enthusiasm. "I've milking at four."

"I really am very grateful."

He made no comment, merely wished her good night, and left her feeling she had pushed him into a corner. Did he think she was trading on their relationship? Very probably.

Daphne's usual Sunday afternoon at Dyers Green relieved Laura of unnecessary explanations as to why Mr Moray was standing in the driveway, evidently waiting for someone, while giving the appearance of having far more important things to do with his time. Her mother would have been appalled by her daughter's plans for the afternoon. The fact Mr Moray was clean and smartly dressed, if a little too casual for a Sunday, would have been irrelevant.

"Where do you want to go?" he asked, squinting against the afternoon sun as she came down the steps to meet him.

"I thought I should choose routes I already know – until I get used to the car. What do you think?

He nodded. "Probably best."

So they set off for Weaversham, a little uncertainly at first, but without her stalling the engine, which was her greatest fear. From then on, it became easier as she settled into the rhythm of the car, pleased the transition had been less demanding than she feared.

He was a relaxed passenger, which she had not expected. Mr Fielding's criticisms were her constant companions, and finding someone who appeared to take her ability for granted, while very gratifying, was oddly disconcerting.

"You're very quiet," she said, feeling she had to say something. "Is my driving so terrible?"

"No – it's fine."

"Praise indeed!" she scoffed, but he did not respond.

They had just turned right off Meeston Road, heading into Weaversham. The roads were quiet, and they reached the high street without hindrance of any sort.

"Do you want to drive a bit further?" he asked. "Go into Lingford?"

"If you can stand the strain."

"I think I can," he said, but offered no further observation.

Lingford too was quiet, its shops closed, and streets empty.

He looked at his watch. They had plenty time to spare. "If you like," he suggested, "we could go back via Smallcross? Make a round trip of it?"

Smallcross and Susan Holbrook, Laura thought. Perhaps he hoped for a glimpse of her as they drove through the village. Perhaps he had not entirely given up the possibility they might renew their liaison – even at this late hour. At heart then, he was no better than John Rufford touring Meeston, hankering after what was not to be.

They drove through the town without incident, heading out along the road that ran alongside the park with its riverside walks. Here, it was busier and there were several cars parked, spaced out along the pavement by the iron railings.

"Do you want to practise parking?" he asked, and without waiting for her to reply, suggested the next available space.

Feeling more relaxed, she executed the manoeuvre faultlessly and turned off the engine with a sense of triumph.

He gave her an encouraging smile, but his thoughts seemed to be drifting elsewhere. His gaze shifted to the view beyond the windscreen – to the railings and the line of cars.

"Do you want me to drive on?" she asked, in the absence of any suggestions on his part.

He turned to look at her. "Can we talk for a few minutes?"

It was an odd request. "If you like." Did he want to talk about her father's legacy, perhaps? He had made no mention of it.

He paused before making his announcement. "I wanted to let you know I've decided to leave Meeston," he said.

She heard herself say, "Oh, whatever for?" in a somewhat peevish fashion, too redolent of her mother for comfort.

"I've decided to go home," was his answer.

"To Scotland?"

"No – Northumberland."

"But why now?" she wanted to know, feeling somehow he was letting her down.

"I've no reason to stay," he said casually, returning to his contemplation of the neatly parked row of cars ahead of them.

It was all Susan Holbrook's fault, she thought resentfully. "But what about William?" she said, knowing she was clutching at straws.

"Alan's old enough to take over," he said, all pragmaticism and solid rationality.

"And the Lodge?" she objected.

"The Lodge?" He shrugged dismissively.

"The Lodge still needs you," she insisted. How could he abandon them like that? On a whim?

"No it doesn't," he said with a shake of the head. "Let's not pretend. Any gardener could do what I do up at the Lodge."

But that was not her point. Who could she talk to, if he were not there? "When will you go?" she asked, finding herself anxious that it might be soon.

"June – at the latest."

"I see." Less than three months. Her fears were justified. He would be gone before she went to college. He would leave her behind.

"It's got nothing to do with your father's legacy," he was saying, apparently eager to assure her of this. "He knew I had the farm. I didn't need his money."

Farm? What farm? Why had he never mentioned this before?

He must have sensed her bewilderment. "I bought it about six years back," he said, at pains to explain himself.

"It's not a big place. Around eighty acres – near Stanegate. Large enough for me to handle on my own."

"At Stanegate," she said, repeating the name, trying to fix it in her mind. She had no idea where it was.

"Just outside the village," he went on. "Near my uncle's farm – south of the Wall – the Roman Wall," he added for good measure. "He persuaded me to buy it when old man Tyson decided to retire. Said Rigg End would bring me back some day." A stillness settled on him, and he was lost in thought for a while. "Seems he knew me better than I knew myself," he said at last.

Rigg End. Stanegate. Places that belonged to his earlier life; an earlier time; before Meeston.

"Who's been running the farm while you've been here?" she found herself asking out of politeness, if nothing more.

He looked pleased that she seemed interested. "My Uncle Geordie and his son, Ian," he said, becoming visibly more animated than before. "Ian and his wife rent the house – or they did until last month. They're expecting their fourth come October, so they needed somewhere larger." He paused, and smiled to himself. "Geordie said it was time I ran the place myself," he said, suddenly turning to look at her directly. "And I think he's right. It is."

She felt obliged to agree, but without much enthusiasm.

He appeared not to notice. "We'd better head back," he said, checking his watch again, "or I'll be late."

She started up the engine and drove to Meeston via Smallcross with her thoughts in a tangle. Robert Moray had no interest whatever in seeking out Susan Holbrook. He was making plans for the future.

Later that night, she lay awake trying to visualise Rigg End, Stanegate, Uncle Geordie, Cousin Ian and his wife, and felt more than just a twinge of irritation that these people, and strange-sounding places, who belonged to a world outside her knowledge, were luring him away. It was paradoxical, she thought, that she should resent his determination to do precisely what she intended for herself. But there it was – she did.

Chapter Forty

The letter from her uncle had arrived.

The plain white envelope was unremarkable, like its predecessor, the handwriting on the front betraying nothing.

Later that evening, she opened it. Inside was a single sheet of folded notepaper. She was in no rush to read it. Whatever he had written would be there, indelibly, whether she read it then, or later.

Outside the study window was a lovely spring evening. The daffodils, growing in groups dotted here and there between the shrubs, were in full bloom catching the last of the sun, their colour almost luminous. Earlier, she had pulled up the lower sash, enough to let in their scent, and with it, a chorus of bird-song from Meeston Woods.

The letter was brief and to the point.

'Dear Laura' – it said.

'Thank you for giving me the news. James wasn't well when he wrote. I'm pensioned off myself now.

'If you really want to come I can meet you the Saturday before Easter. There's a cafe on the prom – The Seagull. I'll be there from two o'clock till five. You can catch a bus to

Collingsby outside the railway station. There's one every twenty minutes or so.

'Regards –

'Andrew'

It was a strange letter: no words of regret; no overt wish to see her; no mention of Jean; no sense of anything at all except a dull acceptance that she might still visit him.

She replied anyway, saying she would meet him at The Seagull as he had suggested in two week's time. But in writing, there were none of the expectations there should have been. Quite the reverse: his coldness implied an obligation, nothing more, and left her regretting her suggestion they should ever meet. But it was too late now, she reflected, as she dropped the letter into the post-box in Weaversham the next day. As the poet said – 'The Moving Finger writes; and having writ, Moves on –'. What was done was done, and could not be undone.

Behind her, a familiar voice called her name.

She turned, prepared to face him with as much presence of mind as she could muster. John Rufford, elegant as always was leaning nonchalantly against the bonnet of his car, attracting the attention of every female passer-by. "How are you?" he asked, as he sauntered over to greet her.

She heard herself say, "Hello, John," in a remarkable casual manner, while her pulse raced and her eyes reinforced everything she had tried so hard to forget. God forgive him for looking so magnificent! "I'm fine," she managed. "And you?"

He paused before replying, engulfing her with a glorious

smile. "Could be better," he said, loading his words with extra meaning.

He was standing much too close, as he always did, the scent of his aftershave exquisite as ever.

"Have you unravelled your family mystery yet?" he was asking. It was small talk, leading somewhere. "It's over five weeks now," he added, reminding her of the last time they had been together.

"Not everything," she said, fighting hard to concentrate. "I said it might take a while."

"Anything you can share with me?"

"No, I'm sorry."

He raised an eyebrow. "Can't you bring yourself to try?" he said, implying incredulity. "I'm a remarkably good listener."

Too glib. The ready answer always there to hand. No thoughtful silence or the carefully considered replies of Robert Moray.

She shook her head. "No, I can't – please believe me."

Whether he believed her or not seemed immaterial: he just kept looking at her, and she was starting to melt, like wax too near a flame.

"Are you doing anything this afternoon?"

Too late, she realised her answer had been, "No."

"It's a lovely day. Shall we go for a drive?" he suggested.

Somewhat lamely, she thought afterwards, she was reduced to pointing out he had agreed not to contact her.

"I haven't," he said artlessly. "I've met you by accident. Besides, I'm only suggesting a drive – possibly afternoon tea in Pickerton. Nothing else."

Did she believe that? With her brain turning to marsh-mallow, she could not think why she should refuse such a seemingly innocuous invitation without sounding churlish, except nothing about an invitation from John Rufford was entirely innocuous.

They drove out of Weaversham, and she sat next to him feeling weak-willed and pathetic.

"I've missed you," he said, glancing in her direction. "Have you missed me?"

She sat mutely formulating an answer which might serve, without reaching an acceptable conclusion.

"Well – have you?" he persisted.

"I thought you'd have found someone else by now," she retaliated, feeling this was honest enough.

He laughed at her. "My God, Laura! I'm not that fickle!"

She said nothing, trying to decide what to do. She should ask him to take her home. But she did nothing.

So instead, they had afternoon tea in a pleasant little café in Pickerton's market square eating egg sandwiches, hot buttered scones with strawberry jam, and delicious fruit cake from a three-tiered cake-stand with paper doilies.

She found herself trying to keep the conversation light and undemanding, picking topics at random from thin air, aware her voice sounded unnaturally cheerful and she was tending to gabble: how it seemed spring had finally arrived; how her driving was progressing; what her plans were for art college – of which he very much approved; enquiring after Michael – had he found a place at university yet? – on and on – snatching at anything she could to keep at bay the awkward subject of emotional attachment.

He listened attentively.

She was frightened, not just by the simple truth this man could reduce her to jelly – he only had to sit there and smile – but by what was worse, her tactics did not seem to be working.

He paid the bill and they walked out into the late afternoon sun. "Will you come out with me this evening?" he asked, getting straight to the point.

She shook her head, fighting to stay rational. "No, John. I'd like you to take me home – to Meeston," she added so he should be in no doubt as to their destination.

He stopped, bringing her to a halt with him. He was looking deep into her eyes, searching for answers. "Have you found someone else?" he asked point blank. "Is that why you're so –" He searched for the right word. " – different?"

"No – I haven't." She was astonished he should think she had. "This isn't about you and me, John. This is about me trying to deal with things I'm finding difficult, that's all."

"I wish you'd tell me. I could help."

"No – no, John, you couldn't. How can I convince you?"

"By telling me something – anything I can make sense of. You're making me feel –" He sought for the right word. " – useless." It clearly pained him.

She wished he would stop pressing her for answers. Words would not come when she wanted them. Explanations collapsed before she could give them voice.

"Is it so bad?"

She nodded, grateful he had seen she was too distressed to speak.

"I'm sorry. I didn't mean to make light of it."

But he had, and she was angry with him. "Just take me home," she begged.

They drove back through the lanes, Laura watching the countryside slip by bathed in a late afternoon sun while her mind wheeled away into a world of its own wishing things were different.

They drove for several miles without speaking. Every so often, he would glance in her direction. Eventually, he pulled into the side of a lane and stopped the car. The sun had slipped behind a fringe of trees, setting the horizon on fire with a band of molten gold. The lane ahead, with its avenue of beeches, was a lattice-work of brilliant light and shade.

He took off his driving gloves and turned to look at her, reaching out to take her hand. His touched seared her. "I don't like seeing you so unhappy," he said softly.

"I told you – I needed time. I meant it. You said you wouldn't get in touch until I wrote. You promised."

"I didn't get in touch," he said with a slight smile.

She was vexed by his willingness to chop logic. "What do you call waiting for me outside the Bank? – touring Meeston in the evenings? – even calling at the Lodge? That was unforgivable!"

"Guilty, as charged, I'm afraid – except I didn't intention-ally call at the Lodge."

"Then what did you mean by it?"

He made a small gesture of hopelessness. "I was giving Jules a lift. I wouldn't have agreed if I'd known where he was going. Your mother invited us in."

"She thought she was being clever. She had the pleasure of taunting me afterwards," she added.

"Then I'm doubly sorry."

"Are you?" she challenged him.

He reached out, tenderly running the back of his fingers over her cheek. "I'm finding this separation difficult," he said, suddenly serious.

She panicked. He should not have said that. His closeness was suffocating her. "I need some air," she said, scrambling out of the car and setting off down the lane at a brisk pace, her hands deep inside her coat pockets.

He followed, easily catching up with her and matching her strides. They walked on under the avenue of beeches into the twilight as the evening filled with bird-song.

Suddenly, he reached out and stopped her in her tracks. "Laura," he said, holding her fast. "For God's sake – I'm in love with you. I don't know what to do."

He was looking into her eyes with that terrible intensity that would undo her. "No, John. No. You just think you are."

He stifled a bitter laugh. "I still can't convince you, can I?" .

Was this the truth? – or just a clever piece of artifice? She dare not answer him.

"You really don't believe I can keep myself to myself, do you?" he went on, his voice catching in his throat. "You're convinced I've had at least a dozen women in the last five weeks. Am I right?"

She swallowed hard. "That's what you've always done, isn't it? Why should you change?"

He looked exasperated. "Because I love you! And I know I love you because I don't want anyone else – and there's been no one else since you."

This was too much to bear.

"At least tell me you believe there's been no one else."

There was a desperation about him she had never seen before, and it frightened her: it made him vulnerable and irresistible in equal parts.

"Tell me," he insisted, his grip tightening.

"I believe you," she whispered, barely able to speak.

"Then tell me how to prove I love you?"

She shook her head. "I don't know."

"Oh God, Laura," he said, bringing her closer, his faltering breath on her face. He rested his forehead against hers. "How can I convince you?" he whispered.

She could not answer because she had no answer to give.

For a moment, he looked into her eyes, searching for something. Then, with incredible tenderness, he did what he had never done before. He kissed her, very softly, on the lips.

She felt herself sinking. There was no defence she could muster against this unfettered tenderness. He was everything she remembered, and more.

After that there was no stopping him. He pulled her into the deep shadow of the trees, all the caution, all the self-control and exquisite orchestration gone. Buckles, clasps, buttons, zips – everything succumbing to his urgency: her skirt hoisted up around her waist; underclothes pulled aside;

his hands everywhere, caressing, leading her on until she wanted him beyond all reason.

He lifted her up, holding her fast, wrapping her legs around his waist and pushing her back against the solid trunk of a tree.

He paused for a moment, the heat of him against her, his breath hard and fast as he looked into her eyes. "I love you," he said, his voice little more than a whisper. "You know I do."

She held his gaze as he brought her down onto him; slowly at first until she had all of him; and then throughout the sweet insistent rhythm until the moment of release, when he shuddered and called out her name, and she abandoned herself to the ecstasy he had conjured in her.

Afterwards, gasping and spent, he kept her close for a few exquisite moments until the strength went out of him.

She slumped against him, her head on his shoulder, listening to the thumping of his heart beating in time to hers, and the panting of her breath mingling with his, and the heat of it against her neck.

For a while they were lost to everything: oblivious. The twilight faded into dusk. The birds stopped singing. Nothing stirred.

He eased her from him gently, the cool of the evening air coming between them. She shivered, missing his warmth. He gave her his handkerchief. "Here," he said apologetically. "You'll need this."

Her thighs were awash with him, the strong scent of his maleness everywhere. She tried to straighten her clothes, but nothing seemed to fit. The elastic in her panties had broken and her nylons were torn. She felt dishevelled, and her back was sore where the bark of the tree had rubbed against her.

He had turned away, adjusting his clothing quickly, and was waiting, shielding her from view, anxiously checking the lane for prying eyes.

She was unsteady when she tried to walk, and he put his arm around her, keeping her close. Neither of them spoke. What was there to say? He had taken her, and she had wanted him.

They sat in the darkened car while he held her hand. "You know I've never made love like that before, don't you?" he said quietly.

She remembered his words at Rothwell Mere. "Yes, you told me."

He gave a forced laugh: sad and regretful.

She did not want to talk. She was exhausted.

He stroked her fingers delicately. "I've never wanted to be with someone as much as I want to be with you, Laura. Please believe me."

She knew, at that moment, he meant every word. But that was not enough. The old doubts still whispered in her ear; they always would. He was too attractive; too charming; too seductive. How could she ever hope to keep him to herself? She never could. Eventually, he would want more than she could give.

"Will you ever feel the same?" he was asking. "Will you?"

What could she tell him? The truth? – that in some ways

he would always be a part of her? – but that she could never trust his love to last? No – she could not tell him that. Not now.

"I'll wait, you know," he said, running his fingers lightly down her cheek. "For however long it takes."

She could not bear the thought of that: it was much too great a burden. "No," she begged. "Please don't. Please – just get on with your life. I don't want to hold you to anything."

He leaned across, kissing her tenderly on the lips once more, undoing her resolve. "Just let me know when you change your mind," he said softly.

Darkness hid her return to the Lodge. The lights were on in the sitting room, and she summoned up the courage to casually announce her arrival from the hallway. Above the din of a variety show there was no reply.

She ran the bath and stripped off her clothes, wrapping herself in a towel. Her undies and nylons were beyond repair, soiled and torn. She found an old paper carrier bag in her wardrobe and stuffed them inside. The problem of disposal would have to wait.

In the bathroom, the steam had fogged the mirror. She wiped it clear with the edge of the towel. Her face looked back at her. She was flushed, her eyes strangely bright, almost feverish. When she let the towel fall, the soft brown hair between her thighs was matted into thick dark strands, the warm stickiness still there, its scent strong and acrid on her fingers, strange and evocative. He had always used rubbers. He had broken all his rules.

She twisted round, straining to see her back. At the base

of her spine, the skin was raw. It would take a while to heal. She felt a sense of triumph at the sight of it. A battle scar. But who had won?

The water was comforting. She let her mind wander as it lapped sensuously against her. His image was still sharp: his dark eyes half-closed, mesmerising her; his lips on hers; his fingers working magic; his exquisite invasion; the ultimate pleasure.

Her body still tingled. He would always be with her.

Chapter Forty-One

The bright sunshine of the following morning was in stark contrast to her mood, which swung from sudden agitation to lethargy and back again in the blink of an eye. She had become a mystery to herself: heart and head in a permanent state of attrition that left her emotionally exhausted and restless in equal parts. She had never imagined she could be so foolish.

She rang Robert's number rather than Aunt Millicent's because she wanted distraction, company and, more importantly, his level-headedness. She would miss that when he was gone.

No, he wasn't busy, he said. It was his weekend off. Alan was doing the milking that afternoon. Did she want to take the car out? A longer run this time?

He suggested the scenic route into the Dales.

They reached Athelstone mid-afternoon and she parked by a row of mediaeval cottages near the green. Opposite, solid and determined to be noticed, the grey, squat tower of the early-Norman church dedicated to St Hilda rose above the dense green of ancient yews flanking the lychgate. A pretty place. Somewhere to return to with her sketch pad and paints when she was at liberty to do so.

"Do you want a break?" he asked.

They left the car and followed a footpath away from the village through a tangled, ill-kempt copse down to a shallow stream where a wooden footbridge crossed into a hay meadow. The water was clear, running over a stony bed, and they hung over the rail for a while watching a pied wagtail bobbing on the stones at the margin. On the far bank, a line of large, smooth boulders arced out from a swathe of close-cropped turf into the stream, and he suggested they sit there for a while and enjoy the sunshine before they drove back.

It was a peaceful spot, with only the sound of larks for company and the distant bleating of sheep and lambs drifting on the light breeze.

"You're very quiet," he observed after they had been sitting there for some time.

"A bit tense, I suppose – with driving," she added, thinking this was an admirable excuse.

"Nothing else?"

She shook her head.

He regarded her with curiosity. "Want to talk about him?" he asked, casually.

"Who?" she asked, feigning ignorance as the most immediate line of defence.

"John Rufford," he said, tilting his head slightly as he studied her. "I was walking back from the Meeston Arms last night," he added, which explained everything.

"Ah – you saw him drop me off."

He ventured an apologetic smile. "You seemed – agitated."

She could feel the sudden rush of heat spread out across her face and turned away to hide it. The skin at the base of her spine was still raw to touch; and so was the memory of how she came by it. And she still wanted him.

"I did warn you."

She glanced up at him. "I know."

"What do you intend to do?"

"I've told him to find someone else."

He stifled an exasperated laugh.

"I'm not fooling myself," she insisted. "I was the one who broke things off, not him. It's his pride that's hurt, that's all." All very rational, she thought, and a perfectly acceptable explanation for John Rufford's unshakable tenacity. It was deeply satisfying to be so certain of his motivation.

Robert Moray remained silent, his concentration on his hands, clasped together as he leant forward. Large hands, well scrubbed.

"I suppose you think I'm heartless, don't you?" she said, knowing she could have added, 'like Susan Holbrook'.

He glanced round. "That's not for me to say."

She hugged her knees. The sun on her back felt warm and comforting, easing the rawness. Somewhere in the distance, a lamb bleated urgently, and its mother called it back.

He seemed disinclined to take the subject further.

"You mustn't be too hard on me," she said, still feeling she should justify herself. "There is another reason."

He turned, waiting for her explanation.

"My father's second letter – I've an uncle I never knew I had. His name's Andrew. He lives in Collingsby Bay. You probably know the place."

Yes, he knew it well.

"There was a younger sister too – Jean. When their mother died, things happened – to Jean – that were …" She faltered, running out of words.

He frowned, trying to catch her drift.

Should she be divulging this? – even to him? She stumbled on, addressing the sparkling water at her feet rather than look him in the face. "They were dreadful – shameful things," she managed at last. And so it all came out, the whole appalling history her father had set down in his beautiful handwriting, its exquisite execution defying the obscenity that lay beneath the words. In the end, she had told him everything, right down to who her father really was – James Douglas, not James Driscoll – and afterwards, she felt emotionally drained. She could not believe how much. "Should I have told you?" she asked.

A sad smile flickered briefly into life. "I'm glad you felt you could," he said. Unexpectedly, he reached out and took her hand, cradling it between his own as he might have held an injured bird. It was a small act of kindness, and she was truly grateful for it. "When are you seeing your uncle?"

"In two weeks time. I was naive, I suppose. I thought I'd try to heal the breech between them, but now – I don't know." She could only give him a flavour of her deep sense of unease. "His reply. It was so odd. I don't know how else to describe it. Cold – definitely. Resentful. I can't blame him for that – but there seems to be something else – perhaps to do with Jean. Something deeper – darker even – although heaven knows what."

"And this is what you don't want John Rufford to know?" There was no criticism – just a bald statement of fact.

"Yes."

"What makes you think he'd care?"

"It's not about *him* caring – it's about *me* caring. It's about how I see myself. Who I am and where I've come from. I can't pretend Andrew and Jean aren't a part of my story. My father could. I can't. That's all there is to it." She felt passionately this was true.

"But if you can share it with me, why not with him?"

"You're family," she insisted. That above everything had made it possible. That was what she would miss when he was gone: her link with another past.

He smiled at her, a genuine smile, a rare thing that lit up his face and softened the harsh lines that framed the sides of his mouth. "Then I must thank you for taking me into your confidence," he said. He was still cradling her hand. He looked down at it, the smile fading suddenly into a frown. "You must think I'm something of a cold fish," he said. "Not given to opening up – talking about things?"

"It wasn't easy for me. Why should it be any easier for you?" She hesitated, sensing he had opened a door and invited her in. "Do you want to tell me something?" she asked.

"If I wanted to talk about my past, would you want to know?"

"Of course."

He paused, thinking things over. "I hid my past – pretended it would go away. It didn't."

"You should have told Susan. It might have helped."

He glanced up at her briefly. "Something held me back. I don't know what. A sense she didn't want to know, perhaps. Maybe I was wrong. But she never pressed me."

"You can tell me. I'm family, remember?"

He tried to smile. "Where shall I begin?"

"At the beginning," she suggested, but her attempt at light-heartedness was lost on him.

He seemed in no hurry.

She prompted him. "If I were to ask you – Who is Robert Moray? – how would you answer me?"

He considered her question. "Robert Moray is the eldest son of Grace Gillmuir of Coldstream and Dr Robert Moray of Edinburgh," he said, addressing her hand still held in his.

"You've never mentioned him before."

"He was an academic. Lived in his own world for most of the time. But I miss his wisdom now he's gone. It's so often the way, isn't it?" He glanced across at her, seeking agreement.

She nodded. "Did you grow up in Edinburgh?"

"No. My parents moved to Northumberland after their marriage – rented a house in Stanegate. I was born there."

"But you sound like a Scot," she objected.

"I had a father I wanted to impress. When I was small, I used to think people thought well of him because of how he spoke."

"So you mimicked him?"

"Yes – I mimicked him." He looked embarrassed to confess it. "Afterwards, I suppose it just stuck."

She thought it was a rather charming image of a serious small boy. "What brought your father to Northumberland?"

"His research – settlements on the Roman Wall. I've a copy of the book he wrote. It's pretty dry stuff, I'm afraid. Of its time, I suppose. But I'm glad to have it."

She was sure he was.

"Well – anyway," he went on, slipping into a more conversational tone. "When my father was on field trips, Auntie Moira would come down from Coldstream to keep my mother company. She met this young farmer – George Robson – Geordie, and fell in love. They married, and set up home at High Oakbank, just outside the village." He smiled, happy memories lingering a while. "It's fine country round there," he said, his voice taking on a softer, dreamier tone. "Facing south over the river. Two-hundred-and-fifty acres of good farmland. Mainly dairy, a few sheep, and some arable along the valley bottom. I spent every spare hour I had on that farm as a boy. Played truant once or twice – and got walloped for it." He coloured slightly, ashamed to admit it.

It was strange sitting next to him, holding hands, listening to his story. He was suddenly opening up his life to her, letting her in to see what few outside his family had seen. She enjoyed the confidence he had placed in her. "You were happy then." she said.

"Yes, I was happy then. But when I was eight, my father thought it would do me good to get some serious schooling.

The family moved back to Edinburgh, and I was sent to Gowrie Academy for Boys – as a boarder." He smiled ruefully. "It was a good school. Very fond of discipline. But I've no complaints. It gave me a sound education."

"But you still chose farming."

"I didn't want the academic life."

"Wasn't your father disappointed?"

"No. What I did with my education was up to me, he said. He just expected me to use it."

"What did you do when you left school?"

"I was too young to join the Army in 'forty-one, and Geordie needed help on the farm. It was hard work and long hours, but I wouldn't have had it any other way." So he had gone back to his roots then, just as he would now. Whatever sorrows there had been between, the place would always call him home. She envied him. Meeston would never call her back once she had left. It lacked the power to hold her.

His mood changed. Like a cloud suddenly passing over the sun, his expression darkened. The tight, familiar lines around the corners of his mouth deepened, his nostrils became pinched and taut, and his brows lowered, shading his eyes. His hold on her hand became a little stronger. She must not ask him questions now. He must make this part of the journey in his own time.

There was a long pause before he continued. "I met Ruth a couple of years after the War," he said, bringing her cold ghost out of the shadows into the warmth of that gloriously sunny spring afternoon. Ruth. It was the first time Laura had ever heard her name. From nothing, it gave this wraith substance: flesh and blood; a place in the world. She had become someone; someone this man had loved so deeply, the light had gone from his life at her loss.

He was concentrating, running ahead of her. "It was when my mother came down with Thomas – my youngest brother," he was telling her. "It was his seventh birthday. Moira had organised games for his party. Fan the Kipper. Pass the Parcel." He smiled wanly. "A neighbour suggested her friend, Ruth Kearsley, could play for them. She taught piano in Bellingham, she said, and she loved children."

The silence that followed had more meaning than any number of words. When he finally spoke, the strength had gone out of his voice. "She was nineteen," he said. "A bonny lass with sandy hair and freckles. Full of life. I was twenty, tongue-tied and gauche. A farming lad who fell in love on the spot, and was overwhelmed by it. I couldn't play a note. I still can't. I never understood what she saw in me."

Laura remembered the afternoon she had walked into his world unannounced, the piano music drifting out of his front door. She could still hear the soft tinkling notes, like the water of the stream at their feet. Susan had gone from his life, and he had retreated into the past.

He drew in a ragged breath, his voice hoarse, ready to break. "We had four very happy years together –" he said, struggling to maintain some semblance of self-control. "Our son was stillborn. Ruth died two days later from complications." Tears sprang into his eyes he did not want her to see. He looked down, fighting against them, his grip on her hand tightening.

She looked away, preserving his dignity, putting her other hand over his, hoping this would help, but having no way of knowing if it did. "I'm sorry," was all she could say. She felt inadequate.

The wagtail returned to its favourite spot on the opposite side of the stream, bobbing on the stones in the shallows. It ignored them, making sudden sallies into the air, catching insects in mid-flight before fluttering back to its stony perch with a harsh chirrup of satisfaction. Its exuberance broke into the gloom, letting in the light and warmth of the afternoon, dispelling the shadows.

He had been watching it intently. When it suddenly took flight and swooped away across the meadow, calling to its mate, he turned to her, trying to be brave. "It's taken me too long to tell that story," he said. "Far too long."

"What stopped you?"

He shrugged. "I was too angry at the time. I didn't want anyone's pity – or help. I wanted to feed the rage I felt inside. I think I was out of my mind for a while," he added. "Later, it was easier not to open up old wounds, just to keep them hidden."

"But time can heal, can't it?" She was trying to sound positive. "You *did* fall in love again – with Susan."

He looked down at their clasped hands for a moment then released his hold. He hesitated. "There was someone else before Susan," he confessed, looking uncomfortable at bringing this into the open. "But I knew it would lead nowhere, so …" He shrugged it off, turning away from her.

"When you'd moved to Meeston?"

He nodded.

"How long ago?"

He considered the passage of time. "About four or five years now, I think."

"Really?" She was quite delighted. There was hope for him yet – despite his doomed romance with Susan. Her curiosity spilled over. "Would you tell me who she was?"

His face slipped back into the familiar mask he wore when emotions became too difficult to handle. He winced slightly before speaking. "You," he said.

Chapter Forty-Two

They travelled in silence.

Laura drove them back to Meeston, her concentration focused on every signal, every change of gear, every manoeuvre. Everything had to be perfect. It was a test of character, she decided, and any over-active thought processes were best left until she could deal with them. They certainly had no place behind the wheel of a motor car travelling at speed.

Robert Moray sat staring straight ahead through the windscreen, locked in his thoughts, as he had been from the moment she had reacted to his confession with astonished incredulity.

The sun was setting when they arrived back at the Lodge. He got out and opened the garage doors, and she backed the car into its space faultlessly. At other times, she would have felt proud of her efforts. Today was different: today there was just a sense of something having been completed, and nothing else.

She remained in the car behind the wheel, gripping it as if her life depended on it. She would have been grateful beyond words if somehow, like the princess in the fairy story, she had pricked her finger, and been plunged into a long, and very deep sleep. A hundred years might just be enough to provide her with sufficient time to rationalise what he had said.

He was waiting for her to get out of the car, and when she showed no inclination to do anything of the sort, he climbed back into the passenger seat, and they sat there, side by side, struck dumb and visibly awkward in the silence between them. "I should never have told you," he said at last, keeping his face turned from her.

She did not answer him – or rather, she could not answer him.

"I didn't think it mattered now – not with us both going our separate ways." He drew in a long breath and shrugged. "And now I've upset you. That was never my intention."

"I'm not upset," she managed. "I'm extremely confused."

"Understandable," he observed, still not looking at her.

"I've known you since I was a gawky adolescent, Robert Moray, and never once – not once – have I had the remotest idea you had the slightest interest in me – not in that way." Why she felt so cross with him, she had no idea, except that she did.

"I learned to school myself," he said dismissively. "It was pointless trying to gain your affection – I was the casual gardener. I doubt if even your father would regard me as a prospective son-in-law. Your mother certainly wouldn't. You were intended for Oliver as far as she was concerned, I knew that much."

She felt dreadful. All those times she had gone looking

for him with her questions about wild flowers; the casual conversations about nothing in particular; the cheerful indifference to him. "Did I lead you on?" she asked, afraid she may have done something silly through some childish thoughtlessness, lacking as she did in her teenage years, much idea about the ways of men.

"No, nothing like that. You were just yourself. Curious. Interested. Someone I was comfortable with. Suddenly – one day – about four or five years ago, I suppose – I looked at you – and you were different. There was –" He sought the right words. "A glow about you. It was as if I'd seen you for the first time – and I began to feel what I thought I'd never feel again."

Martin, she thought. He saw me in love with Martin. Full of joy and the certainty of being in love. Oliver had never noticed any change in her.

"I knew how I felt didn't matter," he was saying. "I knew I was chasing moonbeams – but I chased them anyway, happy to be in your company whenever you came to see me. Happy to day-dream, and leave it at that. Then I met Susan, and thought I could overcome my infatuation – the older man attracted to a younger woman. I was quite pleased with myself at the time," he added, stifling a laugh and turning to face her. His eyes were strangely dark. "It was only later, after she left that I realised I'd done nothing of the sort. You were still there. Still very much there – right at the front of my mind. That day, just before Christmas, when you came to see me … " He trailed off into silence.

"You were angry with me!"

He shook his head. "No. I was angry with myself – because I'd not been honest enough to admit my romance with Susan was a substitute for what I really wanted."

"You pushed me away!"

"Because I had to."

"You're not making any sense."

He was looking at her as John Rufford had looked at her, and it was deeply disturbing. "I knew absolutely at that moment – I wasn't just still in love with you –" He stopped, and turned away, clamming up. For a moment he hesitated, then flung open the car door and strode out of the garage into the dusk. In the gathering darkness, he stood, a silhouette framed in the doorway, head down, hands on his hips.

Bewildered, Laura sat for a moment, trying to unravel his strangeness, and failing. When she finally got out of the car, he turned before she could reach him.

"I'm sorry," he said, clearly eager to escape her company. "Forget everything I said. It was all nonsense. It wouldn't have made any difference. You were still engaged to Oliver. It didn't matter."

"You're rambling," she objected.

"Probably. Look – just please forget what I said. I apologise. Let's leave it at that. Now, I must go."

She took him by the arm, detaining him. "No, I won't leave it at that. You have to explain yourself."

"I can't."

"You can – and you will," she insisted, still holding onto him.

They faced each other across the darkness. She could hear him breathing: tentative, ragged breaths, coming in short bursts.

"You wouldn't understand," he said. "I would offend you – beyond anything I can imagine."

"I think you should give me the benefit of deciding that."

He still hesitated. Then with a boldness she would always remember afterwards as the moment everything changed between them, he released her hand from his arm and put it squarely against his groin. He was hard beneath the thick corduroy fabric. "Now do you understand?" he asked, his voice thick with emotion. "I wanted you that day. I wanted to show you just how much. Like this. And more. It was a kind of madness. It's a kind of madness now."

She had no idea how to answer him. Beneath her hand she could feel his warmth straining against her. It was a dangerous sensation too reminiscent of John Rufford. She was appalled.

He took her hand away. "Now, you see, I have offended you."

"No, I'm not offended. I'm bewildered."

"Then let me go home and rue what I've just done." He stood back, well away from her.

"Don't you think you owe me an explanation? Do you think I'd have told you half the things I did about John and I, if I'd known how you felt about me?"

"No, of course you wouldn't."

"Then why did you encourage me?"

"Because I saw the way he looked at you – the love he felt

for you. Because I thought deep down you felt the same –
that you just wouldn't admit it. And I knew, if you were in
love with him, I could never hope to take his place. I could
be jealous of him, but that was all. I'd missed my chance
when you broke off your engagement to Oliver. He who
hesitates is lost."

It was an astonishing admission for him to make so
openly. She could only imagine how difficult it had been
for him to make it. He was a proud man. "And now?" she
asked him. "Now you know I've given him up?"

"Now? Now, I have to face the truth. I'm not the man
you're looking for. I'm going back to Stanegate because I
know you want to start a new life, on your own, on your
own terms – and you've every right to. I'm going back
because – as I said once before – you can't make someone
love you just because you want them to. I should be
content with what I've got – your kinship – and I hope,
your friendship – despite this evening. That sometime in
the future, you'll want to come and visit me, and I can
show you round Rigg End – no strings attached – nothing
expected." It was too dark to see his face now. But his voice
was filled with regret.

"I don't know what to say to you."

"You don't have to say anything. I'd just be grateful if
you could put right out of your mind what I did – before.
A momentary lapse of good manners – best forgotten."
There was a trace of bitterness in his words.

"I think you're asking rather a lot of me, don't you?
You can't honestly expect me to forget touching you – like

that?" How could she ever forget? Their relationship had been turned inside out, from an undemanding friendship between two equals to a frustrated one-sided love affair.

Silence on his part. Somewhere in Meeston Woods a dog fox barked, its harsh cry slicing through the evening air.

His silence gave her time to think, if not entirely clearly, then at least in part. The genie had been let out of the bottle and there was no putting it back. Something had to be rescued from this wretched business, and it was evident from his state of mind he was in no position to salvage anything, not even his pride. She could at least restore that to him, if nothing else. Finding the right words took a little time. "If I don't know what to say," she began, speaking across the darkened silence between them, "it's not because I'm offended – really, I'm not. I'm trying to make sense of it – what it took for you to show me how you felt – had felt for years. I don't care what you say, there must have been times when you let your feelings show. Something you said. Something you did. A look. I don't know. But something. I must have been walking through my life with my eyes shut – blind – or stupid, I don't know which. I never questioned anything."

A pause, his stillness almost palpable. "Would it have made any difference if you had?"

"It might. Who knows?"

A stifled laugh through the darkness. "Then I was a fool after all."

"Perhaps too cautious," she offered. "For too long."

He thought about this for a moment. "Yes," he admitted. "What do you want me to do?"

"Give me time. I can't forget what's been said – or done, but I don't want to let it destroy what we had. I'd like to save that – if possible. Do you think we can?"

"I'd like to think we could."

But in her heart she knew that was a lie. She would never be able to look him in the eyes again without thinking of his need for her, or how it felt to hold him.

CHAPTER FORTY-THREE

After closing time, Mr Gittings gave a little speech, thanking her for her secretarial services over the years. A little shyly, Laura thought, he presented her with a book token and a card with a Turner landscape on the front, signed by everyone in the office wishing her well in her new career, and she stepped out into the bright sunlight that late March afternoon, like a butterfly emerging from its cocoon, to be met by Mr Fielding, waiting patiently for her to take her Friday lesson. He had good news, he said. The date for her test was the Wednesday after Easter, and he had no doubt she would pass 'with flying colours'. Had she managed to do much driving in her father's car?

Her father's car had become synonymous with Robert Moray's extraordinary revelations the previous Sunday. Since then, she had made strenuous efforts to avoid him, still deeply uncertain how she would face him without being reduced to an embarrassed silence, or worse, silly, inconsequential chatter. There was one saving grace she was relying on to prevent this – the very individual circumstance of their encounter. Their conversation, by pure chance as it turned out, had had the benefit of the welcome shield of darkness. Mercifully, the gloom had given it a dream-like veneer, which under more glaring light would have been impossible. But that did not stop her repeatedly examining every minute detail of what had taken place: dissecting every word, every move, until she had once again come full circle and arrived back at the point where she began – to that unanswerable question – how to maintain the fiction that nothing of any significance had happened between them.

Her image in the dressing-table mirror every morning did nothing to unravel the mystery she had become to her own understanding of herself. No matter how hard she tried, she could find nothing exceptional about her looks that could account for two men, as different as chalk and cheese, vying for her affections. There was, in her opinion, neither rhyme nor reason for John Rufford's persistence nor Robert Moray's devotion. Nor was there anything in her relationship with either Martin or Oliver that came to her aid: Martin's love had been transitory; Oliver's, non-existent. She was left with a fog of confused notions as to what made her attractive to two very different personalities, and consequently with no guidance whatever on how to proceed – except perhaps to quit Meeston sooner rather than later.

Mr Fielding, satisfied she was maintaining her progress and urging her to 'keep it up', ended the lesson outside the Lodge. And she assured him, without the slightest idea how she would achieve this goal, by saying that she would.

Musing on the problem of how she could possibly continue to drive her father's car under the altered circumstances between herself and Robert Moray, Laura would have preferred time to herself at that moment, but it was not to be.

Gwen, as usual, was keen to pass on the latest gossip. She came bustling over from The Village Shop as Mr Fielding drove away. "Oh, Laura," she said, breathless with excitement. "There was such a scene on Wednesday evening outside Robert's place. Mrs Higson told Elsie she'd never heard anything like it in all the years she's been there."

Laura was used to Gwen's roundabout conversations. She knew the part she was expected to play – the curious questioner. But mention of Robert Moray set all kinds of warning bells ringing that needed extra caution in how she replied. So she limited herself to a surprised, "Oh?" and waited for whatever dreadful revelation was to follow.

"Mrs Higson said Susan Holbrook turned up after school Wednesday afternoon and banged on his door like something demented."

A chill ran down Laura's spine.

"Well, it seems when he opened the door, he didn't let her in, just left her standing there – outside. So she started carrying on at the top of her voice about what she'd been told."

Laura tried to look suitable interested, without betraying anything, but her heart was crammed into a very tight space, beating very fast indeed.

"Someone had said they'd seen Robert out in Lingford the other week sitting in a car with another woman, and what had he to say about that? Hadn't he the decency, she said, to wait until the end of term when she'd left St Wilfrid's before carrying on with someone else?"

Laura tried to interrupt, but Gwen was unstoppable.

"And Mrs Higson said Robert just let her carry on – said nothing at all – just stood there, dumb as can be! And then, right in front of everyone who'd come out to see what all the racket was about, she gave him such a whack – right across the face! Molly Smith said she could hear it from her front garden! And Robert just carried on standing there! Didn't to a thing! Not a thing! I said to Harry – a lesser man wouldn't've put up with that. I don't know what she was thinking of. If he'd been the one doing the leaving, it might have been different –"

Laura could stand it no longer. "Gwen," she said, desperate to stop the flow of tittle-tattle. "It was me in the car."

Gwen's eyes widened. Her jaw dropped.

"I'd asked Mr Moray to sit in with me for driving practice. He gave up his afternoon for me."

Gwen blinked, trying to make sense of what she had heard. "Oh, my!" she said, mortified by hearing the truth. "Why didn't he say so?"

"Perhaps he couldn't stop her."

Flustered and embarrassed in equal parts, Gwen could only keep repeating, "Oh, my!" several times.

Laura could only think of one thing – the whole village would be awash with the story, no doubt being embellished in the retelling over cups of tea and garden hedges, pints of ale and the buying of postal orders. It would, without a shadow of a doubt, have already reached the ears of her mother. In this regard at least, Laura was relieved to have been forewarned. Daphne would not know the identity of 'the woman in the car'. Better to tackle this head on, than allow the truth to filter back, benefiting from more colourful interpretations.

Daphne was preparing to leave as Laura entered the Lodge. She was dressed 'for church', evidently attending one of the Friday evening talks Reverend Talbot was giving on 'The Meaning of Lent'. Their conversations were still little more than polite dialogues of short duration, enlivened by occasional barbed comments, or brief forays into topics that required more prolonged engagement, such as discussing the use of the Lodge for coffee mornings. These were Daphne's latest venture into fund-raising for the Bowling Green Committee, usually involving Gwen and Elsie in all the preparations with minimum inconvenience to herself, and preferably with the absence of Laura from the premises.

Daphne raised the subject of the latest scandal without Laura needing to search for the most appropriate means of doing so. "I suppose you've heard about Robert Moray?" she said with her usual tight smile, straightening her hat and checking her image in the hall mirror. "Quite extraordinary."

"Yes, it is, particularly as he wasn't 'carrying on' with anyone."

Her mother turned her head, arching a well-drawn eyebrow at her daughter's tone of voice. "Really? And how would you know?"

"Because he was sitting next to me in Daddy's car while I was driving it – and I was the one who asked him to."

Dropping bombshells of this magnitude was never going to be an easy option, and perhaps with hindsight, Laura thought, she might have managed this particular bombshell with greater subtlety. But there it was – out in the open – and there was nothing to be done about it.

Daphne's expression froze, and Laura could well understand why: two unforgivable indiscretions had been perpetrated; her daughter had *asked* Robert Moray to sit in the car with her; and he had had the temerity to oblige her.

"And before you say anything," Laura plunged in, "I shall be asking him to do the same this weekend – if he can spare me the time – and any other weekend – or whenever – before I take my test. It was extremely kind of him to give up his afternoon. I can't imagine what Susan Holbrook thought she was doing! Now I shall have to explain to the Higsons and the Smiths and apologise to him." On reflection, she thought, this sounded a remarkably essential course of action under the circumstances, although her willingness to re-engage Robert Moray in the rôle of attendant qualified driver, definitely needed more careful thought than she had clearly given it.

Daphne's expression had barely altered, except for a small frown now clearly visible as she digested the latest pronouncement from her daughter. "Well, Laura, your choice of driving companion seems extraordinary. What did you expect? Choosing a man with such an unsavoury reputation? Astonishing. Of course, I realise that what I say means nothing at all to you these days, but some discretion on your part would seem to be required – for your father's sake, if no one else's."

Here at least, Laura managed to hold her tongue. No mention of Robert Moray driving her father to and from Lingford must be made. This wretched fiction must be maintained.

"Well, I shall leave you to sort out the muddle," her mother was saying, turning back to the mirror to readjust the angle of her hat, and tuck in an errant strand of hair behind her ears. "Let's hope we hear no more about it."

What Molly and Fred Smith, and Peggy and Ted Higson made of her story when she knocked on their respective doors, she never did discover afterwards. Uncomplicated folk, they seemed only too glad to have the truth explained to them, but were still largely exercised by the astonishing spectacle of Robert Moray being harangued on his own doorstep by someone they had previously regarded with some affection, and the even more amazing rectitude on his part in response to being physically struck. This above all else had remained fixed in their collective minds as being particularly noteworthy.

And so, having done her duty by him, as she saw it, Laura finally brought herself to stand in his porch, with the heady scent of newly cut logs he had stowed under the bench seats thick in the air. She knocked on his front door, without the faintest notion of how she was going to deal with what followed when he opened it.

He was still dressed in his farm clothes when he answered; still smelling of warm cows and milk. She had interrupted his supper, and she apologised for disturbing him. He was embarrassed at being unprepared for her visit. "I've not long been in," he explained, with a nervous smile. "Do you want to come in?"

Oh, so tactful, she thought. Did she? "Would you mind?" she asked.

He stepped back to let her through. "I've just lit the fire," he said. "If you'd like to wait here, I'll finish tidying up in the kitchen." And he retired through the narrow doorway into the back of the cottage, closing the door behind him, leaving her to sit on his sofa watching the flames take hold more strongly, filling the room with flickering light as the sun began setting across the fields towards Weaversham. From the kitchenette came the sound of plates and pans being washed and rinsed, and then, further off, water being run, energetic splashing, and then silence for several minutes before he returned, freshly scrubbed, wearing his casual cords and plaid shirt, hair still damp, and smelling slightly of carbolic soap. "It still gets cold in the evenings," he said, hunkering down to tend the fire, pulling together the logs before putting on the lamps and settling into his fireside chair. He smiled anxiously. "I suppose you've heard?" he said, clasping his hands together, keeping his eyes fixed on his intertwined fingers.

"Only this evening. I've explained to your neighbours – that I was in the car with you."

He looked up sharply. "You did what?"

"Explained to them – that you were helping me with my driving – at my request."

"Do you think that was necessary?" He clearly did not.

"Yes, I do. I'm tired of gossip in this village. And I – I'd like to apologise to you for what happened. If I'd not asked you –"

He was shaking his head. "There's nothing to apologise for."

"I happen to think there is – but you should have told Susan the truth."

"I don't think she'd have listened. She wasn't in the mood to hear excuses. Besides – I didn't want to involve you."

"That was very thoughtful of you. Thank you."

He acknowledged her thanks with a small nod and turned his attention to studying the fire.

One subject sat squarely between them, unspoken, but nonetheless, very evidently present. Huge, in fact. They had managed a whole conversation without any apparent embarrassment, yet it was here, when it should have been easier, that Laura found herself faltering, while he retreated, as he had so often in the past, into his own private thoughts, waiting – for what? Condemnation in the cold light of day?

"I was wondering," she began, stumbling through a minefield of possibilities, "if you had the time, whether you would sit in with me again – possibly tomorrow afternoon?"

He looked up, eyebrows raised. "Are you sure?"

"I wouldn't have asked if I wasn't."

He frowned. "You'll have to excuse me – I've spent most of this week wondering how I'd face you again."

"Well, so have I, if I'm honest."

He stifled an embarrassed laugh, then looked straight at her. It was an oddly direct gaze that made her look away.

"I thought of driving over to visit my aunts in Broxley," she went on, explaining her reasons. "But obviously, I had to ask you first."

He considered this proposal at some length, making her anxious that he genuinely would prefer not to, under the circumstances. "Does your mother know?" he asked. "About me being in the car – with you?"

"Yes. And I've told her, I'd be asking you again – if you had the time."

His expression displayed some astonishment.

"My mother doesn't rule my life any more, Robert," she said, realising she had used his name without thinking. "But I'd understand if you felt it wasn't … appropriate."

Another long silence. "Do *you* think it's appropriate? You know what gossip there's been already."

"I think I may have put that to rest."

"And it doesn't worry you that you mightn't have?"

"No – not particularly."

"That's all that matters then," he said. "But I've got milking at four. William's given Alan Saturday off."

"You could bring the car straight back, if you like. Aunt Millicent will drive me home if I ask her." How very formal she sounded, like someone arranging an office meeting, but she could not help herself. It seemed the only way to handle the situation. Besides, he had started to study her closely, which was making things more difficult.

He turned away and briefly glanced out of the window. "It's going dark," he said, abruptly getting to his feet, indicating it would be better if she left, without actually saying so.

"Two o'clock then?" she asked, taking the hint and allowing him to show her to the door, while he took great care not to stand too close, but close enough to look her in the eyes, just for a moment, but long enough.

"Two o'clock," he repeated, and opened the door.

She left with a brief "Good night," noticing Peggy Higson was putting out the cat at Number 2. "Good night, Mrs Higson," she called to her, pleased to be seen leaving Robert Moray's cottage after a relatively short interlude, and at such a respectable hour.

"Good night, Miss Driscoll," came the reply.

Everything had been very proper then, except Laura could not quite dispel the notion as she walked up Nether Meeston Lane towards The Cross, that at the moment of departure, Robert Moray was contemplating her in a decidedly John Rufford fashion. But what was more disturbing, was the recognition on her own part, that she might, out of sheer wilfulness perhaps, enjoy his attentions.

CHAPTER FORTY-FOUR

Spring proper, it seemed, had arrived overnight. Sitting on her bedroom window seat day-dreaming about nothing in particular that Saturday morning, Laura was suddenly aware, not just of the return of colour into the garden with its burst of yellows, reds, purples and the brilliant greens of new shoots in the herbaceous border, or of the startling *joie de vivre* in the cadences of chaffinches singing lustily in Meeston Woods, or, for that matter, of the change in the sky, where fluffy white cumulus sailed through a sea of intense blue, and the breeze had become soft and warm – but the unexpectedly exciting, coming-together of all these things at once. It was intoxicating, and she felt the thrill of it running through her as though she was experiencing all this magnificence for the very first time. It felt special, and she wanted to treasure it, and store it up for darker, winter days.

But meanwhile, there was the matter of Robert Moray to attend to.

He appeared promptly at two o'clock, well-scrubbed and presentable, hair newly trimmed, from the look of it, and he waited for her on the driveway under the watchful gaze of her mother scrutinising him from her vantage point at the sitting room window. He turned from inspecting the progress of the pruned dogwoods in the shrubbery as Laura closed the front door. His expression was suitably serious. "Would you prefer I wait for you somewhere else?" he asked. "Your mother evidently would."

"Does she make you uncomfortable?"

"A little."

"Then why don't we meet at the stable in future?"

It was only as Laura pulled back the doors that she realised she had given him the clear understanding they would be meeting on other occasions. She was not entirely sure she had meant to be quite so specific on that point.

He was noticeably reticent that afternoon, confining himself to small comments or brief responses to her questions, and keeping his eyes resolutely forward. He evidently felt this was appropriate under the circumstances.

Laura found herself mildly irritated by this, for reasons she could scarcely understand, except his behaviour seemed to contradict those final moments standing by his door the night before. Better then to concentrate on her driving, and leave the enigma of Robert Moray out of the equation, she decided.

They turned right off Broxley High Street onto the lane down to Hazeldene Court and slowed down.

He cleared his throat. "I'd like you to execute an emergency stop," he said. "Now."

She brought the car to a controlled halt in a manner Mr Fielding would have approved of, applied the handbrake and put the gear lever into neutral. "Was that good enough?" she asked, turning to face him.

"It was excellent," he agreed, only glancing briefly in her direction. "Excellent."

"Shall I drive on?"

"No – not yet." He paused. "I want to ask you something."

She was cautious.

"I just wondered ..." he said, floundering like a horse stuck in a muddy pool, flailing about and only making matters worse. "I just wondered," he tried again, "if you might – possibly –" He broke off, shaking his head. "No – no – it really doesn't matter. You'd better drive on. We'll be late."

How exasperating of him! "Oh, this really will not do! You can't ask me half a question!"

"I'm sorry. I'm finding it difficult. I can't quite get it right – how to speak to you – after –" He made a small, hopeless gesture with his hands.

"Well, I'm afraid I can't help you. I'm doing my best to pretend it never happened." Which was not true, because she could not deny her perception of him had radically changed. He was no longer someone with whom she had a comfortable, uncomplicated relationship, he had become an explicitly sexual individual who harboured a desire to bed her, which was frankly very difficult to ignore. Even now, as he sat next to her, she was wondering if he wanted to make love to her, and she suspected that he did, for all his reticence. And the more intractable problem for her was she was beginning to be curious about him as a lover: imagining him naked; how he would make love; whether he would be considerate or self-absorbed; tender or urgent; where he would kiss her, and how he would make her feel. All terribly dangerous thoughts that were best not considered, because they only served to remind her of John Rufford, and her sense of loss of that vital part of her life. Passion.

He was still considering what to say.

She tried to be patient.

He took a deep breath and began again. "I wondered," he said, concentrating very hard indeed, "whether, if I hadn't done what I did – if I'd been – more circumspect, perhaps – would you, under those circumstances – with the passage of time, maybe – have possibly grown fond of me?"

This tortuous sentence hung in the air between them like a thick fog, and they sat in total silence, until she heard him laughing softly to himself, shaking his head at the sheer nonsense of it.

"That's an impossible question," she pointed out.

"Yes – of course – you're right. It is," he said, clearly irritated with himself.

"Why not say what you mean, Robert? Simply."

He frowned with the effort, taking his time. "Let me try again. You know how I feel about you. Is there anything about me that would make it impossible for you to – to consider me in the same way? My red hair, for instance?"

"What?" She laughed, only to find he was deadly serious. "I'm sorry. Did that ever happen?"

He was embarrassed to admit it.

"No, Robert – your hair is lovely. It's the colour of horse chestnuts when they tumble out of their casings in autumn." She had not meant to be quite so poetic, but it was an honest description, and she was conscious, by his softened looks, that it touched him deeply. He suddenly seemed terribly vulnerable, and the temptation to lean over and kiss him, very gently, was suddenly very real, and very imminent. So she stifled it.

"I just wanted to know," he was saying, "because, if you'd allow me, I'd like to start again. I don't want to stop you becoming who you want to be. I know you need that freedom. But let me say this now, before you say anything – and while I have the chance. I'd like to think it was possible we could be close – closer than we are now. I'd like to be there for you in the good times and the bad."

Laura sat mesmerised, fascinated by his words rather than comprehending them. Meanwhile, it was as if a dam had burst and nothing could stem the flow of emotion he had been holding back so long.

His eyes had darkened. His voice had become slightly hoarse. "I'm trying to tell you I'd like to share my life with you – and that maybe – I don't know when, if ever – just maybe, you might consider the possibility of marrying me."

The loud honking of a car horn broke the spell. In the rear view mirror, an elderly gentleman in a flat cap behind the wheel of a mud-spattered Land Rover was gesticulating that he would very much like to proceed on his journey, and would they mind getting out of his way?

Laura, still reeling from such an unexpected proposal,

shoved the car into gear and covered the remaining distance to the entrance gates of Hazeldene Court in short order, swinging off the road without changing down, and finding herself apologising to him for her lack of control as they swept up the drive, Millicent-style.

They got out of the car under the gaze of Aunt Millicent who had heard them arrive, and was waiting to greet them at the front door.

"My, my, Laura!" she said, advancing down the steps all smiles and enthusiasm. "What a lovely surprise! I said to Sylvie – I'm sure that's James's car coming down the drive – and it was! And there you are – driving it! He'd be so proud of you." She leaned forward and kissed Laura on both cheeks.

Laura turned to Robert, still standing by the car at a respectful distance. "Mr Moray kindly agreed to supervise me," she said brightly, trying not to think too much about what he had just said. "He's taking the car back for me."

"Oh, Mr Moray, that is thoughtful of you. I'm sure Laura is very appreciative of your time."

He acknowledged her kind remarks with a small nod, excused himself politely and got into the driver's seat. He started up the engine and drove away without a single glance in Laura's direction. She wondered how he had managed to be so self-controlled.

By this time, Sylvia had joined her sister, eager to match her enthusiasm. "How lovely to see you again, Laura. So pleased you could come. And driving too! Haven't you come on? And your test in a few weeks too, Millie tells me."

Laura was ushered inside and the afternoon proceeded through the usual series of reminiscences and chatter over tea and cakes, while Laura did her best to deflect her Aunt Millicent's insatiable curiosity.

"It's good to see you've still got roses in your cheeks, my dear," Millicent noted. "Your young man's certainly had a lasting effect on you, I must say – or is there someone new?"

Laura shook her head, lying magnificently. "No, Auntie, there's no one new." Inwardly, she had the satisfaction of noting that her aunt, usually so quick to pick up the slightest clue, had never given Robert Moray a second thought: he was just the Meeston Lodge gardener; a shadow on the edge of their world; someone who rarely warranted a mention. Her aunt had simply failed to register his possibilities, and to her shame, Laura knew, she had always done the same.

As usual, Henrietta had gone to some trouble to receive her visitor, wearing her best frock, her hair newly brushed and neat, a dab of powder and rouge to brighten up her cheeks, and an over-abundance of eau-de-cologne, liberally sprinkled everywhere. "You look radiant, my dear," she said, her podgy hand holding onto Laura's arm as she sat down next to her. "Millie said you still had roses in your cheeks – and just look at you! – you have." There was a twinkle in her pale blue eyes. "But she didn't say who put them there!" she added, implying she had a source of intelligence other than her sister. "Tell me – are you becoming a *femme fatale*? Oh, I do hope so!"

Laura's attempts to assure her otherwise, fell on deaf ears.

"I might be stuck away up her in my room, my dear," she said with great dignity, "but I know what I see. There! I do believe you're blushing. Tell me – have you gone native – like Uncle James? Have you kicked over the traces? Do tell me if you have."

Her aunt's enthusiasm for this possibility made Laura laugh, and gave her the perfect shield behind which she could hide her embarrassment. But perhaps something about her reaction gave her away, for Hetty's grip on her tightened and she leaned forward to scrutinise her niece more closely. "I'm right, aren't I?" she insisted. "I can see it!"

"You really shouldn't encourage me to say anything rash, Auntie," Laura complained, making light of her aunt's persistence.

"Oh, I shan't, Laura. I shan't. There, there. I'm just indulging myself," she said, patting her hand affectionately. "Don't take me too seriously. It just gives me something else to think about."

It suddenly seemed such a small thing to bring some pleasure into her aunt's life, shrunken as it was to an existence confined by four walls and a view over the courtyard. She leaned forward and kissed the old lady's cheek, ignoring the overwhelming scent of perfume. "You never know, Auntie," she said, with a hint of conspiratorial intrigue. "As far as Grandpa Harriman is concerned, there could be another black sheep in the family – but you mustn't breathe a word."

"Not a word," Henrietta vowed solemnly in hushed tones, as if they might be overheard. "But I do hope you're right." And Laura had the satisfaction of seeing her old aunt's face light up with undisguised merriment, while in her own mind, she was running her hands through Robert Moray's warm chestnut hair while he made love to her.

CHAPTER FORTY-FIVE

She packed her satchel with her sketch-book and pastels and wandered out into Meeston Woods filled now with carpets of wood anemones, ostensibly to sketch the primroses she knew she would find nestling in a sunny spot against the boundary wall at Nether Meeston Lane. There was no sign of Robert in the woods, nor was there any when she was bold enough to venture up the lane a little way. His cottage looked deserted, and she presumed he must be working at the farm.

They had made no arrangement to meet, their last conversation being somewhat brutally cut short. Yet it seemed, from his lack of communication, he preferred it that way, purposely putting time and space between them.

Somewhat disconsolately, she returned to the wood and found herself a dry bank on which to sit, folding the tartan rug into a comfortable cushion beneath her. The afternoon light was perfect, intensely clear with sharp contrasts between light and shade. Before long, she had begun to capture the fragile beauty of the the pale petals and their soft green leaves set against the backdrop of the rugged, moss-covered stones. While she worked, a flock of long-tailed tits lisped softly to each other, fluttering overhead through the canopy of branches. It was pleasantly warm.

She did not hear his approach, his footfalls muffled by the soft earth along the edges of the path, so when his shadow fell across the sketch, she was both startled and delighted to see him.

He leaned over to study her handiwork. "You've a natural talent," he said seriously. "What could art college teach you you don't already know?"

"I can't teach Art if I don't go to college."

"My mother does," he said casually, sitting on the grassy bank beside her, arms buttressed against his knees.

"Your mother?"

"She has her own studio and gallery – in Edinburgh," he was saying in an almost off-hand manner. "She's got quite a following."

She was cross with him. "Why have you never mentioned this before?"

He raised an eyebrow, apparently bemused by her reaction. "I don't think you can honestly say Art has been the main topic of our conversations of late."

"I'm not talking about 'of late' – why not all the other times? – in the past – when I used to bring my sketches to you?"

He shrugged. "I was the gardener," he said, as if this explained everything. "Anyway, I've told you now."

"Yes, but you could have told me sooner. Didn't you think I might be interested?"

He turned away, apparently unwilling to be drawn.

She felt a little foolish: he was right, it had hardly been a relevant topic in the general scheme of things. "I'm sorry. That was unnecessary."

He glanced across at her. "Then I'm sorry I never mentioned it before. But you've seen one of her paintings."

"Where?"

"Above my fireplace."

"The landscape?"

He nodded.

"It's beautiful."

He smiled at her appreciation. "Then perhaps I should invite you for tea?" he suggested. "You could study it at your leisure."

She hesitated.

"If you come, I promise not to embarrass you – in any way," he added.

"If that's a promise."

"It's a promise."

"Then I'll accept your offer." She bundled everything into her satchel, while he shook out the rug and refolded it, carrying it over his arm for her.

He led the way down through the iron gate and onto the lane, maintaining a discreet distance. Once inside the cottage, he set the kettle to boil, and laid out two trays with willow-pattern cups and saucers with plates to match, leaving her to contemplate the painting on her own.

"I've not much in the larder," he confessed from the depths of his little kitchen. "I'd not planned on entertaining. Will potted beef sandwiches do? – with sponge cake to follow?"

"Very nicely, thank you."

In the bottom left-hand corner of the painting, she could just make out the name 'Grace Gillmuir' and the date '1935' in the texture of the wood grain of the two lower rails of a stile leading over a broken grey stone wall. The wall itself led the eye into the centre of the painting, following the course of a winding green lane with rising, close-cropped pasture behind it to the left, crowned by a small wood of what appeared to be mature oaks set against a sky of intense summer-blue. To the right, the view opened up across a lush landscape of rising meadow-land where sheep and cattle grazed, and hedges marked out the lines of ancient boundaries. In the distance, a grey stone farmhouse and outbuildings, surrounded by trees, nestled against a hillside. It was early summer, before the fresh green of new foliage had darkened, and the bluebells and red campion, picked out in intricate and exquisite detail against the stone wall in the foreground, were just coming into bloom. It was a beautifully executed piece, something she longed to emulate herself.

There was the sound of the kettle boiling. "What do you think of it?" he was asking over the steady whistling.

"I'm envious," she said. "It's quite stunning. Is it somewhere near Stanegate?"

"It's Geordie's farm from across the river," he explained, coming into the room with a plate of sandwiches. "Stanegate's further north beyond the hills."

"It's dated 1935."

"It hasn't changed much since. She painted it the last

summer we were there. Tea's ready. Would you like to sit down?"

He was the perfect host as he had promised, and after offering her a sandwich, sat in his usual chair to one side of the fireplace.

There was an awkward gap in the conversation she felt compelled to fill. "Is Rigg End nearby?" she asked casually.

He was evidently pleased by her interest. "It's over to the left, behind the oak wood," he explained, passing over the plate with the sponge cake cut into neat segments.

She took one with thanks.

"I've some photographs," he added. "I could show them to you later, if you like."

"I'd love to see them."

They ate in silence, Laura wondering what might happen next. The atmosphere was slightly strained.

"Would you like some more tea?" he offered when their plates were empty.

She declined. Small talk, leading – where?

"When are you visiting your uncle?" he asked suddenly, taking the conversation off into what seemed another direction.

"Saturday." It was a topic she would prefer not to pursue.

"Would you like me to drive you to the station?"

"I've already booked a taxi."

He accepted that. "When are you coming back?"

"I'm not sure. I thought I might take an overnight bag – just in case. I've told my mother I'm visiting a school friend." She was well aware her mother thought her liaison with John Rufford had been resurrected, but that was better left unsaid under the present circumstances. "I had to tell her something," she added. "It was the best I could come up with."

"Sounds reasonable," he said, gathering the plates together and tidying everything away.

"I'll help," she offered.

"No – you're my guest," he insisted and he left her on the sofa, contemplating the painting.

She could hear him moving around; cupboard doors opening and closing; the clatter of dishes, and the swirl of water. She waited, for what, she had no idea. Mention of her uncle had left a cold finger against her heart, at odds with the splendour of the evening sun and Robert's careful manners.

He returned, all smiles, carrying a basket of logs, evidently preparing to light the fire. "It'll go cool now," he said, raking out the grate and setting the kindling in place on top of crumpled newspaper.

She found herself standing up to leave, without being conscious of having made the decision. "Perhaps I'd better go," she said.

"But I've not shown you the photographs," he said, rising from the hearth still holding a bundle of small sticks. "Please stay," he begged, looking suddenly bereft. "I promised I'd do nothing – nothing that would embarrass you."

"I know but I think I ..."

"I only want to show you the photographs, that's all,"

he insisted. "I want you to recognise Rigg End – when you see it."

"I don't understand."

"On Saturday – you'll see it from the train," he said, eager to explain himself. "The track runs along the bottom of the valley by the river – below here –" and he turned to show her on the painting where the sloping pasture in the foreground hid what lay immediately beyond. "And it continues," he said, demonstrating with his finger against the glass until it met the frame, "for about five miles before Wallbridge Station." He turned back to face her, seemed about to say something, then clammed up.

The small distance between them seemed to grow larger. "Have you definitely decided when you're going back?" she asked.

He paused before answering. "The end of May," he said, his expression entirely neutral. "I'll be going up once or twice before."

"I see." She did not know what else to say.

"The place needs some work doing on it," he added, turning away quickly and hunkering down, laying the sticks in the grate with exaggerated care. "I'll write to your mother and recommend Alan for work at the Lodge. I don't know if it'll count for anything."

Laura sat down again. He had made his decision. "You don't need to write to my mother," she heard herself saying. "I'll let her know."

"I should do it properly," he said, striking a match and tossing it into the kindling and crumpled paper bedding.

"You have," she said, deciding there was nothing to be lost now in telling him the truth.

He turned to look over his shoulder.

"I own Meeston Lodge, Robert," she said. "Daddy left it to me, along with a great deal besides. That's why I've resigned from the Bank – why I can start a new career."

He stood up slowly, digesting the implications of what she was telling him. "Did John know?"

"No. I never told him."

He was clearly upset. "I'd no idea, Laura – when I made my proposal," he added. "I'm no gold-digger, I hope you'll believe that." At last he had called her by her name. The soft burr of his voice made it sound like a lullaby.

"I know that."

Behind him in the grate, the fire spluttered into life, sending a shower of sparks up the chimney. He turned back to tend it, seeming to take longer than was necessary. When he was satisfied, he returned to his chair and sank into a reverie, watching the flames lighting up the room as the twilight set in.

"I would like to see the photographs," she said, sensing her news had somehow dampened his enthusiasm.

"Yes, of course." He retrieved an envelope from a drawer below one of the inglenook bookcases, and lit several of the lamps, closing the curtains against the night. "Do you mind if I sit next to you?" he asked tentatively. "Just to show you them?"

"No, of course not."

But he put some distance between them anyway, and

was careful not to touch her as he handed them to her one by one.

They were small black-and-white snapshots, about a dozen or so, showing different views of a sturdy, stone-roofed two-storey farmhouse with sash windows, and an enclosed cobbled yard to the rear with adjoining outbuildings. Behind, on slightly higher ground, was a backdrop of mixed woodland – some mature oaks, a few spruce, and with larch at the fringes.

"This was the old stable," he said, pointing to one of the outbuildings. "My cousin Ian kept his car there – a bit like you do at the Lodge. And these are two small cottages that used to house farm labourers. They're empty at the moment. The other buildings are for the animals and hay storage during the winter." He paused, smiling over an old memory. "I remember old man Tyson showing me a litter of kittens in there one summer. Tiny things – all five of them – ginger, tabby and white – up in the hayloft – and the mother cleaning them up, proud as can be." His love of the place lit up his face. "And this," he said, drawing her attention to the building directly adjoining the house, "this used to be the dairy. It's bright, with plenty of natural daylight from the north, so I thought –" He stopped abruptly. "I thought," he continued more slowly, "that sometime in the future, I could convert it into a studio – for you." He looked up from the photograph, pained at having to admit the truth. "I thought I could lure you to Rigg End with the prospect of somewhere to call your own. But you don't need it, do you? You can afford to make your own life – anywhere." He looked back at the photograph, his voice filled with regret. "In fact, you don't need anything I can offer you."

She looked at the little prints she was holding, and into the face of the man sitting next to her, whom she had known for so long but never taken the trouble to notice, and wondered if this were true.

In the silence that followed, filled by the crackling of the firewood, he was very still, waiting to be told that all his hopes had come to nothing.

"Perhaps I need your love," she said.

CHAPTER FORTY-SIX

The First of April. April Fools' Day. An air of excitement and expectation. Silly pranks and giggling in the dormitories. Miss Arbutnot reminding girls of the limits of acceptable behaviour. Laura having to apologise to Miss Wolstenholme for putting salt in her tea, an escapade that could still make her blush when she remembered it. Not a day, then, she readily recalled, as one of sweet reason and tranquillity. Yet today was such a day.

She lay in bed, luxuriating in the indulgence of wilful indolence on a Monday morning. Her time was her own. Nothing mattered at that moment, except the moment. What lay ahead, beyond this idyllic interlude, was formless, ideas shifting and changing with the passing minutes. What would be, would be. *The Moving Finger writes; and, having writ, Moves on.* A disturbing notion in the past – but not today. Today, it had the resonance of a dismissive shrug, or a casual yawn. She would allow herself this day.

She turned over, watching the light changing beyond the curtains as the sun came and went behind the passing clouds.

Yesterday had been a fork in the road. She had never intended to commit to him so thoroughly. It had just happened. She could not explain why, at that moment when they were sitting side-by-side, the little photographs of Rigg End in her hand, it had seemed the right thing to do. Except that afterwards, she was certain that it was. And still did. Her half-formed fuzzy notions of college life, of belated student days, and all that followed after, had dissolved. They had been a passing fancy, nothing more. There were no more uncertainties. No more doubts. Now her way was clear. She knew where she was going – and who would make the journey with her. It was the completion of a circle. She was returning to her roots. It seemed inevitable – The Douglas Connection calling from the past to bring her home.

Except, of course, it was nothing of the sort. It came as a shock – to both of them. And afterwards, there was a moment's awkwardness between them, that neither of them felt well-equipped to fill. Both needed time to readjust, and for all his previous ardour that might have seen him take her in his arms – and possibly do more, he was reticent, perhaps constrained by his promise he would do nothing hasty or improper. And she had felt the same; unprepared, and not yet ready to reach out to him. The shift had been too sudden and too great.

So they had just talked. She had asked him endless questions – about his family, and who the people were who populated the photographs around his room. She learnt to recognise his brothers, Sandy and Tom with their wives, Mary and Una – and their several children; his Uncle Geordie and Aunt Moira; his cousin Ian and wife Bridie, his nephews Ross and Duncan, and niece Janet, a mischievous little thing peeping from behind her older brother in the photograph of Duncan's christening. And of course, Grace, his mother, with her fetching smile and Douglas looks, and mass of chestnut hair piled high up on her head – like Katharine Hepburn.

He had shown her his father's treatise, the text as dry and academic as he had warned it was. But opposite the title page, was his photograph, and she sought in it some likeness to his son, finding the same intensity of gaze behind the wire-framed spectacles, and general air of earnestness. But she liked the look of him and was sorry she would never know him.

And later, because she was curious, he had let her browse the contents of his bookshelves, to find found amongst the manuals on good farming practice, a wealth of illustrated books on birds and butterflies, trees and garden plants, fish and poultry, and an exquisite volume on the flora and fauna of the British countryside in detailed water-colours.

They had talked of marriage, but in very general terms of how their married life would be, with him devoted to the farm, and she to art. The when and where they would be wed, was left unsaid. Her mother's inevitable objection an accepted, but unspoken fact.

And so the hours slipped by. Near midnight, he had walked her home through the darkened wood, and left her at the entrance to the Lodge with no more than a soft "good night", and chaste kiss on the cheek, and they had parted in a daze of mutual bewilderment to their respective beds.

She woke to daylight, hearing her mother in the hall, and shortly afterwards the front door close.

Gwen and Elsie were sitting in the kitchen drinking tea, embarrassed by their inactivity when she found them there.

"Oh, goodness!" Gwen exclaimed, getting to her feet all flustered. "You'll think us idle things," she said. "Taking advantage of your mother not being here."

Elsie drained her cup. "I was just going to start the sitting room," she explained, clutching a duster to her breast. "Didn't want to disturb you with the hoover." And she scurried off, pink to the ears.

"I don't mind, you know," Laura said, refilling the kettle and setting it to boil. "I know you've both done more than was expected of you over the years."

"Well, I wouldn't want you thinking otherwise," Gwen said, still fussing unnecessarily. "Oh," she said, suddenly. "I've got a letter for you. From Robert. He came in early this morning. All of a rush, he was – and cheerful," she added, handing over the small brown envelope. "Not seen him look like that for years."

Laura put the envelope to one side with studied indifference while she concentrated very hard on pouring water into the teapot.

Gwen, inevitably, was curious. "Obviously, I've not said anything to your mother," she said. "Knowing how she feels about him."

"Always best," Laura agreed brightly, continuing to feign a lack of interest as the safest course of action. "I really

426

mustn't bother him so much about my driving." How plausible that sounded!

Gwen thought about this and nodded understandingly. "Said he was off to Northumberland for a few days. Seeing his uncle, I suppose."

He had said he might, if he could.

"Oh – and Alan would be round to cut the grass later."

Laura was happy to follow this line of conversation. "I noticed it was getting long in the orchard," she said. "All this lovely weather that we're having."

Gwen lost interest in this topic, and sat down again, hugging her tea cup. "I hope you don't mind me mentioning this," she began, "But your mother said you've given up your job."

"Mm. That's right."

"So we'll be seeing more of you from now on."

Where was this leading? – Laura wondered, applying a thick layer of butter and marmalade to her toast.

Gwen was hesitant, a deep frown wrinkling her brow. "It's just that you've not been home much – since Christmas – and she'll find it hard – having you round the place again – if you'll pardon me for saying so."

"I'll try to keep out of her way as much as possible. I shall be out myself a good deal once I've passed my test."

"Well, I didn't want you noticing – without me telling you first."

"Noticing?"

Gwen looked awkward. She got up from the table and opened the cupboard door under the sink. Next to the

427

bucket, and the cardboard box containing the tins of shoe polish and several brushes, was an array of empty drinks bottles. "It used to be just sherry," she explained. "But now there's G and T as well – especially in the evenings, that is. She leaves the glasses in the sitting room, Elsie says."

Elsie was never one for tittle-tattle. Gwen on the other hand, a good soul by and large, was not always so discreet. On the horizon was the prospect of Daphne becoming known as the village alcoholic. If that were so, her status would collapse, and so too would the precious world she had created for herself – and how would that all end?

Gwen was still in full flow. "I do hope you don't mind me mentioning it," she was saying, wanting reassurance.

"I'm glad you felt you could – except I'd be very grateful, you understand, if this was never mentioned outside these four walls."

"Oh my, Laura! I'd never breathe a word to anyone! Not even Harry."

Laura was not so sure, but she was certain the news of her attachment to Robert Moray would only serve to make matters even worse once Daphne knew of it. It was a subject best put aside – not pondered over – not today. Today was for all things uncontentious and sublime. A dream-time of rose-tinted spectacles and pleasant speculation. Daphne, and her drinking, had no place in her thoughts.

Later, in the study, in a calmer frame of mind, she opened Robert's letter.

'Darling Laura' – he had written in his neat script.

'Did I tell you that I loved you? When I got home last night, I wondered if I had, I was so overwhelmed by your accepting my proposal. I hardly slept thinking I may have foolishly forgotten. If I did, please forgive me. I love you very much.

'The reason for my writing, apart from the above, is that I'm catching the early train to Northumberland this morning to put Rigg End into better shape before you see it. William says Alan can do my stint at the Lodge. I've told him I'm going to see my uncle – which is true, but not entirely.

'I'll be away until the end of the week. Do you mind? I thought I'd travel up to Edinburgh as well. I want to tell my family the news.

'Can I confess? – my mother knows about you. I told her over Christmas, when I was like a bear with a sore head, and almost past listening to reason – even hers. She remembered her mother talking about her cousin Annie. They'd been close once upon a time. That's when she gave me the album. She said it might be useful. I wonder if she knew?

'But all this means I won't be back till late Friday night, and won't see you before you set off North yourself. I'm sorry. But try not to fret about your Uncle. He may be just as anxious as yourself.

'Remember if you can, to sit on the left side of the train when you leave Carlisle – so you can see Rigg End – even if I'm not there to wave to you.

'Remember too, I love you –

'Robert

'PS – There's no room for all the kisses I would like to give you.'

She reread the letter, then locked it away in the bottom drawer of the desk, and wandered out into the garden. The week would be empty days without him, but it was a glorious morning and she was filled with hope for the future.

Chapter Forty-Seven

The express thundered northwards, steaming through countryside she had never seen before: the heartland of industrial Lancashire, and the broad sweep of Morecambe Bay; the rising ground of Westmorland climbing to the wilderness of Shap; the slow descent to the softer rural landscape of Cumberland, fringed to the west by the jagged outlines of the Lakeland Fells; and the winding progress through pastures and farmland until it reached the Border City.

The train slowed to a crawl as it entered the station. There was a squeal of brakes, and a jolt as the engine came to a shuddering halt in a burst of steam.

Doors swung open, and passengers spilled out onto the platform.

Laura let them swirl away around her. There was half-an-hour to wait. She sat on a seat nearby, idling her time, hugging her weekend case, and watching the hustle and bustle around her: mail-bags being loaded and unloaded from flat-bed trolleys with squeaky wheels; families going on holiday with excited children; lovers saying their goodbyes, loath to part.

She wished Robert were with her.

The engine sighed and two men in oil-stained overalls and caps slipped down onto the track behind the tender to uncouple it. Outside the station, in the sidings, the replacement locomotive waited patiently, puffing contentedly. The uncoupled engine and its tender edged forward with a sigh, and the snorting black hulk of the replacement backed slowly down the line, the driver hanging out of the cab, inching it closer. There was the clanking of buffers touching, and the carriages shivered. The two men slipped back down onto the track, laughing and joking, handling the heavy linkages with ease. Then they were up again on the platform, chatting to the driver while the fireman stoked the boiler, his face streaked with coal dust and sweat.

"All aboard!" came the shout from the guard, his strong tenor voice echoing up into the rafters. There was a rush of tardy passengers; doors slammed shut and hasty farewells; the wave of his flag to the long, shrill note of his whistle, and a momentary pause as the engine drew in its breath.

A thunderous eruption of steam and blackened smoke filled the air. The massive bulk shuddered and strained, heaving itself forward, its giant wheels spinning and squealing against the rails. A second burst, then a third, its great heart beating faster: a deafening, overwhelming cacophony of sound and energy that drummed in her ears, bombarding her senses. She watched it pick up speed and slip away, the carriages enveloped in clouds of swirling smoke and steam caught beneath the canopy, the air reeking of burning coal and oil. The seconds passed; the noise and vibration slowly died away, becoming ever fainter. The wisps of steam and smoke dispersed, until all that was left was a strange nothingness, filled with the echoing twitter of sparrows in the girders overhead, and a cold wind tumbling a newspaper along the empty grey platform.

She shivered, and got up from the seat.

The cross-country train was waiting on the far side of the station. There were few passengers, and she found a compartment to herself, pleased to be alone with her thoughts.

The journey was slow, the route taking her into a landscape of small villages with tiny stations and interconnecting lanes with innumerable level-crossings. Habitation became sparse, the track swinging north-east for a while to reveal a vista of wild moorland where the tumbled stones of the ancient Wall perched on rugged ridges marked the edge of empire. A little further on, the landscape changed again, slipping into fields and woodland, following the course of a wide, meandering river. A softly rolling land, the higher fields filled with sheep and new-born lambs, the valley bottom freshly ploughed, and pastures ready for cattle to be turned out later in the year. A landscape made familiar, not by personal knowledge of it, but by Robert's eagerness to conjure up its every detail so that she should feel she knew it.

She held her breath, waiting.

The train slowed slightly as it skirted a low hillock, and

then, almost without warning, High Oakbank Farm came into view. She pressed her face against the pane straining to see more. Then, to the west, emerging from behind its sheltering trees and caught in a sudden shaft of sunlight, Rigg End, just as in the photographs, just as he described it: the winding track up from the lane – the sweep of the fields leading down to the river – the hedges and backdrop of woodland – the broad valley bottom. Her heart leapt at the sight of it, like a child's at the promise of a Sunday treat. But it was all too quickly gone, vanishing from sight as the track curved away once more and the train picked up speed, heading for Wallbridge and beyond.

There had been too little time to treasure it. Now there was nothing but a sense of anti-climax and unnecessary loss, and then, as the train pulled in to Wallbridge station, a desire to go no further, but to end her journey there. To forget about her uncle and go back. But it was foolishness. A whim, nothing more. Robert was in Meeston and her uncle would be waiting, not because he wanted her to come, but because she had pressed to meet him. So meet him, she must.

She sank back into a reverie, torn between moments of elation and uncertainty.

The clatter of wheels crossing points intruded on her thoughts. Beyond the pane were ranks of engine sheds and sidings; wagons filled with coal; the detritus of scrap metal stored on weed-filled ground; thick black oil-soaked sleepers, and rusting rails.

There was the echo of screeching brakes ricocheting

off the triple-arched roof. The train slowed to a rumbling crawl and the platform rose up to meet it. A final shudder, and it came to a halt.

Outside the austere classical facade of the station, she found a single-decker bus for Collingsby already waiting, and a group of cheerful trippers clambering aboard for an afternoon by the sea, their merry company too cheerful for her sombre mood.

The bus trundled through streets of grimy terraced housing and empty tracts of land still scarred by acts of war. To the south, across the river, giant cranes towered against the sky, and half-built hulls of great ships stretched out for miles. Echoes of Jack Driscoll, returning here too late before his son was born. A harsh place; unforgiving.

The constant sing-song chatter of those around her lulled her brain. She closed her eyes, fatigued from travelling, and let the time slip by. When she looked up again, the bus had left the city and its suburbs some way behind, winding through a flat, open landscape, following a coastal road. Ahead, a long curving strip of sand merged into a flat-calm steel-blue sea dissolving into a purpled mist smudging the horizon.

The bus slowed and came to a halt. "Collingsby Bay," the conductor sang out, and most of the passengers got up to leave: over-excited children and harassed parents marshalling their offspring; and Laura, solitary among so many who were not. The young conductor helped her down with a smile. "You all right then, pet?" he asked.

"Yes," she said, surprised that he should ask.

"Well take care then," he added, and rang the bell. The bus trundled off to the terminus further down the coast.

She stood on the pavement for a while, dazed and uncertain in this alien place. She had no bearings. It seemed best to follow those who knew their way down a broad cobbled street of grand Victorian terraces which once had iron railings along their walls. Ahead lay the sea. The smell of it was on the wind. The crowd dispersed, spilling onto the broad promenade with lawns and benches set at intervals stretching for miles on either side.

A cool breeze greeted her. Somewhere in the distance, the jangling sound of a funfair organ came and went on the wind. Her heart was jumping. Her head felt strangely light, and she felt sick with unnamed fear. She crossed the promenade and leaned against the heavy railings for support – thick metal tubes strung between corroding concrete posts. Overhead, the gulls screamed. She steadied herself, breathing in the sharp sea air, questioning again why she had come.

She remained rooted to the spot, reluctant to move.

Below her, a beach of fine silver sand curved away to a rocky outcrop, its promontory topped by a squat white-washed lighthouse. Children, heedless of the chill, cavorted on the wet sand; some building great moated castles, little flags of many nations fluttering from their turrets. Adults were huddled in deck chairs behind gaily-coloured wind-breaks: men in their flat caps reading papers; women in their coats and hats, chatting together and keeping watchful eyes on the children. An ice-cream vendor vied with a candy-floss stall to catch passing trade drawn by the siren sounds of a hurdy-gurdy organ and screams of delight from children on a helter-skelter. Further on, a cluster of small shops had their share of passers-by: the newsagent and tobacconists; the gift shop with its rack of postcards, and brightly coloured buckets and spades stacked outside its door; an amusement arcade with a group of teenagers, the girls in calf-length jeans and tight-fitting sweaters, the boys with long jackets and Elvis Presley quiffs, drawn to the slot machines hoping for fabulous wealth at sixpence-a-go.

At the far end was the café, the painted seagull on its facade, faded and peeling.

Laura pushed open the door. The atmosphere inside was hot and stuffy, and smelt of stale cigarettes and fish and chips. The dozen or so tables with their plastic tablecloths were all taken, and there was noisy chatter to the clatter of dishes and cutlery. At first glance, she could make out no one sitting on their own.

At the counter, two cheery young women were deep in conversation. "Can I help you, pet?" asked one, in her sing-song accent.

"I'm meeting someone," she replied, feeling out-of-place. "A Mr Driscoll."

"He's over there, pet – in his usual corner."

At first, obscured by other customers, she could not make him out. All that was visible was a hand holding a lighted cigarette. Excusing herself, she made her way between the tables, fixing a smile in place, and found him, sitting on his own, deep in thought. "Uncle Andrew?"

He looked up, put the cigarette down on an already overflowing ash-tray next to his empty cup of tea, and rose to meet her. "Aye, lass, that's me," he said, offering her a gnarled nicotine-stained hand to shake.

His grasp was perfunctory, his skin colder than hers, and her immediate decision was to keep smiling, come what may. She was shocked, and afraid that she might show it.

He was much shorter than she expected – and very frail. His clothes, from the fawn-coloured jacket with its open-necked beige shirt, to the shiny dark blue trousers, looked several sizes too large, and swallowed him up. His thick straight hair was lank, greying at the temples and kept in place by a greasy preparation. The face beneath was older than his years, the skin leathery, haggard and weather-beaten; his forehead deeply furrowed; and he had the underlying pallor of a sick man. But his gaze was dark, unflinching and intense. "Sit down, lass," he said, returning to his seat. His voice was rough, and talking brought on a fit of couching that racked his fragile frame. When he had recovered, he asked, "Do you want a cup of tea?"

She sat down, her weekend case at her feet. The combined heat, smell of stale fat and cigarettes was nauseating, but she feared refusing might be taken as a snub.

"Another tea here, Maggie," he called out from the table, and one of the women behind the counter nodded her acknowledgement.

"That's very kind of you, Uncle."

He picked up the half-smoked cigarette and squinted at

her through a veil of smoke. "I wondered if you'd come," he said.

"I thought I should."

He made no response to this. After scrutinising her, he said, "I don't see any of my brother in you, lass. Do you take after your Mam then?"

Her mind was empty of anything meaningful to say. "A little," she offered, and was relieved of the immediate burden of further conversation by the arrival of her tea. Her uncle fished out some coins from his top pocket and paid for it without a word.

"So what do you want to know?" he asked abruptly, dispensing with preliminaries that might have been expected. He dragged deeply on his cigarette, still studying her, the smoke curling lazily from his nostrils until he blew a steady stream to one side through his lips.

The proximity of others made her wary, and she wondered if he had known it would, intending to keep the conversation superficial. "I wanted to get to know you, I suppose," she began. The tea was much too strong and left a bitter taste behind.

He flicked ash into the tray dismissively. "Not much point in doing that, lass. Not if you can't tell your mam about me."

His belligerence embarrassed her. "I don't see much of her these days," she said, hoping this would mollify his irritation.

He was not impressed. He finished his cigarette, stubbing it out in the tray next to the others. "Your dad was ashamed of his family," he said abruptly, taking another cigarette from a half-empty Capstan packet.

"He was ashamed of his father," she corrected him, finding confidence enough to stand up to him a little. She would have said more, but the woman sitting closest was evidently listening.

Andrew lit his cigarette from a well-worn lighter and studied the glowing tip for a moment. "Our dad was a hard-working man," he said, oddly defensive. "Nothing to be ashamed of there."

"That wasn't what he was ashamed of," she said, trying to catch his eye.

"Oh it was, lass," he insisted, staring straight ahead at the greasy café wall. "Poverty. That's what he didn't want your mam to know about. Wouldn't have done, would it? Didn't want her to know he'd grown up in the gutter." He nodded, as if confirming this to himself. "He'd gone up in the world. Didn't want us spoiling things, did he?" He inhaled deeply again.

Laura did not know what to say.

He had turned to see her reaction, an expression of quiet satisfaction at her silence. "I don't know what you want from me," he said bluntly. "I can't turn on feelings I don't have, niece or no niece. You may as well be from the Moon as far as I'm concerned." He waved his cigarette at her. "Look at you! All done up, coming from a nice big house in the country with everything done for you."

She was stung by his accusation: she had been careful in her choice of clothes to avoid such criticism.

His raised voice had drawn attention to them. Several other customers were beginning to take notice – their eyes darting backwards and forwards behind their tea cups, missing nothing.

"All very nice for you, pet," he was saying, getting into his stride. "Don't think I mind about that now. You couldn't help your dad." Here he paused. "I couldn't help mine."

She saw the eyes watching them. "Do you think we could go somewhere else?" she suggested, eager to remove him from their audience. "It's very stuffy here."

"I like it here," he retaliated, blocking her suggestion with a scowl.

So, she had been right: he had chosen this place, gambling on her embarrassment not to raise a delicate subject in amongst a crowd. But she had not travelled seven wearying hours to be fobbed off, and if he thought to keep her silent by such a strategy, he was wrong.

She reached across the table and touched his arm. He pulled away from her. "Then tell me what happened to your sister," she asked, making sure the women next to them could clearly hear her question. "What happened to Auntie Jean?"

The muscles in his jaw clenched; his eyes narrowed, and his interest in being overheard diminished visibly. She pressed him further. "She was my auntie. I want to know."

His mood changed: he was wrong-footed and defensive. "What does it matter after all these years, eh?" he demanded, keeping his voice much lower than he had cared to before. "You can't bring her back, lass. Let her rest in peace." And he got up suddenly, scraping his chair across the red-tiled floor, unwittingly drawing a wider audience to watch him as he shambled out the door.

Laura followed in his wake, weekend-case in hand, pleased to extricate herself from the stifling atmosphere and nauseating tea at last.

He kept ahead of her on the promenade making for the first empty bench on the grass. He slumped onto it, breathless and wheezing, huddled inside his jacket. A pitiful sight, she thought. She sat down next to him.

"Have you no shame?" he said, keeping his eyes fixed on the horizon.

She said nothing.

Three children came running past, the eldest flying a blue and red kite with yellow streamers. The other two, a younger boy and girl, followed behind, whooping with delight at its sudden dips and dives.

He lit another cigarette, the smoke wreathing around his head before the wind snatched it away. He fell into another fit of coughing.

"You smoke too much," she said gently.

"Aye, I know," he said, spitting phlegm onto the grass. "Nothing to be done about that now."

They sat in silence for a while, the wind whipping round them.

"I'm getting married in the summer," Laura said, hoping to draw him out.

He glanced down at her hand. "No ring then?" he asked.

"Not yet. His name's Robert Moray," she added, knowing

this would mean nothing. "His grandmother was Margaret Douglas – your mother Annie's cousin."

He said nothing, just looked away, perhaps remembering the past.

"Did you ever meet her?"

"They never kept in touch," he said, still gazing out to sea. "Her family were a toffee-nosed bunch too," he added, the old belligerence resurfacing.

"Don't be cross with me, Uncle," she urged him gently, "Tell me what happened – to Auntie Jean."

He pulled on the cigarette again, exhaling slowly, and squinted into the distance, as if he might conjure her up from the purple mist. It was a while before he answered. "She went mad," he said, his voice flat; colourless. "That's all."

Laura could hear the hurdy-gurdy and the screams of children on the slides. She could hear her uncle's words, but their meaning slid away, out of her grasp, lost in the din and the unpalatable truth.

He inhaled again. "She was carrying on, the neighbours said," he was saying, his voice a rasping croak. "Kept telling them her dad had married her." He paused. "Well he had, hadn't he? He'd been shagging her for years." The brutality of his words hung in the air between them. Another, longer pause. A seagull screamed overhead. "They said he'd better get the doctors in. They locked her up. In Dodwell Asylum. He went back to Ireland." He turned at last to look at her, his expression worn out; empty. "Well – now you know. Does it make you feel any better, lass?" He looked away again, dragging on the cigarette. "It didn't make us feel better – your dad and me – when we saw her in that padded cell. Wasting away. Raving on about not eating till her Jackie came home for his supper." He retreated into silence again, the wound reopened, jagged and raw.

What could she say to him? All she could see was the image of a frightened little girl marked by a cross on a school photograph. For a while, her mind refused to focus, content to be diverted by the smallest thing: a sweet wrapper tumbling along the promenade, its silver paper glistening in the sun; the rasp of her uncle's breathing next to her; the sounds of children playing on the beach. But in the end, she knew she must acknowledge his disclosure with something solid; something he could accept.

"Daddy said he'd never forgiven himself for neglecting her," she said, hoping this would ease the pain.

He turned to look at her. "We never forgave each other," he said savagely.

There seemed nothing left to say. He finished his cigarette and threw down the stub, grinding it under his shoe. He stood up suddenly and checked his watch. "If you get yourself down the road, lass," he said, "you'll catch the quarter-to back into town." He wanted rid of her, and she had no way of holding on to him.

She gathered her case from beside the seat. "I hoped we'd have more time together." She was desperate to detain him a little longer. "I could stay, if you like."

He shook his head, beginning to back away, stuffing his hands into his jacket pockets. "You've got your life. I've got mine. Let's leave it at that, eh?" And he gave her a thin smile before he turned, shambling off down the promenade into the crowd still mulling over their postcards. He never looked back. In no time at all, his slight figure had been swallowed up, and all that was left was the jangling of the hurdy-gurdy and the raucous cries of the gulls.

Chapter Forty-Eight

Miss Arbutnot held fixed opinions on individual responsibility. "Don't blame others," she would say to miscreants. And so it was for Laura, with Miss Arbutnot's condemnation ringing in her ears. She could not blame her father: he had not suggested meeting Andrew, only that she contact him; he had not revealed his sister's ignominious end, because he wanted it kept hidden. No one was responsible for the dreadful outcome of that afternoon, except herself. She had been curious beyond reason, and now must pay the price. Regret would alter nothing. *The Moving Finger writes*.

She began her journey home fatigued and fretful, surrounded by others whose existence barely registered, except to irritate her fragile state of mind: the little girl, laughing and shouting, who ran into her chasing a soap bubble; the noisy crowd of trippers heading home, their bodies crammed against her; the children standing at the window of the train, blocking out her longed-for glimpse of Rigg End Farm and her only consolation.

She closed her eyes, shutting herself away as best she could. But her uncle's words stuck fast.

She went mad. That's all.

The rhythm of the wheels grew more insistent. Clickety-clack. Clickety-clack. Clickety-clack. Soon, it was all she could hear, and that was enough.

The train to Crewe was late, the waiting room cold and uninviting, the snack bar closed. She waited on the platform, disconsolate.

Arriving home a day too soon would rouse her mother's interest. There would be curious questions and no ready answers. She telephoned Robert from the grubby phone box outside the ticket office and asked if she could stay with him. She did not say why, and he did not ask – nor did he demur.

An hour later, the express was steaming south. Beyond the window, the scenery faded into lengthening shadows. She slipped into an exhausted doze, the endless loop of thoughts and images giving way to brief, but necessary sleep.

She opened her eyes. The lights in the carriage had come on. Beyond the window, silhouettes of trees and buildings sped past, lit by a rising moon.

What had she expected from her uncle? It was clear right from the start he had no great wish to see her. But she had not guessed the extent of his resentment harboured all those years; she had been unprepared for it. Nor had she imagined he would totally reject her, and how much this would hurt her pride. But *she* had opened old wounds for him, and he had felt it keenly. Why should he not firmly close and bar the door between them?

And what of Jean? Jean – elusive and intangible – slipping out of reach every time she tried to think of her, like the ghost she truly was – the timid little child, never wanting to be seen. It had seemed such a simple thing to ask – what happened to Jean? Simple, for someone lacking in discretion; lacking the wit to imagine there might be good reason for her father's reticence. And she had blundered on, relentlessly, not imagining there might be something more degrading or more shameful to uncover. How wrong she had been.

She went mad. That's all.

A simple statement with the keenness of a blade.

Was she truly mad – at first? Or had she only told the truth that no one would believe? – or wanted to believe? Had Jean been sane when locked away, and only later lost her wits among the lunatics? Was this what Andrew and his brother had suspected? Was this the great sin which neither could forgive – either themselves – or one another? Had it left an indelible scar? Yes, it had. And in her head her uncle's voice kept repeating over and over again, *Well, now you know. Does it make you feel any better, lass?*

No, she thought. It doesn't. It never will.

It was gone eleven when the taxi dropped her off at Robert's door. At Meeston Cross, a group of youths, fresh from the Meeston Arms, were laughing and joking, going their separate ways. They were raucous as only young men can be, their voices strident, still uncertain of themselves.

Laura struggled with her purse, the catch stiff and awkward for her fingers, numbed with cold. The driver waited patiently. Too fatigued to care, she gave him notes instead, and let him keep the change. He tipped his cap and drove away before she changed her mind.

Coming down the lane, someone whistled tunelessly. She turned to look. Robert opened his front door, the light from his living room spilling out along the path, illuminating her.

Alan Benyon stopped whistling.

"Evening, Alan," Robert said, standing in his doorway, barefoot, a jacket thrown over his pyjamas. "Don't be late for milking."

The boy nodded dumbly and stumbled on down the lane, hunched up, hands stuffed into the pockets of his jeans.

Robert ushered her inside. "You look cold," he said. "Sit by the fire. I'll make you a hot drink." No questions. No comment on the awkward fact she had been seen arriving at his door, quite evidently to spend the night. Just Robert, being practical and dealing first with what was needed most.

She did feel cold – to the core. She sat on the rug by the fire, warming her hands.

"Have you eaten?" he asked, handing her a cup brimming with hot chocolate.

She shook her head. "I don't want anything."

He put a hand to her forehead. "You don't look well," he said. "I'll fill a hot-water bottle. Get you to bed. I'll sleep down here."

"No –"

"I'll be up at four with Alan. I can sleep on the sofa."

Alan. Alan, who had seen more than he should have seen.

He read her thoughts. "You don't have to worry. He won't breathe a word."

"How do you know that?"

He leaned forward and kissed her gently. "Because he knows what happens if he does," he said.

She did not understand.

"He saw Susan leaving here last winter," he said, turning his face away to mask embarrassment. "She never knew. Alan was up earlier than usual and saw her from the yard." He glanced over his shoulder. "He never meant to cause trouble," he said dismissively. "Young men like to brag, that's all."

So the Higsons had been innocent – and Molly Smith, and all the others who she had been so quick to blame. "How did you find out?"

"He told me – once all the fuss died down. I thought it took some courage to do that," he added, with a faint smile.

"You're very forgiving."

"We all make mistakes," he said softly. "Now, drink up, and get yourself to bed."

An unfamiliar upstairs room, with white-washed walls and sloping ceiling: faded floral curtains; a small oak wardrobe by the window with a matching chest of drawers and bevelled oval mirror on a stand; a simple bedside cabinet with a clock, and a lamp, with a floral fabric shade.

His double bed was newly made, with fresh linen, just for her. She sank into its softness, a hot bottle at her feet, and pulled the quilt around her, knowing she was drifting into sleep.

It was a night of fitful dreams – of multi-coloured kites and sweet wrappers blowing in the wind – of almost catching them, and always failing. She woke at dawn to a chaffinch in full song. The bedside clock said almost six. Her head was aching, drumming to the rhythm of train wheels clickety-clacking.

She padded down the stairs to his bathroom with its pre-war fittings and lemon-yellow egg-shell paint. In the medicine cabinet by the tiny window, she found among the disinfectant, cotton wool and plasters, a small bottle of aspirins. She took two of them, replacing his toothbrush in the glass on the shelf above the basin. It was still damp from recent use. Next to it, his shaving brush and razor had been left to dry. She was an intruder in his private world and hoped he would not mind.

She sluiced her face, surprised by her image in the mirror: she was pale, fragile-looking, like a porcelain doll, and there were dark rings beneath her eyes. She went back to bed, curling herself against a spare pillow, pretending it was him, and was soon asleep again.

When she awoke, her head had cleared. She lay on her back staring at the ceiling, strangely calm; a blank canvas. The previous day had faded like a dream. There was nothing left except a better understanding of herself. Perhaps she should be grateful. Her uncle's rejection had been a blessing in disguise: the last link to her Driscoll past, with all its guilt and shame, broken for ever. She had learned the truth; she had grieved for Jean, but Jean was now long dead.

You can't bring her back, lass. Let her rest in peace.

Her uncle had been right after all.

She turned over, thinking of Robert. Robert and Rigg End. Her future – and what she made of it. That was what mattered. The rest was history.

Chapter Forty-Nine

She knew everything about him now: the pale smoothness of his skin, kept from the fierce heat of the sun because it would burn; the red-gold of the hair that ran down from his chest to the plateau of his belly, and down again to frame his groin; the fine down on his arms and legs that glistened golden in the firelight. She knew every curve and every muscle; the strength of him locked in the lean, hard frame she had never seen before; and the softness, there in his face in the after-glow of loving, and the gently beating pulse lodged at the base of his throat.

He was dozing, letting her run her fingers over him, ruffling the hair across his chest. In the dark, she could no longer see its brightness, but its texture felt like silk to the touch, and she could not get enough of it. He seemed content, happy to allow her an unfettered exploration; happy to let her rouse him once again.

They had come so far in so short a space of time.

The previous day, he had let her sleep, waking her at noon with tea and toast and she had struggled to sit up, confused by where she was.

He had sat by her on the bed, not presuming anything

too soon, sensitive enough to know that all had not gone well.

"It was wrong of me to go," she had confessed. "I opened up old wounds he'd buried in the past."

"Will you go again?"

"No. He doesn't want me to."

"Then let him be."

She had nodded, feeling he was right. "As you said – you can't make someone love you."

He had smiled at her remembering it.

Later, he had brought her soup and buttered roll, and feeling better, she had gone downstairs to join him and talk of other things: of Rigg End, and all their plans for it; of Geordie and Moira's delight, and of his mother's joy.

It had grown dark, and a light rain had become heavier with a rising wind, pattering softly against the window pane. He had set the fire to keep her warm and held her close, her head resting on his shoulder. He had kissed her hair, and then her lips, softly at first, and then with more insistence, seeking out her breasts, and she had wanted him.

In the firelight, they had undressed each other, unsure and hesitant: Laura anxious not to lead too soon in case it might offend, or hint at other tutelage; Robert, cautious at first, then bolder, finding her ready to accept his touch.

He had taken her there, on the rug by the fire, and she had held him close, even at the end. So he had poured himself into her, unrepentant, his love-making, tender but intense, although not so well choreographed or finely tuned perhaps, but erotic nonetheless, with a fierceness that could match her own the second time around, breaking John Rufford's spell at last.

The fire had died to nothing and they had come to bed, tired and replete, falling asleep in each other's arms. And here they were, in that dark hour before first light, rested and content: he, stirring once again beneath the lightness of her touch; she, wanting him to hold her fast, and fill her to the brim once more.

He turned over, obliging her with wanton cheerfulness that left them breathless and gasping with delight.

A blackbird burst into song as the greyness of dawn spread out across the sky.

"We're shameless," she whispered, pleased to find him so.

He ran his hands over her again with quiet satisfaction . "We've certainly been careless. Do you mind?"

"No. I love you." In truth, she had enjoyed the spontaneity, pushing from her mind echoes of another time.

He unwound himself from the sheets and padded naked to his chest of drawers, heedless of her pleasure in the sight of him. "I've something for you," he said, handing her a little heart-shaped box, as red as blood.

He sat beside her as she opened it, his eyes filled with love.

Inside against the velvet lining lay an antique ring, its chased gold band set with oval rubies round an iridescent opal, like a strange exotic flower that shimmered in the paleness of the morning light.

"It's beautiful," she said.

"It was my grandmother's – and her grandmother's before that."

"Janet Fairburn's?"

He was pleased that she remembered. "My mother wanted you to have it as a token of the bond between us. Will you take it? – with all my love? – from one Douglas to another?"

"You know I will," she said. He was beautiful, she thought. The harsh lines of his face softened by his loving, the seriousness succumbing to a smile; and his chestnut hair all tousled from her fingers running through it. Her heart was full.

He held her hand. The ring slipped easily in place. He laughed at it. "You have such slender fingers," he said, kissing them. "We'll take it into Kerrigan's when I buy your wedding ring. They'll make it fit you better." He replaced it in the box and put it by the bed.

Their wedding. A subject lightly touched upon so many times, but never properly discussed.

"I need to tell your mother I've proposed," he said at last, serious once more. "I owe her that at least."

No, she would not have him so humiliated. "You owe her nothing, Robert."

"Then let's say that I owe it to your father," he insisted, mindful as always of what he felt was right. "When shall I tell her?"

Never, was the word that sprang to mind. "Can we leave it for a while?" she hedged.

"It won't get any easier, you know."

"I'm not sure I can cope just yet." There had been too much emotion in her life of late. She needed time to arm herself again, against the inevitable recriminations; the fear of what might be said that could never be undone.

He smiled. "Yes, of course. I understand." He glanced up at the clock. "I'll have to go. We're off to Paxton market with some calves. William's expecting me at seven." He got up quickly and began to dress, content to let her watch him, knowing why. "I should be back for six. Can you stay?"

She shook her head, resenting the intrusion of reality's harsh light. "Mr Fielding's due at five."

He stopped buttoning his shirt and sat down on the bed again, embracing her. "Forgive me. I forgot."

She did not want to leave. "I should be here, Robert. Not up at the Lodge. I don't belong there any more."

"I'll come up and see you tomorrow afternoon," he said, kissing her softly. "Now I must go. I don't want William wondering why I'm late."

"I'll make you breakfast, if you like?"

"No, stay here." He turned at the door. "Don't look so sad," he said. "I shall think of you all day – and how I left you in my bed."

She listened to him moving through the rooms downstairs: the kettle boiling; water running in the bathroom; crockery and cutlery being laid out and later cleared away; the opening and closing of the front door – then silence. It crept up the stairs and into the room, surrounding her. She lay abandoned, curled up in the tangled sheets, thick with the scent of their loving, and waited for the comings and goings in the lane outside to cease. She listened to the birds singing, her thoughts drifting, until once more she fell asleep.

She awoke with a start. It was almost eleven. She dressed hurriedly and tidied up his room as best she could, then waited until just past noon before she left, trusting that his neighbours were too preoccupied with mid-day meals to see her slip out through his gate.

There was no choice but to take the path up through the woods. The way was wet in places with shallow pools on harder ground, and when she reached the kissing-gate on Meeston Road, her shoes were rimmed with mud. She found a patch of fresh young docks, their leaves just large enough to wipe away the worst. Such subterfuge, though necessary, did not sit well with how she felt. It seemed so wrong to hide their love.

No one was at home.

Unwillingly, she ran the bath, needing to wash away the scent of him out of necessity and nothing more, resenting the loss of his maleness and longing for his loving once again.

Later, changed and ready for the afternoon, she went downstairs. In the quiet of the study, she reflected on the past few days and her father's photograph, his placid features caught forever in that single moment of paternal joy. There had been so much for him to hide. Now she would do the same.

She removed the tin box from the drawer and took out her writing pad. On a fresh page, she wrote in careful, even script for posterity to note, "Sometime in 1924, Jean Driscoll was committed to Dodwell Lunatic Asylum. She died there the following year, aged 20."

A simple statement. What more needed to be said?

She tore the sheet from the pad, folded it, and placed Jean's photograph inside, then laid it in the box. It was done. Let her rest in peace.

She turned the key, and put everything away.

The clock chimed four. There was still an hour to go. She would have time before Mr Fielding was due.

It was a sunny afternoon, the churchyard filled with the heady scent of new-mown grass.

She picked her way along the well-worn path, dappled with sunlight, her thoughts elsewhere. Ahead, there was an unfamiliar sight: a black granite headstone, solid and defiant, standing at the head of the grave, the sunlight glinting off its polished surface, dazzling her eyes. The uneven mounds of turf had gone. Instead, slim grey granite curbstones and newly-raked gravel marked the plot, and a gun-metal flower holder stood empty and forlorn.

The stone was warm and smooth to touch, her fingers tracing round the edges of the letters chiselled out with stark efficiency and then picked out in gold.

To the memory of James Driscoll 1899 – 1962 R I P.

Nothing else. No 'Much Missed', or 'Dear Departed'. No 'Treasured Husband and Father'. No fond farewells of any kind. Just a statement of his passing, emotionless and hard: an inscription carved in stone that would defy the years and perpetuate a lie, just as her father knew it would. James Douglas had died unrecognised, unrecorded, and unmourned.

She had come, humble and contrite, intending to apologise; to denounce her reckless folly; her naivety; and then to ask forgiveness.

The wind stirred in the beech tree, fluttering the fresh young leaves; the birds were singing. But his presence no longer hovered round the place. Like the past, he too had gone.

Quietly, she turned and walked away.

As she reached the road, Mr Fielding's bright red car drew up outside the Lodge. It was five o'clock. Life went on.

Head up, she forced a smile; waved, and crossed the road to meet him.

Chapter Fifty

Deception and waiting: she was well versed in both, but the waiting was less easy.

"I don't know what needs discussing in a downpour," her mother had observed. "Can't it wait?"

But it could not. Every fibre of her body was on fire, and she cared not one wit for the discomfort of the workbench while he worked his magic on her, or afterwards returning home – after too short a time – soaked and out of breath, as if from running.

Two more lessons in the car, and Mr Fielding, displeased at her sudden lapse in concentration, remarking that a similar mistake could cost her dear.

Good Friday, and time standing still. More rain during the morning that spilled into the afternoon. Robert had gone over to Park Farm to help with lambing and would not be free that day. She mooned around the study pretending to be busy, but unable to settle, and idled the time away watching rain run down the window, day-dreaming of her life to come.

After tea, a late burst of sun drew her out into the garden, where she unexpectedly discovered Alan with his girlfriend in the garden store: she, a slip of a girl, barely sixteen, from one of the houses up on Smallcross Lane, who fled, half-dressed, red with embarrassment; Alan, apologetic but defiant nonetheless, knowing what he did of another close relationship. So they reached an understanding that silence by all parties would be best all round. A lucky find then, ensuring Alan's absence from the place on future evenings.

Easter Saturday, and unwelcome news.

"Ah," Daphne said with satisfaction, slicing open the white envelope over one of their rare breakfast times together. "Word at last!" Inside, was a deckle-edged card with silver bows, bells, and horse-shoes on the front. *Mr and Mrs Richard Gorst and Mr and Mrs Horace Parr request the pleasure … RSVP.* "Did I mention there's to be a double wedding? – the last Saturday in June?"

Laura said nothing, knowing there was nothing she could say.

"At St Barnabas' in Lingford, of course. There'll be *so* many people, St Wilfrid's would be far too small." Daphne looked across the table, apparently expecting some response. "You could at least show some enthusiasm."

"Really, Mother? – should I?"

"You are invited after all."

"I don't know why. I told Oliver I didn't want to be. It would be embarrassing for everyone concerned."

"How very perverse – considering you were so set against marrying him yourself. And what about Rosemary? You used to be such close friends?"

How could she accept – even for Rosemary and Julius'

sake? In two months' time, she hoped she would be gone, living far to the north with the man she loved, Meeston a distant memory of times past. But she could not say as much. There were no wedding plans in place. Nothing absolutely fixed – because she had stayed his hand and would not talk of it. "I'll send them cards, of course," she said, and wondered if either happy couple would reciprocate.

"Well, I shall certainly be going," Daphne was saying, finding it necessary to qualify her eagerness. "For Rosemary's sake, of course – not Oliver's. What he sees in that Parr girl, I'll never know. She'll lead him a merry dance I'm sure."

"Quite probably," Laura agreed. "Now, I must go. I need to brush up on the Highway Code."

Daphne looked up with mild curiosity. "Wednesday isn't it? – your test?"

"Yes."

"Well, at least you won't need to ask *that man* to accompany you any more once you've passed. Dreadfully embarrassing to have Dorothy Villiers mention it last week. Quite dreadful." And she turned back to the invitation, apparently satisfied at being able to express her contempt for him again.

"Then perhaps you should know I've asked him to go with me to Lingford this afternoon," Laura said. "I need all the practice I can get." But she did not say precisely what she meant.

They went to Kerrigan's to have the ring adjusted and he

arranged to collect it the following Tuesday, after market, and buy a wedding band to match in size. They wandered by the river for a while before she drove them home, and had the heartache of letting him go earlier than she wanted because he was needed elsewhere.

Easter Sunday. St Wilfrid's full to overflowing with the doors flung open wide, the swelling notes of the organ filling the air; voices echoing out across the fields "... O Lord of all, with us abide, In this our joyful Easter-tide ..."

He met her in the walled garden, and they spent a reckless hour in her bed while the Lodge was empty; dressing hastily and repairing to the vegetable plot to regain some semblance of a casual meeting discussing the progress of the potatoes, or when to sow the beans. And then he was gone again, back to Park Farm and the lambing sheds, and she was left with the memory of his loving and longing for the days to pass. Which eventually they did, and Wednesday came round.

She returned to the Lodge triumphant, Mr Fielding shaking her hand so enthusiastically, she was almost sorry their prickly relationship had now come to an end.

"I was just saying to Elsie, don't you think Laura's done well, Robert?" Gwen was saying when he appeared later that afternoon. The two women had greeted her arrival home with hugs and eagerness, wanting to know everything. "You must be pleased," she added. "All that spare time of yours you gave up for her."

He was standing in the doorway to the kitchen, grubby, still in wellingtons and smelling of sheep. He nodded, his expression showing satisfaction, but betraying nothing more. A well-practised art. He had spent years hiding his emotions behind a mask; now was just the same.

Laura smiled at him, knowing she was blushing, but it was easily dismissed, considering so much praise was being heaped upon her.

Gwen was all smiles. "Will you join us for a cup of tea, Robert? I know it's not the same as a sherry, but it's a bit early in the day for that, and I don't want Harry thinking I'm turning to drink." An awkward topic, quickly dropped.

"Can you stay?" Laura asked, hoping that he could.

"I'm sorry, Miss Driscoll. I only took half-an-hour off to come up and see how you'd got on."

"That's very kind of you, Mr Moray. Thank you for taking the trouble."

He smiled enigmatically. "I need to have a word with Mrs Driscoll," he said, as if this were a common-place event. "Will she be in tomorrow afternoon?"

Gwen was eager to be helpful. "I think she's seeing Mr Stockdale at two," she said, cheerfully unaware of what was being discussed.

"Perhaps if you called at around one-thirty then," Laura suggested casually. And he agreed he would. So she walked out with him through the walled garden and onto the drive, keeping a discreet distance apart, as was necessary, although he quickly pressed into her hand the tiny heart-shaped box. "Wear it with my love," he said, his eyes betraying everything. "I'll tell her tomorrow."

She nodded, slipping it quickly into her pocket. "Can't you stay?" she begged: she had wanted more of his than this.

He shook his head. "After tomorrow, we'll have all the time we want. Now I must go," and he pulled back so that nothing looked amiss. "Remember I love you." And he turned to briskly walk away. At the entrance to the Lodge, he met her mother coming in. "Afternoon, Mrs Driscoll," he said politely, and walked on.

Daphne turned to watch him go. "He looks very pleased with himself," she said tartly.

Laura merely smiled. "I thought I should thank him for helping me – to pass my test," she said. An easy lie.

"Well – if you felt you must," she said, advancing up the steps to the front door. "Are you coming in?"

"Yes. Gwen and Elsie are in the kitchen. We're having a celebratory cup of tea."

"Oh, really?" A brittle smile.

Daphne left the business of complimenting her daughter to her domestic staff, consulting her watch with ever-increasing frequency, implying it was time for them to leave. They took the hint.

"Goodness, I thought they'd never go!" she said irritably. "Richard's collecting me at five. Some Law Society Dinner or other this evening. Cynthia has invited me for supper."

"But you will be in tomorrow afternoon?" Laura asked casually.

Daphne frowned. "Only until two. Mr Stockdale is driving two of us over to Tapston Heath Bowling Club – to see their clubhouse. It's splendid by all accounts. Just what we need in Meeston." She paused. "Why do you need to know?"

A deep breath, and a casual shrug. "Oh, Mr Moray asked if he could have a word with you, that's all."

"Can't you deal with it? I really don't see the necessity for me to speak to him."

"He particularly asked to speak to you."

"I really can't think why. Most peculiar," she added, checking her watch again. "Well, I can't stand here wasting time. I need to change." She paused at the kitchen door. "If I'd known sooner, of course, I could have asked you to drive me over," she observed, looking pained at Laura's lack of thoughtfulness. "But it can't be helped, I suppose."

It was at that moment Laura resolved never to drive her mother anywhere, at any time, for any reason.

The following afternoon, Daphne, was resplendent in a pale-pink silk blouse under her elegant light-grey woollen suit, ready for her afternoon out. Her dark-grey leather gloves and handbag were waiting to be collected from the hall table, and she was hovering close by, checking her image in the mirror and fretting over the apparently unnecessary, and definitely unwelcome, interview with Mr Moray. "I do hope he won't take long, Laura. Mr Stockdale is always so very prompt," she said.

"Perhaps if you waited in the sitting room …" Laura suggested, trying not to sound as anxious as she felt.

"I'm sure what he has to say can be said in the hall," her mother responded, brooking no contradiction. "Or the kitchen, for that matter, if he comes here smelling of the cowshed as usual."

At which point, Robert Moray, immaculately groomed

and looking every inch the country squire in his sports jacket, checked shirt and twill trousers, could be seen mounting the porch steps.

Laura let him in with a warning smile.

Her mother surveyed him critically, still visibly offended by his presence, not least by his entrance through the front door. "Can't this wait until another day, Mr Moray?" she asked crisply.

"I think it's better that I speak to you today, Mrs Driscoll" he said softly, courtesy itself in the face of evident antagonism. "In private."

Laura opened the door into the sitting room. "Perhaps it would be better if you both sat down," she suggested, eager to remove her mother from the hall in case Mr Stockwell should arrive.

Daphne frowned, perhaps sensing something momentous in the air. She led the way and he followed, closing the door behind him, leaving Laura pacing in the hall, tense and dry-mouthed. Beyond the door, his words were muffled, measured and calm.

Laura took out the beautiful Douglas ring from its little box and placed it on her finger. She waited, heart in mouth. There was the briefest of pauses, then he opened the door and invited her to join them.

Daphne was sitting in her usual chair, ramrod straight. The colour had drained from her face; her expression frozen; her eyes staring at them both in disbelief; and one hand clutched at the pretty pink bow at her neck, seeking its support.

Robert remained standing, the model of rational moderation. "Laura," he said, giving her an encouraging smile, "I've told your mother of the affection I've felt for you over the years – about my prospects – and what I can offer you – that I've made a proposal of marriage, and you've felt able to accept it."

Daphne turned her adamantine gaze upon her daughter. It was not difficult to guess what she was thinking.

"We wanted you to be the first to know," Laura said, trying very hard to sound sincere, and presenting her left hand for inspection.

Her mother's eyes fastened on the ring, evaluating it, and evidently coming to the conclusion her husband's legacy had purchased it. An unpleasant tightness fastened round the corners of her mouth.

"It's a family heirloom," Laura was quick to tell her. "It's quite beautiful, isn't it?"

Daphne remained mute, struck dumb.

"I can see this has come as something of a surprise, Mrs Driscoll," Robert was saying with masterly understatement, valiantly trying to fill the chasm of silence that had descended on the room. "But I hope in time you'll feel able to accept me as as your son-in-law."

How he managed to utter these words and sound convincing was beyond Laura's comprehension. No one who knew Daphne Driscoll could possibly imagine her ever looking favourably on Robert Moray as a son-in-law: casual gardeners did not become sons-in-law in the Harriman scheme of things, particularly when they had an unsavoury reputation.

Daphne had begun to recover herself. Her colour had returned, and she was working herself up to give vent to her feelings. The early arrival of Mr Stockdale prevented the eruption. His car pulled into the drive, and Laura ran down the steps to greet him. He found himself ushered inside and brought into the sitting room to witness what he later referred to as "a most awkward situation".

The atmosphere was electric. "Well, Mother," Laura said, perhaps a little too brightly. "Aren't you going to tell Mr Stockdale our news?"

The necessity of maintaining her dignity in front of her visitor generated sufficient politeness for Daphne to mask the extent of her true feelings. She rose from her chair with regal dignity, straightened the front of her skirt, and with a forced smile, said in distinctly strained tones, "My daughter and Mr Moray have got engaged, Edwin."

Mr Stockdale's reaction was a mixture of anxious astonishment, tempered by good manners. "Oh," he said, looking nervously between mother and daughter. "Congratulations."

Robert smiled expansively. "There'll be a formal announcement next Friday in the *Lingford Herald*," he said, providing Daphne with yet more unwelcome news.

"And when's the Happy Day?" Mr Stockdale asked, doing his level best to be enthusiastic.

"As soon as practicable," Robert assured him.

There was an appalling bottomless silence.

In the absence of further conversation, Mr Stockdale felt compelled to add, "Perhaps in that case we should toast the happy couple?" And after consulting his watch observed, "There's plenty time before Mrs Barnes expects us."

"I'm afraid we'll have to defer that pleasure for another day, Edwin," Daphne said, tight-lipped, recovering herself sufficiently to put an end to the proceedings in as short a time as possible. "I'm sure she expects us before two." And with that she removed herself into the hall to collect her handbag and gloves, leaving Mr Stockdale to excuse himself with some embarrassment, and follow in her wake. The front door closed behind them with considerable force.

There was a terrible silence.

"You'll have to make allowances," Robert said, reaching out for Laura's hand. "This was the last thing she would expect."

But Laura was shaking, too angry to make allowances for anything.

He put his arms around her. "Don't be upset on my account," he whispered. "I've known her too long to be offended."

But Laura was beyond such mollifying. "I've known her far longer, Robert, and she offends me more each day."

He just smiled at her. "Enough," he said, planting kisses in her hair. "Don't waste your time on anger. There are more important things. Take me upstairs, and when we're done," he added, "you can drive me over to Broxley, and give your aunts our news."

CHAPTER FIFTY-ONE

At Hazeldene Court, Millicent was on the steps to greet them, waving cheerily as they both got out the car. "Hello, Laura. Congratulations on passing your test!" she said, kissing her enthusiastically on both cheeks, and briefly noting Robert's presence. "Do you still need to be chaperoned?" she asked with a quick glance in his direction. "Probably best for a day or two. Very easy to become over-confident." And turning to Robert, she smiled graciously, and said, "Very good of you to keep an eye on her, Mr Moray." A slight pause, noticing he showed no sign of leaving. "Are you staying for tea?"

"Thank you," he said, with a slight nod, acknowledging her invitation.

"Well, do come in both of you. There's no point in hanging about outside. Goodness! I do believe it's starting to rain. Such disappointing weather this week." And she ushered her visitors into the sitting room where Sylvia was hastily plumping up cushions and fussing over the need to find an extra setting of the bone china tea service for their unexpected guest. Henrietta, they were told, was having her usual afternoon nap.

"We do so enjoy having young visitors, Mr Moray," Millicent informed him. "But we rarely see the Gorst children these days. They seem to be far too busy to spare us the time. Of course, there are all the arrangements for the weddings, so it's not surprising. We must be dull company for young people."

"I'm sure you're not dull company at all, Miss Harriman," Robert said, smiling at her winningly and leaving her somewhat flustered by his observation.

And so the casual chit-chat proceeded as Sylvia enquired as to how he liked his tea, and offered him a generous slice of Victoria sponge, which he accepted. They were both fascinated by him, never having really noticed him before, and seeing him from their perspective, Laura had to admit, he cut rather a fine figure, red-headed or not.

With her aunts' attention diverted from her by their determination to be good hostesses, and by careful manoeuvring, Laura was also able to keep the tell-tale ring hidden beneath her plate until such time as she thought best to bring her news out into the open.

Millicent, always slightly more astute than her younger sister, was beginning to show signs of curiosity as to why Mr Moray should be staying for tea – and possibly more importantly, why her niece had chosen to sit on the seat next to his. Laura could see her casting sideways glances at him when Sylvia was talking, and a small frown had appeared as she wrestled with the conundrum of his presence.

At last there was a lull in the conversation which allowed Laura the opening she had been waiting for. She cleared her throat, aware she was slightly nervous of making her announcement. "Actually," she began, "Robert didn't need to chaperone me today," she said, noticing Millie's raised eyebrow at the use of his Christian name. "We've got some news for you, and we wanted to tell you together."

Her aunts looked at one another and then at Robert with renewed interest. The plurality of those involved in bringing the news had been noted, and Laura had no doubt Millicent was already getting the drift of where the conversation was leading: her expression had become one of intense interest, and she was leaning forward slightly in her chair waiting for her suspicion to be confirmed.

"I know this is going to be quite a surprise for you," Laura went on, hoping the announcement was not going to have the effect of a thunderbolt, "but Robert and I have decided we'd like to get married."

Sylvia, deferring as always to her older sister, nervously glanced in Millicent's direction, seeking guidance as to what her reaction should be. Millicent, momentarily caught off-guard, rapidly regained her composure. "Goodness, Laura! How wonderful!" she said, looking between the two of them with obvious fascination at this seemingly amazing turn of events. "Are you officially engaged?"

Robert reached for Laura's hand, revealing the engagement ring for their inspection. "We are," he said, giving Millicent another expansive smile. "I'm glad to say Laura accepted my proposal."

"Oh! – such a beautiful ring, my dear. Quite exquisite!" Millicent exclaimed, inspecting it closely.

"It belonged to Robert's great-great-grandmother."

"Exquisite," Sylvia echoed.

"Well, congratulations! – to both of you!" Millicent said, sounding genuinely pleased.

"Oh – yes," Sylvia repeated valiantly. "Congratulations."

Everyone stood up. Millicent and Sylvia embraced her warmly, and Robert shook their hands.

Millicent put both her hands round his, not letting go until she had satisfied herself she had seen in him what she had been looking for. "Every happiness to you both," she said, bestowing a smile on him.

"Thank you, Miss Harriman," he said, bewitching her once more with his good manners.

And Sylvia, not wanting to be seen as tardy in any way, was happy to repeat her sister's good wishes with equal enthusiasm.

After which there might have been an awkward silence if Millicent had not been willing to advance her understanding of what had happened. "Well, Mr Moray – I'm sorry, I should say Robert, shouldn't I?" she said, beaming at him again. "We're very pleased you wanted to come with Laura to tell us your good news. We oldies aren't used to such old-fashioned courtesy – and I mean old-fashioned in the nicest possible way, of course."

He responded with a smile. "It only seemed right to introduce myself properly to you – and I very much hope Aunt Henrietta will be able to see me later too."

"Hetty? Oh – she'll be delighted," Millicent was able to assure him. "Absolutely delighted. Goodness me – yes, she will."

It occurred to Laura that in all the years Robert had been at the Lodge, this was the first time either Millicent or Sylvia had had any meaningful conversation with him. It must have surprised them both to find him more acceptable than they might have supposed. But did they think he was simply a charming man who had spotted the chance to catch an heiress – and succeeded? Laura was given no opportunity to speak in his defence: Millicent had already opened the interrogation.

"Do tell us something about yourself, Robert," she began. "We're rather ignorant, I'm quite ashamed to say – after all the years you've been at Meeston Lodge too. Most remiss of us."

Laura was relieved her aunt had been circumspect, and not used the term 'worked' to describe his connection with the Lodge. Robert for his part was unruffled by Millicent's evident curiosity, and the more he spoke of his family, and his background, the more Laura saw her aunt reappraising the situation.

Having grilled him for half-an-hour or so, detained under the pretext of a further slice of Victoria sponge, Millicent directed Sylvia to see if Henrietta was awake, and suggested Laura should go up first to see her, so that she should not be flustered by the unexpected arrival of someone she did not know. And having got the necessary assurance that Henrietta was indeed awake and looking forward to seeing Laura, Millicent accompanied her niece out of the room, leaving Robert discussing the origins of rhododendrons with Sylvia over another cup of tea.

"Goodness, Laura!" her aunt said, as soon as they were safely out of earshot in the hall. "What a pleasant young man! So softly spoken too, with that lovely Scottish burr. And those gorgeous green eyes! How could we have been so blind all these years?"

"I was just as blind, Auntie – until quite recently."

"How long has he been smitten?"

"About five or six years."

"Heavens, Laura! So long! But does he know about – you know – "

"John Rufford? Oh – yes."

"Good gracious! My – my – I'm amazed. What can I say? Young people these days ..."

"You could say you liked him," Laura suggested.

Millicent gave her a very old-fashioned look. "Whether I like him or not doesn't matter, my dear – but I do. And he's obviously in love with you. Oh my!" And she clapped her hands with excitement. "Hetty said you were up to something last time you came, and I said, 'nonsense,' – which goes to show how much I know about things. But I hardly dare ask," she said, becoming suddenly serious again. "What does your mother think?"

"Do you really need to ask?"

Millicent shook her head sadly. "She won't be pleased, I'm sure."

"I think that might be an understatement, Auntie. If Mr Stockdale hadn't arrived just after we'd told her, I think things could have become very unpleasant."

"I presume she thinks he's a gold-digger."

"He's just the gardener as far as she's concerned."

"Well he's clearly more than that – and he's got property besides. What can she complain about?"

"She's never liked him, and there was some gossip in the village last year – about his relationship with a mistress at St Wilfrid's Primary."

Millicent raised an eyebrow. "Ah, I see – so that's why he's not too concerned about Mr Rufford, is it?"

"Possibly."

"Well, as long as he makes you happy, Laura. That's all that matters."

"He does, Auntie."

Millicent studied her closely. "I can see that," she said, patting her hand. "Well, we mustn't keep poor Hetty waiting any longer. You've got a lot to tell her, and she'll be wondering why I'm keeping you."

Henrietta was bright as a button sitting by the window, all agog to know the news. "Sylvie tells me you've got something exciting to tell me," she said, her pale blue eyes twinkling at the prospect of some delicious gossip. "I said, 'She's gone native, hasn't she? She's kicked over the traces – just like Uncle James.' And she said I had to ask you myself. Tell me I'm right, Laura. I told Millie the last time you were here. 'Just look at her,' I said. 'She's up to something.' And she wouldn't believe me."

Laura bent over and kissed the carefully rouged cheeks, and was overwhelmed as usual by the abundance of sweet perfume. "I've not exactly gone native, Auntie. But I think I might have kicked over the traces."

"Oh, do tell," Hetty said excitedly, and taking hold of Laura's hand caught sight of the ring. "My goodness, Laura! You're engaged! And such a lovely antique ring! Rubies with an opal centre – like a flower! Sit down – sit down. Tell me more. Who is he?"

It was difficult for Laura to tell her without her aunt bursting in with some observation or other. And the prospect of meeting this mysterious gardener who had been at the Lodge for ten years, and who plainly had more about him than just green fingers, was almost too much for her to bear.

"Oh, do bring him up, Laura. Let me meet this disreputable man who's captured my niece's heart and intends to run off with her to the wilds of Northumberland! How wonderful!" And her unlovely features suddenly took on an inner glow which might have been kindled years ago, Laura thought, if the right man had come along for her.

Laura imagined Hetty's enthusiasm to meet Robert would rescue him, although he seemed to be having a perfectly amicable discussion with both sisters when she entered the room.

"She's terribly excited about meeting you," she warned, as she led the way up the oak-panelled staircase. "Don't be surprised by anything she says, because she has some strange ideas. It's all to do with her Uncle James who was the black sheep of the Harriman family. She's always had a bit of a soft spot for him."

"I'll bear that in mind."

Laura opened the door into her aunt's room. "Aunt

Hetty," she said, letting Robert step through after her. "I'd like you to meet my fiancé, Robert Moray."

"Oh my!" said Hetty, clasping her hands together in delight. "So you're the gardener! Come and sit next to me and brighten up this old woman's life!" And she patted the chair Laura had occupied earlier.

Much later, and over-fed with cake and sandwiches, they eventually took their leave to the sound of chorused 'good-byes' and 'come again soon' ringing in their ears. And having been talked at and scrutinised for so many hours, they both lapsed into silence as Laura drove back to Meeston through the dusk in a fine drizzle, the windscreen wipers flapping to and fro in a gentle, leisurely way.

"I like your aunts," he said. "Hetty's quite amazing, isn't she?"

"She's very struck with you."

He laughed softly. "You were right, I wasn't entirely sure what she was talking about half the time. Who's the Edward Harriman I'm suppose to be 'one in the eye for'?"

"My grandfather. A horrible old man. Made her life a misery – and everyone else's come to that. He's the one who decided Oliver and I *had* to marry."

"In that case I'm delighted I've helped to thwart his plans."

She turned to look at him. "So am I."

They had reached Redbridge. It had been a lovely afternoon, filled with joy and laughter. What lay in wait on her return to Meeston Lodge was quite another matter.

Chapter Fifty-Two

She had persuaded Robert to go home, insisting she must face her mother on her own.

Daphne must have heard the car returning. By the time Laura had reached the front door, she was waiting in the hall. She was still wearing the grey suit and pink blouse from lunch time, something she would not normally do, and her face was visibly flushed. Laura had barely crossed the threshold before the tirade began. "How dare you!" she raged. "How could you do such a thing!" Behind her incandescent fury was the tell-tale slurring of her words.

Laura took her time, gathering her composure. "Keep calm," Robert had said. "Let her have her say. Gales always blow themselves out." Laura was not so sure.

"Have you taken leave of your senses? Wanting to marry *him! That man?* A nobody after your money! Not to mention his morals – or lack of them!" her mother added for good measure. Abhorrence and disgust oused from every pore.

In the pause that followed this initial salvo, Laura had time to fire her opening shot. "How much sherry have you had this evening, Mother?" she enquired casually, adjusting her hair in the hall mirror. "Or have you moved on to gin-

and-tonic already?" She turned back to look at her. "You really shouldn't drink so much. It's becoming a habit."

"I don't need lectures from you on my conduct," Daphne fumed, clutching the bannister rail for support.

"Perhaps you do," Laura said. "People are starting to notice your fondness for it. I wouldn't want you becoming known as an alcoholic."

Daphne had been unprepared for this attack. Her concentration wavered. "What I drink in the privacy of my own home is *my* business. You making a fool of yourself in public – with *that man* – is something else entirely!"

" 'That man', as you so insultingly call him, is my fiancé," Laura reminded her. "And I'd be obliged if you'd remember that."

"Fiancé or not – you can't marry him."

"Oh? And why not?"

"Why not? I should have thought that was obvious! He's our *gardener*! He doesn't *belong* to our set. Harriman girls don't marry their gardeners!"

Laura smiled inwardly. "We've had this conversation before, Mother," she said pointedly. You seem to forget – I'm not a Harriman."

Her mother's advance faltered. She regrouped and reinforced her position. "You're my daughter!" she retaliated, evidently feeling this was much the same thing. "A situation you appear to disregard at every opportunity!"

"Yes, if I can. It's hard to take you seriously when you never listen to anything I say. Now – are we going to continue this conversation in the sitting room, like two civilised people? Or are we going to stand in the hall while you continue to rant for the rest of the evening?"

Sweet reason was not Daphne's strong point at that moment. "We'll stand here for as long as I want to!" she thundered. "You knew Mr Stockdale was coming this afternoon – and you made sure I wouldn't be able to tell *that man* exactly what I thought of him – and his proposal!"

"On the contrary, you made your feelings perfectly clear. Robert was left in no doubt whatever. And I'm sure Mr Stockdale was in no doubt either."

"I speak as I find," she said, indignantly. "What did you expect? How can you think of marrying him? – after that business with Susan Holbrook?"

"That's over and done with."

"Oh is it? Has it occurred to you it was barely four months ago? What will people think?"

"I'm not interested in what people think."

"Then you should be!" Her mother's hand played nervously with the bow at her neck, her concentration shifting to other matters, clearly nearer her heart. "I don't know what I'm going to say to Cynthia – I really don't," she said bitterly. "I'll be a laughing-stock. My daughter throwing herself at the gardener – "

"I didn't 'throw myself' as you so indelicately put it. I fell in love with him."

"What rubbish!"

"Don't be so melodramatic!"

"I'm not being melodramatic, Laura! He's beneath you!"

"He's our gardener through choice, Mother, not because

he has to be. You've never bothered to find out more about him, have you? And when you're told, you don't want to listen. He doesn't need my money. Don't you understand?"

Her mother's animosity rose above her gin-fuelled petulance. "I know all I need to know about him," she said venomously, choosing to close her mind to any defence on his behalf. "And what I know, I don't like! He's a snake in the grass! Wheedling his way into your affections. He did the same with your father. Contemptible man!"

Laura's patience finally snapped. "I think that's quite enough, Mother," she warned, biting her tongue to prevent herself revealing secrets in the heat of the moment. "I love Robert Moray, and I intend to marry him, and that's all there is to it. And this time," she said, advancing across the hall until there was barely an arm's length between them, daring Daphne to strike her as she had done once before, "there's nothing you can do, or say to stop me."

For a moment, there was silence.

Then Daphne drew herself up to her full height, a tight-lipped smile spreading across her face. "Hah! Isn't there?" she said triumphantly, tilting her head back imperiously. "Well don't expect me to be at your wedding!"

The tension collapsed like a burst balloon. Laura could barely contain her laughter. So this was the ultimate sanction? Did her mother really believe this was a threat? "You're pathetic," she said, too angry now to listen to Robert's urgings. "Drunk and pathetic. Listen to yourself. You're a self-righteous, self-opinionated, narrow-minded, ignorant woman, puffed up with your own sense of importance. This is all about you – not me. You and your precious position in this community. Your so-called 'good works'. Your 'status' as Lady Bountiful. Your sheer arrogance and intolerance. Let me tell you something, *Mother*, you're the last person on earth I'd ever want at our wedding. I can't imagine anything worse. Oh, and by the way," she added for good measure, wanting to be certain their relationship was completely and utterly destroyed for ever. "Here's something else for you to ponder on over your next bottle of gin. In case you're wondering, Robert and I have already been to bed together – several times in fact – including in this house!"

Daphne relinquished her hold on the bannister and sank onto the hall chair, the colour draining from her face.

There was an incredibly long silence, filled only by the steady ticking of the clock.

Daphne had turned to stone.

Laura surveyed her handiwork with satisfaction. "I suggest you have that drink now. You look as though you need it," she said, and leaving Daphne speechless in the hall, went upstairs, determined to take some very positive action to remove herself from this woman forever.

She began by making a list of what she needed immediately; what she could leave behind; and what she wanted to protect, once she had gone.

The next morning, after what had been a sleepless night, she politely avoided Gwen and Elsie's anxious enquiries. Was Mrs Driscoll all right? She was still in her room, refusing to come out. Laura suggested they both take the rest of the day off, which they agreed to, although somewhat reluctantly, fearing perhaps their absence might be the cause of unnecessary friction the following day.

Once they were gone, Laura telephoned Mr Weightman, the locksmith in Weaversham, whose services had been required once or twice at the Bank. He obliged her by coming over to Meeston immediately, and fitting a mortice lock to the study door, handing the keys over to her when the job was done. "You can't be too careful these days," he said understandingly. "Always best to have internal locks as well – just to be sure." To which sentiment, Laura was happy to agree.

When she had waved him off, she set about transferring the listed items from her room into the security of the study. She packed her satchel with the art materials and put this, together with her portfolio and easel, by the front door. With everything else safely locked away, she filled two suitcases with essential clothing and took these down to the hall, made herself a light lunch, and telephoned Robert when she knew he would be at home. He understood her reasons, and said he would square their arrangement with William that afternoon. He did not argue against her decision.

"I'll drive round this evening," she said. "There are a couple of things I need to do first." She did not say what, and he did not ask.

With her preparations complete, she wrote a brief note to her mother.

There was no polite salutation.

'After yesterday evening,' she wrote briskly, 'I have no wish to see you, or communicate directly with you ever again.

'I am moving in with Robert tonight, and have taken with me everything I need in the short term. Other items I shall want in future, I have stored in the study, out of your way. If I need to access these, I shall do so on Sunday afternoons when there is no likelihood of you being at home. Once I am settled after my marriage, I shall arrange for these to be removed. Everything else left in my bedroom can be disposed of.

'Any future communication necessary between us regarding the running, or the maintenance of the Lodge, should be made via Mr Parr at his office address.

She ended the note with the single word 'Laura', folded it and left it propped up against the clock on the mantelpiece in the sitting room.

Then she telephoned Mr Parr and arranged to see him at his office.

Throughout, Daphne remained closeted in her room, most probably with a suitable bottle of sustenance. Her absence signalled her defeat. But no doubt she was watching from her window when Laura piled her belongings into the car and drove away without a backward glance.

It was almost five o'clock when she reached Lingford. She parked in the Market Square and waited long enough to be sure both Oliver and her Uncle Richard had left the office before making her way there. This was one occasion when she had no desire to meet either of them.

She rang the doorbell, and Mr Parr let her in with a welcoming smile, inviting her to sit down in his office.

"I'm sorry I wanted to come so late," she said. "You must have thought it very strange of me."

He seemed unperturbed. "No, not at all, Laura," he assured her. "I'm assuming this visit involves circumstances where you would prefer the absence of the other partners."

She was glad he had such a precise understanding of her motives.

He tidied together the papers on his desk and placed his pen and pencil neatly beside them. "Now," he said, clearing his throat. "How can I help you?"

She got straight to the point. "There'll be an announcement in next Friday's *Herald*," she said. "Robert Moray and I are engaged to be married."

Mr Parr's expression betrayed only mild surprise at the news. Perhaps it relieved him of any residual guilt he may have felt over his daughter's awkward liaison with Oliver. "Ah," he said with a slightly raised eyebrow. "Let me offer my congratulations to you both."

"My mother objects to our marriage."

He only nodded, apparently taking this for granted.

"Which is one of the reasons why I asked to see you." She paused. "Firstly, I'm taking your advice. I'd like to make my Will."

He nodded again, reaching for his pen and note-pad.

"I want Robert to inherit everything."

Mr Parr's hand remained poised above the pad for a moment. "As of now?" he asked tentatively.

"Yes."

"Mm," he said thoughtfully, putting down the pen.

"You disapprove?"

He made a small noncommittal gesture with his hands. "It's not for me to approve or disapprove," he said. "Merely to advise."

"And you think I should wait until we're married?"

"It might be prudent."

"If anything happened to me tomorrow, Mr Parr, I'd still want Robert to inherit everything."

"Does he know this?"

"No. We've never discussed it – and he has no idea of the amount involved."

"Mm. I see. No other individual bequests?"

"No. None."

He considered the implications, allowing her sufficient time to do the same. "This is hardly a complicated document, Laura," he said after a prolonged pause. "It certainly won't take long to have it drawn up for you. If you're absolutely certain this is what you want, I could have it ready by tomorrow lunch time. Would that suit?"

"Perfectly."

"In that case, I'll phone Mr Gittings first thing in the morning. I'm sure he'd be willing to act as a witness for you. Shall I suggest we meet at the Bank, rather than here? Two o'clock perhaps?"

"That's very kind of you. Thank you."

He made a note in his diary and sat back in his chair, regarding her with some affection. "So what's the other thing you wanted to speak to me about?"

Laura felt her mouth go dry. "I've come to a decision. Last night, my mother and I almost came to blows."

"About your marriage?"

"Yes. Things were said that can't be unsaid, and I've – I've decided to move in with Robert – immediately – at Nether Meeston Cottages."

Mr Parr pondered this intelligence, most probably reflecting on his daughter's less-than-perfect conduct.

"It won't be for long, Mr Parr. We're intending to get married as soon as possible."

"I see."

"It's very regrettable, I know, but I don't wish to have any further direct contact with my mother. Obviously, with my responsibilities for the Lodge, I realise this will cause difficulties – so I've asked her to raise any matters through you in future. I'm sorry. I know this puts you in a very awkward situation."

"No more than in the past," he observed, as if used to this state of affairs. "I presume you have no intention of returning to Meeston after the wedding?"

"No, we'll be living in Northumberland."

"Ah, yes. Mr Moray has a farm there, I believe," he said. "I think your father mentioned it."

She was surprised he knew. "Yes. Rigg End – near Stanegate."

"Lovely part of the world up there apparently," he said. "Yes, it is."

He looked surprised. "Oh – you've seen it?"

"Oh – yes," she hedged, realising she was saying more

than she intended. "I was in the area a few weeks ago – visiting a friend. I saw it from the train."

Mr Parr nodded, apparently satisfied with this explanation. "Interesting man, your Mr Moray," he added after a moment's reflection. "More to him than meets the eye, as they say. I know your father enjoyed his company."

"Yes, I believe he did."

"Well, you clearly do, which is more important."

She found herself blushing.

He sighed and got up from behind his desk. "I'm sorry your mother is being so difficult, Laura," he said with a pained smile.

"She doesn't know the harm she does."

"No," he said pensively, walking with her to the door. "No, she doesn't, I'm afraid." And Laura wondered if he had had a similar conversation with her father.

"Thank you for time," she said, shaking his hand.

"Not at all. Until tomorrow lunch time then," he added, beaming at her.

For a while she sat in the car considering the consequences of her actions. Was it just a petty act of revenge – and nothing more? Possibly. But she no longer cared.

In a perverse way, she realised, her own behaviour was following the Harriman tradition: taking whatever measures necessary to keep a legacy within the family. She had cemented The Douglas Connection absolutely. Edward Harriman would have understood her motivation; whether he would have appreciated his philosophy being used against his daughter was quite another matter.

Chapter Fifty-Three

As scandals went, Laura's removal from Meeston Lodge to live with Robert Moray, was by far the most noteworthy anyone in the village could remember. It far outweighed the Susan Holbrook-Robert Moray scandal of the previous Christmas, not least because 'the man in question' was the same man. By and large, it seemed to do him no harm whatever, certainly among the men who frequented the Meeston Arms. In fact, it seemed to add an extra gloss to his already enhanced persona, and there were certain young bucks in the neighbourhood who clearly wondered what he had got that they were singularly lacking. The female members of the community were divided on the subject. The older ladies frequenting the Village Shop and Post Office registered their shock, gossiped copiously amongst themselves, and went home, possibly wondering what was missing from their lives. The younger women, Laura noted, were not averse to casting their eyes in his direction, and openly flirting with him.

For Laura, however, it was a different matter. She had imagined she could 'brazen it out', once something more titillating came along. But the 'something' failed to materialise. The men would smirk when she passed. The women tended to ignore her, particularly those who relied on her mother's patronage, while others, who had no immediate acquaintance with either party, felt it incumbent on them to disapprove of immoral behaviour in a young woman from a Good Family as a matter of course.

Gwen and Elsie occupied an uncomfortable No-man's Land. They made strenuous efforts to avoid contact in public – fearing, no doubt, that any overtures would reach the ears of Meeston Lodge. But after the official announcement in the *Lingford Herald*, the postman brought greetings cards from both of them offering their congratulations.

For others, the situation was equally fraught. Reverend Talbot, fresh from his sermon on the forgiveness of sins the previous day, was struck dumb when he bumped into Laura outside the Post Office, rendered mute by the conflicting demands of his Faith, his Humanity, and the Church Organ Fund. Laura was faintly amused by his evident confusion.

Of Laura's immediate relations, Millicent was eager to keep in touch, only too happy to pass on titbits she thought of interest. It was from Millicent, Laura learned Daphne had been whisked off to Dyers Green by Cynthia, and that once restored to her old self, had returned to Meeston Lodge with such an aura of affronted dignity, no one had dared express any opinion – even a sympathetic one – on the subject of Laura's defection.

"All this excitement, my dear," Millicent told her, "has quite perked up your Aunt Hetty. She's positively blooming.

We're arranging for one of these electric chair-lift things – so she can come downstairs again and join in all the gossip!"

From the Gorsts, there was a stunned silence.

Meanwhile, Robert's neighbours remained scrupulously polite, their proximity to the source of the scandal once again the cause of some embarrassment.

Laura's isolation increased, and the date of their wedding became a matter of urgency. Where they would marry, who they could invite, and who would come, raised awkward questions. From not being discussed at all, the topic began to dominate their lives.

"We can marry in Edinburgh," Robert said, providing all the answers. "I could arrange to see the Registrar next week, if you like."

So the date for the wedding was fixed: they would be married on the last Saturday in May. It would be a quiet affair at Edinburgh Registry Office. Millicent and Sylvia were content not to be invited; Henrietta would not have been able to travel in any case. There was no one else Laura wanted to invite. For her, it was enough to have the love and goodwill of Robert's family around them to wish them well.

But Robert's absence in Edinburgh, even for so short a time, was almost more than she could bear.

April had given way to May: the mornings bright, with heavy dew sparkling on the grass; the hedgerows and orchards bursting into extravagant displays of blossom; the evenings filled with the echoing cries of swifts and the twitterings of swallows.

Alone, Laura became restless, wanting to escape the

confines of the cottage, and a sunny evening saw her in the car, setting off to seek inspiration for her art elsewhere.

In her haste to change, she had left her ring on the chest of drawers, and by the time she remembered, it was too late to go back. She had travelled several miles, taking the car down winding lanes, past hamlets, and into the more open countryside of pastures and scattered farmsteads that merged into semi-wilderness and wetlands.

There was a sudden familiarity about the scene: a vague remembrance. She slowed down. Around the bend an empty lay-by came into view, a weathered signpost on a wooden stile by a hedge. Rothwell Mere.

She pulled in, and for several minutes sat, the engine running, wondering if she should drive on. She had never thought to return here, with its memories of another time – and another man. But it was tempting now to see the mere shake off its wintry garb and put on the softer robes of spring.

With her satchel slung over one shoulder and clutching the travel rug, she clambered over the stile and into the field, finding herself hurrying towards the top of the rise. When she reached the spot, the scene laid out before her was beautiful; serene. More than she expected. In pure joy, she half-ran down the slope, found a flat shelf of turf and laid out the rug, to sit, hugging her knees, absorbing everything around her. In the distance, blackbirds vied with one another to out-sing all the rest. Her blood sang in her veins.

The mere was like a mirror bathed in sunlight. Along the

margins, the new season's reeds, sturdy and upright, were topped with feathery bronze fringes, like plumes on cavalry helmets. Beyond, the trees were no longer dark forbidding skeletons, but a study in vivid greens, their outlines hazy with new leaves. Behind them, the sky was turquoise blue with peach-tinted clouds; and every stone, every blade of grass, every leaf was tinged with yellow-gold.

From deep within the reeds, a duck and flotilla of ducklings set off across the shallows, weaving an exquisite zig-zag plait of colours in their wake.

She sketched quickly.

The sun began to dip towards the trees. The scene was changing. The shadows spread, slipping across the grass, plunging the mere into darkness, swallowing it up. She worked feverishly. Her senses seemed too sharp; too finely tuned; too near to breaking. In the end, it was finished and she sat back, exhausted; drained.

Late spring evenings are usually the best.

His words came back to her unbidden, somehow melancholic. She closed her eyes, remembering him standing there, wrapped in his duffel coat against the cold, camera at the ready, smiling down at her.

"Laura?"

Her heart missed a beat, then clamoured in her head. *His* voice. Unmistakable.

She swivelled round, her pulse racing. She had conjured him up.

He was there, standing at the top of the rise – John Rufford, in light grey slacks and open-necked white shirt, his cricket sweater thrown casually around his shoulders. He came down the slope with easy strides. "I wondered whose car it was," he said, leaning forward unexpectedly to kiss her lightly on her brow, overwhelming her as always with his aftershave. His face was soft, filled with pleasure, his eyes consuming her. "You passed your test then? Congratulations!"

Her throat was dry. She could not speak.

He ignored her silence, bathing her in his glorious sensual smile. "It's wonderful to see you. I came here on a whim – and here you are! What made you come?"

"I – I don't know," she said, hearing her voice coming from a great distance away, like someone else's.

"Ah – so it wasn't the possibility of finding me here then?" he said, slipping effortlessly into his usual banter. He hunkered down to examine the sketch. "God, Laura," he said admiring her work. "You really are good at this. It's beautiful." He paused to look at her, his expression changing to one of reflective contemplation filled with tenderness. He was close, much too close, invading her private space.

She felt paralysed. This was how he looked the last time – while he was loving her – and she had wanted him beyond all reason. He was potent still, even now. There was danger here. She pulled away, standing up to put more space between them. "The light's going," she said, gathering her things together hastily. "I can't do any more today."

"I'll carry the rug," he offered, folding it carefully and following her as she walked quickly up the slope. After a moment or two, he asked, "Did you find out what you wanted to know – in the end? – about your family?"

"Yes."

"As bad as you expected?"

She could not look at him. "I've come to terms with it."

He seemed undeterred by her unwillingness to talk. "It's strange," he said. "I was going to phone you this weekend. I wanted to apologise again – about what happened – last time. Everything's all right, is it?"

"Yes, everything's fine," she assured him.

"Good."

She stumbled slightly, and he took her arm. "I noticed you've not been around recently in Weaversham," he observed, conversationally. "Have you been away?"

She was bewildered. Something was terribly wrong. For him, nothing had changed: he was still waiting. She clutched her satchel close, like a protective shield: something physical to put between herself and this seductive, beautiful man, who could still make her want him.

He was waiting for her answer, his head slightly tilted, brown eyes engaging hers, a questioning smile on his lips.

Was it possible he did not know? – about Robert? She clutched the satchel closer, her fingers overlapping, bare of ornament, reminding her she had come without her ring; her talisman against temptation.

At the top of the rise she stopped, forcing him to do the same. She freed herself from his grasp. "John," she said, listening to her voice falter as she spoke. "You do know I'm engaged, don't you?"

It was hard to watch the destructive power of words: her words, heard by him but not fully understood at first. For a moment there was no response: nothing, just his eyes looking into hers, holding her fast. The change came slowly, remorselessly as his self-assurance drained away. A slight frown gathered on his brow, then deepened; his gaze wavered, betraying disbelief, then pain; his smile froze, then faded. He said nothing, reduced to silence, and his face became a lifeless mask. She had destroyed him, utterly.

An assassin's knife could not have done its work so well.

She floundered, trying to explain. "There was an announcement – in the *Herald* – after Easter."

He blinked. "I see," he said, his voice flat; emotionless. "I must have missed it."

"Didn't Jules mention anything? I thought he might."

He shook his head and turned away, thrusting his hands deep into his pockets. "I've not seen Jules for a while."

"Oh – I see." What else could she say?

His face was still turned away from her. "He works in Chester now – County Offices – easier for him and Rosemary when they're married ..." He trailed off, his voice breaking under the strain.

She should have written; should have been honest and told him everything. Instead she had embarrassed him; humiliated him. He did not deserve that. "I'm sorry," she said. "I should have let you know."

"No. No," he insisted, with a forced smile, trying to preserve his dignity. "You mustn't be sorry. Not your fault.

You told me to get on with my life. I didn't. I've only myself to blame." He paused, studying his shoes. "God knows what you must have thought of me – of my behaviour. I wouldn't have been so – so – no, I really wouldn't."

"It's not your fault. You didn't know."

Suddenly, he looked up at her, seeking answers. "A sudden decision was it?"

She nodded.

"Who's the lucky man? Do I know him?"

She paused. Telling him was hard. "Robert Moray."

"Really? The revenge of the Pale Knight!" He stifled a hollow laugh.

"Please don't say that."

"I'm sorry. I didn't mean to be rude." He turned away, facing into the sun as it reached a fiery crescendo on the horizon. "Ignore me," he said, his voice thickened with emotion. "I'm not handling this very well."

She wanted to explain; to make it easier. "Robert and I – we're related," she said.

He nodded, his face still turned away from her. "Ah – I see. Part of the family mystery?"

"No. Something that came out of it."

He cleared his throat, recovering a little. "A common bond then."

"Yes."

A pause, filled with bird-song.

"When's the wedding?"

"Two week's time."

He glanced round. "So soon?"

"Yes. We're marrying in Edinburgh."

"Oh. Will you live there?"

"No. Robert has a small farm up in Northumberland."

He did not appear to find this in any way astonishing. Perhaps he was beyond astonishment. He merely nodded his acceptance of the fact. "So – we'll never meet again." A statement rather than a question. He was looking right at her now, fighting back tears.

She shook her head. "No. I don't think so."

The sun had finally sunk behind the trees, filling the field with jagged shadows. It had grown colder.

They had run out of words. They turned and walked back to the stile in silence. She let him help her over, conscious as he did so, he did not let her go as quickly as he might have done.

In the lay-by, they stood facing one another, a world apart.

"Thank you for everything, John," she said. "I mean it."

He smiled bravely, a ghost of a smile, gone as quickly as it came. "I shall always love you," he said. "Always."

"Please don't say that," she begged. "I'm sure you'll find someone else – some day." Empty words. Thoughtless words. She hated herself for saying them.

He shook his head. "No, I don't think so." There was a long pause. His eyes were searching hers. Dark chocolate eyes she could drown in. "Promise me something," he said softly, " – that you'll remember me fondly."

She nodded, unable to speak.

He leaned forward and kissed her lightly on the cheek,

lingering for a moment, the scent of him filling her head. "Goodbye then, Laura. Take care of yourself."

She tried to smile, but her heart was heaving into her mouth. She turned away and hurriedly scrambled into the car. In her mirror she could see him standing by his Roadster, watching her go. Solitary. He waved, and she drove off, not knowing, or caring where she went, tears streaming down her face.

She lost all sense of direction, driving blindly until at last she headed home.

It was dark when she reached the cottage. She threw herself onto the sofa, emotionally raw; lacerated. Fresh tears welled up and spilled over in an inexhaustible torrent. Her head ached. She needed Robert, and his absence left her weak. Eventually, she fell asleep.

A tawny owl's eerie cry awoke her. It was still dark. The ache in her head had become a fog. She sat up slowly, aware her eyes were sore and her nose blocked. She had no idea of the time.

For a while, she sat in the dark, not wanting to think or feel. Eventually, the mood passed. She put on the light and closed the curtains, steadier with familiar things around her. The clock said just past two.

The sketch-pad was on the floor by the door where it had slipped from the satchel. She retrieved it, finding her study of the mere. It no longer seemed a picture of a golden evening captured in late spring: it had become something darker. The deep shadows among the reeds were strangely menacing, challenging the brilliance around them as ephemeral, doomed to die with the passing of the sun. It had become a scene of shattered hopes and dreams, and unutterable despair. It would forever remind her of John Rufford's pain; his humiliation, and not how she wanted to remember him. He belonged to another time: to a January day, when ice glazed the surface of the mere and caught the reeds along its margins in its grip; when the sun offered little warmth, but they had walked there hand-in-hand ignoring the cold; when she had been entranced by him, and he had brought her into the light making her shine.

She would destroy the sketch.

Impulsively, she reached to tear it from the pad. But something stayed her hand. He had admired the piece; thought it beautiful. She surveyed it with fresh eyes. Would he think so still? Would he want it as a keepsake? – a gift to mark their brief bewitching time together? She had his Rubaiyat; he had nothing that was hers. Perhaps she should leave its fate to him. He could destroy it if he wished.

She removed it from the pad with care, and turned it over, writing on the back, 'To John. A memento of an enchanted place. May 1963. From Laura.' She paused, and after a moment's hesitation added, 'with love'.

Chapter Fifty-Four

November 1988

A grey November day, like so many others in his twenty-four years, Tom thought, yet not like any other.

He had been up before dawn and gone out to the sheds in the teeth of the gale to feed the stock and check over the sheep on the lower pasture, taking Brack, the favourite of his Border Collies.

It was a raw morning, the valley filled with thick curtains of rain buffeted by a gusty wind. The river had risen several feet overnight, the thick brown waters swirling in smooth eddies between the banks, taking with them whatever they found up-stream. It was a scene of tumult and deceptive calm. He watched it for a while, ignoring the rain running down his neck and Brack's undiminished exuberance. His mind was empty, devoid of emotion or sense of time until at last the dog's insistence made him turn back up the field to the shelter of the farm.

The rich smell of smoked bacon and sausage drifted out of the kitchen as he discarded his wellingtons and hung up his sodden coat and leggings in the porch. He padded into the warmth in his stockinged feet and rubbed his numbed hands by the range. "What time are you leaving?" he asked his brother.

Jamie, younger by two years, and the image of his father with his chestnut hair, solemn face and green eyes, was serving up the meal. "Straight after breakfast. I want to get Flora to Carlisle for ten."

"I said I'd catch the train," Flora said defensively, pouring hot strong tea into their mugs. "I'm not a child." There were dark rings around her eyes.

"I know," Jamie said softly. "But I'd rather drive you over."

"Is Dad up yet?" Tom asked.

The latch on the kitchen door announced his arrival, and he took his place at the head of the table silently, waiting for Jamie to dish up the eggs alongside the sausage and bacon.

His father suddenly looked much older, Tom thought. His hair was streaked with grey since the summer; his mouth more set, framed by the creases etched on either side; and the joy had gone out of his eyes.

"The animals settled?" his father asked, making a start on his meal.

Tom nodded.

"Do we need to move the sheep?"

"Not yet. The river's up, but it's not into the bottom field."

"It's been a bad night."

But Tom knew it was not just the weather that had kept his father out of bed, wandering the house: his face told half the story; his long silences the rest. He had lived through this before.

"I'm taking Flora back to College after breakfast," Jamie said. "I'll call in later if you like."

His father shook his head, but did not look up. "No, Jamie. Get yourself back to Durham. It's time you both got on with your lives. Tom and I need to get on with ours."

"I offered to go back by myself," Flora objected, the image of her mother for a moment: determined; forthright.

Her father looked up at her and smiled, a thin smile, quickly gone. "Your portfolio's too big to carry on the train, Flora. Let your brother take you back."

"I just wanted Mam to see my project," she protested.

"She was glad you took the trouble. So was I." He paused from eating. "She was proud of you, you know. All of you," he added with conviction, looking at each of them in turn in that intense way of his.

They ate the rest of the meal in silence, words suddenly intrusive. And afterwards, everyone gathered in the hall to say their goodbyes. It was a hasty affair: too much emotion had already been spent, and no one wanted to linger. Jamie swung into the driver's seat, the engine shuddered into life, and the battered VW disappeared down the track into the rain.

The house sank back into silence, as if waiting for other footsteps and another voice. For days it had been filled with people: at first close family; later, friends and neighbours, and the previous day a crowd of strangers mingling with more familiar faces. Now everyone had gone, and the house, already quieter than it should have been, was quieter still.

His father turned to him as he closed the door. "Your mother left this for you," he said, taking an envelope from his jacket pocket.

Tom took it, wondering what needed to be written down that had not been said before. "I'll read it later, Dad. We need to move the bales."

"No, read it now. I can move the bales." He paused. "Read it in the studio, Tom. She'd have liked that."

This was her domain: a bright and airy place, the simple white-washed walls hung with paintings and sketches, some of her own, some of her father's. All around was familiar muddle: the last students' easels and stools spread around the place; boxes of paints, pastels and pencils; sketch pads and notebooks in heaps; stacks of brushes in jam jars. And most poignant of all, the unfinished piece she had been working on before the pain became too great – a study of Brack, ears pricked, sitting on the cobbles in the yard waiting to be called for his day's work.

Tom sat behind the old mahogany desk with its pretty glass paperweight, the letter opener with its ivy leaves on the handle, and the black-and-white photograph of his mother with her father in its silver frame. He felt an intruder. This was where she sat to write her letters in the mornings, and he slipped into remembering other times: mother and son, talking about his future and what he wanted from his life – the farm before everything; Jamie upstairs in his room with his nose in a history book as usual, always living in the past and intent on teaching Classics – and now at university; Flora sprawled in the corner of the studio with her crayons and paper, creating a fantasy world of vivid shapes and colours that was becoming her trademark style.

He studied the plain white envelope, feeling the smoothness of the paper in his hands. She had written his name on it in elegant italics crafted like a medieval manuscript. He slit open the flap using the letter opener. Inside was a single sheet of folded A4 paper.

'To my special son:' it read.

'Darling Thomas,

'I'm writing this because there are things I've never talked to you about before.

'After my father died, I became curious to find out more about my family history. You'll find what I discovered written down in the blue ring-binder in the bottom right-hand drawer of my desk, together with the documents and photographs referred to. It proved an emotional journey at the time, until I became able to put things into perspective.

'If I learnt anything from this painful exercise, it was that truth isn't always plain – or simple. Circumstances at the time can prevent people from being entirely honest, and sometimes precious relationships depend on a necessary fiction. But often, whether we like it or not, the truth will come to light in the end.

'I've been extraordinarily lucky, Thomas. I've had three splendid children, and twenty-five happy years with a wonderful, loving man. Please look after him for me – and look after yourself too. I only wish I'd been given longer to see you settled. Sarah is a lovely girl. Don't take too long to decide if you love her enough. Time slips away too quickly. Remember that.

'Your loving Mother'

There were four kisses at the bottom. He reread the letter before putting it aside, uncertain what to make of it.

The bottom drawer of the desk was unlocked. He pulled it open and surveyed the contents. The blue ring-binder was sitting on top of several large buff envelopes and folders, all neatly labelled; there was a battered tin cash-box, and a small well-used notelet box with a tulip pattern on the top, held together by a red elastic band. He took everything out of the drawer and laid it on the desk in front of him. He was uncertain where to begin.

His father was quiet over lunch. Several times, Tom caught him looking anxiously in his direction. "I'll come out with you this afternoon," he offered, thinking he was needed.

His father shook his head. "No, son. You carry on. I need time to myself."

"If you're sure."

"I'm sure."

By late afternoon, a watery sun was filtering through clearing skies, raking the valley with shafts of white light. Tom had been engrossed, surrounded by his mother's history: the details; the photographs; the documents and scraps of paper.

His life, he thought, had been uncomplicated, so easy when compared with those laid out before him. The Driscolls, a sad record of frustrated lives and thwarted hopes;

of degradation and despair. The bitterness and resentment taken to the grave by his great-uncle Andrew; the tragic early death of his great-aunt Jean; his grandfather living a lie to preserve his social standing. And the Harrimans, locked into another age, out of step with the times, their fortune dwindling into nothing as the years passed. He remembered his lovely old great-aunts in their sprawling house at Broxley; their kindness and generosity when he visited; and talk of his grandmother at Meeston Lodge, stiff and unyielding, who had remained estranged, and in the end, unloved and alone, a chronic alcoholic blaming everyone but herself.

Amongst everything around him, nothing had been mentioned of the contents of the notelet box. He was curious. He slipped off the elastic band and eased back the lid. Inside was a slim volume bound in black tooled leather, the title worked in faded gold in an exotic style of script – *The Rubaiyat of Omar Khayyam*. There was a less ornate edition among the poetry books his mother kept on the bookshelves in the sitting room. This smaller and more elaborately decorated book, with exquisite illustrations, must have been read often: the edges were worn and the pages fell open naturally at different places. A small deckle-edged photograph fell out from one of these, and slipped onto the floor. He picked it up, giving it little more than a cursory glance, more interested to read the poem it marked.

Ah, fill the Cup: – what boots
it to repeat
How Time is slipping underneath

our Feet:
Unborn To-morrow and dead
Yesterday,
Why fret about them if To-day be
sweet!

One of her favourites.

Idly, he turned his attention to the photograph. He was confused. It was a black-and-white studio portrait of a man a few years older than himself. He stared at it. The expression, the striking facial features, and thick dark hair, exactly matched his own.

He turned it over, reading the dedication on the back, 'To Laura from John, with love – February 1963'.

For a moment, a great stillness filled him. The image blurred. Others took its place: the crowd of strangers in their funereal black filling the house, paying their respects – art dealers, collectors, reporters even – a sea of indistinguishable people milling round, except for one – this face in the photograph – older of course, but not much changed by time: the hair still thick and dark, slightly greying at the temples; a vigorous, elegant man, softly spoken, gracious, with deep brown eyes, just like his own. He remembered him now with startling clarity; remembered the look of him that had been so familiar, without knowing why; remembered the visible reaction on his face when his father introduced them – surprise, shock even, smothered immediately by careful politeness; remembered the warmth of the departing handshake afterwards, the leave-taking longer than expected; the intensity of gaze; the tears held back.

"Thomas, I'd like you to meet Mr Rufford," he could hear his father say. "He's got a fine collection of your mother's work." He could remember the expression in his father's eyes: anguish that was more than grief. He must have known the truth for years.

Sometimes precious relationships depend on a necessary fiction.

He sat for a long time holding the photograph, feeling numb. After a while, he packed everything away into the drawer and sat watching the scudding clouds as the evening drew on, listening to his heart thudding with a dull relentless beat against his ribs. It was easier than thinking.

Later, the skies cleared and the pin-sharp brightness of the stars heralded an early frost. He went out into the yard, eager to clear his head.

Once the animals were settled for the night, father and son came in to warm themselves. Tom poured out a large tumbler of whisky for them both, and they settled by the fire in the sitting room trying to ignore the empty chair between them.

The air was heavy with the acrid smell of wood-smoke, a warm familiar smell of winter evenings in the past. Tom closed his eyes, recapturing the memories of easy conversations, laughter and music that had been a part of all their lives, holding them close. He was at a loss what he should do – or say; how to raise the subject of the photograph – or even if he should. But the knowledge of it lodged stubbornly inside him, wanting answers.

His father was watching the firelight caught in the patterns of his glass. "Do you want to ask me something, Tom?" he said, his face set firm – stoical.

The choice of silence was no longer his, but still Tom paused, needing time to think and pick his words with care. Finally he asked, "What can you tell me about Mr Rufford, Dad?" He had wanted the question to sound casual, but it came out differently – more like a challenge.

His father took a long, unhurried draught. "John Rufford?" he said, not looking up from his glass. "Didn't your mother mention him in her letter?"

"No. I found an old photograph among her things."

There was a long silence. His father withdrew into himself: defensive; in no hurry to take the matter further. Eventually, he sighed, stirring himself. "We were rivals once," he said at last. "He was in love with her. More than he knew until it was too late."

Was this what his mother meant? – Tom wondered. *Don't take too long to decide if you love her enough.* He and Sarah had been dating for a year. Was she warning him?

His father was waiting.

"What happened?" Tom asked.

"She chose me," he said with a tinge of pride, then looked away. "But it was a close run thing," he added, as if talking to himself. "They were good together. Given time, he would have won her in the end."

It was an awkward revelation. Tom waited, unsure now how he should proceed.

One of the logs collapsed into the heart of the fire, and

his father hunkered down to add another to the blaze, watching the flames take hold before returning to his chair. He reached for his tumbler again and drank slowly. He seemed far away; unreachable. "I stole her from him," he said quietly at last, keeping his eyes on the glass. "He'd played the field, you see – before they met. She thought he'd never change. I'd loved her for years – I seized the moment." He looked up defiantly. "But I'd no illusions, Tom. I knew I was the safe haven she needed at the time. I could never light the spark in her the way he did."

Tom looked away, embarrassed by such openness. He took a long draught himself, letting the strong liquor numb his tongue and burn his throat.

His father had sunk back into his memories. "Your mother was a passionate woman," he said at last, glancing up at him. "And the truth is, Tom, I still can't believe she's gone. I reach out for her, you know – at night – and I still can't believe that she's not there." His loss was etched into his face. "But I can't complain," he said, fighting his emotion, his voice much stronger now, "She's left me three wonderful children – and years of loving to remember." There was a strange fierceness in his eyes Tom had never seen before. A kind of triumph. "And that's what I stole from John Rufford. That's what he never had."

The fire crackled in the grate sending a flurry of sparks dancing up the chimney.

"Did they ever keep in touch?" Tom asked, afraid they had.

His father shook his head. "No – not after we were

married. She sent him a sketch after they last met, that was all. A memento she didn't think he'd keep. But he did – started collecting after he saw that piece about her in the Sunday supplement."

"When did you find out?"

"About a month ago. A receipt was sent here by mistake. His name was on it. I checked with the dealer. He'd been buying them for years."

What had that knowledge cost him? "Did you think he'd come – to the funeral?"

His father finished his drink, hunching over the empty glass. "She thought he might." He sounded weary.

So, they had talked about it – about the possibility. It must have been hard for them. The ghost from the past. Was this the reason why his mother wrote? – to explain herself?

The truth will come to light in the end.

He remembered the tragedy written in John Rufford's face when recognition dawned; his loss. "Did he still love her, Dad?"

His father put down his empty glass. "Yes," he admitted, looking at his son. "He said he envied me."

Was this why he had introduced them? To acknowledge the past on his own terms? To give the man his due and let him know the truth? – to ease his pain?

There were too many questions Tom wanted to ask. But not yet. Maybe when his thoughts were clearer; when his father's sense of loss had lessened. Maybe then. Maybe never.

His father was silent, hunched forward, staring into the fire: a man bereft; the past laid bare.

Did the truth matter? Did it diminish the love this man had given him? He had loved him wholeheartedly from the start, without reservation, knowing everything.

I've had twenty-five happy years with a wonderful loving man. Please look after him for me.

Tom stood up, downing the last of his drink. He laid a reassuring hand on his father's shoulder. "Would you like another whisky before we turn in, Dad?" he asked. "It's a cold night and we've a hard day ahead tomorrow."

His father looked up hopefully, searching his face, a faint smile acknowledging he understood.